THE RED ADMIRAL

THE JESSICA KELLER CHRONICLES: VOLUME 6

BLAZE WARD

KNOTTED ROAD PRESS

The Red Admiral
The Jessica Keller Chronicles: Volume 6
Blaze Ward
Copyright © 2018 Blaze Ward
All rights reserved
Published by Knotted Road Press
www.KnottedRoadPress.com

ISBN: 978-1-943663-70-5

Cover art:

© Yuliia Lashyna | Dreamstime.com - Space battle. Science, astronaut.

Cover and interior design copyright © 2018 Knotted Road Press

Never miss a release!
If you'd like to be notified of new releases, sign up for my newsletter.

I only send out newsletters once a quarter, will never spam you, or use your email for nefarious purposes. You can also unsubscribe at any time.

http://www.blazeward.com/newsletter/

ALSO BY BLAZE WARD

The Jessica Keller Chronicles:

Auberon

Queen of the Pirates

Last of the Immortals

Goddess of War

Additional Alexandria Station Stories

The Story Road

Siren

The Science Officer Series:

The Science Officer

The Mind Field

The Gilded Cage

Doyle Iwakuma Stories

The Librarian

Demigod

Greater Than The Gods Intended

Other Science Fiction Stories

Myrmidons

Moonshot

Earthquake Gun

Moscow Gold

Fairchild

White Crane

The *Collective* Universe
The Shipwrecked Mermaid
Imposters

PART ONE
OVERTURES

OVERTURE: JESSICA

DATE OF THE REPUBLIC MARCH 22, 399 KELLER
PALACE, WERDER, ST. LEGIER

Jessica Keller considered the view from the mezzanine, overlooking the training floor below.

Unlike the canvas-covered, packed sand in her own dojos, this was a concrete slab with a thin, padded layer over it. Enough to keep you from breaking a bone if you tumbled, but not enough to prevent some wicked bruises. It would, however, teach you to fall correctly, and quickly.

There was a young woman training. Jessica knew that the local media liked to play up comparisons between the two of them, but the likenesses were rather sparse.

Jessica was a few fingers below average height for a woman of the *Republic of Aquitaine*, around 160 centimeters tall, with brown hair just past shoulder length, impressively streaked with gray. The woman on the training floor had the towering stature of the *Fribourg* Imperial Family, nearly a head taller than Jessica, with golden-blond hair in a braid that hung past her shoulder blades.

Jessica was built broad. Not stocky, but with hard curves. On another woman, a less-driven one, it would have turned to flab easily enough, leaving her a squishy, middle-aged *hausfrau*, like Jessica's own mother. Jessica would not allow it, fighting a constant battle in the pool, the gymnasium, and the dinner table. So far, she was winning.

Down there, the young woman was long and lean, built straight, like a volleyball player, only starting to develop muscles as she finally grew into herself.

At forty-one years old, Jessica felt every one of the light-years she had covered in more than twenty years of hard naval service. The trainee was just eighteen, poised to take life by the horns and twist it to fit her need, something that would have been impossible even as recently as six months ago.

Jessica was simply astounded at how much had changed. Not nearly enough, but if she died tomorrow, Jessica Keller could go into hell knowing that she had permanently altered the course of human history in her time. She didn't know how many generations it would take to finally rid the *Fribourg Empire* of their toxic notions of gender, but she could see that day out there in the distance.

She turned to the man standing silently beside her. Studied him briefly before he glanced her way with a wry grin on his face.

Tall. Even taller than the woman on the floor, but obviously a close relative, both in coloring and features. Fully gray now, as his fifty-fifth birthday had passed. Broad in the chest, but with a vee-shape that tapered down to a narrow waist, the kind that came from serious time in the weight room and careful attendance to his diet. Nothing at all like the man she had first met in the flesh nearly seven years ago.

At their first duel. Not the one to the death that *First Ballard* had wanted to be, but just as fraught, when she had foiled his plans and his minions at *First Petron*.

In her mind, she still thought of him as *The Red Admiral*. Everyone did. If you used that term in casual conversation, anyone in either the *Fribourg Empire* or the *Republic of Aquitaine* would immediately flash to this man.

Emmerich wore black now, no longer *The Red Admiral*, but *The Grand Admiral*. Commander-in-Chief, *Fribourg* Fleet. Third, only behind the Emperor and Crown Prince Karl Ekkehard, commonly known as *Ekke*.

These days, Jessica wore red instead: a scarlet jacket, buttoned up the front with gold fripperies stitched here and there, rather than the tight tunic she still unconsciously expected, plus the dark blue slacks that made up a *Fribourg* naval uniform, so much baggier than the uniform she had worn seemingly her whole life. And impossible to fit quickly into an emergency suit.

The only place she deviated from a *Fribourg* uniform was her shoes. She would be damned if she was giving up the comfortable walking shoes *Aquitaine* used, for the hard-soled leather her companion was wearing.

His stare lingered before he turned his head the rest of the way, drawing those wide shoulders in a little.

"I suppose you intend to blame me for this, as well?" Emmerich Wachturm asked in a dry tone, gesturing at the scene below. His eyes twinkled mischievously.

"The thought had crossed my mind," Jessica replied with a grin, turning back to watch.

The blond woman was moving like a dancer, with a thin, straight sword in her right hand, turned sideways to her foe, a taller man with longer arms. Both wore mesh masks and heavy, quilted chest pieces, plus protection on arms and legs.

In a more-formal event, they might have called this fencing, as the woman was using a sabre, a straight blade ninety-six centimeters long, but there was no carpet to dance on. And the woman's opponent wasn't an Olympian. Instead, he was Imperial Army, and a close-combat expert.

The rules here were simple: don't get killed while killing your opponent. Points were measured in limbs declared wounded. An arm injured must be held behind you. A leg caused you to have to stand in place and pivot.

This was dancing with steel. Not quite the *Valse d'Glaive* that Jessica practiced, but much closer than many modern martial practices. The *sabreuse* below also fought with only one blade where Jessica used both a saber and a *main-gauche* interchangeably.

Still, the young woman was learning quickly, gaining skill consistently from that first awkward lesson Jessica had watched. After twenty minutes, the man was ahead on points, but only seven to five, which was amazing against a trained foe like the soldier.

Especially for an Imperial Princess.

"It was her choice, by the way," Wachturm said after a pause.

"Uh huh."

He sounded a touch defensive. Jessica could appreciate why.

Imperial propaganda had done a damned good job originally, making Jessica Keller over into an exotic barbarian so as to dissuade impressionable Imperial teenage girls from emulating her. A pirate queen from beyond the pale of civilization. That she was then a lowly Command Centurion in the *Republic of Aquitaine* Navy was glossed over. Later, those same bards played up the elements of the doomed romance that saw

Jessica crowned and her first, great love, Daneel Ishikura, the famed pirate known as *Warlock*, slain in battle.

Today, they were making her over again, only this time as the woman who had just helped save the Empire as a *Fleet Centurion*, and now, the new *Red Admiral*.

Jessica considered rolling her eyes at the whole situation, but she understood politics and diplomacy well enough these days to let it go. The *Fribourg Empire* needed an anchor around which to coalesce. The young woman below would serve as inspiration for their dreams, but Jessica had to be the rock upon which those dreams could be built. Just as Em was the mason who would build them.

A whistle sounded, ending the bout. Both opponents stepped back and saluted each other before removing their masks and turning to the gallery, which today consisted solely of one referee keeping score and two Imperial Admirals.

Even from here, Jessica could see the immense grin on the Princess Kasimira's face. She had lost on points, but only barely, to an expert with decades of experience. Four hard months of rising early every single morning in order to train with weights, dance, swim, and practice gymnastics, coupled with youth and good genes. Plus occasional lessons with Jessica herself on the finer points of a woman using edged steel, so different in movement from a man, and yet so similar.

Kasimira, *Casey*, would go as far as her dreams took her.

That was another thing Jessica could count on her side of that cosmic ledger.

"Are you convinced, Jessica?" Emmerich asked, his voice gone more serious now.

"I was never worried about Casey, Em," she replied, looking down. "Her father, and her brother, will be the harder sell."

She stared at the man again, *intent* written on her features.

"Convince them, and then I will believe."

OVERTURE: JOH

Karl Johannes Arend Wiegand, *By Grace of God Almighty His Sovereign Imperial Majesty of Fribourg, Karl VII*, known as *Joh* by his family and close friends, sat at the far end of the big conference room table, facing the closed door, alone with the requisite, dozen bodyguards, and his thoughts.

As much as the Imperial Palace and Fleet Headquarters represented his authority, this room was probably the actual seat of his power. The massive table, cut and polished out of a single piece of blue granite, resting atop heavy wooden legs, dark with age. The walls were austere, sheathed over in a dark jade covered with a few tapestries that represented many of his ancestors in the founding and history of the Empire.

This was the place where the Inner Staff met. Flag Officers only, and only members of the Imperial Blood. They were the men who truly made Imperial policy, but they did it by keeping the important decisions under their personal control. His cousins, since he had no brothers and had become emperor sooner than expected, after the terrible accident that killed both of his parents.

This room, right here, was the *Fribourg Empire.*

Hopefully, it would survive what he was about to do today.

All protocol had been cast to the winds for this…*moment.* Now was not a time for conservatism, or halfway measures. The avalanche had already started, and he could only hope to successfully ride it to the bottom of the mountain while trying to steer it to a safer place.

Joh knew he was probably destined to fail, but he was looking with eyes measuring centuries, and not the mere decades of his remaining lifetime.

He took a moment to check his uniform, it having been hours since he got up and worked out this morning. Tailored navy blue slacks. The same dark fabric in the jacket, over a lighter blue shirt. The single, gold spiral galaxy embroidered on each epaulette, symbol of rank as supreme commander, *Emperor of Fribourg*.

He was prepared.

Beside the door, a light changed from green to red.

Joh knew he could remain seated. It was his prerogative to do almost anything that suited his fancy. Today called for more.

He rose from his seat and nodded to the bodyguard closest to the door.

"Open it," he ordered in a deep, firm voice.

The man made no acknowledgement but to reach out with one hand and palm the sensor. Joh's men, his Imperial guards, took themselves much more seriously today, having failed him six months ago, when his cousin, Sigmund Dittmar, sought to overthrow the Empire.

They would never make that mistake again.

Joh drew a deep breath to settle himself as the door opened and the group assembled outside began to enter.

The term *motley* had a negative connotation, historically, but it also communicated the amazing diversity of humanity represented before him.

Come to his *Court.*

Emmerich Wachturm stood in front, *The Grand Admiral of the Fleet.* Joh's strong right arm, his Best Man, his best friend for more than fifty years. Dressed in the black day uniform of his rank, rather than the more formal affair he was occasionally forced into by circumstances or company.

Jessica Keller walked behind him. *The Fleet Centurion* who had been the bane of his Empire, as well as its savior. Recently, she had taken to wearing the day uniform of a *Fribourg* Fleet Admiral of the Red, but today she had reverted to her Fleet Centurion's attire. Joh preferred women like his beloved Kati, long and willowy, but there was something to the compact, athletic curves shown off by Keller's uniform.

Perhaps it was just the being who inhabited the flesh. One of the most dangerous people in the galaxy. And slowly, awkwardly even, becoming something of a friend.

Behind Jessica, one of the most daring minds out there, contained in a tiny body under a thatch of black hair. Lady Moirrey *zu* Kermode. *Ritter of the Imperial Household.* Advanced Research Weapons Technician, *Republic of Aquitaine* Navy. According to his spies, a goofball of the first order, capable of quoting amazingly-obscure literature and modern pop songs in the same sentence.

And a woman who had killed two Imperial assassins in single combats. Never forget that part.

zu Kermode wore what Joh assumed was a homemade outfit today, based on the intelligence files he had read about her. Tight, slate-gray slacks under a top that split the gap between a tabard and sundress, front and back panels hanging to her boot tops and slashed to her thigh, with a black, leather belt containing it. Interestingly, the dress had been done in dark maroon, edged and embroidered in white. Over her heart, also hand-embroidered, the Imperial Crest: *Golden Eagle Elevated and Displayed.*

Moirrey had taken the style of her formal cloak as a *Ritter* and gone fashionable with it. As one of only two women alive with the *zu* designation, there were no official guidelines for how a female *Ritter* should dress.

Still, he approved. It was demure but still flattering on a woman that barely came up to his collarbone. And it conveyed her importance and place to anyone who wasn't immediately familiar with her face.

As if such a person actually still existed on this planet.

Joh smiled a secret smile with Moirrey as she came in, rather like the one they had shared when she had shot Geoffrey Grundman, who had happened to be standing just behind Joh, the shot passing beside his ear close enough that he still remembered the heat.

She blushed and glanced down, obviously fighting to control a bout of giggles that threatened to erupt. Moirrey was like that.

Behind Moirrey, Joh's greatest surprise. Not that she was here, but how she presented herself.

The Imperial Princess, Kasimira Helena. Casey *zu* Wiegand. His youngest child, and only surviving daughter, since her sister Steffi had been killed during the coup, while saving his own life.

Casey wore an identical outfit to Moirrey's, scaled up, obviously hand-made by Moirrey in secret, probably for exactly this occasion. Joh could sense a new fashion trend breaking out, although Imperial woman would be careful not to match the exact color, nor the Imperial crest.

Perhaps he should suggest the simple logo of the Imperial fleet in gold and white, on the dark blue fabric the navy used.

Patriotic, but demure.

Another aspect of the avalanche that threatened to bury him.

The last person to enter was a man Joh had never formally met. Oh, he had read any number of hastily-compiled dossiers on the fellow, but there was little actually known about him, except what his spies had learned, mostly from Jessica Keller or her Prime Minister, Desianna Indah-Rodriguez. And even that was sparse. The man was something of a cypher, and quietly went about his business with the care of a blacksmith making horseshoes.

Yan Bedrov, pirate.

Mid-forties. Tall and skinny, with dark hair buzzed tight against his skull, both receding and graying. He wore a charcoal-gray outfit that conveyed formality, but retained hints of the barbaric underneath, mostly in the patterns sewn into what might otherwise be a simple jumpsuit. Fitting for a man who had been a pirate most of his adult life, and now served the *Queen of the Pirates* herself, Jessica Keller.

Joh had heard enough from Em to make up his mind. Em and Jessica had put the entire thing together in strict secrecy, since what they had proposed was technically treason of the highest order. At least until Joh gave his personal assent.

Being *Emperor of Fribourg* meant that some things required official sanction. It had to happen here, in this room, with all the symbolism and history contained therein.

"Please," Joh said warmly, gesturing to his visitors. "Be seated."

Jessica ended up across from Em, on Joh's left, with Moirrey and Casey on that side, and Bedrov next to the Grand Admiral. An interesting balance, female to his left, and male to his right. Hopefully not a psychological separation, but just luck of the draw.

Joh rested his right hand on the small, leather satchel he had brought with him. There were easier ways to have done this thing, but someone, somewhere, would get the wrong impression.

Treason was contagious. It did not exist in this room, but he had to inoculate an entire interstellar empire against it.

Joh studied each of the seated faces, starting with Em and working his way around the table.

Calm. Poised. Excited. Grinning. Serious. Thus he would always remember them.

"Will the Peace hold, Fleet Centurion?" he asked Jessica in a formal, canted tone. History would record this conversation, and replay it for centuries.

Jessica fixed him with eyes like emeralds on fire.

"On my oath," she replied simply. Nothing more.

Joh felt the immense power of those words.

Empires could be built on them.

If *Fribourg* was to survive, he would have to do exactly that.

Joh nodded slowly and turned to Em next.

"Is this the best way forward?" he asked his oldest friend.

Em nodded slowly.

"It is perhaps the greatest gamble any of us will ever take, Your Majesty," Em replied. "I do not believe anything less will succeed."

Joh nodded again. So much of this was playing for the galleries, but it had to be done.

Future historians would pore over this day, writing entire volumes of Imperial history that started now, Chapter One, with that door opening.

"Lady Moirrey?"

"I'll makes ya proud, Sire," she chirped in that thick, barbaric accent she always carried with her, a reminder of a home on distant *Ramsey*. Joh made a note to visit it, someday, circumstances allowing. Moirrey deserved that much.

He had no doubt about her words, or her calm confidence. No less than Emmerich Wachturm had been convinced that Lady Moirrey, *zu Kermode of Ramsey*, held the key to defeating *Buran*, *The Eternal*, the self-styled *Lord of Winter*.

"Lady Casey, will you speak with my voice?" he asked his youngest, no longer a child, but turned now into a fierce warrior by association with other such folks. Folks he trusted and respected.

"I will, Your Majesty."

Avalanche. No woman had ever spoken for the throne.

Ever.

Before Casey did it.

His Imperial Majesty Karl VII turned to the last person at the table. He picked up the leather satchel, weighing it both physically and emotionally for a second, before reaching out and placing it into Yan Bedrov's firm hands.

"The complete technical specifications of the *Paladin*-class battleships, including as-builts of the IFV *Amsel*, the *Blackbird*, as she has been repaired, following the raid by *Buran*. Also, everything we have been able to learn about the naval architecture of the star nation known as *Buran*," Joh said formally. "Yan Bedrov, do you understand the task at hand?"

"Aye, sir," the man replied, even now acknowledging no liege but Jessica, as was proper. His voice was a high baritone that conveyed an utter conviction that made even Jessica's word seem doubtful by comparison. "I will forge you a sword."

A sword? Yes, Joh supposed so. But not just any sword. No, this one would, by the everlasting Grace of God himself, be wielded by Jessica Keller.

Joh drew in another breath. Released it.

He studied his daughter, aware that no father wanted to push his children out of the nest, but that the survival of everything Joh and his predecessors had spent their lives building might possibly rest on her shoulders. It would be a test even greater than saving the Empire from Sigmund.

Her blue eyes stared calmly back. She reminded him of her mother, that same poise, that same strength.

It would be good.

"As my representative, you will be provided a staff of experts," Joh said simply. "It is my understanding that Jessica's flagship, *Kali-ma*, has space on the final ring to add another transport shuttle, similar in size to the vessel known as *Baxter*, and that she has agreed to transport it, and you, as a diplomatic mission to *Ladaux*. We will also send a courier vessel, as well as a fast freighter loaded with trade goods, the latter of which will accompany *Kali-ma* on to *Petron*."

Casey nodded silently. This had all been worked out ahead of time. This was just the legal paperwork to absolve these people from guilt and responsibility, if something went wrong later.

By Imperial Command…

Joh glanced over at Em and received the slightest nod of assent.

"There will be one addition to your team, Lady Casey," Joh continued. "An expert transferred from the Imperial Naval Staff who will advise you on economic issues, given the nature of your task."

That broke through his daughter's calm poise. Joh could see the slightest hint of confusion in the back of her eyes, morphing quickly into nothingness as she got control of her face an instant later. An Imperial Princess understood the power of projecting calm.

"Who, Your Majesty?" she asked, taking the obvious cue with grace.

Joh let his glance trail over to Jessica Keller. This was the greatest risk. Hints had been suggested, but nobody had been willing to simply walk up and ask the woman's opinion.

Joh realized now that he had made a grave mistake, not asking Em to simply throw diplomacy to the winds on this one and ask her, but everything he had heard, from everyone with even tangential knowledge of the situation, suggested that this was the right course of action.

Avalanche. Only history would be able to say if he had judged correctly.

"A captain from the Fleet side," Joh replied. "An expert economist with a solid naval grounding who can speak capably on obscure technical topics with Republic engineers."

Jessica's eyes flared, just the slightest bit. Nothing else. No change of breathing. No blush.

No palm slamming angrily down on the table top, either.

"Captain Torsten Wald will be joining your mission."

OVERTURE: KIER

URAL STARBASE: SAMARA. STATUS: AT REST

In one of the ancient tongues, *Chéngbǎo* meant castle, when the term suggested stout stone walls on the surface of a planet, proof against wild and dangerous barbarians raiding across borders. Before foolish emperors built grand walls that spanned continents.

From her conference room just off of her ship's bridge, Xi Derag Ahma Kier considered nearby space, the wall of hollow darkness that filled nearly a quarter of the display screen in front of her.

In historic terms, *geographic ones*, a nearly-impassable desert, such as once separated the homelands from the decadence of the coastal nations. Or the endless marshes and forests on the western frontier, behind a single wall of mountains that had kept those barbarians at bay for a time.

As The Eternal, *the* Lord of Winter *reminds us, time is on a circular track, returning again and again, as humans are unable to break out of the biological patterns of entropy and destruction. Even today, a new tribe of barbarians threatens once more to bring it all down. Only we will protect* The Holding.

She looked around from the viewscreen at the rest of her bridge and the men and women who commanded the *Buran Angustidens Steadfast at Dawn*. As a Nightmaster, the vessel was the anchor of the entire border fleet on this swathe of the terrible gulf that both sides called *M'Hanii*, stretching sideways for light centuries in the gap between arms of the galactic plane.

At *Samara*, the *Lord of Winter* had decreed a Barricade, a stronghold, a line in the dirt drawn with a saber. A mark that even the barbarians could understand, one that proclaimed *"Here, and no further."*

Time and again they had come, only to be thwarted, as their supposedly advanced technology failed in the face of the greatness that was *The Holding. The Eternal.* Humans were too fallible to face the might of *Sentient* systems.

Thus would they always fail.

Five faces stared back at Kier from around the conference room's table, representing not just the normal three of a *Buran* warship, but a fourth for the child vessels that *Steadfast at Dawn* carried with her between worlds and the fifth who was her new master of spies, one recently returned from personally witnessing the barbarians known as *Fribourg*.

He was a hard, lean man who somehow looked subtly wrong to her. Unconsciously, she recognized that the man was from an obscure genotype, rare in *The Holding*, but common in the lands of the barbarians. Eyes at once too round and too flat, lacking the subtle fold at the outer edges. Skin that looked utterly washed out without the golden undertones of the homelands. Irises that were rimmed in green, rather than the uniform brown so prized for conformity.

It made him stand out as an individual, rather than a member of *The Holding*, which must have been painful when he was younger, but put him in a position to better serve by impersonating one of the outsiders regularly, the better to understand what foolish deviltry they would be up to next.

"What have they learned?" she asked the spy.

Even his mannerisms were strange, but this was a man who lived inside the life of another, behind a mask whose slippage would inevitably lead to his own execution.

"The warlord-queen Keller has returned to her own distant holdings," he said simply. "What few of my sources remain safely in place can report little without risk greater than any possible reward, so little is known, but we surmise that she will not return soon."

He stopped to take a drink of water. Each of them had containers secured to the table top, but only his actually held anything. This was a crew of warriors, not scholars. There would be time for refreshment after the briefing.

Kier waited while the man drank and composed his thoughts.

"The plot having been thwarted, the men who might have been able to tell the Emperor anything useful all died in the coup attempt," he continued. "The hereditary leader of *Osynth B'Udan* and several of his immediate staff knew more, but wisely fled as soon as possible and escaped to *Buran*, where they have been given asylum. The man is an inveterate conspirator, so he will eventually be settled in a golden cage on a world much closer to the Core, to live out his days in isolated splendor."

"And the risk of another Imperial assault on *The Holding*?" Kier pressed. This was the one thing that concerned her. Assassins could handle the rest.

"With Wachturm promoted to supreme command, the risk is greater than it has ever been," the spy replied. "Previous Grand Admirals were political creatures. Wachturm is a Warrior."

Enough said. Scholars loved to talk, to dicker, to *maneuver* their foes into traps. Warriors would go for the throat.

Kier had studied Emmerich Wachturm as much and as closely as his greatest fan might have, aware than the *Fribourg Emperor* has been planning to dispatch the man to finally face *Buran*, to face her, directly.

With him in supreme command, he would not come personally, so would have to rely on lesser commanders, weaker tools, to try to execute his will.

Xi Derag Ahma Kier understood in her soul that only Emmerich Wachturm was good enough to threaten *Buran*'s hold on this frontier, this beachhead holding all of *M'Hanii*. Most of the rest of *Fribourg*'s admirals barely rated a footnote.

If the one known as Keller had indeed returned to her own barbaric holdings on the distant fringe of the galaxy, *Fribourg* was doomed.

PART TWO
EMISSARY

CHAPTER I

The most interesting thing about the hall, now that Jessica had gotten thirty minutes to size everything and everyone up, was the way the small hearing room had been organized, small by government standards anyway. It had been arranged such that a speaker could address the Committee from a slightly-raised platform, one that still put his head several steps below that of the men and women facing him at a long angle, safe atop their own high stage, behind a heavy and official table, the one with their names and planetary ridings spelled out in front of them.

The nineteen men and women who sat on the *Senate Select Committee for the Fleet of The Republic of Aquitaine.*

The Committee.

The exact group that *were* the civilian control of the Navy itself. Most of them were long-serving politicians with significant experience on the topic. Several were retired fleet officers of one type or another, usually from one of the Fifty Families that formed the social backbone of the Republic.

At the center was Senator Tadej Horvat, former *Premier of the Senate,* former Command Centurion, and, for the last several years, Chairman of the Committee after his party had lost control of the Senate, brought down in the same scandals that destroyed Jessica's old nemesis, Bogdan Loncar.

Tadej was a tall and broad-shouldered man sporting a round build, with sandy-blond hair finally fading to white, although she doubted that the original color was natural. The man was in his sixties and known to be a touch vain.

But at the same time, he and Nils Kasum, First Lord of the Fleet and Jessica's mentor, seated opposite at another table, had been friends since boarding school. Horvat had become one of her guardian angels, and one of the reasons Jessica had gotten as far as she had, as early as she had, promoted to Fleet Lord younger than any other person in more than a century.

She owed Horvat, and Kasum, a debt she doubted she could ever repay.

Jessica wondered how far today would stretch that. Angry scowls were brewing.

Interestingly, from her seat in the audience, she had the best view of all the players.

On her right, the Committee, dressed like resplendent peacocks in colorful tunics and suits. On her left, the seven men and women who were the Lords of the Fleet in black. Civilians, but frequently at odds with the Committee, from whom they took orders and tried to carry them out.

In the audience, several random groupings of folks, some she knew and some she did not, with two very special characteristics about them: important and interested enough to be invited to something this secret, as well as possessing a security clearance at the highest possible level that would allow them to be here.

Even the man at the podium, having finished addressing the room and now taking questions, didn't meet the second, especially as he wasn't even technically a Republic citizen, but Yan Bedrov was the reason they were all here. *He* looked out over the room like a lion beset by feisty rabbits. Anyone who didn't know the man probably mistook the serenity on his face for calm.

Jessica knew he was angry enough to chew nails right now by the stiff way he held his shoulders and the fact that both hands were palm-down and flat on the lectern. Normally, Yan fidgeted when standing and addressing a group, hands going all directions. Movement helped him think, so he said. But he was handling their questions with grace and even occasional charm.

Probably measuring throats for knives in his head, though.

While she waited for the unconscionably-long-winded Fourth Lord of the Fleet to perhaps finally get around to possibly making his way to some meaningful point, Jessica studied the rest of the audience.

Down at the end of the front row furthest from her, the current Premier, Judit Chavarría, a stocky fireplug of a woman with mahogany skin, black hair, and perfect nails, sat next to Calina Szabolski, President of the Republic, an erect, lean lady with laugh lines on her face and long, silver hair. The President was a former professional athlete of impeccable family, in direct descent from the Founder of the Republic himself, Henri Baudin.

A few others of note amidst the three to four dozen people in the audience, mostly politicians with an interest in naval affairs, or busybodies lacking better hobbies. A goodly number of bodyguards and aides in addition, mostly toward the back of the auditorium until called upon.

Jessica was in a first-row seat, almost in the center. Moirrey was on her right and Casey on her left, the two women wearing the identical maroon outfits Moirrey had originally sewn for their audience with Karl VII. Vo Arlo had ended up one row behind them, a quiet Gibraltar of a man in a Centurion's uniform custom-made for the giant.

Beside Vo, the one true stranger in this group, even now, so many months later.

It wasn't that Captain Wald hadn't been a perfect gentleman, and even a touch shy. Jessica had found him charming and quite witty once he got over his natural reticence, the outsider in the larger group. And Casey truly had needed an economist of his skill for what was coming.

Jessica still had not decided if she was going to kill Emmerich Wachturm for presuming. Or thank him.

It didn't help when Wald leaned forward to tap Casey on the shoulder and whisper some key, arcane point into the woman's ear. The ear on Jessica's side. Where she could smell his after-shave lotion.

Fourth Lord finally seemed to be winding down. Perhaps. The man was a long-winded blowhard who seemed in love with the sound of his own voice more than anything. Still, it broke her concentration on things that were superfluous right now.

"And in conclusion," the man said, angrily slamming his hand down on a binder on the table in front of him and making several people jump. "These designs are insane. You propose to throw away over a century of accumulated knowledge and wisdom about proper naval architecture. Why should we even entertain the notion of listening to such rank imbecility from a foreigner? A barbarian pirate, no less."

Rabbit, challenging lion.

Jessica wondered if Bedrov would actually yawn at the man before replying. She could tell even from here that he was fighting the urge to roll his eyes. Which was a step up from actually, publicly threatening the man.

The silence stretched as Yan seemed to look for the right words. Presumably, less profane ones than he would normally use on his gun deck, given the delicate and august company he found himself addressing today.

Yan eventually settled on a vague shrug.

"Because your ideas are stupid and impractical," Bedrov replied. "It would require a logistics train some seven months long each way, just to support the border. Perhaps Seventh Lord could explain the absurdity of that task to you in smaller words."

"How dare you?" the Fourth Lord snarled, starting to rise.

"I was given this task by someone I like and respect far more than you, buddy," Yan countered with a voice edging finally into an angry snarl and a finger coming up to point at the Fourth Lord.

For a moment, Jessica wondered if Alois Dominguez was going to let his temper get the best of him and cause the man to issue a challenge to the pirate, a man who had previously killed three men in duels. With blades.

"And I don't personally give a damn what you think of the designs, pal," Yan continued, grinding broken glass into the wound. "You aren't being asked to adopt them, and if you don't want to build them, I have several other interested parties I can talk to instead."

"This information is classified at the highest level," Dominguez snarled. "I'll have you arrested for treason."

"No, you will not," Yan snapped the whip on the man with an audible crack. "I am not a Republic citizen and not subject to such laws. And, as of yesterday, I have resigned all of my commissions: here, *Fribourg*, and *Corynthe*, so I am a private businessman, protected by your own commercial laws, which I *have* studied rather closely before this. So bring it, you stupid, fat clown."

"I'll have you know-"

"That's enough, Alois," Nils Kasum broke in on the man.

Jessica was always amazed that such a deep voice could emerge from such a skinny chest, but he still did that better than anybody she had ever met. Especially when he was angry and willing to let everyone within earshot know it.

Like now.

Fourth Lord snapped his head around angrily, focusing his rage on First Lord, having already forgotten Yan.

"I do not answer to you, Nils," Dominguez barked. "As Fourth Lord, all design and construction decisions are mine. You'll get what I decide to build."

"While you may not report to Nils Kasum," Tadej Horvat suddenly called out in a dry, sharp voice that seemed to fill the entire auditorium. "You do answer to me, Alois Dominguez."

Sudden stillness filled the room. Pregnant. Stagnant. Angry.

Dominguez fell quiet, his breathing audibly labored. Tadej pointedly glanced slowly right and left, taking the temperature of his comrades as the room held on the edge of a precipice.

"The Committee feels that it has lost confidence in you as Fourth Lord, Alois Dominguez," Tadej pronounced. "I will expect your resignation on my desk in one hour."

"And if I refuse?" the man challenged in a rising voice.

"That would please me," Horvat replied in a chilling tone, another lion provoked by the same, angry rabbit.

Alois Dominguez turned white. Jessica suspected that there were probably decades of bad blood playing out right now, in public, although she knew next to nothing about the man about to become the *former* Fourth Lord of the Fleet.

Tadej Horvat was probably the most dangerous opponent a person could have in this room. Many people had found that out, usually the hard way.

Fourth Lord was already standing. He turned and stomped out of a nearby door.

"Sergeant At Arms," Horvat called in a lighter voice, a rapier rather than a battle axe. "You will enforce my will."

Jessica watched the tiny blond woman rise from a spot at the left end of the front row they shared. Svetlana Ognianov had the long, lean build of a dancer, a voice like a history professor, and moved like an assassin. Jessica had met a few of those, now.

"As you command, Chairman," the woman said in a tone that conveyed no emotional loading whatsoever.

Dominguez must be truly hated around here. Or he was being made an example of.

Either way, dangerous games.

Jessica let a small grin escape her rigid control.

These people had NO idea what really dangerous political games looked like. They had never stopped a coup, or faced a warship dropping nuclear explosives on an inhabited world.

Lady Casey could give them some pointers, if she chose. As could Jessica.

Tadej extended his serenity over the room.

"My apologies to the rest of the chamber," Senator Horvat said, as if nothing had happened. "Unfortunately, that wasn't even the stupidest, most asinine thing that man had said, even this week. Yesterday, he asked me why Fleet Centurion Keller has not been brought up on official charges of treason, for her role in the recent events at *St. Legier*. Apparently, even his own vote to send her on that mission had escaped the man's memory."

The Senator scanned them all now, slowly, settling his eyes on Jessica for several long seconds before he finally turned back to Yan.

Lions, having cowed the rabbits back into submission.

"Now, Sri Bedrov," Tadej said firmly. "You have resigned all official stations, is that what I understood you to say?"

Yan actually nodded to the man, almost a slight bow. One lion recognizing another.

"That is correct, Senator," Yan replied. "As of this morning, *Bedrov & Keller, Registered*, opened its first business office, down in Penmerth, *Ladaux*."

Jessica found it highly amusing that *every single head* in the room turned to look at her at the same time. All of them, including the ones who should have known better. Shocked looks. Amused. Curious. Angry.

"No," Yan continued. "Not her. Miguel Keller is the Chairman, being a Republic citizen. Vyacheslav Keller, his son, is my Chief Legal Officer. Having not passed *Aquitaine*'s rigorous educational and credentialing requirements, I may not call myself a Naval Architect, so my title is simply Principle Designer. I will, however, stack my warship specs up against anything that any of you want to submit. I will guarantee you a distant third place, behind me and *Pops* Nakamura, Crown Naval Designer of *Corynthe*."

All the emotions turned to confusion at that point, except for the very few people in the room who actually knew who Iorwerth Nakamura was, and who therefore understood that he might be the most original and skilled starship designer alive. At least until he and Yan finally went head to head. Jessica looked forward to that competition, and not just as the woman who would get to build those lovely designs, someday.

Corynthe might be a poor star nation, but necessity truly was the mother of invention. Nakamura and Bedrov had both come out of that poverty with dreams of building starships, and, further, with the understanding of the need to make them compact, efficient, and deadly. And to do so at an acceptable price.

No Fourth Lord had ever had to measure costs to the fraction of the Lev when building a star fleet.

"I see," Senator Horvat replied diplomatically. "Based on?"

It was a simple question. And a bear trap was a simple piece of steel. They both looked innocent and harmless, until you put a foot in them.

Jessica wouldn't have put Yan up there today if he hadn't hunted his own fair share of bears over the decades.

Yan actually grinned at the Senator. It was unnerving in what should be a very sober and serious discussion.

Lions, discussing rabbits.

"You people have no conception of poverty whatsoever, Senator," Yan said, encompassing the entire room with one, rude sweep of his long arm. "Your entire war with *Fribourg* could be described by an outsider such as myself as an argument over who had the prettier mansion and the most mistresses."

Yan paused to glance at the rest of the gasping audience before returning his attention to the one place that really mattered. The murmuring slowly subsided.

"Until I was fourteen I lived in a slum, Chairman," he said in a calm, hard voice. Emotionless only because any emotion now could be interpreted as a challenge and Yan was smarter than that. "With a brackish well that was a thirty minute walk each way. Power that blacked out regularly because the generators overloaded, or a line failed, or because someone had pissed off the man with his hand on the switch and got made an example of."

Yan took a deep breath. Jessica watched him almost literally shake off the cloak of his past as his chin came up.

"Your ships, your entire navy, are built around spending Levs like you own the printing press," Yan continued. "Primaries by the pallet. Missiles by the gross. *Corynthe* doesn't use either of those because we can't afford them. With the logistics train you and Karl VII envision, they will not be possible, so I eliminated them. The result are a set of designs that are smaller, deadlier, and specifically tailored to the task the *Emperor of Fribourg* demanded of me. The next step is yours."

Jessica thought Moirrey might be able to throw a glitter-filled water-balloon at someone right now and not be noticed, from the sudden, shocked silence. She did not lean over and suggest it to the woman, as much as she wanted to.

Instead, she turned to look past the Evil Engineering Gnome.

Jessica had whispered in Judit's ear, as the Premier had first entered today, that the woman might need to engage in the conversation at some point, without mentioning why. But Judit was a canny politician. She saw her opening now and stepped boldly into it.

"Sri Bedrov," she called over the murmuring. "You say you have gone into private practice? Who, then, are your backers? This may become a matter of national interest for the Republic."

Technically, even the Premier wasn't supposed to speak in this setting, given that this was something of a secret Committee hearing. At the same time, no one the least bit intelligent was going to gainsay *that* woman.

Yan actually smiled, for the first time in twenty-some minutes.

"Based on the advice of my Chief Legal Officer, Slava Keller," he replied in a lighter tone, "we have recruited two Bond Investors at present. Stock itself is severely curtailed, with the Chairman, board members, and other officers collectively voting just under forty percent of the shares, while I retain a significant controlling majority."

"Bond Investors, Sri?" Tadej called. His tone had gotten light and almost playful, but he had known most of these people for decades, and knew that Jessica had vouched for Yan. And finance was a realm where his expertise probably rivaled Captain Wald, seated behind Jessica and waiting.

Tadej had probably never actually met Jessica's little brother, at least not yet, but Slava was a well-known chandlery attorney in this town, working on both civilian and military contracts. It had made him quite successful. This venture was likely to make him filthy, stinking rich.

Not as rich as his sister, but she was a Queen with a government and a treasury behind her.

Still, Jessica's niece and nephews would never be hungry.

"That's right, Mr. Chairman," Yan replied. "The financing was structured around an eventual goal of three major investors to provide initial funding and maintain a joint, personal interest in our affairs, without being able to dictate terms or seize control."

"I see," Tadej said in a tone that would have made most people take a step back. "You'll pardon me for not having had a chance to study your incorporation documents yet, Sri Bedrov. Who are your two current investors?"

Anyone else might take umbrage at the tone. Jessica had prepped Yan for exactly this occasion. It was going to happen, best that it be done right.

Lions, talking over the heads of the rabbits.

"Two private, galactic citizens, Senator," Yan's smile had broadened. "Women with impeccable political credentials, given the sensitive and serious nature of the business. My plan at present is to recruit a third person to round out the group. The two are Casey *zu* Wiegand and Jessica Keller, strategically representing *Fribourg* and *Corynthe*."

Again, every head turned her way. Most were probably seeing the pretty, blond girl seated next to Jessica for the first time.

Oh, certainly she was a beautiful, Imperial Princess, and thus something of a unicorn in this land, but she was also a *Ritter of the Imperial Household. Aquitaine* did not even have such a concept, although they would be more willing to accept such a woman here than *Fribourg* would, *Aquitaine* lacking the foolish gender notions of the Empire.

"Princess Kasimira?" Tadej asked in a very stilted, very formal tone. Someone would be recording this conversation. Probably several someones, if for no other reason than future blackmail.

Politics in *Aquitaine* wasn't blood sport, mostly because actual blood was so rarely shed. It still came close, from time to time.

Jessica twitched the slightest bit when Casey suddenly stood. They were going off script, but Casey probably had a better nose for politics than Jessica did, having been raised to it her whole life. Jessica smiled serenely at the few faces that hadn't followed Casey upright.

"No, Mr. Chairman," Casey called across the room. "As a *Ritter*, I of course am authorized to speak for the Emperor, and do so occasionally. However, I made this particular investment as a private citizen, out of my own funds that are not tied up in anything official. My personal, majority inheritance was quite substantial. Income from my Duchy is also significant."

Judit had a calculating look on her face when Jessica glanced over.

"And yet," Judit interjected. "You *can* speak for the Emperor, when you choose?"

Casey nodded. At her core, the woman had been raised an Imperial Princess. She was made of extremely stern stuff. Most people here just weren't aware of that, with the exception of stories they largely discounted. And nobody had truly understood Casey's role in defeating Sigmund Dittmar's attempted coup.

Fools.

"Why should we engage?" Judit pounced, making it clear that *We* represented the entirety of *Aquitaine.*

Before Casey could speak, Yan laughed out loud. The man had spent a great deal of time in meetings with her, Casey, and the rest, on the flight from *St. Legier* to *Ladaux.* Planning, evaluating, questioning.

"Because Lady Casey is one of only two women alive entitled to wear a blade in the *Imperial Presence*, m'lady," he said. "Not even Jessica Keller has that privilege. I considered asking the other one, and I might, one of these days, but she's already deeply involved with this project, and most of her funds are currently locked up on *Thuringwell.* That's a better investment, both for *zu* Kermode and the Republic, right now."

Without even looking, Jessica could feel Moirrey's blush. Her very skin turned warm, sharing the arm rest with Jessica. She would be red to the tips of her ears, uncomfortable at being the center of this kind of attention.

"And you propose a third, Sri Bedrov?" Judit pressed.

"That would be a private affair, madam," he fired back. "I have not had the chance to make an approach, and it would be inopportune to name the person, that being the case."

For a pirate, Jessica was always a little amazed at how well the man could handle his diction, when pressed into a corner. Probably too much time spent with Imperial busybodies.

Judit seemed satisfied, however. She nodded to Yan and let it go.

Tadej had remained quiet through the exchange. He might represent The Committee, but this woman politician, rival though she be, *was* the government. He had been there. He understood how things worked. Better than anyone else, probably.

"And your designs, Sri?" Tadej finally asked. "I have studied the vessels. Impressive, but the weapon systems are experimental, and my experts do have their reservations."

"Battle-proven for two of them and then improved on in both cases,"

Yan answered, matter of factly. "*First Thuringwell. Battle of St. Legier.* The third is an obvious and logical extension of the existing systems it will replace."

"And the fourth?" Judit suddenly asked. Her voice was ever-so-slightly playful. "The one you refer to as a Bubble Gun?"

"Really?" Yan was surprised. "I thought I had corrected all the notes and references in the schematics."

"You missed one on diagram 193," Tadej added tartly.

"Oh. Oops," Yan grinned and shrugged. "Still, I trust my expert that the *Reversed Field, Pinch, Plasma Implosion Generator* will work as designed. Her opinion was enough for the Emperor. It's certainly good enough for me. And you people made her an Advanced Research Weapons Technician. You don't get to complain when she comes through and invents new stuff. All these weapons designs are hers, by the way. I just built the ship around them."

Moirrey's blush got worse, if that was possible. She really had called it a bubble gun, after a late-night brainstorming session that involved bubbles blown in liquid soap and left to float about the salon chamber. And copious inebriation.

There had been weirder inspirations. Newton had his apple, and Archimedes his bath. Moirrey could have her bubbles.

And the glitter that was her signature.

Jessica just thanked the powers that be that Moirrey had never figured out how to scale glitter up to a naval weapon.

So far.

Judit turned back this way.

"*zu* Kermode?" she asked simply.

Moirrey rose, mirroring the already-standing Casey in their matching outfits, to make Jessica feel tiny. And protected. She could do much worse than those two beside her and Vo at her back.

Jessica fought down the giggles when Moirrey spoke. Normally, excitement made the woman fall back into a cant so thick you had to parse it with a knife. When she got focused, she could give diction lessons to Republic politicians. Like now. Obviously, she and Yan were both up to no good.

"The design for the so-called bubble gun is based on battle reports and empirical research provided by Imperial scientists," she said in a voice that sounded utterly alien coming out of that mouth. "It will exploit technological aberrations in the defensive systems that *Buran* uses instead of the powered shield designs on our vessels. We should be able to kill a *Buran* vessel without fully rupturing that defensive fabric, and capture it more or less intact, which is something that *Fribourg* has never managed."

"Which reminds me," Tadej spoke up. "I will note that the starship designs you submitted all have an excessive number of gyroscopes, especially for this mass tonnage. Why?"

"Alber' d'Maine," was Yan's whole reply.

Jessica noted the five heads that nodded at that, while the rest looked on in utter confusion. Those were the ones that knew her crazed berserker. Nobody else could envision executing a high-energy turn on gyros in anything larger than a shuttle, let alone something the size of a battlecruiser.

"And the other designs, Sri Bedrov?" Tadej pressed.

"You will need escorts for the Expeditionary Cruisers I have envisioned," Yan said flatly. "Your destroyers are, kilo for kilo, the least efficient use of space I have ever seen. *Pops* and I actually discussed the replacement design years ago, but never got around to proposing them. I dusted those off, updated them to Moirrey's new technology, and included them, but *Pops* gets most of that credit. And the licensing fees if you decide to build them."

"But, corvettes?" Tadej let some level of confusion and disbelief into his tone.

"Nomenclature, for the most part," Yan grinned. "Smaller than your basic destroyer design, but larger than the cutters you phased out a generation ago. Using your standards, the first one would be Corvette/Escort hull number 401, bumping up from where you stopped, seventy-five years ago."

Jessica watched Tadej flip open the notebook before him a touch theatrically, rifling pages and then putting a finger down to mark his place. She suspected he had already memorized most of it, but the man was playing for the galleries today.

"Escort, Minehunter, Patrol, and Assault variants," Tadej noted dryly. "Plus proposals for several others, at a future date. Why a Corvette/Assault, Sri?"

"I am reliably informed of the need by the Fleet Centurion, Senator," Yan replied. "Tomas Kigali will want to kill things. *CA-264* will do that rather well."

Jessica noted the tiny shake of the head and nascent eyeroll that Nils Kasum was trying to suppress. Kigali had refused to be promoted out of his tiny Cutter/Revenue, *CR-264*, into a Survey Cruiser when his comrades had upgraded, because "they don't kill things…"

Silence descended.

"If there are no other questions for Sri Bedrov?" Tadej asked the room. Pause. "Hearing none, the witness is dismissed."

Jessica took a deep breath. Up until now, things had been technical and straightforward. This was when it would get interesting.

Tadej took a moment to study the audience, focusing this way like a lion spotting a whole new herd of rabbits.

"The Committee calls Casey *zu* Wiegand, *Ritter of the Imperial Household*, to the stand."

CHAPTER II

The man had a cruel mouth. That had been Casey's first impression of Senator Horvat, at that very first, informal meeting, when she had arrived with Jessica several weeks ago and been privately introduced to the power players of the Republic.

Horvat had wanted to discount her. Not because she was a woman, although Casey had spent her entire life fighting that battle. No, he just didn't think an eighteen-year-old was capable of moving mountains.

Ask Sigmund about that, if you both end up in hell, Senator.

Casey walked slowly, regally, to the little podium, Captain Wald's briefing packet in one hand, a five-ring binder as thick as some of her favorite novels. Her mother had taught Casey how to enter a room and compel every person there to acknowledge you.

And the Empress was compelling at it. Casey might not have her mother's coloring, but she had that same long build, plus the muscles from father's side of the family, as evidenced by both Dad and Uncle Em. And she had committed fully to her training on the flight to *Ladaux.*

Jessica might not have fore-seen this particular scenario, but Casey had not been fooled. The Empire had been winning the war, at least until Jessica Keller arrived. And then they had started losing. Slowly, to be sure, victorious on other fronts.

But Jessica Keller had upset the apple cart in other ways, inspiring a whole generation of young women to ask their fathers why they couldn't do things.

Young women like Casey.

zu Wiegand, *Ritter of the Household*, about to speak with her father's voice, binding the Empire itself with her words.

She took the one shallow step up and rested the book on the inclined surface. Yan Bedrov had worked without notes for forty-five minutes, but he had not been called upon for arcane miscellanies. And Casey suspected he might have been able to answer those off the top of his head, as well.

Yan Bedrov was a man who ran deep.

Casey glanced to her right first, acknowledging her uncle's greatest foe in the days before Jessica, Nils Kasum, with a smile. The remaining five Lords were strangers to her, but she did not sense any great animosity from them.

Down front, Jessica and Moirrey, with Colonel *zu* Arlo and Captain Wald supporting them. Casey had taken on the entire *Fribourg* Fleet with their help.

And won.

The Premier and the President farther down. Casey could only dream of the day a female led the House of Dukes. Perhaps she needed to suggest that one of the empty duchies be granted to Queen Jessica. Casey could imagine her friend retiring to a life of Imperial politics, a shark encountering a school of sleepy tuna.

The Committee. An exotic thing. The closest equivalent might be Staff High Command, the group led now by Uncle Em in his black uniform, and only open to Princes of the Blood. She thought that they might have to relax their recruiting standards a bit, with Sigmund Dittmar dead in the coup, and Artur Marquering executed for treason not long afterwards. There weren't that many competent, seasoned commanders with the right heritage, these days.

Casey suppressed a grin at the thought of Jessica taking *that* room by storm, as well.

So, nineteen men and women of power, prestige, and old hatreds of *Fribourg*.

Jessica had told her that the Peace between nations rested on her words. She understood that now, looking at the many hostile faces.

At least Senator Horvat was neutral. Visibly.

"Raise your right hand," he commanded formally.

Casey did, pulling her shoulders back and down, and jutting her jaw, just a bit. These people would not intimidate an Emperor that had seen off a coup attempt and the first raid on *St. Legier* in three centuries.

"Do you swear under penalty of perjury that the testimony you are about to give is the full truth as you know it?"

"I do," Casey swore simply.

"Lady Casey," Horvat began slowly, taking her measure carefully. "You have witnessed the presentation given by Sri Bedrov, regarding several new warship designs he proposes that the *Republic of Aquitaine* construct. Did you have any questions for Sri Bedrov?"

"I did not, Senator," she replied.

Casey and Captain Wald had spent many hours poring over the designs with the pirate. And the implications.

Her father had suggested an absolute revolution in the Peace between *Fribourg* and *Aquitaine*, and entrusted her and Jessica to execute it.

Her biggest obstacle so far was seated before her, a graying Senator Jessica trusted, one of the woman's so-called Guardian Angels, along with Nils Kasum.

Senator Horvat picked up a piece of paper and pretended to study it for a second. Casey was not fooled by the mannerisms, although she suspected many would be.

"I have a letter from the *Fribourg Emperor*, Karl VII," Horvat said in a grand voice. "Offering to fund the construction of a number of naval vessels, on two conditions. One: that they be crewed exclusively by the Republic. And Two: that they be allowed to serve with the *Fribourg* Fleet on a neutral, distant frontier."

Casey could tell how many people had been privy to that secret communication, before now, by the location of the gasps, murmuring, and shouts emerging around her. Or rather, the gaps. About half the Committee had not known, but most of the other key players had: Kasum, Chavarría, Szabolcsi included.

Casey updated her mental notes regarding the still, dark waters that flowed in the Republic Senate. Father and Uncle Em would find her observations priceless when she got home. Perhaps she would need to write some non-fiction for a bit.

Senator Horvat actually had to reach out, grab, and slam the gavel down once on the table, a hard, ringing thump that cut through the rabble.

"There will be *order*," he called in a voice that would not be brooked.

Casey suspected that Horvat was keeping score right now, as well.

Silence eventually snuck into the room.

"Now then, *Ritter* Wiegand," the Senator continued, his tone ever so exasperated by the interruption. "Pardon me, *zu* Wiegand. You are familiar with the contents of the letter?"

"I am, Senator," she said. "And the implications."

Let them chew on that one. Remind them that *Fribourg*, while younger than *Aquitaine*, was much larger, and largely an unknown to these people. There would be wheels turning within wheels.

"To put it simply, then," Horvat stared at her. "Why?"

He really did have a cruel mouth. Thin lips pressed together, rather like a librarian about to shush someone. Beetling eyebrows drawing slowly together in the middle as he awaited her. Hot, dark eyes that had seen it all, done it all, and were not convinced that an eighteen-year-old *Princess Imperial* had anything new to show him.

Jessica had warned her that Tadej Horvat was something of a control freak. Casey could see that as she moved to introduce a whole new playing piece onto his otherwise-carefully-crafted chess board.

"There is Peace between our nations, Chairman Horvat," Casey replied simply. "Karl VII will see that it runs the entire length of the treaty, while looking for excuses to extend it beyond the quarter-century originally agreed to. We would enlist the aid of *Aquitaine's First Expeditionary Fleet* to help us address what we believe to be a threat to all humanity. Jessica Keller has assembled one of the best fighting organizations in a century, but *Buran* is something entirely new to all of us."

"*Buran?*" the man asked, still following a formal script in his head.

"*The Eternal*," Casey replied calmly. "The so-called *Lord of Winter*. One of the ancient evils from humankind's past, in control of an entire star empire that rivals *Fribourg* for size and power. Citizens of *Aquitaine*, hear me: *Buran* is a *Sentience*, a deathless artificial intelligence, of the kind that destroyed the homeworld and nearly our entire species. It is one of the *Destroyers*, threatening the modern age. *Fribourg* will not allow that."

Bedlam.

Casey shut her mouth and serenely rested her hands on the podium. It would be minutes before Horvat managed to regain control, as the entire room was consumed.

One Senator, an older man at the far end of the table, had apparently passed out, although medical staff were on hand and quickly moved the man to one of the audience seats, rather than transporting him to a hospital, so it must have been shock and not a heart attack.

Not that Casey was above using that as a weapon.

She hadn't told Jessica the complete truth, but Father and Uncle Em had instructed her that regardless of the outcome of her mission, they would fight. On two fronts, if necessary.

Without *Aquitaine*, though, they only expected to damage the beast while in the process of dying themselves, leaving Jessica to finish it off.

If she could.

CHAPTER III

Nils had been planning to have lunch here anyway, so he had a reservation already. Thirty seconds after Princess Kasimira had dropped her bomb on the Committee, he had sent a text update that he would need a larger table, possibly the entire room. The reply had been almost instant.

Someone had probably gotten bumped to a different room, a less prestigious one. A First Lord, he could do that. Not that he liked to wield such authority recklessly, but today it was necessary.

And so Nils found himself seated in the Marquette Room, tucked clear at the back of Fleet Headquarters, a twenty-minute walk from where the Lords of the Fleet had been entertaining the Committee. Tad, Jessica, Judit, and the Princess had joined him.

There were others that might be needed later. Captain Wald, from the Princess's staff, and Yan Bedrov, for instance, and Moirrey, one of these days as well, but momentous decisions would rest with the people right here.

Nils found it amusing how often the future of the Navy, and the Republic itself, had played out in this room. Important decisions made over wine and good antipasti plates. He made a note to check if any historian had ever made that connection, and written up a history of the room itself. It certainly needed one. He might have to suggest it to someone. A First Lord could do that, too.

They had added a leaf to the booth, extending it, and added a chair. As host, Nils had taken that, seating Tad and Jessica on his right and Judit and the Princess on his left. The wine came from one of Tad's estates, a sweet merlot that would sit well with freshly-baked sourdough bread.

Nils smiled at Tad's grumpiness. The man never liked losing control of his hearings, and he had certainly underestimated Lady Casey. Once. Most likely the last and only time that would happen.

Nils had warned him. At least Senator Nalani had not suffered a serious medical event, although the corpsmen medics had eventually convinced him to go to the fleet hospital for observation.

Nothing more of any use likely to be accomplished, Nils had suggested lunch, although he had been afraid Tad would break his gavel, pounding the table so angrily to get everyone to shut up.

So he made sure the first glass poured went to the Chairman, followed by Judit. And that the cheese plate landed at that end of the table.

"Better?" Nils asked his friend, who had only much later become his boss.

"Scamp," Tad replied around his glass. He turned his attention to the Princess. "And that, young lady, was certainly an interesting way to make sure you were on the evening vidcasts."

Nils watched the Princess affect a surprised look that fooled nobody, followed by a slight, mischievous smile.

"Whatever do you mean, Senator?" she asked lightly, tilting her head just the slightest bit. "I was given to understand this was to have been a secret hearing."

Nils laughed out loud.

"I can think of at least a half dozen people probably already leaking the good bits to friendly reporters," Nils said. "Not the parts that would get them prosecuted, mind you, but *Buran* as a lurid monster from the depths of history. Too good to let someone else get the headline."

"No doubt," Tad agreed. "Judit, how will this impact the elections?"

Nils let a little sourness color his face. The Senate sat at will, but it also had a fixed duration. One that was fast approaching. Elections would be required in a little over six months. Already, people were sharpening their pencils and their knives.

And Tad and Judit represented different parties. They still went to the opera on double-dates with their spouses, but that was after hours. The business of the Senate was beginning to turn from governance to politics, like the progression of the seasons on the planet below them.

Judit shrugged.

"Assuming I don't call a snap election late in the game, we should have time to negotiate a deal, all parties being interested," she said. "I suspect that it will then become a major campaign theme."

Tad nodded sagely.

Nils could already see the spin forming into little vortices. The Peace was popular. At the same time, sending a fleet off to fight in one of *Fribourg's* wars might not be, regardless of the public's fascination with Jessica. And the press would fall utterly in love with Princess Kasimira.

Casey.

She preferred to be Lady Casey, or *zu* Wiegand, since this was official business as a *Ritter*, a Knight representing the Imperial government, and not her role as the youngest daughter of the Imperial family.

Nils compared the woman to his own daughters when they had been that age. Anaïs, the elder, might have been up to the technical aspects of the task, but Estelle would have brought Casey's panache to it. Still, he could see his granddaughters growing up in a world colored by Jessica Keller and Lady Casey.

Interesting times, indeed.

Nils decided to break the ice wide open with a sledgehammer. With the elections coming, nothing less would do. And they wouldn't have the luxury of time on this one.

"Brass tacks, Lady Casey," he said, addressing himself to the woman as if she were one of his prize students, back in his teaching days. A younger Jessica Keller, perhaps. Not necessarily all that far off from the truth, from everything he had heard so far. "Assuming our government supports you in this task, what is your budget?"

He was amused by the way Casey slowly turned her head to face him, like she was lining up a turret for a shot. Measured, methodical, deadly.

"Based on the last set of notes from Captain Wald, First Lord?" she said to his nod. "The two cruisers in their current design incarnations take us to roughly seventy-eight percent, with construction contingencies built in. Four escorts on top push us to roughly ninety-seven percent. The alternative would have been to ask you to build a brand new Star Controller from scratch, using either plan seven or number nine, either of which would have been over ninety percent of the total budget allocated themselves."

Nils nodded but kept his surprise to himself. He hadn't really expected that honest nor that technical of an answer from the girl.

No. Woman. Grown woman who had personally seen off a coup attempt that would have resulted in her death. Lady Casey might give Jessica most of the credit, but Nils had skimmed Jessica's full report within eighteen hours of their arrival in-system three weeks ago.

Woman. Very much a young Jessica Keller, if she desired. Even at eighteen, Nils could see the same fire underneath.

Nils was impressed that she had the numbers at her fingertips. This was not a helpless princess on a photo op or a lark.

"And what do you actually propose to do with such a revised First Expeditionary Fleet?" Nils asked.

He could see the questions Tad and Judit wanted to ask, but they were probably going to let him drive this, being the expert. And this might be a nice way to finally ease into his retirement. Build this fleet and then take off the uniform so he could take up politics. Or raise cattle.

Nils was looking forward to being the sort of pain in Petra's ass that Tad usually was in his. Grumpy old senators who used to be Fleet Lords were the worst kind.

It would be tremendous fun.

Lady Casey studied his face for several seconds before she answered.

"Why should *Aquitaine* help *Fribourg* conquer the galaxy, First Lord?" she asked. "Is that the real question you want answered?"

"Your words, Lady Casey," he replied solemnly. "But yes. Why? Why should I, we, help our fiercest enemy when we might take the opportunity to reclaim a number of worlds that used to be part of the Republic? And perhaps more?"

"*Fribourg* is a militant culture, First Lord," she said in a calm, heavy voice. "It has been thus since the Founding, and before. We were not forged on a trade compact, as *Aquitaine* was by Henri Baudin. Father believes that *Fribourg* can be forced to change. Slowly. Painfully. Fretfully. But eventually successfully. Ekke, my brother, feels the same. They think that with fifty years to work at the project, two full Imperial generations, it can be done."

She paused to take a sip of wine and study the other faces before returning to him.

"But if we do not stop *Buran*, now, the beast will consume the Empire entirely before then. And you will be next."

"And Jessica Keller and First Expeditionary can prevent that?" Nils asked, careful to conceal the sarcasm that wanted to escape. She would misread it as mockery.

"*Fribourg* is also a very conservative society, First Lord," Lady Casey said. "Fleet tactics are based on a slow, methodical strategy, one that cannot quickly adapt to radical, newly-changed circumstances. Uncle Em, Emmerich Wachturm, could probably manage to drive them back, but he cannot be two places at once, and the hands that held the fleet's reins at *St. Legier* were not trustworthy. Sigmund Dittmar died during the coup. Artur Marquering was executed afterwards for treason. Kunibert Marquering was retired in semi-disgrace. We will be a generation rebuilding."

"And Jessica?" Nils pressed.

"Uncle Em considers her to be the best commander in the field today, First Lord," she explained. "Better than him, and at least as good as he was on his best day. His words, First Lord."

Jessica blushed furiously as everyone turned to look at her, but remained silent. Her debrief had taken three days, and there were still details to go through, as well as mountains of reports and logs to read.

Nils watched Lady Casey's head suddenly come up and look around the room. Her eyes settled on the woman tending the bar across the room, fierce, but not angry. At least, not that he could tell.

He turned to look, and noted the bartender grinning as she worked. A cat with a canary.

It was Lady Casey's turn to blush as he turned his attention back to her. She gestured to the ceiling.

Nils became aware of music that was playing, low and steady. A full string section slowly winding themselves up to lift the rafters, but still poised just at the verge of a dead gallop. A wave of cavalry building to a canter in the morning fog.

Half a league onward…

"That's the opening to my second symphony," she murmured by way of explanation, blushing ever so slightly.

Second? Symphony?

Nils made a note to go back and re-read this woman's dossier much closer. And perhaps purchase her musical catalog. You could learn a great deal about someone from their art.

"So we defeat *Buran,*" Tad suddenly growled. He was still fuming, but coming back to control with a little wine. "Then what, Lady Casey?"

"Then I will be ten or twenty years older, and ready to retire, Tad," Jessica suddenly injected into the conversation. "And the future will be safe from the demons of the past. Trade and culture will cross back and forth and we won't have to fight. I swore an oath, ladies and gentlemen. To end the war with *Fribourg*. This is one way to do it. The next generation will be left with the task of holding that peace, but I intend to deliver them the option."

Nils fixed his attention on his favorite student now.

"We were on the brink of pushing them all the way back, Jessica," he said. "You were. Winning back everything that had been lost. Possibly even destroying them, given enough time. Why should we give that up? Why hold the Peace, if *Fribourg* cannot stop us?"

"Emmerich Wachturm asked me that same question, Nils," she replied. "On the flight deck of *Amsel*, when he took me out to show me his brand new battleship. He told me that I held the balance of power in my own hands. That I could get the Senate to break the treaty, if I set my mind to it."

Jessica stopped to take a drink of wine and a deep breath.

"I have thought long and hard on that topic in the six months since," she said, turning her head to include everyone, even if the conversation really was just between the two. "In the heat of the moment, I reacted to protect Casey, and then to drive that son of a bitch Dittmar into the ground. Killing the *Buran* raider was just a lucky break. On my head, on my conscience, there can be a generation of peace, or a generation of war. Not for me. I will be at war for the rest of my life, I expect, but there are trillions of people out there who will have a chance to know a different galaxy, due to the choices we make, I make, today."

She fixed him with a cold stare that he felt all the way to his soul.

"*Buran* must be stopped," she whispered. "If I have to go fight them alone, I will, but I have the best team in the galaxy available. I would like your blessing to use them."

Nils felt cold death reach out a hand and just brush it across the back of his neck.

Jessica was serious. Enough so that she might actually resign everything if she had to. Fleet Centurion. Queen of the Pirates. Give up everything, like Yan Bedrov had, in order to face this new future.

And if she did, how many of the men and women of First Expeditionary, of the entire fleet, would do the same, just so they could follow this woman into the gates of hell?

Tad's face had closed. But that was a good sign. It meant he understood how closely balanced the stakes were, and would let Nils talk.

Judit had a fierce grin on her otherwise silent face. No doubt, this would be on a campaign poster, one way or the other, since Judit had largely built the Peace on Jessica's work and words.

Even Lady Casey had a wry smile on her face. But this was an Imperial Princess, and she should be expected to be something of an expert on politics as the art of the possible.

The decision was really rather easy. Like Jessica, Nils had given his entire life to the war effort. He could see the sun starting to rise in the distant, dark east.

Nils speared Tad with a smile.

"I'm going to need a new Fourth Lord if you're serious about doing this," he said simply. "A friendlier one."

Tad nodded.

"Pity we can't hire Bedrov," the Chairman mused, his face softening. "But I have a candidate in mind. Which reminds me. Bedrov was discussing a third investor in his mad scheme when all hell broke loose back there. Without him present, are the two of you willing to discuss the topic?"

Nils watched Jessica and Lady Casey communicate with a few quick shrugs and nods. They really had turned into a team over the last half year. What did that imply?

Jessica tapped a finger on the tabletop.

"No further than this room," she said. "And this group."

She waited for the rest to nod.

"Yan's a crazy genius," Jessica continued. "I knew it before. I learned even better on the flight home. He wants to approach the President herself, but as a private citizen. He figures that to be the single highest vote of confidence he can get anywhere."

"That's boy's got brass," Tad observed. "Let me chat her up privately and see what she thinks."

Judit's nod was the critical one, the one that sealed the deal.

A moment of tension passed.

Tad turned a beaming look on the princess.

"With that concluded, I have one last thought. Lady Casey. I used to be a Command Centurion, in my younger days," he rumbled, an angry bear about to chase a smaller rival off from a favorite berry bush. "Yours and Bedrov's plan has only one flaw that I can see, but also one I think we can fix, as soon as Arott Whughy gets back with *Auberon*."

"What's that?" she asked.

Nils could hear the edge of reserve under her words, the challenge, like a knife hidden in folds of cloth.

"You didn't dream nearly big enough," Tad replied with an evil grin.

CHAPTER IV

Because Jessica spent so little time actually working in her office, as opposed to being in the field, this last year, being on a mission to *St. Legier*, the space was still rather sterile. She hadn't bothered decorating the walls with artwork. The only modification to the furniture was a small sideboard Jessica had added to hold Marcelle's antique coffee service, the altar that traveled everywhere with them.

Marcelle grinned at her as she worked to grind the beans with a hand-held rotary burr. The woman claimed that using a powered device cut the beans too fine and you ended up with a more bitter tone than you got with a coarser grind and a slow brew.

And Marcelle had spent decades perfecting the technique, since she first got Jessica addicted to the delicious outcome of her art.

Fresh honey from her uncle's farm. Fresh cream that had been inside a cow on that same farm three days ago. Beans carefully frozen for transport and just now grinding, before they could thaw. A small vial of bourbon, hand-infused with a sliced vanilla bean and left to gestate for three weeks.

Jessica didn't spoil herself with much, or very often, but her coffee was still the one indulgence she allowed herself. Especially today, when she needed to upend the entire galaxy again, and needed the assistance of the most dangerous pixie ever born to do it.

Marcelle checked her watch and plugged in the self-heating teapot. Not for her a battery-powered version, but another unit made to modern specs from an ancient design. Jessica had told her to fill it all the way today, which would be enough water for four mugs.

Three, and a refill if someone wanted.

A chime filled the room. Willow had approved of someone getting past her, and there was only one person on the list. Anyone else would have caused Jessica's other bodyguard to ask. Or just turn them away.

The hatch opened and Moirrey entered.

Centurion *zu* Kermode. Lady Moirrey of Ramsey. The Evil Engineering Gnome.

Pint-sized.

"You wanted t'see me, ma'am?" she asked in a light tone, coming more or less to a semblance of attention. Maybe.

Jessica pointed at the chair on the left, farthest away from Marcelle.

"Sit," she ordered. "Marcelle is making us coffee."

Jessica looked at Marcelle and included her in the conversation.

"And make yourself a mug," Jessica continued. "I would like your input on this topic as well."

That got an arched eyebrow in response. Marcelle had spent a good portion of her life waiting outside in the hallway, protecting Jessica from people and problems, or standing quietly back against a wall in case her charge needed something done or retrieved.

Things were different today. They needed to be handled differently, and Moirrey might not have the cultural depth that Marcelle did, at least not yet, to answer this need.

They waited in comfortable silence as Marcelle committed art. Moirrey got the first mug, flavored just so. Jessica was next, enjoying an extra dash of cream just because it tasted of home.

Finally, Marcelle sat, eyeing Jessica through a squint that promised a sarcastic tongue when she finally got around to speaking. With Marcelle, that might be a while.

"We are most likely going to war," Jessica began simply. "The Senate appears inclined to back us in our task, and to do so with a serious amount of support."

She paused to let them absorb that. The deliberations had been mostly secret, but of course details had been all over the vid last night and in all the news magazines today.

"Rights," Moirrey nodded sharply. "What's ya needs to take't t'the next steps?"

Jessica sipped her coffee and let the warmth fill her belly with *comfortable.*

Then she took a step off the cliff. That was always the risk, when asking Moirrey to color outside the lines, but she had never been disappointed.

"Bedrov went and decided to out-Roman us," she said with a conspiratorial grin. "His cruiser designs are named after ancient Roman Legions. So I did some research into the deep archives last night. Ancient Rome, the Republic that birthed the famous empire that so much of our history derives from."

Jessica watched Marcelle struggle to not roll her eyes. The woman had never been the bookish type, usually finding more trouble in bars and with boys and girls, where Jessica had preferred the dojo and the library. But that was part of what made them an effective team.

"Dunno them folks much," Moirrey replied. "Ramsey were more Nordic folks 'long those lines."

"Which is why I wanted Marcelle in this conversation," Jessica said. "She can help with some of the cultural context that might not translate well. The word I want you to look up is *fetial.* Then I want you to build me a spear."

"A spear?" Marcelle asked in disbelief.

"Yes," Jessica agreed. "When you read the details, you'll understand."

"So nots just any spear," Moirrey said. "Yer wantin' som'thin' big, right? Impressives."

"I want *2218 Svati Prime, Pint-sized,*" Jessica said simply. "This is going into the history books, one way or the other, so we need to make a grand, formal gesture. *Aquitaine* was at war with *Fribourg* in one sense or another for nearly one hundred and fifty years. Most people still think this is just a lull before we start everything up again, like last time. And we don't have the formality about this sort of thing that Republican Rome did, opening the gates of the Temple of Janus and all that. I need *Auberon*'s Art Department to fix that for me, with a blank piece of paper, a history book, and a reasonable budget. You two tell me what you need, as I'm going to be in a hellscape of meetings until all this works out, and won't have any time to dedicate to it."

"That's we can do," Moirrey said, glancing over at Marcelle for confirmation. "Will that be all, ma'am?"

"It will," Jessica said.

Within moments, she was alone in the bland, empty office.

War was coming. Best to do it right.

CHAPTER V

They were almost home. For *Wiley*, Command Centurion Shiori Ness, commander of the Corynthe flagship *Kali-ma*, it had been a long year at sea, but she had no real life beyond sitting on this command deck, commanding.

Nobody waiting for her to open the door. Everyone else would be happy to be home, if for no other reason than to see what Jessica's people had done with a year to work and enough firepower to crack any two heads together.

Hopefully, those fine folks from *Aquitaine*, in their pretty uniforms, had kept the peace, and she wasn't about to drop into a palace where someone other than David was regent, but her intelligence was weeks old, picked up at their last food-and-supplies stop.

Times like this, she missed that old rascal Bedrov. Anders Himura was probably a better officer, but Yan had developed a knack for gunnery she had rarely encountered. He might have been the best tactical officer she had ever served with. Still, he had trained a good crew, and Himura had driven them to be better people, better officers, and not just better killers.

But she might need killers in four minutes when they dropped out of JumpSpace.

"Anders," she called from her command station, waiting for him to turn. "Status?"

"All gun crews green, Top," he replied with a hard, predatory smile.

"Flight Wing reports green and ready to hot launch on command. Damage Control teams suited up and ready to play."

Yes, they had spent too much time training with the Imperials, those weeks when the ship was dry-docked for repairs. At least they had been able to fly way sooner than the *Blackbird*, but nobody had mauled *them*.

"Science Officer," *Wiley* continued, circling her bridge. "We'll be coming out low, down on *Petron*'s south pole, and relatively hot. We'll need probes fired over both horizons."

Bryn Maki looked up from his boards a second later and met her eyes across the space. His was a rare genotype on *Petron*, a descendent of one of the early families, colonists originally from *Nihon*, themselves almost pureblooded Japanese from the Homeworld, however many millennia ago. He was tall and slender, with straight black hair, brown eyes, and a golden hue to his skin that was so much brighter than her own tone. And rare, with all the pale-skinned Anglos that made up so much of the rest of the crew.

"Already programmed, Command Centurion," he said crisply, never once losing touch with his boards.

It was good. Wouldn't do to drop out of jump on top of a hostile fleet that had taken over while they were gone, even if *Wiley* couldn't imagine the circumstances where that happened.

She opened a comm back to *Baxter*.

"Desianna, this is *Wiley*," she said. "Final warning before we drop out. You should be on station in about two hours."

"Already packed and set for a spiral launch, Shiori," the Prime Minister said in her happy voice.

That woman would be happy to be back. To see her son, her friends, her home.

Not for the first time, *Wiley* wondered if she should convince Galen Estevan to make good his threat to build some warships, rather than motherships, and sail off to help Jessica.

How are you going to keep them on the farm, after they've been to *St. Legier*?

But that was a tomorrow problem. She had a year to get caught up on.

"All hands, prepare for insertion," came the call, followed a few seconds later with "What the hell is that?"

CHAPTER VI

Denis Jež looked up from his book when the ship-wide alert chimed. They were already two months overdue for Jessica and *Kali-ma* to return and send them home, but he understood why, from the regular packets First Lord had sent.

He was just mad the woman had gone off and had a major adventure without him.

"All hands, this is Nina Vanek aboard *Auberon*. I have the flag," her voice came calmly through the speakers. "Possible hostile insertion detected. All hands to battle stations."

Denis was off his bunk, into his shoes, and out the hatch in two seconds. It wasn't his watch right now, so he was in his quarters, rather than his day office, but this Star Controller had been well-thought out when she was designed. He was on the bridge in less than thirty seconds.

Nina bounced out of the command station as soon as she was sure it was him and took up the Tactical boards. Fleet Centurion Whughy would be down on the Flag Bridge. Tamara Strnad would normally be bringing up tactical as his First Officer, but she was over on their newest ship, playing command centurion for them. Below, Flight Deck was prepared to fire three alert fighters, and probably a GunShip, into space as soon as they were needed.

"Status?" Denis called.

Around him, the bridge had fallen into that calm poise that told him everyone was ready for battle. There had only been a few of those over the last year. Nobody in this entire sector was big enough to challenge a Star Controller, let alone one with her escort team in close contact.

Still, there were always dumbass pirates out there. Fewer today, but it was like a disease, and the vaccine was slow to act.

"One vessel just came out of jump, Command Centurion," Nina replied, cycling her boards and bringing up firing solutions. "Launched two probes immediately, and she was running hot to begin with. Passive scan reads her as a 4-ring mothership, and none are scheduled to arrive this week."

"Nav, plot a course to intercept, but wait for the command," Denis commanded. "All weapon stations stand by to engage."

After a year, he had a feel for the Fleet Centurion down in Jessica's chair. *She* would have expected him to begin moving immediately, friend or foe. Whughy wanted to give the order himself.

Denis would be glad to have Jessica back.

"Bridge, this is Whughy, I have the flag," the man's voice came through. "Do we have positive ID?"

Spit and polish. By the numbers. None of the elegant curves compared to Jessica's thinking. She would have used anything as an excuse to keep the crew sharp, not that Arott Whughy had let them get dull.

Senior Centurion Daniel Giroux had been with Denis for his entire professional career, always serving on a vessel named *Auberon*, first the Strike Carrier, and now the Star Controller. And he had refused the promotion that would have made him a command centurion on his own scout or survey vessel. That would have taken him away from the center of things.

Another one infected by Tomas Kigali's warrior ethos.

But he was among the best at what he did, and Denis was happy to still have him, even if it had required the First Lord to pull a few strings. The man had apparently done it to keep this crew together, when normally officers would have cycled in and out much more frequently.

"Stand by, Flag," Giroux said, face down over a readout. "Confirm mothership. Confirm 4-ring mass. Confirm *Kali-ma* on engine signature, but she's had some work done somewhere in dry-dock since last we met."

Denis laughed quietly. Nina grinned at him from across the room. They had all read the reports about the coup. Most of them felt the same jealousy at not being where *Kali-ma* was.

"All hands, maintain battle stations while we maneuver," Whughy ordered over the comm. "*Corynthe*'s Queen has returned, aboard her flagship. All vessels stand by to acknowledge *Kali-ma*. Bridge, move to rendezvous. Assume they'll want to board the orbital platform soonest."

Only *Aquitaine* would greet a Queen of the Pirates with 21-gun salutes over her own capital. But it was one of the reasons these people were pirates, and not civilized folks, all his efforts over the last year notwithstanding.

"Jež, this is *Wiley*," a new voice broke in suddenly from the comm. An angry, exasperated one. "What the hell have you done to my station?"

Denis joined the whole bridge laughing before he signaled everyone to silence and replied.

"We have nearly a thousand marines and a heavy construction Ala of engineers available, *Wiley*," Denis replied, grinning ear to ear. "So we brought the place up to Republic standards and expanded it a little. Wait until you see the new ring highway connecting the outer boroughs of *Corynthe*."

Over nine hundred very bored marines, one of two battalions they normally carried, seconded to *Digger* Wolanski and his group of lunatic construction specialists who had replaced the other security battalion. Those folks had only gotten a taste of fun when they were unleashed on *Thuringwell*. Now there were schools, hospitals, water treatment facilities, and reservoirs.

And not just here. Goodwill tours to eight other planets, dropping pre-fabbed facilities or cutting new roads as a reward for being good, little, civic-minded pirates who paid their taxes on time and took care of their citizens. Plus visits to three places where they didn't. Or hadn't, until Arott Whughy and First Expeditionary Fleet, under direction of David Rodriguez, Regent, had brought them more firmly into compliance.

"*Kali-ma*, this is Whughy," the Fleet Centurion joined the conversation. "Do you have a flag aboard?"

"Negative, *Auberon*," Wiley replied. "We outran all news, including *Marco Polo* and the Imperial TCL accompanying us. I have dispatches for David and orders for you from First Lord."

"Roger that, *Kali-ma*," Whughy replied. "See you aboard the station shortly."

CHAPTER VII

DATE OF THE REPUBLIC SEPTEMBER 04, 399 ROYAL PALACE FACILITY, PETRON ORBIT

Because Jessica wasn't aboard the ship, David Rodriguez, *Regent of Corynthe*, king in all but name, was able to go straight to meetings, without having to have a slow round of formal receptions welcoming her home.

Jessica had always grumbled privately about the effort, but she did understand the visuals of the task, and how much she meant to the people who were beginning to think like members of a polity, and not just the next victim-in-waiting. Or working to make someone else the next victim.

So he was in Jessica's favorite boardroom, seated in her chair at the end of the table. Uly Larionov and Flag Centurion Enej Zivkovic were on his left and right, representing the government. Arott Whughy was next to Enej, representing the military might of both *Corynthe* and *Aquitaine*.

At the far end of the table, David observed his mother, Desianna Indah-Rodriguez, widow of Arnulf, former King of the Pirates. It had been six years since Jessica had avenged Arnulf and taken the throne, keeping it just warm enough that nobody would challenge her, or David as her regent.

Not that anybody of that mind had survived the original purges, but there were always fools. Jessica herself had thought it would take three generations for civilization to fully take hold. He had bet her that they could do it in two.

His mother had taken the role of Prime Minister. If there was a more-dangerous politician left in all of *Corynthe*, it was probably Uly, seated next to the throne as Comptroller of the Crown.

Uly's nephew, Galen, had accompanied Desianna and Jessica to *Fribourg*, and sat now on Mother's right, with *Wiley* on her left, as Shiori finished her update.

An awkward silence descended as people absorbed her words, but her smile had not dimmed one bit in the time she was away. Grown, if anything.

David was acutely aware that he was only Regent, serving at Jessica's whim, even though she had made it clear that her duties might never allow her to return full-time, at least until she retired from active duty in another decade or two. And even then, she might abdicate in his favor, once people got used to the idea of him in charge.

But he also knew that she trusted him to do things right. Slowly, overcoming centuries of inertia and tradition, but correctly and properly. As much as it pained him sometimes.

"Mother, *Wiley*, Galen, thank you for what you have done, and welcome home," he said. "We'll have a small party tomorrow for everyone, that will additionally serve as a going-away for the First Expeditionary Fleet."

David turned his attention to the man in white. But for Jessica Keller, Arott Whughy would be the top prospect to become First Lord in this generation of *Aquitaine* officers. He might still be, since Jessica was obviously going to be doing ten thousand other things, and Arott had spent a year here effectively acting as Vice Admiral of the *Corynthe* Fleet.

A useful training program. Maybe he should suggest it to Jessica.

Whughy's recruiting drive had been very successful. David would miss the hundreds of young people, more than three to one female, who had taken *Aquitaine* up on the offer of service, but he also knew that many of them would come back in a decade and make *Corynthe* a better place.

And he didn't have to worry about *Wiley* deciding she wanted his job. Or anyone getting through that woman to try to take it from him.

"Fleet Centurion?" David asked formally. It was a mere formality, but Whughy prized form probably more than content. In that, he differed greatly from Jessica. "How soon can your squadron be prepared to depart? From Desianna's descriptions, you won't be needed immediately for the war effort, but I also know your folks want to go home."

"There are two remaining projects on the ground that I would like to wrap up, sire," Arott replied quickly. "But we have been prepared for seven weeks now, so we should be able to depart within a week and not leave things undone."

Undone. A man intent on seeing things to completion. Tax revenues had gone up fourteen percent in the last year, as his teams built and improved facilities, freeing up capital for investment in people and training. And had worked to weld *Corynthe* into a thing, and not just a place.

Arnulf's dream, brought to fruition by his widow, his successor, and his oldest son.

David nodded. He glanced at his principle advisors. Enej and Uly nodded as well. A week would be sufficient.

"*Wiley*," he said. "I want to hear about the *Buran* attacker now. And what it is that Yan Bedrov and Galen have cooked up. *Pops* will be ecstatic if there are new things to build."

CHAPTER VIII

It wasn't a place he liked to visit. Too many bad memories. Too much risk of running into some of his old comrades, the few of them that weren't dead or in prison. Of the rest, very few of them would ever recognize him, especially today.

But Vo Arlo had made a promise to himself.

That he would come to Anameleck Prime. To see who he had become.

It was a cool morning, late spring at mid-latitudes. The boulevard he was walking along was wide and straight, lined with big trees and small shops. The city known as Anameleck Core was the capital of the Republic's industrial might, the center of finance and manufacturing, and existed in the shadow of some of the biggest shipyards in known space.

At the intersection, he paused, looking left down a street where things got…more interesting. Z'Shani was down that way, the slum where he had been born, lived until he was sixteen, had escaped from. A kilometer and a half walk would pass him through the Dragon Gates and into the old warren of cramped streets, tall buildings, and laundry hanging from lines strung between balconies.

Mankind could fly between stars, and yet there was still a core of rich folks who demanded that people be poor, just to give them someone to be superior to.

Vo caught himself grinding his teeth and stopped. He wasn't here to be a cat burglar any more, not like the old days. And he wasn't here to change the world down there, although he understood now what levers could be applied to do that.

And he knew who to talk to, about changing things, but she wasn't here, and didn't need this on her plate right now.

Maybe, when he got back to *Ladaux*. And maybe not. He had other options now.

Vo caught a reflection of himself in a glass storefront that made him pause. The weather had promised mist or rain later, so he had worn his third-best dress uniform today, the one for regular events. *Auberon*'s patch on his shoulder, as always. Tags for Security and Command on the right breast. The Big Four awards on the left. It was impressive for a simple Centurion, if he could be said to be one.

Vo wasn't sure what he was anymore, except that he was a thirty-one-year-old, active-duty marine with a job to do. So he was here.

He crossed the street to the monumental edifice that took up the entire block, slate and tan stone rising fourteen stories into the gray sky like a semi-malevolent pyramid. An altar squatting angrily on the roadside, chewing up young lives and frequently not spitting them out until it was too late.

The Temple of Law.

He had escaped. Luck, timing, something. Being the right person on the right morning, perhaps. Vo figured he might never know, and that was okay.

Through the door, two middle-aged men in security uniforms looked up from their morning gossip. The day was early, so not many people had come to the Anameleck Courthouse yet. It would get crazy later, he knew.

The one on the left sat bolt upright as Vo approached. He rose suddenly and saluted smartly, staring intently at the ribbons on Vo's chest. Not many people survived winning the Republic Cross. Almost none did it twice.

Vo returned the salute anyway, even though it was unnecessary for the man to have done it in the first place: indoors, and a civilian to boot, but the guard had obviously served his hitch.

"How can I direct you, Centurion?" the guard asked in a scratchy tenor.

"Judge Metharom's chambers," Vo replied simply.

It was nobody's business but his, why he was here, in dress, unannounced.

"Fourth floor, sir," the man said, turning to point. "Lifts are on your right."

"Thank you," and Vo was gone.

He ignored the murmured conversation the two guards struck up as he walked. Presumably, the one explaining the uniform and the medals to the other. Vo did catch the word *hero* being bandied about. He shrugged, but only internally.

The fourth floor was a long, quiet hallway with closed doors, frosted glass for the most part. Senior Judge Holman Metharom's door was on the very end, down that protracted walk.

Vo took a breath and opened that door into a small office.

A woman sat behind a broad desk, looking up slowly as he closed the door behind him. She had a heavy-set kind of bulk to her. Not fat, but solid with an extra ten kilos about her. Gray hair with only traces of brown still in it. Crow's feet and lines. Sharp eyes.

Vo would have guessed a rough mid-fifties. *Anameleck Prime* was not a soft place to live, unless you were one of the blessed.

Her eyes got an appraising cast as he approached her. Hard, but with a small grin tucked in. She reminded him of one of his teachers, back when he was ten, with that same knowing look.

Vo felt like a side of meat as she caressed his whole frame with her eyes. He still didn't understand how an ugly grunt like him could have that effect on some women, but he did. He had learned to live with it and keep his opinions to himself.

"You were a lot skinnier, then," she said by way of opening.

Vo blinked in surprise, but the woman did look familiar. Fourteen years ago, she probably would have been about forty and still a brunette. Skinnier, too, but never skinny.

And he had been skinnier, too. 198 centimeters tall and built like a pencil, but that was when he was climbing walls and breaking into buildings for a living. Or whatever you called the occupation of a cat burglar. No extra mass because there was never enough food for a sixteen-year-old from the wrong side of the Gates, and anything extra he got always went to his little sisters and his family.

Vo smiled with sudden memory. She had been the bailiff, that day. He remembered her now, a woman who looked tough enough to handle any punk who got hauled in by the gendarmes.

Like him.

"The Navy has treated me well," Vo rumbled back at her.

Again, that appraising look. Meat, on a hook.

"Yes, it has, Centurion Arlo," she replied. "What can I do for you?"

Or to *me?*

She had that look in her eyes, too.

"I was hoping to see the Judge, madam," he said. "To let him know that things turned out well. Is he in?"

"No," she said. "He only works two days a week now, as a Senior Judge, but I know where he should be today."

She rose abruptly and stepped around the desk.

He remembered her well, now. 160cm tall and all business. Probably could have taken him then. Probably not today, but you never knew.

"Shall we?" she asked. "It's a short walk."

Vo nodded.

"Alda Greet," she held out a hand. "We've never properly met."

"Vojciech *zu* Arlo," he replied. "Was I that bad that you remember me, fourteen years later?"

"Oh, no," she laughed musically, opening the door to the hallway and gesturing for him to proceed. "I looked you up when the papers ran a story about you three years ago. Local boy made good. And then again after the trouble at the Imperial palace last year."

Vo nodded and walked.

Local boy. Made good.

Wonders.

The place wasn't sure if it wanted to be a bar, a restaurant, or a fraternal organization, judging by the way it was decorated. Probably a little of each, Vo decided as he followed Alda into the room. White tile floors, and rough concrete walls. Vaulted ceiling with exposed pipes. There were twenty tables scattered about, with a dozen or so people, usually alone, having breakfast, or just coffee, or a reading.

It was too quiet to be a restaurant or a bar, even mid-morning, and the clientele were all older folks, averaging somewhere north of sixty, at first glance, up to the wizened, little troll in the corner doing a crossword puzzle on paper as fast as he could write.

The judge wasn't dressed as a judge, today, wearing nothing more than a semi-formal suit, perhaps the kind normally covered by robes.

And he hadn't changed appreciably from Vo's nightmares. Mostly bald then. Completely now. Wrinkled and hunched more.

That same sharp gleam in those eyes as they came to rest on Vo's face.

Vo felt like a mouse hiding in the grass as a hawk suddenly appeared overhead.

"Holman, look who came to visit," Alda said kindly as they approached. "Vo *zu* Arlo."

The judge rose from his seat slowly, with the kind of care an elderly man took, unsure of his physicality. He held out a hand for Vo to shake.

"Welcome, Sri Arlo."

The grip was that of a much younger man.

The judge powered off his reading tablet and gestured for them to join him at his small table.

Vo sat and let the silence descend around them. The Fleet Centurion had taught him the trick of using awkward pauses in conversation as a weapon.

"In my decades as a judge, I have sent more than two thousand young men and women into military service," the judge said in a slow grind. "As an alternative to a life of poor decisions and dead ends. Those were the ones that had some glimmer about them. That they might make something of themselves, if given a blank slate upon which to write."

Vo nodded. That just about described his life and his entry into the *Republic of Aquitaine* Navy. Everyone was equal in basic training. Nobody cared about your past, your education, or your future. They only wanted to know about your capabilities. Could you do the job handed to you? Could you learn to rise above yourself and become a leader of others?

"Most served out a three year hitch and were done," the man continued. "Of those, I have a very low recidivism rate. Something like four percent ever ended up on the wrong side of the law again for anything more serious than a traffic ticket or a row in a bar."

"What was it about me?" Vo asked in a compact voice.

That was the question that had haunted him, all these years. Had brought him back to this planet for the first time in…

Vo noted how both of them smiled at that. Obviously, he had been a topic of conversation, probably more than once.

Local boy, made good.

"Brains, young man," Senior Judge Metharom smiled. "I had all your test results from school in front of me when you appeared. I always do. Crime is frequently a moment of bad luck, so I want to see the years that led up to it. The fleet doesn't want to deal with a rotten apple any more than the justice system does. You had potential, if you could be put into a system that gave you purpose, structure."

"I still got lucky," Vo said. "Senior Security Centurion Crncevic, *Navin the Black*, was my first commander, back on the *Cahllepp Frontier*. Later, Jessica Keller."

"And each recognized in you abilities you didn't even know you had, Centurion," the judge replied. "Both have written me letters in the last few years, letting me know how you had turned out. They wanted me to know that my system did work."

Both of them? The Fleet Centurion had gone that deep into his files, his background, that she could write a letter to this man?

Yeah, he supposed so. Jessica was like that.

Vo could only imagine the level of background scrutiny he had been subject to when a letter from the *Emperor of Fribourg* had come with his name on it.

"So you knew?" Vo asked.

The judge's eyes got shrewd all of a sudden.

"I knew that you had succeeded beyond even my wildest expectations, Centurion," he said with a solemn smile. "Until you walked through the door just now, I had no idea what kind of man you turned out to be."

Vo nodded.

Neither had he.

CHAPTER IX

Jessica wondered at the small group as they contentedly trooped from exhibit to exhibit. Trust Moirrey to decide that they needed a day off and that it should be a visit to the zoo. And then convince everyone to go along with her.

The Evil Engineering Gnome and Casey wore matching, perfectly contrasting sun dresses for the warm weather. Marcelle and Willow were in outfits that might be interpreted as paramilitary tactical gear, at least by a civilian. Jessica wore one of her older green and black Command Centurion uniforms, minus all patches and identifying badges of any kind.

That was for the benefit of the last member of the troupe, Captain Wald. Torsten, since he was also wearing a semi-civilian outfit that might just as easily pass for that of an economics professor, which he might have been. And might yet be once he retired from active duty. Average height for a man meant that he was shorter than both Marcelle and Casey, although taller than Willow, Moirrey, or Jessica. His dark brown, curly hair was clipped exceptionally short today, enough so that Jessica could see the gray hairs starting to infiltrate everywhere.

The zoo was mostly empty of visitors, this early in the day and late in the season. A few other groups of tourists were wandering about. Several parents with young children in strollers or tow, exploring the sights and smells.

"What's next?" Casey asked Moirrey, arm in arm like long-lost-sisters.

Moirrey carried a map in her free hand. She lifted it up and studied it for a moment.

"Dinna know," she chattered. "T'ink I'd ken do th'birds next. How's ya feels 'bouts holding an owl on yer hand, Case?"

"An owl?"

"Aye," Moirrey beamed. "They does falconry here, but night critters, with trained owls. Always wanted me an owl when I were a kitten. No place fer one onna ship, thoughs."

"I like it," Casey replied. Jessica watched her turn and bring everyone into the conversation with her gaze. "How about you?"

Jessica glanced at Torsten and caught a ghost of a grimace. He apologized with a shrug.

"If I may," he said carefully. "I think I would like to rest here on a bench for a bit. You ladies go enjoy the raptor house and come get me in a bit?"

"Ooh, we can waits." Moirrey chirped. "Is no goin' nowhere."

"I'll be fine," he said, making a friendly motion to shoo the woman and all her energy along.

"You go," Jessica decided. "I'll stay and keep him safe from nannies and pigeons."

Willow started to say something, being the way-too-serious bodyguard, but Marcelle cut her off with a look. After several years together, nothing more was needed. And Lady Casey was a bigger target than Jessica, out of uniform and hiding in plain sight. The rest left.

Jessica followed Torsten to a concrete bench at a crossroads in the walkway, watching the man walk with a hint of a limp. Across the way, the four women made their way to a giant, red barn, wood-sided and with big, sliding doors. It reminded Jessica of something one of her uncles once had on his own farm. A place to store harvesting equipment for the most of the year it was unneeded, but must be protected from weather.

The whole zoo had that feel to it, which made sense. Penmerth might be the capital city of the Republic, but it had never grown into anything bigger than a medium-sized college town surrounded by millions of hectares of farm country in every direction.

Bankers went to *Anameleck Prime* to make money and fame. The Navy preferred a small-town feel to what it did. Kept the staff humble, to live among the farmers and ranchers that really represented the backbone of the nation.

A slight breeze picked up as they sat. There would be clouds later, just peeking over the horizon, but the sun was out now, so he had chosen the side of the walkway with shade.

Seated, Jessica could see the straps that held the man's prosthetic leg in place through the normally-baggy cloth. Then-Lt. Commander Torsten Wald had won the *Imperium Medal for Bravery* for his actions, saving several members of his crew from death in a hull-breach. He had lost his left leg about mid-femur when he got caught in a slamming emergency bulkhead, pulling the last of his men to safety instead of himself.

Afterwards, he had gone back to school from his hospital bed and rehab assignments, discovering a penchant for numbers theory. A PhD in economics had been his ticket to a staff job, a year before he would have been ready to return to active duty on a warship. He had never looked back.

With Lady Casey walking away, she watched Torsten relax enough to show the amount of pain he must be in.

"Bad?" she asked, watching him massage his left thigh.

"New planet, new gravity, new weather," he said through gritted teeth. "Didn't realize the walking would aggravate it this badly, or I would have brought something for the pain and the swelling. I'll be fine by the time they remember they left us here. And it was a good excuse for us to talk, semi-publically, but without everyone around."

"I see," Jessica replied.

She did, too. The four weeks since they had arrived on *Ladaux* had been a whirlwind of activity. This was the first day since then that Jessica had been able to schedule time for her and Moirrey to take their guests touristing without it interfering with meetings or other official duties.

She hadn't been completely alone with the man in nine months. Not since the reception where she first met him, and even then hadn't been alone, instead surrounded by all the women of her traveling household in the midst of a formal, Imperial reception. It had merely felt like just the two of them, until Emmerich Wachturm intruded.

She studied Wald's eyes. Green, like hers, with depths of pain and uncertainty visible, even now. Serious face. Utter stillness.

Like that first time they met, she watched him hesitate, a naturally-reticent man forced to speak up in a potentially-awkward situation. A minefield stretched out between them, even if only a psychological one.

Jessica had been waiting for him to get comfortable enough to confront her. It appeared he had arrived.

She watched the faintest grin cross his face.

"This is not a question for the Fleet Centurion, nor the Queen," he said carefully. "Possibly, the *Wildgraf.*"

Jessica smiled, suddenly back in that reception and watching this man work up the courage to confront *Fribourg's* greatest enemy. Alone.

"Ask, Captain," Jessica replied mildly, just as she had then. "I will judge."

Still, he hesitated, probably reliving that night as well.

"I understand the reason I am here, on *Ladaux,*" he said with a tone verging on angry grimness, but never quite succeeding. "Reasons. Two-fold, in fact. Lady Casey really did need a naval construction specialist, a fleet officer, and an economist on her staff. I was handy, an expert in all three, and the Grand Admiral trusts me."

"But?" she pressed carefully.

"I am concerned at Emmerich Wachturm's ulterior motives," he continued. "And possibly His Majesty's as well, since something like this had to have been approved at the highest level."

"What did Em say?" Jessica asked.

"To me?" he replied. "Nothing. Nothing at all. But there were questions. And rumors. And Desianna asked things as well, both before we left and on the trip here."

He ground to a halt at that point, confronting a chasm Jessica could see at the man's feet.

"I am an Imperial officer," he spat out quietly, gesturing with the hand farther away. "I know my duty. But, this…"

And that was where words failed.

Jessica nodded. She had been down this same logical path. There had been days she wanted to head straight back to *St. Legier* and strangle Admiral Wachturm for presuming to send Torsten Wald along on this mission, with all that it implied.

And days she wanted to thank the Grand Admiral for that same presumption. Possibly the Emperor, the old Emperor, as well.

She smiled again to put Torsten at ease. He had wanted to ask a question of the *Wildgraf,* and not the Fleet Centurion or the Queen. In Imperial culture, that made it a *personal* question.

"And you are concerned at the expectations placed upon you by your superior officers," she said. "The personal implications of sending *you,* rather than any other officer."

Silently, Torsten nodded, an officer facing the gallows, but doing so without flinching.

"Because there was a spark between us that night," she continued. "Something we have not discussed, but both recognized, however silently we did so."

Again, he nodded. The pain was back in his eyes. Physical, as his thigh muscles screamed in agony. Emotional, as the two of them came face to face over a topic that they had only danced around, ere now.

Sitting, Jessica had been very careful to retain a space between them. Two acquaintances on a bench, chatting, rather than lovers on a rendezvous.

She reached out her right hand, slowly and carefully, but not tentatively, placing it on his shoulder.

"In *Fribourg* culture, it would be incumbent upon you to make your feelings and emotions known, Torsten," she said. "And, thus, you must confront the *Wildgraf* on a personal topic that touches too close to home. Especially as she outranks you socially and militarily."

He nodded, still silent. She could feel how hard his heart was pounding right now. Almost as much as hers, which surprised her.

"How fortunate we are, then, to be in *Aquitaine*, Captain," she continued. "This topic can be addressed on a personal level, and not as an affair between nations."

He started breathing again at that. Shallow. Rapid. But breathing.

"Am I wasting my time, pursuing the woman Jessica Keller?" he asked. "The *Wildgraf*? Should I retain the distance between us, and act only as Lady Casey's Aide d'Economics?"

Jessica realized that she had stopped breathing as well, poised on this man's response.

"I don't think so, Torsten," she replied, looking inside herself. "There has been nobody in my life since I lost *Warlock*. There hasn't even been an interest in looking on my part, until now. I will make you no promises on the topic, except an open mind."

He smiled suddenly. It lit up his entire face.

"That's all a man can ask, *Wildgraf* Keller," he said.

He held out a hand, which she took. His palm was warm, but not drenched. Firm.

The smile reached all the way to his eyes, washing out much of the pain.

Jessica realized she probably had the same look in her eyes.

Nobody had gotten close enough to look in six years.

CHAPTER X

Moirrey peeked.

Because of course she did. Ya hadta know how t'in's would shake out, if'n yous were gonna rattle cages.

Casey were all googly-eyed at the teensy owl resting on her fist, gripping the big, leather glove and starin' back som'tin fierce. Predators talkin's silent-like, even if the one were no bigger'n a teacup Chihuahua. Marcelle and Willow were watching the room, and the bird, and the bird-keeper. Professionally-paranoid, heavily-armed girls were like that.

Her sister and the captain were just visible from a window, sittin' careful on the bench. Stiff, kinda. Not at all relaxed 'til they shook hands.

That were good. She watched the man flow into mellow. Jess dinna move any closer physically, but she were leanin' in more now. So were he. Was good. Moirrey remembered to breathe and turned around to the others.

Marcelle asked about a half dozen questions with a single raised eyebrow, but the chick could do that. Moirrey settled for a quick grin and a thumbs up. After th'last two years in each other's pockets, it were 'nuff. Marcelle grinned as well.

Big Bad Red Admiral prolly though he were bein' all sneaky'n'stuff, sending the captain with them, but Desianna'd done snift it all out pretty early. And made sure everyone but Jessica were enough in on it that nobody'd say nor do nothing stupid, like make a pass at the man.

Not that Willow would. Too non-professional. And Moirrey had Digger to look forward to in another few weeks. Marcelle found her own fun on the flight deck, entertaining Gustav, the pilot known as *Eel*, of all people. Er, maybe being entertained *by* him. Marcelle weren't gonna settle for no selfish lovers.

Bird-house-keeper collected the little burrowing owl by bribing her with a caterpillar. Moirrey figgered they'd been gone long 'nuff.

"Seen enough, Lady Casey?" she asked all nice like.

Casey might be a princess back home, and a bad-ass here, but she were still only eighteen, and had never really been out of the palace. Had no idea how to sneak past watch geese or nothing.

Not that Moirrey was gonna teach her today. That could wait a few weeks. Certainness.

"I believe so, Lady Moirrey," Casey fired back with an evil grin, catchin' the zoologist folks sideways. She'd been sneaky, introducing the tall, blond girl as important folk and leaving herself out of things. Trust Casey to play rough.

Crap.

Everyone were staring at her now, like she done growed another head.

Moirrey scowled as hard as her giggles would allow, but let the good people fawn o'er her fer a bit. T'weren't no schedule today besides sun. And maybe ice cream when it got warmer.

'Cause, you know, ice cream. Real stuff, too, and not the bulk containers *Mendocino* brought them, regular as clock-work out in the deep cold.

Took another five minutes to finally get clear of the owl and raptor folk. Didn't need no more birds-on-fists. Fed enough critters to enough hunters, thankyouverymuch. Gots places to go, peeples to see.

Finally.

Sunlight and air. Barn weren't bad, just weren't sky. Couldna have no windows open, er the birds'd fly off quick-like.

'Sides, the prey she were trackin' were sittin' over here on a bench, all calm and unknowing and stuff. He saw them coming, nodded at her sister, and put down his right hand.

Moirrey watched him lurch to his feet in one quick, ugly motion, like a turtle finally getting upright after fallin' off a log in the terrarium.

Moirrey knew'd there was a stump there, and a little pocket the captain stood up inta. Hook on a few places like a one-sided garter belt, pull up yer pants, walk like nothing at all. From the lines around Captain's eyes and cheeks, were right painful today.

"Got a silly, technological question fers ya, Captain Wald," she said as they all gathered back up, four of them with two satellites wandering around being armed and dangerous.

"Yes, ma'am?" the captain said.

Once he got to walkin', ya couldn't tell, but standing up and that first step were dead giveaways.

"Why a peg-leg?" Moirrey asked. "Why don't *Fribourg* do a modern, computerized version like we do?"

She'd spent enuf time 'round the captain to know this were safe ground. His silence now were mostly lookin' fer words. Translatin' cultures, which he were good at.

"The single greatest threat to humanity that *Fribourg* can imagine is an AI, a *Sentience*, the kind that nearly destroyed us all, Lady Moirrey," he began.

He looked close at her. *Eyeballin' her soul*, Ma useta say.

"There is something worse," the captain continued. "Something from the very early days of technology. Humans used to implant computers directly into their bodies, madam. Cybernetic systems capable of replacing your eyes with artificial sensors, or your limbs with enhanced, robotic versions. Or worse, connecting your brain directly to the *Sentience* itself, turning you into a member of a giant hive, like a worker ant."

"We're talkin' 'bout a leg, Captain," Moirrey retorted lightly.

Some peoples were just too serious about things.

"We're talking about the first step towards evil, Lady Moirrey," he replied. "Would I like a leg that worked thoughtlessly? Painlessly? Absolutely. Wire it right up and let me at it. If I was never going home again, I would seriously consider investigating the state of the art in the Republic. But this is just a mission. I would have to give up everything and be completely ostracized. Never go home. That will never be worth it."

Moirrey felt her mouth screw up kinda sideways as she stared at the man.

Thinkin'.

She'd done some research afore now, just to talk tech with the dude, but hadn't expected that level of calm *No*.

Figured. Man weren't no slouch, er the Red Admiral, the other Red Admiral, the Grand Admiral, woulda never tried a stunt like this.

They had stopped walking. Well, she had, and everyone else had kinda petered out with her.

Whoops.

"Not wired, I get that," she finally said after a second. "There's gotta be a better way to do it, though."

"*Shades* of evil, Lady Moirrey?" he asked in a tight voice.

"Shades of *stupid*, Captain Wald," she snapped back. "Ya lives in near-constant pain, 'specially since planets ya visits'll have a wacko gravity field and atmospheric pressure. Kin only 'magine what a storm'd be like. Is unnecessary. Makes it a bad design solution."

Man weren't dumb, just stubborn. Of course, weren't like nobody within two meters weren't stubborn, too. If they coulda distilled it, she'd be rich.

Moirrey stepped back one stride to see his leg better, to visualize things. Captain Wald stood stock still and faced her, as stubborn a guy as even Digger, which were high praise. Moirrey blocked out everyone else.

There. Huh. Maybe? Dancin' on the edge, but this side, so even the captain oughts to not bitch much. And I can always yell at the Grand Admiral and Karl VII about it. Start a new trend. Something more civilized.

Moirrey smiled up at him.

The stubborn had been replaced with concerned. Kinda sideway looking at her, which meant he were smarter than he let on, too. Knew she were up to something. And knew her rep as a crazy woman.

Whole damned Empire knew *that*.

"So," she said in a voice that had stolen every cookie out of the jar when mom weren't looking. "Wired neuro-implants is out. Got that. What's about a pure osseointegrated solution?"

"A what?" he asked.

Moirrey liked the way everybody got that confused look, but remained silent. This were just the two of them, at least until her sister needed to come rescue the poor guy, him being out-numbered five to one, 'n'all.

She turned to Casey, included her in the grin.

"So's," Moirrey continued. "Ya implant a hunk of something, traditionally an alloy of titanium, usually with a threaded end, like a screw, and an open structure, kinda mesh-like. Bone'll grow around it, given time. Other end sticks out the stump, right out of the skin, with a connection socket at the far end."

Casey nodded slowly, aware that she might suddenly be on the hooks in an official-like capacity n'stuff.

"With you so far," she said warily.

"With us, we attach a custom limb with artificial muscles and wire it all to the existing nerve endings," Moirrey chirped. "After about six months, you can walk like normal, once all the bone stabilizes and yer brain rewires itself. After that, you can start training fer marathons, if'n yer crazy enough."

"Okay?" Casey continued.

"What if we left just the stump and the socket bits?" Moirrey asked. "Build him a detachable titanium peg-leg with a foot. And maybe some racing stripes, but no electronics. No *cybernetics*. Just chrome."

It were fun, watching everybody's face go confusered. Moirrey decided that were her cookie of awesomeness fer today, and just started walking. Let them catch up, physically and metaphorically.

If'n they could.

Seriously? The Fribourg Empire *were all about black and white, some days. Useful, but stooooooopid.*

Moirrey already had three-quarters of the design built in her head. Only real question were if he were right-hand dominant, like a lesser being, or a lefty, like all right-thinking people. Drop a hex-head bolt in and add a cute little carrier for the wrench right into the shin.

And maybe some flames.

CHAPTER XI

The light was subtly wrong, Jessica decided. About half a notch too dark for her preferences. It gave the bridge an ominous cast that just unsettled her.

Probably by design, she decided after a moment of thought. Keep everyone just a shade off center. She checked her control boards once more and looked around, pulling her sleeves down for the umpteenth time.

Jessica hadn't worn one of her old black and green command centurion tunics in years, and this one was tight in the torso. She decided that maybe she hadn't spent enough time in the gym and the pool, or on the dojo floor. Time to shave off those last three kilos she'd never gotten around to.

And maybe two more after that. Get back down to her original Academy graduating mass, two decades on.

This was not her lovely flag bridge on *Auberon*, all round with the big display in the center of the conference table. It was instead long and shaped like an arrowhead with the very tip chopped off blunt where a display screen showed *Ladaux's* horizon turning below them.

RAN VI Ferrata. Meaning *Iron-clad.* Trust an outsider like Yan to out-Roman a culture that had consciously shaped itself after one of the greatest cultures in history, naming the first Expeditionary Cruiser after one of Rome's most famous legions, rather than using the normal naming schema for a ship in the battlecruiser class.

Of course, Jessica wasn't sure that the battlecruiser designation fit, either. Yan had called it a *pocket dreadnought,* among other things, including fire-breathing dragon. An all-big-gun, fast, super-heavy cruiser with only energy weapons, against a foe that specialized in some sort of power absorption system, rather than the traditional ship's shields everyone else used.

Jessica shook her head and focused. She knew he was out there, lurking. In that, she had an advantage over the average ambush those bastards sprang. And she knew she was facing what *Fribourg* called a *Mako.* All of *Buran's* ship classes were named after terrestrial sharks. Makos were pure, energy-weapon-based, heavy cruisers, unlike the new type that had bombed *St. Legier,* the missile-and-bomb-armed variant called a *Roughshark.*

She knew looking for it would be a waste of time. Even this deep in a gravity well, the damned thing could blink on old-fashioned JumpDrives, like an electron hopping from one valence shell to the next. You could do that when your ship was *Sentient.* It was just a massive math problem to navigate across the gravity well.

Jessica would have thought it impossible for a human to accomplish, until she met the Twins: Asra and Saša Binici. *Neon Pink* and *Rocket Frog.* Two of Queen Jessica's best pilots, trained by *Pops* Nakamura to do the impossible.

No, it was just patience and planning, two things Jessica also excelled at.

"Tactical," she called to the young man who was her First Officer today. "Confirm all batteries are cleared and charged."

The man looked at the two officers facing him across a small area on her right. Gunnery and Defense Centurions with serious faces. Quick words flowed back and forth.

"Confirmed, Command Centurion," the man called back less than a second later. "Bubble gun is holding a charge in the tube. Type-1-Pulse are set for incoming missiles and fighters. Type-3-Tuned are charged. Two are set for long range, the rest for close work. Both Type-4's are cleared and charged."

"Pilot, bring us up five and accelerate a touch," Jessica ordered. "Make him chase us a little."

The waiting was the most frustrating part. Dark space around her and a thief in the night.

Only this one was holding a knife and measuring her kidneys, rather than trying to flee.

"Contact," the science officer yelled across the space. "Ship just appeared off our port bow."

"Engage," Jessica ordered.

She had already briefed her new crew, but this wasn't the team she had spent years building.

Honing.

Denis would have been a half-breath ahead of her, giving the order, and even that would have been too long. Aleksander and Nina would have opened fire as soon as Giroux made a sound, confident that nobody innocent was going to *just appear* on their sensors.

Because they made very little sound themselves, each weapon was coded to a tone so the bridge crew could identify them as they fired. The Music of War, some wag had called it, once upon an epoch ago.

The defensive array, a series of Type-1-Pulse beams on the flank, chirped like an angry squirrel as they fired. The Type-3 beams were lower, individual notes down a half octave or so as they joined the symphony. *VI Ferrata* didn't have primaries, but the Type-4 beam sounded like a truck horn, angry and compelling. Jessica appreciated the penetrating nature of the sound, but she would have had them redone as something more like a tuba after this.

Less likely to induce headaches.

"Pilot, shut down and execute your roll," Jessica ordered over the rising din.

The Expeditionary Cruiser had been designed, in part, for Alber' d'Maine to fly into battle. High-Energy-Turns, pivoting an entire warship on an axis to bring weapons to bear at a target that thought he was safely behind you.

The Mako unleashed his mauler, the weapon called a Mag-Shear that went through standard shields like a knife through warm butter. The Expeditionary Cruiser had very light shields for a ship this size, basically what a normal, smaller heavy cruiser would array, relying instead, in part, on insulation and physical armor plating on the outer hull itself to protect them.

Everything lit up at once as the Mako's Pulse beams and Flicker beams ripped into *VI Ferrata*'s hull like a school of piranha. Smoke and sparks filled the bridge and it sounded like Surtur, the bringer of fire himself, was trying to beat the door down with an axe.

And then darkness.

Jessica had made sure she was strapped in, which was good, since they lost gravplates and she found herself pushing upwards against the seat belt.

Emergency lights came on in places, showing one crew member floating helplessly in space across the way, cursing like the sailor he was.

"All hands, stand down," a voice cut through the noise and smoke. "This exercise is complete."

"Damn it," Jessica said, grinding her teeth together to keep the longer string of profanities inside her head. These people didn't need to see her rage.

"Lights up, please," Yan Bedrov's voice was easier to hear now, as people quieted. "Bring the gravplates to five percent until our little bird lands safely."

That brought a round of laughter as the blushing man dropped. Hopefully, his belt had broken in the excitement, and he hadn't just forgotten to attach it.

Of course, the whole point of a training exercise like this was to knock all the bad habits out of people in controlled circumstances.

"Good," Yan continued, rising effortlessly from his station in a rear corner as Jessica turned her head to look. "Gravplates to standard."

Air systems had already gone into overload to suck out the fake smoke and ozone from the air as the lights came back on.

Yan was holding a clipboard in one hand, taking notes. He reminded her of *Navin the Black*, Jessica's long-time Security Centurion who did everything on paper first, and only entered it into a system later. Jessica did the same thing.

Notes on paper were personal, until she chose to commit them to eternity.

"Good news," Yan said as he strode close.

Jessica tried not to snarl at the man in frustration.

First Lord Kasum was here as well. He had been manning the Science station. His voice had called the encounter.

"How could that be good?" Jessica was exasperated.

"You just got the second highest score of anybody going through this training exercise," he smiled evilly at her. "Forty percent."

Ouch. Everyone else had been even lower?

"Who has first place?" she asked, naturally competitive, especially in her field of expertise, combat maneuvering.

"Me," he grinned as he leaned on the side of her chair.

"You cheated," she fired back. "You wrote the scenario."

"No, ma'am," he said. "I only programmed it. It runs itself along a very sophisticated decision matrix, once you fire it up."

"So how do you beat it?" another voice joined in.

Petia Naoumov. First Centurion, Home Fleet. Previously seated quietly in a rear corner, watching. And learning. A tall woman with long, black hair and Japanese ancestry. Jessica's boss. Everybody's boss as senior flag officer serving, answering only to the First Lord himself. And the person most likely to replace that man when he retired.

Yan grinned. He looked almost like a weasel spying a lame chicken.

"You people are fantastic tacticians," he said, encompassing Petia, Nils, Jessica, and the rest of the bridge crew with one hand. "But you have never been pirates. And never had to out-think them."

"Pirates?" Nils asked, coming up to form the fourth side of the diamond.

"Correct, First Lord," Yan replied. "You think in Cartesian space. Maneuver to optimum position for your shields and guns. Overwhelm the other guy when he finds himself out of position and facing the wrong way."

"So what's the answer to *Buran*?" Jessica asked, knowing that Yan wasn't just showing off. Although there was an element of that, as well, this pirate from the galactic fringes getting to show up the rich cousins.

"We pirates never want to kill the other guy, Your Majesty," he replied with a sardonic look. "Why bother going to all the effort? No, we want to sneak up on him, disable the bastard, and steal all his stuff. You had the right idea at *St. Legier* when you suckered that Roughshark in by flying *Kali-ma* too far off the *Blackbird*'s flank, putting us out of close escort. You have to think like a pirate here, as well. He'll do the same thing. At least until he learns better."

"And that would be?" Petia's tone was getting frosty, so she was probably right at the edge of her patience.

Yan could be something of a showman, but he had just spent six months nose-down in every bit of technical intelligence available on the topic of *Buran*. It made him much wordier than normal.

"The bubble gun is an obvious solution," Yan said. "Once they figure out it's there, you'll never see another centerline pass from the rear. They'll come right over the front of you at full speed, just like at *St. Legier*. Maybe cross your T, if they can time it right. Seriously, Kigali would have seen the solution immediately. Gator roll the bastard."

"Gator roll?" Jessica asked. "Seriously?"

"He went down your port flank at high speed," Yan said, ticking off things on his scoring sheet. "All the point defense systems got five rounds off with a very high hit ratio. The Type-3's each fired twice. The Type-4 on that side fired once. The bubble gun would have come to bear eventually, but he would have hopped himself somewhere else by then, so that shot would have been wasted, as well as the flip on the gyros."

"And?" Nils chimed in with an edge.

In his day, he had been the top-rated battle commander in the fleet, a mantle he had handed off to Jessica some time ago.

"You shot at him with exactly half your beam weapons," Yan said, losing the easy grin and getting grim finally. Nasty. "Half. Everything I built has at least a 190 degree hemisphere of fire. That's on purpose. You roll your skull or your belly at him, and everything, *everything* on this ship except the bubble gun can hit the bastard, especially at jousting range. I promise you he'll feel that, especially the fours. The oversized gyros are so you can snap over a roll faster than he can dodge, not to spin lengthwise. d'Maine will pull some crazy shit, but that goes without saying. I've seen the reports on *Second Thuringwell*."

Jessica nodded. They were still working out how to fight a new way. Command a new way. Engage an opponent they had never encountered, never even heard of, other than from her and Yan.

"So why do I even have two, puny missile launchers, if there is barely space for them?" she asked. "What? Sixteen rounds?"

Again, that pirate smile.

"Twelve, and it's even worse than that," Yan replied. "The tubes and the rails are set to Imperial standards, not Republic. Nothing around here will fit. The Emperor and the Grand Admiral will supply us housings with fuel, but no warheads. Those are for whatever Moirrey comes up with."

It made a rude, and weird sort of sense. At least as much as anything did, when you threw out everything and started over with a blank screen.

She could see Robbie taking *VI Ferrata* into battle easy enough. And Alber' in the sister ship, *VI Victrix, Victorious*. Jessica would be a sitting duck, even in a Star Controller.

She turned to Nils.

"Three corvettes won't cut it," she said. "Not for *Auberon*. We won't have the sort of close-in firepower that the Expeditionary vessels have."

"Yeah," Yan said. "I talked to Senator Horvat about that over lunch the other day."

You did what?

"He agreed," Yan continued. "Need a full ring of coverage to protect the big girl."

"I see," Jessica said. "Six, like we currently have with the destroyers?"

"Close," Yan replied. "Seven, with a CP added in. Oh, and he suggested an Expeditionary Carrier."

CHAPTER XII

Jessica had carved out the entire evening, and had Marcelle enforce it with the sort of ruthlessness that she and Willow would bring to protecting their boss from fools and last-minute interruptions. It wasn't the Marquette Room, as much as she would have preferred it, mostly because of the hassle of getting a civilian in and through all the necessary security rigmarole.

No, it would be a quiet evening down on the planet, having steaks and wine at a tiny, family-owned restaurant, clear out on the edge of town. A place that had been there Jessica's whole life. Her parents had come here on occasion, celebrating life events or just having a fantastic meal.

Jessica grinned as the waitress took their orders and departed. The young woman, not much older than Casey, was the granddaughter of the current owners. Jessica had watched her grow up in this restaurant: from a rambunctious toddler, to a teenager doing homework in a back booth, to a young woman learning how to own and run a restaurant.

Her departure left them alone in a cozy, back corner, as far away from everybody else as the proprietor could seat the famous local girl he had known since she was also a youngster. Exotic plants in pots filled almost every available space: on shelves, in corners, even bolted down to the flat board behind Casey's head that separated this booth from the other one.

As befit the evening, both women were dressed in sedate, civilian attire. Blue in Jessica's case, maroon in Casey's. Marcelle had eaten earlier, so she could sit at the table closest to the door into this room while sipping tea, watching for trouble, just as Willow was doing out in the skimmer.

This was as private as Jessica was ever allowed to get, these days. Unless she hid herself in her cabin or the head with a book, just to have nobody around. Which she did occasionally.

Jessica studied her…*charge* was probably as good a word as any. Casey was an adult now, by both Imperial and Republic standards. Capable of making binding decisions for herself, whatever those might be.

At the same time, both Emmerich and Karl VII had impressed upon Jessica that she might be the only person in the galaxy from whom Casey would accept a *No*. Frightening, but after so many months with the woman, Jessica had to agree. Casey was smart, capable, and driven. Nils could probably convince the young woman to do something, eventually, but it would take him time. Jessica could stop her.

Casey practically fidgeted as she sat. The sudden hand out to grab a glass of red wine and take a sip. The head cranking around to watch the room before returning to watch Jessica.

Fidgets.

Jessica smiled. It was obvious that Casey had been working herself up to something, but still hadn't gotten there in her head.

Another sip from the glass. Fortification, Jessica supposed.

"I have a plan," Casey began suddenly, perhaps in the middle of a conversation in her own head that was spilling out to engulf them both. "Understand that much."

Jessica cocked her head slightly to the side and grinned at Casey.

"What am I talking about?" Jessica asked, throwing the woman sideways with the awkward phrase.

Most women were afraid they were going to grow up and be their mother. Jessica had apparently turned into Nils Kasum. How many times had he asked her that question, early on, to for her to ground herself back at the beginning, from the middle of a paragraph, in exactly these same sorts of conversations?

Casey blinked. Blinked again. Blushed like a teenager again, suddenly. Composed herself.

Deep breath. Pause.

"I need your help with something, Jessica," Casey said in a nearly-formal tone. "And your advice, although I might not follow it."

"Fair enough," Jessica replied evenly.

It was like watching tapes of herself at that same age. How had Nils survived?

"I had a long conversation on the topic with Yan," Casey continued. "Both before we got here, and since everything else has happened."

Jessica nodded. Let the woman build up a head of steam. The sooner she got to her point, the sooner Jessica could maneuver.

"He went through a Reserve Commission program," Casey stated flatly. "One designed for foreign officers who will serve with Republic forces."

"He did," Jessica agreed. "I needed him to understand us when I had him supervise building *Kali-ma* for me in an *Aquitaine* yard. And then to take that training home, and infect *Corynthe* with it."

And he had. *Kali-ma* under *Wiley* and Yan had approached *Republic of Aquitaine* standards in almost all things, even before the flight to *St. Legier*. Afterwards, on the long journey home, they had arrived fully. *Lincolnshire* probably wouldn't appreciate the changes to Jessica's fleet over the next decade, staring across that long, porous border.

Jessica really didn't give a shit.

"I would like to do the same," Casey said simply.

Fortunately, Jessica wasn't holding her wine glass at the moment of that pronouncement, else she might have dropped it. Or choked on a mouthful of wine, possibly spraying Casey with it.

"Why?" Jessica finally settled for, having discarded a dozen other responses along the way.

Casey's grin broke through her fierce, formal mien.

"Every *Emperor of Fribourg* has been a fleet officer first, up until now," she replied. "This one should be as well."

Jessica opened her mouth, and closed it again. Casey had a point. For several hours, this stubborn woman had been *Emperor Karl VIII* in name and in fact. Had seen off her cousin and his treasonous comrades. Had even rallied the fleet to her cause as a seventeen-year-old girl.

Jessica could only imagine what a thirty-year-old version of Casey would be like.

"But there are two other reasons," Casey continued, once she was sure Jessica wasn't immediately arguing with her.

"And they are?" Jessica replied forcefully.

Truly, Nils Kasum brought down from the heavens above and speaking into her ear and out her mouth. *Spooky.*

"One, you yourself said that the war with *Buran* will take a decade or two. Perhaps forever," Casey said. "With you expecting to serve on that frontier for as long as you wish or can, the *House of Wiegand* needs to be present also. Just as Uncle Em has to stay home and keep things going, my brother will not be able to serve in a combat setting. There are far fewer Princes of the Blood, today, who can serve. Em's son, my cousin Tiede, is one of the few of this generation. His brothers-in-law, Carson and Bernard, are both exceptional, but they are not family. Steffi's husband, when her turn came, would have been the same."

Casey paused, and gulped.

"My husband, when it comes time, will have impossible standards to meet," she said in a quieter tone.

Of that, Jessica had no doubts whatsoever. It was one of the reasons Jessica had been single most of her life, opening herself up only for *Warlock*. And possibly considering an Imperial economist.

Impossible standards.

"That's one," Jessica said carefully.

Casey's grin was back.

"If I can do it, so too can every other girl out there aspire," Casey said. "*Wiley's* not the only one."

Jessica let a shark-like grin appear, just for a second. This was the outcome of *Thuringwell*. Right here. Daughters asking their fathers "*Why not?*" when the men had no better answer than "tradition." That wasn't going to work much longer.

I swore to see the Empire overthrown. Sitting across from me is the proof.

Jessica got serious.

"Do you think your uncle and your father will allow it?" she asked.

"Do you think I'm going to give them the option?" Casey fired back. "The alternative is I have to sit around the palace all day, making noises about the Charter of Man to news outlets. I think they would much rather I be far away from the centers of power, if I'm going to be a radical."

Jessica became even more serious. There was no arguing with Casey on this path. Or even the politics. The woman had been born and raised to it.

"Will they, in retaliation, try to find you a husband early?" Jessica asked. "Find a man to control you?"

"I would make his life a living hell," Casey swore, eyes flashing angrily.

"Plus, the more I'm on the frontier with you, the less chance there'll be that any traditionalist will want me."

Those blue eyes turned silly for a second.

"No chance of a political marriage to one of the great families after I've been off to war, Jessica," Casey grinned. "Soiled. Fallen. Lost. Father might have to marry me off to a barbarian warlord or something."

Jessica grinned back.

"I know a few I could introduce you to," she said slyly. "Just be happy that David Rodriguez, my Regent back home, is happily married. And to the quietest woman you've ever met. Else you might get your wish."

"Ha," Casey said. "What about you? The great Jessica Keller? I've heard rumors that you might be seeing someone."

Jessica shrugged. Felt herself close down emotionally.

"Nothing so serious as even that," she said. "We have talked. Considered the options. Nothing more."

"Still, an economist?" Casey grinned ear to ear. "You?"

Again, the shrug.

Words had been enough, especially with the implications.

Jessica waved a hand to metaphorically shove everything to one side. None of that mattered. Not tonight. Had nothing to do with what Casey wanted.

"You truly wish to become a Centurion, Casey *zu* Wiegand?" she asked, letting Nils Kasum place the words in her mouth.

Perhaps it would only be a footnote, but Jessica knew that they had reached another one of those points that the history books would take note of.

"More than anything in the galaxy, Jessica."

CHAPTER XIII

Marcelle let silent feet carry her into the engineering space where Moirrey had taken up residence. First Lord had offered the woman a bigger space and a full support team, but Moirrey had waved them off as a distraction from what she needed.

Looking around, Marcelle figured that more people would have just gotten in the way of *stuff*. And Moirrey had stuff piled everywhere about the place. Hopefully, Saana Robles would be back soon from *Petron* and could start sorting this crap out.

Looking at the engineer at work, Marcelle decided she could have stomped in here as loud as she wanted, with a full marching band, as long as she didn't actually threaten any of Moirrey's projects. Moirrey was head-down on some welding project, black shield in place and sparks dancing in the air, oblivious to anything else.

Moirrey.

Marcelle carried the long, metal case lightly in one hand, a superlight alloy in a style still called an anvil case from the depths of history, when apparently you carried anvils in them. Or something.

The box was one hundred and seventy centimeters long, twenty thick, and sixty wide. Matte black. Marcelle would have thought it perfect for most electric guitars, if she still played regularly and needed something so grossly overdone to protect an axe from the hazards of travel.

It rang with a dull thump as Marcelle up-ended it and slammed one end down onto the marble floor with enough force that she might have chipped tiles. Heaven knew she wasn't going to damage the case unless she brought a hand weapon to the fray.

Moirrey flinched, powered off her laser, and slid it blind into a cute, leather holster sitting by her right hand on the counter. She flipped up the faceplate with a grin that most people might need the welding mask to be protected *from*.

"Wazzat?" Moirrey asked.

Marcelle leaned her long frame forward and rested her chin on her hands on top of the case.

"You said somewhere between a meter and a half, and two, right?" Marcelle replied.

"Did."

"So I went and found you a case," Marcelle grinned.

"Looks like one of Jessica's sword cases," Moirrey observed. "She gon' miss it?"

"Same manufacturer," Marcelle said. "Contacted them and got a smoking hot deal, on account of my connection. They are apparently making bank on these things now, once everyone found out Jessica used their model. Will this work?"

"Gimme."

Moirrey was up off her stool and grasping at the box, so Marcelle let go and stepped back. Moirrey spun and flipped the case up onto the counter, next to whatever she had been welding, and pulled a tape measure from some hidden pocket.

You could never imagine how much gear Moirrey carried with her at all times until you had watched the woman strip to do laundry on someone else's starship.

"Perfects," Moirrey exclaimed after a second.

Marcelle watched the tiny woman pull open the second drawer down and extract a wooden dowel rod, tapping it once on the floor with a ringing thud and then placing it into the hollow interior of the case.

The stick was a golden brown, with wavy, oil-like patterns in the wood. Marcelle guessed it to be right around a meter and a half long, and at least two centimeters across.

"Where did you find that?" she asked.

Moirrey grinned.

"I mights be a bits famous," she admitted. "An' tole someone it were a present for Jessica, whens I were done. Gots a good deal. Still freakin' 'spensive."

"I would hope so," Marcelle said. "That's wild olive. Those things grow for centuries, and not on *Ladaux*."

"Yup, but grows good on *Pohang*," Moirrey agreed. "They exports it and furniture makers mostly buys the stuff. The iron were the easiest part, once I figured out how bendy I wanted it."

"Bendy?" Marcelle asked. "It's a spear. It's not supposed to bend."

"Ah, but it were," Moirrey countered. "Is a *pilum*. Ya heaves it at th'ther guy. Diamond-shaped tip punches through a shield like a bodkin and maybe hits him anyway. Either way, the middle of the shaft is supposed'ta bend when it lands, so's you canna throw it back, and canna even pulls it outs yer shield. Serious troubles when crazy Roman dude with a gladius comin' fer yer liver."

Marcelle nodded. Her job had been finding Moirrey the books, not actually reading them herself, beyond skimming enough to know what questions the crazy engineer would ask next.

Her job was finding things. What people called a dog-robber, because in the old days, sometimes you had to take a bone away from a hungry dog to feed a pissy admiral. Jessica had needs, Marcelle found her things. No incriminating questions asked.

Same with Moirrey.

Marcelle watched the woman pull a metal piece from the same drawer as the spear body. Marcelle figured it was about as long as her arm, with a cup at the bottom to fit over the end of the wood, a four-pointed punching tip like a special dice at the other end, and a shaft behind the head about as big around as one of her fingers.

Moirrey placed the spear-head into the box along with the olive rod and gave a satisfied grunt. Marcelle walked close enough to study the result. Just needed some foam, maybe some ugly fake fur, like her first guitar case, and a few spots to store spare strings, picks, and towels. She'd be all set.

"Okay, so I get that part," Marcelle said to her tiny sidekick. "The *fetial* is a priest, and he walks up to the border, says the magic phrase, then throws the spear across the border as a formal declaration of war."

"Yup," Moirrey agreed. "More to it, historically, but we's not about to give them thirty-three day's notice that a sneak attack's comin'. But we gots ta be formals."

"Right," Marcelle reached out one long arm and rested it atop the strange, metal contraption taking up most of the countertop. It looked vaguely like a cross between a robot spider and a coffin, roughly octagonal in cross section, something like four meters long, and nearly a meter across. "So what's all this for?"

Moirrey's smile lit up the room again.

"We throws the pilum as a formal declaration," she chirped. "Then we attacks. But Jessica wants a big, grand gesture fer th'historical folks. So we's gonne throws this thing from orbit, and it carries the pilum down close 'nuff that it can drop the thing unto enemie soil. Boom. War is begun. All formal-like."

It made a bizarre sort of sense, when you considered that Jessica had asked Moirrey to top *2218 Svati Prime*. This thing would probably be a lovely shooting star crossing a night sky, which primitive cultures had usually considered a sign of impending bad luck.

And Jessica Keller declaring war on your poor planet was going to be the ultimate bad day for somebody.

CHAPTER XIV

Jessica had been trying to fall asleep at a reasonable hour, a rare enough occurrence these days considering all the work she had to do. There were never enough hours, and rarely a day off, but all of this work would bear fruit soon.

Out there, docked a long ways away from her across the station, the first ship had been born, of what would become a completely rebuilt First Expeditionary Fleet. Her fleet.

Her sword, as Yan Bedrov had promised an emperor.

CE-401. The first of a new generation of Corvette/Escort vessels that could serve on any frontier, with any fleet, but which would first be traveling to face *Buran.* At least until Jessica was able to work with David and order a few to go to *Corynthe.* As Yan had said, you have to think like a pirate to fight *Buran.* And he did. And they would fight pirates just as effectively. Probably more so.

The Senate had moved quickly, once they decided to go. Models approved and orders placed. A quiescent Fourth Lord accepting the designs rather than tinkering endlessly. The wheels of government could spin, when the occasion demanded it. On distant *Anameleck Prime,* three much-bigger hulls were also taking shape. Shipyards everywhere, convinced a year ago that they might have to turn to civilian construction, had ramped up to three shifts instead. Third Lord Philips had begun a massive effort to rearrange crews, as absolutely everyone wanted to transfer to First Expeditionary, the new warfleet, rather than just chase pirates and rescue lost sailors for a career.

A chime caused Jessica to open her eyes. Sleep wasn't coming anyway.

She keyed the door open and admitted Marcelle, sitting up and pulling the pillow up behind her back. If it was important, Marcelle would have just opened the door and entered. If it was an emergency, sirens would be waking the dead.

"Good news," Marcelle said as she caught Jessica's eye. "The Gray Lady just arrived in system and transmitted. They're about ten hours out from docking."

The Gray Lady. Marcelle's pet name for SC-006, the Star Controller *Auberon.* Jessica's ship. Her friends.

Her home.

It had been sixteen months since she had seen them, one last look back from *Kali-ma*'s observation deck as they climbed out of orbit to make the long run to *St. Legier.* For them, a year of serving under Arott Whughy as Fleet Lord in an independent command, far from home.

Hopefully, the crew had stayed sharp. Had infected Whughy with the concept of coloring outside the lines, rather than learning to stay inside them from him. Reports had looked promising, but there was only so much you could read.

Jessica needed to see them in the flesh. She needed to know that the sword was still sharp.

She would be using it soon.

Activity at the big hatch triggered the alert siren, letting everyone in range know that the primary airlock was about to open. Jessica waited with a small mob of people, most notably Nils and three of the other six Lords of the Fleet. She had been on the other side of that door often enough, but standing here was weird.

Still, she wouldn't have missed it for the world. Especially not today.

Jessica wore her Fleet Centurion uniform, rather than the dress whites of a Fleet Lord. As a nod for the event's importance, she wore all of her important awards, including the special, custom ribbon that Karl VII had commanded, for the crews of the *Blackbird* and *Kali-ma,* veterans of the *Battle of St. Legier.* Jessica normally would have said *First St. Legier,* following *Aquitaine* naming conventions, but she really didn't want to tempt the fates that there might ever be a second.

Beside her, Nils Kasum was dressed to the nines in his best uniform, including the longcoat he wore for special occasions. The other Lords wore their normal day uniforms, except Third Lord. Glenfeld Philips was in as full a dress uniform as regulations covered, and he had a smile like a cat with a mouthful of canary.

Jessica really didn't know the man all that well. He controlled all Personnel decisions for the Navy, just as Fourth Lord was responsible for naval construction and Seventh Lord handled logistics.

As a person, he was barely taller than Jessica, and squishy around the middle, but there was a delightful fire in his eyes today.

The hatch cleared.

Normally, people would be cheering, but everyone had been instructed to remain quiet for the surprise ceremony that was about to occur. And they were all Fleet here. They would obey.

Jessica craned her head for a better look, around taller men and women blocking her view from the side of the main corridor.

There. Arott Whughy. Good.

The man was dressed in whites, but he was wearing his Fleet Centurion uniform, and not dress. It was a hopeful sign. On the first row, next to Whughy, Denis Jež, also in day uniform.

Because there wasn't space for everyone to dock at the same time, First Lord had ordered the other Command Centurions and senior officers from the rest of the squadron to assemble aboard *Auberon*, and then debark with her crew. They probably guessed that something was up, but they had no clue how big.

Next to Denis was Robbie Aeliaes, his dark skin and curly hair contrasting with Denis's lightness. Alber' d'Maine was next, his dark hair buzzcut short and showing off all the gray that was starting to appear. He'd never cared what he looked like, as long as he could fight.

Thomas Kigali, tall and blond and gorgeous. Just as much a warrior as Alber', just in a different direction.

Doriane Matveev, off *Ishfahan*. Jessica would miss the woman, but there was no place in the upcoming campaign for a missile cruiser, when *Buran* could short jump away from any strike Doriane could launch.

Kanda Cosmina Lungu. *GSC Ballard.*

Command Centurions Teuta Uzodimma, Yezekael Jarogniew, and

Siran Akpabio. RAN *Brightoak*, *Rubicon*, and *Vigilant*. Jessica's old squadron command, nearly a decade ago.

Tonći Östberg, Calista Katsaros, and Ionuț Yannic. The escort carriers, *Andover*, *Albena*, and *Advocate*.

How many of them would stay with their current commands and be promoted later into larger vessels? How many of them would rather stay with the war?

Time would tell.

Command Centurion Waldemar Ihejirika. The Fleet Replenishment Freighter *RAN Mendocino*. The Milkman, as far as *Auberon*'s crew was concerned. A friend that had been there with them at the very worst of *First Ballard*.

Command Centurion Illiam Kovack, off *Mendocino*'s counterpart *Duncan*. Food, fuel, and spare parts.

And, yes, best of all, one extra smiling face on the first row.

When First Expeditionary had ambushed and captured a small pirate force, most of the vessels involved had been so badly damaged that they were stripped for parts and destroyed. One, however, had been taken intact by *Auberon*'s marines.

Given the nature of *Auberon*'s deployment, as a friendly patrol but not technically under David's control as regent, the various lawyers involved had gotten together and hammered out an agreement that resulted in the vessel being impressed into *Aquitaine* service as the *Republic Support Vessel Bulldog*, commonly referred to as the *Junkyard Chihuahua* from her tiny size, smaller than even *Mendocino*.

Still, the vessel was a fully capable Salvage Transport, what folks in *Corynthe* frequently called *strippers* when they served the pirates to dismantle a captured ship as quickly as possible for cargo and spare parts. In Whughy's hands, she had been turned into a mobile drydock and front-line repair facility for a task force so far from home.

And had been put under the command of a prize crew led by *Auberon*'s First Officer, Tamara Strnad, another one of those who had been with her from the beginning. Only Robbie Aeliaes had known Jessica longer.

Those years had forged Tamara from the Strike Carrier's awkward Second Officer into Denis's right hand. She was much taller than average, at 1.9 meters, and perfectly proportioned. That intimidated most men. Tamara had finally learned to use that as a weapon, rather than an excuse.

Her raven black hair was long and braided and her eyes were bright green emeralds today, walking with the other commanders for what she expected would be the last time.

Tomorrow, she would have to go back to being *Auberon*'s First Officer, as far as she knew. Taking off the third stripe she was technically only entitled to for now as a Brevet Command Centurion with an independent command.

Jessica smiled as the front line marched forward and came to a fairly professional-looking stop in front of the assembled Lords.

Behind them came the First Officers and senior crew from all vessels, plus a mob off of *Auberon*, everyone trying to whisper quietly about the strangeness of the situation.

Only Arott and Denis knew what was coming.

"Assembled crew, come to attention," Arott barked, barely suppressing his grin. You had to know it was there to see it in his eyes.

Surprise lost out to training. Heels snapped together, shoulders came back, heads came up.

Utter silence.

Nils and Third Lord both stepped out of group as if a sudden, snap inspection had been called. Nils looked from right to left, Whughy to Strnad, with a proud smile, extending it to the rows of First Officers and senior staff standing just behind the command centurions.

He let the moment stretch just long enough that people were starting to get nervous over there, before he pulled a folded paper from an inner pocket of his jacket and opened it.

"By order of the Senate of *Aquitaine*," he began in a voice Jessica could only classify as proud, "on this day signed by Senator Judit Chavarría, Premier, and Nils Kasum, First Lord of the Fleet, we declare to all that Tamara Vanesa Strnad of the planet *Ereshkigal* is hereby promoted to the rank of Command Centurion. May she exercise this responsibility with authority, intellect, and care, for she is our representative in all things."

Tamara had turned white. Her eyes looked like fried, green eggs. Her mouth even fell open, just the slightest bit, before she slammed it shut again.

Behind and around her, cheers erupted. Jessica smiled, but remained still. Things weren't done yet, even if they were operating well outside normal methods.

Before things could get out of hand, Nils raised his left hand overhead in a very obvious STOP motion. Such was the man's authority that things settled as quickly as they had started.

Again, Nils studied everyone in the front row, a hawk sizing up chickens. He had not moved to congratulate Tamara, which caught her and everyone else off guard.

Again, silence engulfed the scene.

Finally satisfied, Nils turned to his compatriot.

"Third Lord Philips," Nils preened. "She's all yours."

Like Nils, the Third Lord pulled out a parchment, but he was grinning ear to ear. Glenfeld Philips had a voice like a mountain moving, a bass so profound that Jessica sometimes wondered if he and Vo Arlo could talk to whales. He could still bounce it off bulkheads when he wanted.

"By will of the *Republic of Aquitaine* Navy and First Lord Nils Kasum, the undersigned, Command Centurion Tamara Strnad, is hereby ordered to report aboard the *RAN II Augusta* at the earliest opportunity and take command, subject to the normal rules and regulations. She will exercise excellence and demand the same of her crew, that the whole reflect the greatest acclaim in serving the needs of the Republic and the will of the Senate.

Signed on the Date of The Republic October 29, 399 by Third Lord Glenfeld Marlborough Philips."

He stepped close enough to place the document into Tamara's suddenly-shaky hands. Jessica would have guessed the woman was utterly numb, but she deserved everything. She should have been given her own command long ago, but Jessica and Nils had worked to keep as much of the old crews of *Auberon*, *Brightoak*, *Rajput*, and *CR-264* together as wanted to remain, bending all the normal rules of promotions to keep the core of warriors together. And people had asked to stay.

Plus, Tamara wasn't going far. The Senate had decided to build an *Expeditionary Carrier*, something Yan had included in his catalog, based on the Expeditionary Cruiser design, for First Expeditionary. They needed an expert in strike carrier operations to command her. At the same time, *RAN Audacity*, a strike carrier that was one of the old *Auberon*'s sister ships, had reached her effective end-of-service. *Audacity*'s final command centurion, Vendula Van Bueren, was retiring, and her first officer was being promoted to Fleet Operations and a position on Nils Kasum's staff.

Tamara would inherit much of *Audacity*'s crew, on a brand-spanking-new vessel. Jessica would gain another command centurion, one she already knew and trusted. Much of the rest of her task force would be strangers, but Jessica would have Denis, Robbie, Alber', and Tomas when she needed them. And, now, Tamara as well.

People had remained silent this time, unsure what other shoe was going to drop, since the two Lords of the Fleet still hadn't dismissed everyone.

Nils turned to Jessica and smiled.

She stepped up to Fleet Centurion Arott Whughy, that movie-star handsome, tall, blond man who had been commanding *her* fleet for the last year. Again, everything had been quietly worked out ahead of time, but this was for the benefit of all the assembled crews and officers.

Arott's chance to shine, to be in command of all this, rather than only getting to watch from the sidelines, as Jessica had just done.

He smiled down at her from that great height.

"Fleet Centurion Whughy," Jessica began in a firm voice. "You are relieved."

"Fleet Centurion Keller," he replied evenly, a voice filled with smiles. "I stand relieved."

She took his hand and shook it. Nils had plans for this man, as well. Nobody had told Whughy what they were, yet, but Jessica smiled as she traded places with him, standing at the right end of the line facing out as he took his spot next to First Lord.

"First Expeditionary Fleet," Jessica called out. "Dismissed."

Rather than fight the mob embracing Tamara, Jessica let it pool around her.

There would be time tomorrow. She was only getting started.

CHAPTER XV

There was no permanence in man, nor his works.

Only the gods were allowed to claim eternity, and even then it was necessary for them to overcome the petty spitefulness of men and their will to build anything lasting. Thus was it decreed by The Eternal, *the* Lord of Winter, *that man should have no great monuments save Him. No buildings cast in the permanency of stone.*

Naught, but wood walls and a simple tile roof. For in that seasonal transience would man find happiness with his place in the universe, seated contentedly at the feet of the Great One, there to receive his wisdom.

Ul Banop Cheani Yuur, Khan of *Trusski*, looked out over the empty meadow behind his magnificent palace compound and considered what eternity meant.

The fog was just beginning to thin in the face of the autumn morning. Dawn revealed the quiet stream meandering from right to left, seeking its eventual way to the sea, once it crossed all manner of boundaries, ponds, and challenges. Low grass was just tall enough to hide small creatures from predatory birds if they remained cautious.

Magnificent stands of trees beyond the wild, open space framed the palace grounds, a kilometers-thick belt on two sides that formed a game park for the residents of the Capital city, Taymyr, with the wealthiest of them able to afford their own palaces on the meadow itself.

Each generation had torn down this palace and rebuilt it, frequently moving so slowly that the construction was eternal: adding a wall here and removing one there; transforming an arcade into a patio, a guardhouse into a museum, or a mogul's palace into a tea room.

When no man or woman owned the land, they could not pass it to progeny. And *Buran* himself, the *Lord of Winter*, had decreed impermanence, so there was no silly sentiment attached to the old. One would hold the land in trust and put it to use for a time, until your lease or your life expired and it moved on to the next occupant's temporary custody.

Yuur had been Khan for eight years now, a Scholar who had managed the seemingly impossible, to rise to become a *Minister of the Eighth Rank* and be appointed to govern this sleepy world. Far from the grand lights and bustling metropolises of his youth, but welcome, nonetheless. It was a simple, quiet place. The fading darkness overhead drew his eye.

At this time of year, one could rise well before dawn and stand on this porch facing the southeast as the sun rose at your left shoulder, crossing slowly behind you. Until the stars faded, you could face the darkness, that great gulf known to men as *M'Hanii*, light-centuries of empty darkness filled with great clouds of cool gas and pitifully few stars.

Beyond, somewhere in the grand distance, the star *Ninagirsu*, gateway to the *Altai Sector*, and eventually *Winterhome* itself, master of the *Protectorate of Man*. Perhaps Yuur would be blessed to retire there, once his days of usefulness to *The Eternal* drew to a close. It would be a lovely reward for a lifetime of service in the distant hinterlands, colonizing an abandoned world wrested from under the nose of the distant barbarians known as *Fribourg*.

Perhaps the barbarians feared the darkness, its empty, black skies visible from Taymyr seven months of the year. Only in the summer did the sun generally set in such a way that the thin band of lights representing the galactic disk filled the skies, leaving most to simply notice the few orbital platforms and rare freighters as sudden shooting stars overhead in other seasons.

The sun finally turned the sky golden. Yuur knew he should give up hiding here and go face his day. There was tea to steep and bureaucrats to face. Perhaps he would get lucky and something interesting would happen today, to break up the monotony of living on a farming world that was only now, after four generations, able to export enough goods to import expensive fineries, rather than the barest minimums necessary for life.

Under Yuur's steady hand, his government was nearly half a generation ahead of the Great Plan laid out by *The Eternal* for *Trusski*, the outcome of diligence in the face of daily tedium.

A touch of excitement would be a pleasant change.

PART THREE
ENGINEER

CHAPTER XVI

Yan was careful with his tumbler of expensive whiskey as he moved. The enclosed warehouse dock was enormous, but most of the lights at this end were off, leaving only emergency illumination and pathway markers. All the noise was down at the other end of the building, audible as only a faint buzz in the distance.

Around him, the first generation of her Starfighter designs had been completed and certified to *Aquitaine*'s standards. Maybe they would be good enough for his standards, as well. It would have been nice to have Gustav or the Twins here. Those three could put a fighter like these through its paces far more readily than the boring test pilots the Republic used.

He reached out one hand to just stroke the bronze-colored metal of the craft before him, probably the oddest design he had ever drawn up. A revolution in everything and everywhere, with his signature at the bottom in red ink. Because if you were going to do it, you should do it in vermillion.

It was almost as good as holding his first granddaughter for the first time had been.

"That is still the ugliest damned thing I have ever seen," a woman's voice intruded on his reverie.

Yan pivoted slowly. It wouldn't do to spill that fantastic, liquid smoke, either on the floor or his expensive suit or, worse, brush up against something covered with grease or the other kinds of crap you found on a flight line.

She was tall and lanky. Almost the opposite of Jessica that way. Laconic and occasionally foul-mouthed enough to fit in with his pirates back home. Mostly, Yan knew Ainsley Barret to be a very high-functioning introvert, a maths nerd, rather than a barroom brawler, like so many of her comrades.

Still, *da Vinci* was an expert. Possibly *The Expert*. And would be seated in this very craft, when the time came. She slowly sipped her own glass of whiskey.

Yan smiled at her like a Buddha and left his hand on the fighter's hull. He silently glanced up at the craft. He supposed a simple fighter pilot would find the craft annoying and clunky. After all, they had each of them grown up wanting to fly the sleek, elegant javelins of the Fleet. They probably all had posters of them on their walls as kids. *Aquitaine* was rich like that.

Engines at one end, guns at the other, pilot in the middle, stubby winglets with missiles and pods on each side. It was a design as old as technology. Totally worthless in space to have all that streamlining built in, but woe to the poor engineer that suggested otherwise to former fighter jocks turned Fleet Lords and Senators.

Lucky for him he didn't give a shit what politicians thought. Same went for pilots like Ainsley.

Still, it would be her life on the line in this craft. Even if she thought it was ugly.

"It's also faster than anything in the fleet, *da Vinci*," he finally said, turning back to look her in the eyes.

Like him, she was dressed for the occasion. On him, simple grays in good fabric that stood out against everyone in their pretty dress uniforms. On her, black and green that stuck to every curve in mildly distracting ways.

"You couldn't even put a beam on it?" she asked.

Ah, so that was her issue. Not that his new design was a forward-facing horseshoe, with the cockpit on the left bar and a weapons platform on the right, with two big engines out the back, flying like a stubby *Y*. Not that it had an order of magnitude more power than the design it was replacing, or better shields, or the sensor array and nav computer off of a dedicated scout corvette.

No, *da Vinci* wanted to be able to shoot people, like everyone else on the team.

"No," he said simply. "You're already down to cold rations and bottled water for any extended mission. I started with what the Twins did to rebuild *Eel's* strike bomber, and took out everything to give you enough shields to stay close with the hornets while running your jammers at full power. Thought about mounting Archerfish beams like the Twins have, but you're going to be so many light-centuries from a logistics yard that every spare consumable I could cut, went away. Would it make you feel better if I bought you a beam pistol and a shoulder holster?"

"Already got that in the emergency survival kit," she replied, stepping close enough to run her own free hand across the fighter that would be her second home. "What's this give me?"

"Second *Thuringwell*," Yan replied evenly, holding his place but glancing sidelong. She was near enough he could smell her perfume, but he didn't want to make it obvious he was stepping away from the woman. "Except running at full speed, and loud enough to impersonate *Auberon* instead."

She slipped under the nearer hull and stood fully upright in the space between forward nacelles, cockpit on her left, sensor array on her right. The body was still streamlined, just not elegant. Not like *da Vinci*.

Rather than bend, and risk spilling the contents of his glass, Yan stepped around the nose of the craft. Ainsley was a Flanders mare in a carpeted stall when he did.

"And if it doesn't work?" she asked, meeting him with a hard stare.

"Then the two Strike teams and the Escort Wing will be up shit creek," he said.

Just because, Yan stepped closer. Not quite into her personal space, but enough that they could talk in low tones. Subdued.

Intimate.

"The Emperor wanted something that could take on a pack of hungry sharks that can blink in and out of RealSpace," Yan continued. "And do it clear the hell over on the far side of the Empire from your logistics train. And he tasked me with doing it."

Her head came up, just a bit, and her jaw jutted, ever so slightly.

"So you'll design it, and then send us off to die?" she sneered quietly.

"No," Yan countered. "I'll be right there with you. Probably have to break out some of the spares from *Andorra* and fly alongside on the run out so I can teach you kids how it's done."

That lit something in her eyes. Competition. Competence. Challenge.

Talking to the fighter jocks in a language they understood.

I'm better than you. Here, let me show you.

Wouldn't last long. Yan knew that. Those same kids had better reflexes than he did, and more experience in the little ships. He hadn't flown a Starfighter full-time in almost two decades, since he rated a move to ship-side crew and worked his way up to be Ian Zhao's second in command.

Before Jessica. Before the future.

Before Yan Bedrov had to grow up.

She stepped a half-stride closer herself. Again, not intimate, but personal. Confidential.

"And you think you can beat me?" she asked.

"Not for long," he murmured back. "I just have to teach the rest of you where the new corners and boundaries are. Then you'll start pushing them."

A normal voice now might sound like a yell, confined on three sides by a brand new P-6 *Vanguard* fighter. And Yan Bedrov on the fourth.

"Pushing boundaries?" she teased lightly. "Is that what you like?"

Yan grinned lightly at her, nearly on a level as they spoke.

"I've been hanging around pirates for nearly three decades now, *da Vinci*," he said. "It's what you brigands do best. The good ones, anyway."

There was something in her eyes now. That same fire, perhaps, turning darker.

"And that's me?" she asked.

"I studied your missions in great detail when I was building this design, madam," he said. "*Petron. Ballard. Thuringwell.* Even the early stuff when Jessica was just figuring out how to get crazy on *The Long Raid.* Anybody less than the best wouldn't have been able to pull all that crap off."

"Studied me closely, did you?" she continued, easing forward another half-step. "How closely?"

Yan was breathing on her now, but still never touching, although if either of them moved, a circuit would close. Probably with a blue spark of electricity.

"Pilot leaves her signature in every blip of the throttle," Yan said. "Every word spoken. Every shot fired. You're as good as *Jouster*, but you never wanted to fight. You wanted to fool everyone else into mis-thinking. A master of misdirection."

Her breath smelled like whiskey and mint. An odd combination, he thought, wondering what she tasted like. She was close enough to find out, if he wanted.

Did he want?

A few Imperial ladies had thrown themselves at him on *St. Legier*, afterwards, but that was mostly the exuberance of near-death and victory. And they knew he was leaving shortly anyway.

da Vinci was a different story. He would be working very closely with Ainsley, perhaps for years, depending on how this campaign went. Interesting woman, but she held her cards very close.

Yan wondered how much of her behavior now was just bravado. A new stick against which to measure.

She was studying him just as closely. Yan noted how her eyes half-closed as she took a sniff.

"Mis-direction, Bedrov?" she finally said. "So you don't really know what I want?"

It felt like there should be slow music, as close as they were.

"Does anyone?" he countered. "Do you?"

That jibe got home. The eyes grew shrouded, piercingly intense.

Suddenly, Ainsley Barrett was an eagle spying a trout swimming too shallow.

"Are you married, Bedrov?" she queried. "Is that the root of your reticence?"

"*Corynthe* views these things differently, *da Vinci*," he replied. "I had a woman when I was younger, but after two kids, she decided she didn't want to deal with someone who was away all the time, and likely to come home dead anyway. Still gave her most of my money, back in the days when thirty was old and nobody I knew expected to live long enough to retire. Have a second wife, but that is more of convenience. She was already twice a widow when I settled down enough to maybe see forty. That was a decade ago. I'm home more these days, stationed at *Petron*, but I haven't seen her in a year and she won't be waiting up for me."

"So you think I'll just be a fling?" she asked tartly.

Yan noted that she hadn't moved away from him. Or closer. Neither did he.

"I think you'll be whatever you want," Yan replied quietly. "Any man or woman who thinks otherwise is a damned fool."

Neither of them moved, planets tidal-locked now, letting the universe rotate around them.

"And if I wanted more than a roll in the hay?" she snapped at him.

Yan shrugged nonchalantly. He took another sip of the superb whiskey as a way of catching his breath.

Kissing this woman sounded dangerously fun.

He fixed her with his own predator's stare, like a soon-to-be-dead man entering the fighting circle. There had been three of those along the way. It had stopped after three. Nobody wanted to be the fourth once they realized how deadly he was under all the unassuming poise.

"You've got however long Karl's war lasts," he replied. "After that, I might go back to *Corynthe*. I might stay on *Ladaux*. I might become a Baron in *Fribourg*. If you want more than that, you and Aaliyah will have to have a personal discussion. Or end up sharing me."

"That's all you have to offer?" she sneered.

"Anything more would be a lie, Ainsley," he retorted hoarsely. "Anything anyone offered beyond that would be pure fiction."

"So you'll give me honesty?" she asked.

Something had changed in her voice. A new flavor that hadn't been there even a second earlier.

"For starters," he said. "I'll call your bullshit. I'll expect you to call mine. I snore. And I'd enjoy snuggling up against your back, first thing in the morning, even before you woke up to a warm hand wrapped around your breast. Past that… Karl, Wachturm, and Jessica have shit that's going to need to be done, and nobody but me that can do it, at least until someone decides to go get *Pops*. And you're going to be flying against opponents so strange that they might as well be an alien species, so there's a pretty good chance you don't come back, some day. Honest enough?"

He liked the little flare thingy her nostrils did when she got her back up. The little squint that crinkled the bridge of her nose.

What the hell.

He leaned in and kissed her, noting how carefully they each held a half-empty whiskey glass away from their bodies as the other hands found flesh and muscle.

And pulled.

CHAPTER XVII

Emmerich Wachturm looked at the pile of five-ring binders holding down the conference table, separating him from the four men seated down both sides. They wore the uniform of the Imperial Fleet, but weren't his people, except in the extreme abstract.

He would be hard-pressed to remember their faces tomorrow. Spies were generally chosen for that characteristic, among others. All the best intelligence operatives were unremarkable, forgettable people, existing in shades of gray, even the analysts who took the thousands of raw reports, mostly snippets of conversations and fragments of documents, and turned them into infuriatingly-ambiguous recommendations.

He reached out a hand and touched the pile, mostly reassuring himself of its immense solidity. After a year, these men had gotten better about just reporting what they knew and not worrying that he would be offended by the results. Both of Em's predecessors as Imperial Grand Admiral, his cousins Hans Huff and Kunibert Marquering, had let the naval spooks and Imperial Security folks intimidate and bamboozle them.

Em had made it clear that ass-covering would be punished harder than truth. These binders held the new truth. Once those bureaucrats began to fear him.

Em smiled grimly at the men.

"Is there any good news?" he asked the eldest, a fleet captain in a spotless uniform.

"Actually, there is, sir," the captain replied carefully. All Em ever remembered of the man was the way the gray coming in at his temples contrasted with the dark brown skin. "Since Imperial Security was untrustworthy, we were able to clean up a number of leaks and deep cover agents in the aftermath of the coup attempt last year. Additionally, several double-agents were identified and have been fed bad-enough information to cover other things."

"And the Princess?" Em asked.

"Princess Kasimira's journey to *Aquitaine* is known, but not the specifics of her mission, Admiral," the man replied. "We don't believe *Buran* even has agents there, at least not yet, and all important information is strictly need-to-know at our end."

"So while we are confident that everything Grand Fleet does will be leaked almost immediately, we have that one ace up our sleeve?" Em asked. "That's what we have to rely on?"

"Yes, sir," the man nodded grimly. "They have some method of getting information back to *Buran* faster than should be possible, according to notes we confiscated from Admiral Dittmar's operation. Supposedly four months round trip from their capital to ours, when it should easily be three months each way. There are theories, but anything we do to investigate them will likely tip the Sharks off, so we have waited and listened."

"Nothing a blade in the night can solve?" Em asked.

He hated dealing with that side of his job, but history was replete with examples of a single assassination preventing a war, or ending one. It was a fact of Imperial life.

"The Emperor didn't ask for Admiral Keller to bring a stiletto, Admiral Wachturm," the captain said in a dark voice.

The other three men nodded. They had been the ones that had failed, even during Keller's Raid, but nobody could have predicted Jessica Keller. Even today, the models were barely better than a coin toss. Em knew Jessica liked it that way. Worked at it.

Something else they shared.

"No," Emmerich replied. "And if you don't plan to eat the egg afterwards, a sledgehammer is just as effective as the edge of the pan."

He took a deep breath and nodded.

"Thank you, gentlemen," he continued. "I'll take it from here. Dismissed."

Em rose and left the mess on the table, along with the men. Nothing would depart that room except under strict guard and the watchful eyes of the four men with guns that were waiting in the hallway outside.

Even he didn't do more than have the papers available during his weekly briefing, so that arcane and obscure points could be looked at more specifically, when questions inevitably arose.

At least the messages from *Ladaux* had been promising.

Jessica and her people would be leaving soon. And he would travel to meet them, rather than risk all the spies and leaks at *St. Legier*.

Would it be enough to save the Empire from *Buran*?

CHAPTER XVIII

Nils didn't like it. Not one damned bit. But he also knew there wasn't a single thing he would have done differently had they done it over. He looked around the shuttle's small conference room and thought about the necessity for secrecy that had him sneaking across deep space, rather than holding the big ceremony in the traditional way.

For luck, he touched the bulkhead closest to him. Jessica happened to glance up from her reading at the moment. She grinned at him.

Nils had read her many reports. Emmerich Wachturm had a vessel just like this, designed as a compact flag transport, built specifically to get fleet lords or admirals rapidly between systems without tying up a larger vessel. Wachturm's was newer and apparently much faster.

Nils had confiscated the one originally outfitted by Bogdan Loncar before the man had been cashiered for treason. Nothing wrong with the vessel itself other than the utter decadence of the fittings. The gold plating everywhere. The deep carpets halfway up the green walls.

But it shouldn't be necessary. It offended Nils that he had to sneak around.

Jessica had insisted. And she had been the commander on the ground long enough to know how to fight this particular battle.

She sat at the far end of the cabin, facing him. Petia was closer, turned sideways, reading. Arott Whughy had the apparent ability to fall asleep the instant his butt hit a comfortable chair. At least he didn't snore. More like soft purrs.

Nobody else.

Or rather, everyone else had already snuck off, or been consumed in the various Builder's Trials that would precede *Acceptance Into The Fleet*. Even *Mendocino* and *Duncan*, First Expeditionary's normal Fleet Transports, had been loaded up and sent off with sealed orders, only to be opened in deep space.

Nils suppressed a sigh. Or thought he did.

Maybe Jessica was reading his mind. Again.

She did that.

"*2218 Svati Prime,*" she said in a low voice. "*Xi-Shi. C'Xindo. Surat Thani.*"

Nils knew the names.

He knew she preferred a different nomenclature, but he also knew she was going to lose that argument with the historians.

Keller's Raid.

Her signature move, the sudden explosion out of JumpSpace onto an enemy system that was unprepared, overwhelming all local opposition before it had a chance to do anything. At *Thuringwell,* she had added the twist.

Staying put and fortifying.

Strategic offense. Tactical defense.

Petia was paying attention now. She closed her reading slab and prodded Arott awake with a toe, aware that perhaps it was time for *that* conversation.

After all, it was just the four of them right now, the inner core of participants in the crazy adventure set in motion by a distant *Fribourg* Emperor. Only two of them of actual importance, when push came to shove.

The others had retired to their own, aft section of the small ship: Marcelle Travere, Willow Dolan, Kamil Miloslav, and the dozen or so officers and crew who supported their commanders with the daily paperwork. Not even Enej Zivkovic and Cheng Yin Dominguez, respectively the Flag Centurions for Jessica and Arott, were present.

No, this was just the principals.

Arott squared and stretched his shoulders like a bear awakened mid-winter. Nils and Jessica both grinned at him at the same time.

"Because I simply don't know how much *Buran* has penetrated the

Republic's political apparatus," Jessica began. "In that, Loncar did us a favor, because you've spent several years now aggressively digging out moles and spies when you might not otherwise have put that much effort into it. But *Buran* is coming. *Fribourg* is utterly riddled, or was when I left. I suspect Em's unleashed the hounds of hell on Imperial Security."

"Em?" Arott asked.

"Grand Admiral Emmerich Wachturm," Petia interjected in a disinterested-sounding voice. "Casey and Jessica both refer to him as Em."

Jessica turned a surprised look on the woman, got a grin in return.

Arott nodded confirmation. "Go ahead."

"So the Senate vote for a massive construction program wasn't exactly a private affair," Jessica continued. "And all the various shipyards suddenly ramping up to spit out a dozen new ships will make the news. I want to keep our capabilities as quiet as I can. As long as I can."

"But a secret commissioning?" Nils asked. "Vanishing like a thief in the night?"

"You agreed with me then that it was the best way to do it," Jessica replied carefully. "What's changed?"

"I've gotten old and grumpy," Nils realized, feeling a weight suddenly heavy on his shoulders. "Set in my ways. What you are doing overturns every tradition I've spent my whole career upholding."

Nils stopped and considered his next words. What he needed to say.

Like so many other things about Jessica, it would be an important footnote argued histrionically by historians, probably for centuries.

But now, more than ever, it felt right.

"When this thing is done," Nils said, gesturing to include Arott as well as Jessica. "When I've blessed the two of you and sent you into battle, I intend to resign as First Lord of the Fleet. I have spoken in vague terms with both Judit and Tad, and they are in agreement. Petia will most likely replace me as First Lord. As you've reminded me countless times, the Great War is over. I got to be the lucky bastard who was in office, so I'll get the credit for being a genius, but the three of you are about to start a new Great War. I just don't have the energy to pursue it, certainly not if you're right about it taking decades to complete. No, this is a good place to round it off."

It was hard to say whose face had grown the palest of the three. Which mouth had fallen the farthest open.

Intellectually, all of them had known this day had to be coming.

Eventually.

Nobody lived forever, except the very *Sentiences* they were going to be fighting, or the one they had fought so hard to protect, once upon a time.

Nils suddenly felt lighter. As if a great weight had been pressing him down, and now it was gone.

He smiled, looking forward to being that grumpy, ex-Navy Senator on the end of the first row, bitching about kids these days.

Petia was closest to him, both historically and emotionally. The other two had been his prize pupils, but Pet had been a close and dear friend for many years.

She reached out and put a comforting hand on his knee. Jessica and Arott were still in shock.

Good. That meant it was going to catch everyone off-guard, both *Fribourg* and *Buran*.

He could promote Kamil to Senior Centurion and leave him with Petia to retain continuity until she figured out how she wanted to run her office. And two of the most dangerous Fleet Centurions in the galaxy would be steaming to the far horizon of the *Fribourg Empire* at the head of the most formidable fleet in memory.

"Senator Kasum?" Jessica finally managed to get out past a mouth that looked like it had gone dry.

"Eventually," he said. "I know the trip to *St. Legier* was supposed to be a vacation for you, in spite of what happened. I need a break. Hopefully nothing so exciting happens to me."

Nils accepted congratulations and condolences in equal amounts. It wouldn't be official for a few weeks, but in his mind, he was already gone. The hard part would be keeping the grin off his face.

Let Petia handle things for a while. Nils didn't see Jessica ever taking his spot at the top, but Arott might, one of these days.

That was as good a legacy as he could imagine.

CHAPTER XIX

It had started here, looking back. Just over seven years ago, Jessica had first boarded the old Strike Carrier *Auberon* at *Kismayo*, taking command in prelude to *The Long Raid*. The first step in ending the Great War with *Fribourg*.

Fitting that she would return here to do something even bigger.

The First Lord's transport had eventually docked with the dreadnaught *RAN Bellerophon* after the hard run to this system. The first time, Jessica had been headed on to *Simeon* with Denis and the new crew to see if she could break them, or forge them.

A lifetime ago. Several lifetimes.

She looked around the small office she had claimed, down and aft from the ship's flag bridge. A standard metal desk with old dings that probably told many interesting stories. Oak sidebar for beverages that was currently empty. Two chairs lurked across from her awaiting their next victims.

She still had six minutes until her next meeting. Possibly the most complex of them all. Certainly one of the riskiest. With commensurate potential rewards.

Jessica turned her shoulders past ninety degrees to the right first, and then the left. Pretty good for forty-two years old and working at a desk so much. At least the fighting robot kept her sharp and trim, even if she wasn't running it above Six very often. Probably needed to change that, going forward. Things were going to get sharp. She would need that killing edge honed.

She rose from the seat and turned to the port on the outer bulkhead, at her left hand. She had left the armored panel closed earlier, to reduce distraction, but she keyed it open now and stared into near space separated only by a hand span of transparent metal, and catching her own reflection in white from the glass as she did.

It took her a moment to locate them all, parked at rest in relation to one another and to *Bellerophon*, the whole group hiding more than a light hour away from the planet itself. Again secrecy.

Closest was *Auberon. SC-006.* The Star Controller for First Expeditionary Fleet. Looming like a tremendous whale more than twice *Bellerophon*'s size. Enormous and powerful, and already out of date, a new-born dinosaur that would eventually need to be retired to a distant, less-dangerous frontier, away from the one she must first challenge.

Needs must, and we had to balance time against secrecy. Certainly, we could have rebuilt her, or built a new one, but not without telling everyone in the galaxy what we were up to. We'll just have to be better than them, and I've got Denis for that.

Below and further away, side by side like two attack dogs on a single leash, *VI Ferrata* and *VI Victrix. Ironclad* and *Victorious.* Robbie Aeliaes and Alber d'Maine, Command Centurions in charge of vessels that could possibly each take on a dangerous dreadnaught like *Bellerophon*, even though they were barely bigger than battlecruisers.

Below them, forming the point of the triangle, *II Augusta. Majestic.* Tamara Strnad finally given her opportunity to shine aboard history's first Expeditionary Carrier, a cold-built variant of her sisters, the Expeditionary Cruisers. Smaller than a Fleet Carrier, but still much more than a Strike Carrier, able to walk right into the middle of battle with *Buran* and fight as well as any ship in the fleet.

The others were too far away to be more than points of light to the naked eye, but she had no doubt they were out there. Gone were the six destroyers that had been *Auberon*'s boon companions since launch. In their place, a pack of smaller vessels. Sleeker, faster. Able to achieve sailing feats that would make Tomas Kigali's mouth water with envy, were he not here now, leading the way.

It had taken the forcible retirement of an obstinate Fourth Lord, but the *Republic of Aquitaine* Navy was building corvettes again. The first such craft in generations, after the long experiment with cutters and destroyers in their stead.

CA-264. Corvette/Assault. Tomas Kigali in a chariot that *killed things*, while still being able to easily sail for six months without stopping for food or directions.

Three CE models: *401, 402,* and *403. Corvette/Escort.* The backbone of the new fleet, the new war with *Buran.* Armed with a pair of Type-3-Tuned beams, capable of long range sniping or short range hammering, as decided by the commander before the battle began. Further protected by four Type-1-Pulse beams, the variant Moirrey had dreamed up after watching *Buran* shred the skin of *Amsel* with a similar weapon. The old Type-1, but with bigger capacitors and more generators in-line behind it. A lethal woodpecker, on defense.

CM-404. Corvette/Minehunter. She didn't carry any mines herself, but was tuned to detect and shoot them from a very long ways off. No Imperial intelligence had suggested *Buran* used mines. What good would a net of explosives be, against a vessel that could make impossible leaps from inside a gravity well? But they would learn, soon enough. Moirrey had spent a year studying the logs of *St. Legier.* And a decade dreaming.

CS-405. Corvette/Scout. The weakest hull of them all, sacrificing both of her Type-3's for giant sensor arrays, like those off of *RAN Ballard,* but intended for combat on day one, rather than as a side gig while exploring.

All of those vessels would fit into the array Jessica had built in her head. Battle plans, strategic calculus, logistics trains. *Buran* could jump right on top of her fleet and attack, but she and Yan would guarantee them a savage mauling in the process, especially when the two Expeditionary Cruisers carried Type-4 beams, in the hands of people who knew how to use them in battle.

No, it was her last meeting today that left Jessica…not *concerned,* but *focused.*

Ballard would be joining the mission. There was so little data available, in the way of surveyed routes, that the big Survey Cruiser would be necessary, just to leave a trail of breadcrumbs for future fleets.

But Yan hadn't limited himself to only thinking about fleet maneuvers and warfare. He'd managed to convince Tad to fund an experiment that Yan eventually wanted to build back home. Jessica, too, perhaps.

CP-406. Corvette/Patrol. A survey carrier, or pocket strike carrier, depending on how you wanted to think about these things. A corvette that kept the forward and aft Type-3-Tuned turrets: *Anna* and *Zebra,* and the rear two Type-1-Pulse turrets: *Wiley* and *Yalu*. Up front, where *Boren* and *Chester* turrets would have resided, a trio of fighter craft perched on external launch rails. It was the smallest mothership Jessica had ever seen, not even a full 1-ring like *Petron's* merchants and pirates flew, which usually carried six to eight fighters.

Jessica remembered the conversations with Yan and Nils, when the subject had first come up.

"What kind of a Command Centurion would even know what to do with something like this?" Nils had asked.

"Gimme a pirate," had been Yan's grinning response.

Aquitaine didn't have pirate commanders. *Petron* did, but none she could recruit and train in the time available. Maybe tomorrow.

So Nils had gone to Third Lord Philips with a vague set of requirements from Yan, and the four of them had culled the resulting list down to a set of candidates.

Nils had selected a rough dozen. Yan had read the stack of files once, pulled one, and handed it to Jessica.

"Her," was all Yan said, voice registering the sort of intransigence she rarely heard from the man. The kind where he was actually willing to argue with her in public, something he rarely did, generally happy to close the door before voices were raised.

Jessica had flipped the document open and quickly scanned the contents.

Nothing that immediately jumped out at her, but she read closer. Family: check. Education: normal. Scholarship student, but so many were. Academy notes: exceptional, but within normal range. Good ratings from commanders and subordinates both.

"Okay," Jessica finally had said, unable to identify anything that would move Yan like it did. "Why her?"

"She's you, ten years ago," he had said smugly.

"You've only known me six," Jessica had retorted, flipping the file open and reading again.

She quickly gave up and handed the file on to Nils. "I can't tell. Your opinion?"

Nils had smiled frostily himself, until he started reading. Silent minutes passed before he looked up.

"What are you seeing, Bedrov?" Nils asked in a sharp tone.

"Jess is aggressiveness incarnate," Yan had said. "That's good, but a Half-ring Mothership like this needs to balance that with an understanding that sometimes the odds are too long, and you don't have to win the war with one shot. Sneak up on the bastard and study him. Pounce from an odd angle if you can. Run like hell if you can't. Our Fleet Centurion here runs just far enough to turn and ambush you, again and again. But this one will find someone, fix them, and then go get the big boys and girls to come in and hammer the guy into the mud. Pirate-think."

And he had crossed his arms, like the decision was already made.

Ten years ago.

Jessica thought back to when she had just taken command of her first destroyer squadron from the bridge of *Brightoak*. Had been obliged to surf the politics, spending too much of her time answering to a dilettante Noble Lord, rather than to one of the Fighting Lords. At least until after *Third Iger*, when that idiot Loncar had finally decided that he had had enough and that Jessica Keller needed to be broken.

Instead, she had been forged.

Jessica had memorized the command centurion's file that night. She called up the stats now in her head, studying the stars in the window as if looking for inspiration.

Taller than Jessica by a hand span. Considerably paler, of Anglo-European descendant with dark red hair and a stern smile, as if pausing long enough for the camera to do its job was interrupting more serious work she could be doing. Notes about not suffering fools gladly, mixed with a tart tongue that had gotten her into trouble on more than one occasion, balanced by the many people willing to go to bat for her when she did.

Driven.

Yes, that was the description. That was what Yan had seen in the file. Probably not as crazy at risk-taking as Jessica knew herself to be, but this newly-promoted Command Centurion had been marked for possible greatness and guided along the way. Not one of Nils Kasum's disciples, but she easily could have been.

The woman might end up being one of Jessica's, which was part of why she found this meeting so unsettling. Jessica's team had been composed of men and women with her for a long time, colleagues and comrades. Now, she was old enough, senior enough, that she would be training a new generation of students.

Her disciples.

And, in at least one case, a pirate, to hear Yan talk.

A knock at the door.

Jessica turned, but remained by the porthole.

"Come," she called.

The door opened to reveal Enej, looking serious, and the woman behind him.

"*CP-406*, Fleet Centurion," he said simply, standing to one side as he gestured the Command Centurion to enter before he closed the door.

"Sit," Jessica commanded in a light tone, already taking this other woman's measure.

Marcelle would be close by, ready to make coffee if needed, but this would be formal. At least at first.

How often do you order a subordinate to "Cry havoc, and let slip the dogs of war…" to quote Moirrey's favorite playwright?

Jessica suddenly understood how nervous Nils must have been that day, asking her to set the *Cahllepp Frontier* on fire.

Command Centurion Jennifer Glenn. The oddest of her commanders, if only compared to the other corvette commanders. On paper, a good match with Alber' or Tomas for warrior ethos.

Jessica returned to her seat and just studied Glenn for a few moments, aware that the command centurion was returning her gaze just as intently. Like she had done to Nils in those early days.

So do we come full circle.

"We haven't met before, at least not that I'm aware of, Command Centurion," Jessica began. "But you come highly recommended by people privy to what I'm about to unleash. I've had this meeting with all of the other commanders individually, to make sure they understand my goal and their place in it. What I'm about to tell you does not go beyond these walls…"

———

Jessica leaned back and watched Command Centurion Glenn absorb all the ramifications. The possibilities. The risks.

The rewards.

"Questions?" Jessica asked simply.

"We'll be at the very tip of the spear?" Glenn replied. "*CP-406*, that is, and not just us and *Ballard*?"

"Correct," Jessica agreed. "*Ballard* will be out looking for all the things a Survey Cruiser does. You'll usually be her escort."

"And we'll be the ones to interpose and distract, if we stir up a hornet's nest," Glenn completed the thought.

Jessica could see unasked questions on the woman's face.

"Ask now," Jessica said. "I'd rather we work all this out today. Yours is likely to be the most open-ended task, compared to everyone else."

"Yes, it is, sir," the Command Centurion replied with a stern face. "Why me? What was it in my file that drew the eye, rather than one of the destroyer commanders you have worked with for years?"

Jessica already knew that Jennifer Glenn was the right person for this task. The calm assurance under those words just reinforced those conclusions. She wasn't plagued by doubt, but rather by concern that she might be missing something the Fleet Centurion expected her, needed her, to be doing.

And doing it right, the first time.

"Yan Bedrov thinks you would have made a great pirate, had you grown up in *Petron*, Glenn," Jessica said. "High praise from him. An understanding of which battles to fight, and which to avoid. Or rather, how to sneak up on the bastard and then get out of the way of your ego and come get me when you need to annihilate someone, rather than trying to do it yourself."

One sharp, curt nod. Nothing more. That sword had gotten home. One of these days, Glenn just might be sitting on this side of the desk having this conversation.

Silence stretched between them. There would be more questions, later, but those would be operational. Tactical in service of the strategic and the logistical.

Winning.

Jessica had her team. Her commanders.

Her *Sword*. And Moirrey's *Spear*.

Now she had to take them into Imperial space. And beyond.

CHAPTER XX

It galled Judit to no end, watching Saturday's election results come in from all points of the Republic. It had been five long, ugly days. Fortunately, she had a closed door and a private office. And the government was only a caretaker today, tasked with keeping the lights on, but not making any significant decisions until the election was certified.

Most ridings had not been in any doubt, the result of local influences, popular senators, and voter inertia. Still, her margin of control had been thin to begin with.

If current trends held, she would lose her majority.

Not as badly as some had predicted, but still. Enough.

Late-breaking votes usually went for stability. Many had. And news leaking out had confirmed that the war with *Fribourg* was effectively over, and that Jessica Keller was going off to rescue the Imperials from something worse at the head of a newly-constructed fleet.

That had helped.

But not enough.

Her party would still be the largest in the Senate, barring odd, post-election maneuvering, or the rise of an unforeseen personality cult. Tad's party had regained some of the seats they had lost in the *Tennerick Affair*, but not enough.

And she still thought of it as HIS party, even though he had stepped down from operational control following the previous elections, five years ago. Stepped down, and taken possibly the second-most-important job in the government: *Chairman of the Senate Select Committee for the Fleet of The Republic of Aquitaine.* Civilian control of the Navy itself.

An aide knocked quietly at the door, and then opened it a moment later.

"Your lunch date has arrived," he said simply, waiting for her nod before opening it the rest of the way and ushering Tadej Horvat into her office.

Judit suppressed the scowl that lurked. She had known Tad for nearly two decades. Respected him. Liked him.

Trusted him.

She closed the binder on her desk and checked the antique clock over his left shoulder as he sat down in the comfortable chair she kept for visitors.

Silence.

She studied his face closely, saw the years finally etching themselves, in spite of everything Tad had done to pretend to be young forever.

"What do your spies say?" Judit asked.

"Forty-six percent, forty-one, seven, three, one, and a handful of leftover oddballs," Tad replied evenly, as if unsurprised at where the conversation had begun, or where it was headed. "Rigid enough that you will not be able to form a stable government, with the various ideologues involved. I would be even worse off, trying to replace you."

"Hung or minority?" Judit asked.

Either option sucked to put it bluntly, but the alternative was six months of maneuvering to try to form a new government, before inevitably failing, then having to call a second election and hope for better results.

Tad drew a heavy breath. He was a big man, tall and impressive with a leonine mane of thick, white hair that made him look august rather than merely old.

"Years ago, I made Nils Kasum, and more importantly, Jessica Keller, a promise," he said, impersonating a desert holy man with his tone.

Judit listened closely. There had only been rumors about that private conversation, up until now, so she was aware of how small a circle of people must have had access to this information, to keep it secret this long.

"And today, we are about to send Jessica off to war again," Tad continued. "The old government supported it enthusiastically enough to fund a crash construction project with emergency funding."

Judit nodded as he paused, unwilling to interrupt his flow before he got to the juicy bits.

"It would send entirely the wrong message now, to pull the rug out from under her feet by not voting to send her off, something neither a Hung Parliament nor a Minority government has any duty to take up."

Judit raised her right hand, palm up, as if to ask "*What, then?*"

"I have spoken with my people, privately," he said, his voice dropping to a conspiratorial whisper. "We are prepared to support your government from all votes of no confidence for at least eighteen months, and negotiate certain things ahead of time, so that you will not fail to govern. *Aquitaine* will remain strong."

"A War Government, then?" Judit asked. "A Grand Coalition for the period of the emergency. Not much changing, but your full, patriotic support?"

"Just so, madam," Tad replied, seriousness itself.

"What did you promise Keller?" she asked, awestruck that one of the greatest political animals of the era was willing to lie down with the lambs peacefully, if just for a short nap.

"She told me that with the government's support, my support, she could win the Great War, Judit," he replied. "Sat right here in this chair, while I sat in that one, and told me she could do it. And then she went and did the damned thing."

Judit nodded, privately shocked beyond all words. There had been a similar conversation later, over *Thuringwell*. And a similar promise kept.

"And now *Buran*, Senator?" Judit asked.

"Are you willing to bet against that woman, Premier?"

No. No, she was not. Only fools would do that. Jessica Keller, and Lady Casey with her, might be fighting *Buran*, but they would likely completely overturn *Fribourg* in the process.

She held out a hand. Tad shook it.

Promise kept.

Judit took her own deep breath and pushed back her chair to rise.

"A celebratory lunch, Tad?" she asked.

"Indeed," he agreed. "Hopefully not a last meal for the condemned."

CHAPTER XXI

It would be an ending, though only three of the people in front of him knew it.

Nils stared out at the faces in front of him from the small riser and podium and memorized as many details as he could, aware that he might never see some or perhaps any of them again. Certainly not as their commanding officer… although he was aware-enough of his influence on their lives to know he would always be that, at least in their hearts, even after Petia took charge.

In all endings, beginnings. In all beginnings, endings.

A score or so of Command Centurions in green and black. Two Fleet Centurions. One First Centurion. All three of them in the white uniforms. Three *Ritters* of the Imperial Household, dressed in the red cloak that was their badge of office.

The future of *Aquitaine*, or at least the Navy he had served for more than forty years. Guarantors of the Republic.

Protectors.

He would be able to sleep at night, knowing they were guarding the walls.

Nils let the moment stretch.

Jessica knew why, as did Petia and Arott. The others might think him taken of a maudlin turn, and there was some of that. But that was not why he waited.

"I had hoped to promise you a generation of peace," he finally began in a quiet, somber voice.

This was not the last time he would wear this uniform, nor this particular longcoat, but it would be the last with these people, this team. He and Petia would go home shortly, and there would be one last ceremony, one last mission, to attend.

"After what you did at *Thuringwell*, the Empire was shaken to its core," he pointed at Jessica, and then let his gesture encompass much of the rest of the audience, also veterans of what had become the last battle, although none had known it at the time.

"And I asked each of you, privately, if you were done," Nils continued. "Perhaps ready to enjoy the peace that you had carved out. Nobody took me up on the offer, but that will surprise none of you. I could not list all the people who chose to remain at rank and station in order to stay with their friends. Even the Senate itself recognized that, and altered the rules of promotion and seniority, to keep First Expeditionary intact and then make it up to you later, when you were done."

Nils took a breath, faltering internally, but unwilling to lay that burden on these people, his other children.

"Yours will not be a generation at peace," he said. "But we will not necessarily find that a terrible and grave sacrifice. Each of us found a home in the Navy as a way of protecting the weak and innocent from the monsters of this galaxy. You have simply gone beyond *Aquitaine* and made it your place to protect *Fribourg* as well. To protect Humanity itself. There will be kind words for you from the man we all still know as the Red Admiral, Emmerich Wachturm. I have no doubt you will meet *Karl VII* as well. And all of you have now met and worked with Princess Kasimira, Lady Casey, Centurion *zu* Wiegand."

All eyes turned to the tall blond standing between Jessica and Pet. He watched her simply nod to the murmured congratulations. Hers was technically a reserve commission for foreign officers, but she had passed every test in the top ten percent. Casey had earned her spot on Jessica's staff.

Given a full course at the Academy, Nils had no doubts that the woman would have graduated in the top dozen. And she still had the third highest score on Bedrov's never-to-be-sufficiently-damned *Buran Interceptor Course*, having taken the lessons of *First St. Legier* and put them to deadly-efficient use.

"Understand this," Nils finally let the raw emotion of the moment color his voice. "It has been my singular privilege to be your commander. To watch each and every one of you rise above all challenges and to do so with honor and dignity. So if I cannot go out there into the darkness with you now, rest assured that I will never let the light in that window be extinguished. You will always be able to find a way home. Now, Fleet Centurion Keller, if you would."

Nils let the tears show in his eyes. He owed these men and women that much. They replied with cheers and applause perhaps inappropriate to a ceremony that was supposed to be a solemn affair. But Jessica's Merry Men: Kigali, Aeliaes, d'Maine, and many others; had rewritten the book more than once.

Nils Kasum had no doubt they would do so again.

According to that book, he was supposed to stand to one side as Jessica made her remarks, but Nils stepped down into the crowd and let their warmth, both physical and emotional, embrace him. They would learn the terrible news in a year or so, long after he had retired and taken his well-deserved rest. It would be good.

He studied the apparition that had taken hold of everyone's attention.

Jessica had a reputation as a hard and serious commander. Aggressive. Ruthless. A force of nature utterly unstoppable.

Nils was surprised at the wide grin that filled her face as she took his spot above the mob.

"I have often heard the turn of phrase about good commanders being the kinds of men and women that others would gladly follow into hell itself," she said in a bright, cheery voice completely different from what Nils had been expecting. No doom, nor gloom. Perhaps discussing the fresh crop of blueberries just picked. "And that may be necessary yet. But I have studied the galactic architecture on the far side of *Fribourg*. That space where the stars peter out into a darkness light-centuries across, before you enter into *Buran*. A gulf of stygian darkness intent on swallowing all of our souls. My friends, they cannot have them."

Nils made a note to inquire later. This sounded like something Moirrey Kermode had dug up from one of her ancient playwrights in rhythm and timber. The fellow who had written that thing about St. Crispin's Day that he had heard her quote on more than one occasion.

Certainly, the whole audience was up on their toes now. Nils had known it was coming, and still felt the pull.

"We are not going to charge into hell and storm the place, 'though they may think it," she continued. "Instead, we are going to take the gate itself and bar it from our side, so that none of them may escape us. I know that in normal times, a fleet like this would warrant a grand ceremony. *Acceptance Into The Fleet* of all these vessels at once should have required three weeks of ceremonies alone. But I asked the First Lord to forebear, even forego, such a thing."

She paused now, long enough to fix everyone in the room with her stern gaze, from Robbie Aeliaes, probably her oldest friend, to Glenn, her newest Command Centurion. There was fire in that promise. She would be on that front line with them, facing whatever monsters another of *The Immortals* might bring.

"Comrades, we are on the clock," she said simply. "*Buran* is coming for us all. They do not know who we are, where we are, or even that we are coming, and I plan to keep it that way. We will leave as soon as everyone is fully loaded and the last engineer has departed. The fleet will rendezvous deep in Imperial in space, with the Grand Admiral alone, so that not even the Empire knows we are coming, and so nobody's spies can warn *Buran*. And then we are going hunting, my friends. Or rather, since all the *Buran* vessels are apparently classed after Homeworld sharks, we will be going fishing. And Moirrey has forged for me a harpoon of legend."

Nils watched that smile grow to encompass the whole room.

"Ladies and gentlemen, one last hearty meal for the condemned," she said. "In the morning, we ride."

CHAPTER XXII

Jessica let the warm hum of human energy surround her as she took her place at the great circular table commanding her flag bridge.

This was her home.

It was only partly a running joke between her and Arott Whughy that he had personally taken her chair from this table and put it into storage while he commanded the squadron at *Petron*. He actually had, but that had been a statement to her people that he wasn't trying to usurp her place. And that had secured his with them during that long mission, guiding *Petron* a few more crucial steps into a more civilized place, reminding her team that they were more than just warriors.

She sat and nodded to her newest staff member. Enej used to sit directly across from her, but he had moved sixty degrees to her right, letting himself and Centurion *zu* Wiegand see each other as well as watch her. Denis was her right hand, commanding *Auberon*, even as Enej was her left, the chief of staff and Flag Centurion that could translate her words and thoughts into concrete-enough orders that her team knew where they needed to be next as the music played.

First Fleet Lord Loncar had always placed maximum emphasis on the exact placement of his task forces, even delaying an attack until every destroyer was in the proper plane and alignment.

Fool.

Jessica just had to dance, with the enemy, much as she would an unpredictable fighting robot. Robbie and Alber' could seamlessly switch between sword and shield, saber and *main-gauche*, on the fly. Tamara as well. They all knew Enej and had worked with him for years.

Fingers in a glove.

The third point of the triangle would be more interesting, but Jessica had no doubts that Casey was up to the task. Her training did not include the sort of rigor that a four-year Academy training course would include, but then, she was never going to pilot a starship and need to calculate orbital paths and gravitational deflections.

Probably.

Instead, Jessica had created the role of Imperial Flag Centurion. Just as Enej handled squadron communications, Casey would talk to Imperial Captains, if any happened to be part of her task group once they arrived. And while they might complain about taking orders from an *Aquitaine* vessel or a woman, nobody was going to argue with Admiral of the Red Keller, especially not when the order came from the mouth of a woman who could legally introduce herself to them as Emperor Karl VIII.

Jessica looked around the rest of the room, spotting familiar faces and newcomers. Unlike the warriors, her flag staff tended to be more fluid, as Nils and Petia worked to seed other squadrons and fleets with veterans of First Expeditionary's flag bridge, as a way of quietly transforming the entire Navy.

Jessica counted noses on the various displays projected around her like ghosts. Everyone was here, ready.

Primed.

Even Kigali had gotten into the act, swapping places with *CS-404*, the scout who normally rode in the van, instead of *CA-264*'s accustomed place at the rear, just so he could lead. As the Command Centurion with the longest time in grade, to go with perhaps the biggest legend other than her own, he could do that.

"Casey," Jessica said all of a sudden. "You do it. That's the most appropriate, I think."

From three meters away, it was hard to tell if the young woman blushed, but she did smile carefully and nod, reaching down to press a virtual button on the console in front of her.

"First Expeditionary Fleet, this is Casey *zu* Wiegand, aboard *Auberon*. I have the Flag," she said in a firm voice, no doubt aware that those words would be recorded for posterity. "*CA-264*, come to zero-three-zero, up ten, roll three-five-zero and accelerate to flank speed."

Kigali's ghost nodded at all of them and looked down.

"Zero-three-zero, up ten, roll left ten, roger," he called back, far more formal than was normal with that man. He understood the new legends that would be born today.

"All vessels," Casey continued. "Conform to *CA-264* and prepare to transition to JumpSpace on my order."

Jessica found it amusing that Casey's first glance was to Enej, to make sure she had said it all correctly and in the right order, smiling at Jessica only after the Flag Centurion nodded.

Next stop, *Fribourg* and the Grand Admiral.

CHAPTER XXIII

"Are you happy to be able to finally go home, *Uller?*" *Jouster* asked with a tease.

The two men were flying point on a mass formation. All twenty-seven birds from *Auberon*, all eighteen from *II Augusta*. Three from *CP-406*. Hell, even the three ready-fighters from *Andorra*. Plus the two Gunships and four DropShips from *Auberon*, led by a brand-new, bright-red *Cayenne*. And the ScoutShip *Whisper* from *II Augusta*.

Everybody who could fly.

It was an impressive wall of craft, even if he had traded in his beloved *M-6 Gungnir* for the radical new design of the *E-2 Scorpion*, an improved upgrade of *Eel's Petron* craft that that pirate Bedrov had dreamed up.

But *Jouster* was finally happy. It had taken him this long just to figure out how to tweak and override all the damned controls and safety features the pirate had added so that his craft finally flew the way he wanted: right out on the edge of insane. The edge he needed in combat.

Jouster supposed he could have gone for one of the *C-1 Templars*. It was, after all, much more of a melee fighter than the strike fighter *E-2*, but he had seen the tapes from *St. Legier*.

Buran fought like pirates, those folks he and his team had just spent the last year teaching manners. Bounce out of nowhere and clamp on like a shark. And while a Type-1-Pulse might be fun against other fighters, nobody had ever seen anything like Starfighters on that frontier. So he was much happier sitting behind a big gun. Or beside one, as it were.

The horseshoe layout still threw him off. The Type-3 should be in front of him, so it was between his legs when it fired. Not that he would ever say that out loud.

At thirty-seven, Command Flight Centurion Milos Pavlovic, *Jouster*, was too old to be flying combat missions, but he refused to admit it. And only the Fleet Centurion was going to be able to pry him out of that cockpit. That she hadn't yet done do said volumes about what she thought was coming.

"What is home?" *Uller* asked, after a pause to collect his thoughts. "I have lived on *Ladaux* for thirty years."

Forty-year-old Senior Flight Centurion Friedhelm Hannes Förstner, *Uller*, was almost as good a pilot as *Jouster* and they both knew it. And nowhere near as crazy. And just the man to break in all the new pilots that the expanded wing got as kids came and went.

Jouster was in command of the squadron, but he still stayed in the cockpit, even though a Command Flight Centurion was supposed to be a desk billet. Strike Squadron One was his, just as *Uller* commanded Two and *da Vinci* was in charge of Escort Three.

First Lord had kept the senior people together as much as possible with retirements, school, and casualties, while running younger pilots in for a year of what *Jouster* liked to call *Advanced Combat Flying*.

The crazy shit.

And *Uller* had nowhere to retire to, either. Or hadn't. The Förstner family had been officially proscribed nearly three decades ago, finding asylum in *Aquitaine* one step ahead of the headsman's axe. Chartists in the age of Empire.

Besides, *Uller* liked to fly. He was a big man, right exactly at the top end of height and weight allowable in the cockpit, limited by safety systems and ejection seats. A blond bear of an old-school Viking with a petite wife back home on *Ladaux* and a passel of kids getting ready to be grown-ups soon.

"You don't miss *St. Legier?*" *Jouster* called across the vacuum between then

"Lady Casey gives me hope," *Uller* said. "The pardon arranged by Fleet Centurion Keller was wonderful news to my parents and siblings, but it can be just as easily undone later. I will be the first in my family to return, and even then it will only be to pass through to a far frontier."

"You don't think it will work?" *Jouster* asked.

"Imperial Security executed my grandfather for his political views," *Uller* replied in a tired voice. "Paper is only paper."

"What's he so bitchy about, now?" *da Vinci* suddenly added her voice to the conversation on the private, command channel.

"He doesn't trust people," *Jouster* said.

"Well, duh," *da Vinci's* voice smirked. "His second kid was born before *you* even knew he was married, you remember."

"It is hard, lowering my guards, even today," *Uller* managed to impart a shrug to his tones. "It will be harder to go back and look at those places that my family knew, even if I have so few useful memories of the homeland."

"Do you miss it?" she asked.

"It is not my home," the blond pilot said. "*Ladaux* is home. Where we are going is just a place."

Jouster was about to make a sarcastic reply when a single, loud tone overrode him. And every other pilot on every comm channel.

"Flight Force, this is *Auberon*," a woman's voice intruded.

It took him a second to identify the Princess. She was new, but good at this. Keller had warned him in no uncertain terms not to make a pass at the girl, or the Fleet Centurion would simply ground him and drop him on an Imperial planet for the duration.

It was the only threat that really had teeth. He had minded his P's and Q's, so he had not spent that much time around her, unlike *Uller*, *Bitter Kitten*, and *da Vinci*.

"*Jouster*. Go ahead," he called back.

"Four asteroids designated by the flag," the woman said in a calm, almost bored voice as little stars appeared on his nav console. "All craft initiate a multi-vector strafing run at high speed. Points will be awarded for accuracy, damage, and bonus for destruction. You have the wing."

"Roger that, *Auberon*. *Jouster* has the wing," he said, reaching down and starting to dial some of his controls past their safety points, lockouts having already been disabled. He confirmed the path he wanted and transmitted it to the mob of killers behind him. "All ships, you heard the lady. Guns only. Form on me and let's bring the thunder."

Jouster had already slammed the throttle to the stops. There wasn't much extra available, since Bedrov had put the biggest engines possible behind him and added a generator for the gun and onboard systems, but he could still eke out an extra two percent over anybody else by judiciously overriding in places. Maybe he could get three percent on the closest fighter, as big as *Uller* was physically. Mass still figured into the equation.

On his console, a small gap opened. Not much, just enough that everyone else would notice and try to catch him. Nobody was ever going to.

Target One was a small asteroid, as they went. Maybe a kilometer on the long axis and half that wide, shaped vaguely like a barbell. *Furious* had invented the technique, once upon a time. First Expeditionary had refined it in the years since.

Jouster dialed the engines back to idle, unlocked his gyros, and snapped the nose of his craft down and sideways, until he was flying forward, upside down relative to his previous flight orientation, while facing left nearly forty degrees. He shifted his hand from the throttle to the gyro control and fired the first shot, knowing the parallax of three meters was going to knock him off center just enough. Better to fly these missions now and learn that, rather than find out in combat.

Dead center hit. At high speed. Flying sideways.

Just like the book said to do.

He shifted on the gyros, twisting on his nose and side like an eel as he triggered a second shot. On his console, the little trailing stars started to blink as *Uller* got off his first shot into the same rock.

That annoying voice in his ear as he triggered the third shot, as fast as the guns could cycle.

"Warning. Hazardous thermal load detected," she said, a recording that followed him everywhere like a nagging wife.

It took time to bleed off heat when a Type-3 cycled. Even a system as well-built as this one wasn't instant. And you weren't supposed to fire three that quickly. The little temperature gauges on the console certainly weren't happy.

Still, that was what combat was all about.

Jouster took his finger off the trigger before he fired a fourth. Rode the gyros up and over like a man off a ten-meter diving board, until he was aligned with the second rock. Slammed the throttle to the stops and let the sudden power press him deep enough into his seat that his suit inflated a little.

This was flying. This was *living*.

Second rock, coming up.

He checked the various readouts as the rest of the team finally got into place to take their run at the first rock, zeroing himself down on the second rock and triggering his first shot.

Uller hadn't even completed his first re-alignment to chase.

First shot was high and wide. Over-compensating for drift when his unconscious brain saw the arrowhead shape as an enemy warship moving right to left.

Jouster forced the nose of his craft down and around with gyros and the slightest blip on the engines.

Master-piloting-class, children.

The second shot was on the beam, carving off a chunk of what was probably nickel from the way it showed up on his scanners.

"Warning. Thermal load critical."

She was back. She was annoying. She was why he was still single.

But she was probably right.

Just because he was tired of listening to her, *Jouster* reached under the console and found the fuse interrupt that would cut the voice off.

Still, *Jouster* withheld the third shot with a muttered curse and rolled like a space-borne gator instead, buying time for the coolant systems to catch up as he found target number three and opened the engines to maximum thrust and narrowest nozzle settings.

Catch me if you can.

On his boards, something was off.

Wrong.

Readings were going the same way.

"Not good," he muttered, mostly under his breath.

"Whole sentences, please, *Jouster?*" *da Vinci* called back over the comm.

Apparently, he was talking louder than he thought.

"Problems over here," he said, off-hand, still pressed flat by the acceleration.

"Declare an emergency?" *Uller's* voice joined Ainsley's in mothering him.

"No," he growled. "I got this. Just a problem with the coolant system. Gimme a sec."

On his board, something suddenly went red.

And then everything went white.

"All vessels, we have an emergency," Casey called to the room, trusting than the flag bridge comm was open and the signals routing software would pick it up.

It had been a routine training exercise, so Jessica and Enej were off-duty. Available, but not in the room with her.

That wouldn't last much longer as alarms began to scream everywhere.

She took a moment to draw a breath deep into her lungs and close her eyes.

The page she needed in her memory took a second to find, because it wasn't one she had ever expected to need.

But that was why you studied those regulations. Committed them to memory.

Anything could happen.

Like now.

"*Uller*, take charge of the wing and get everyone clear," Casey ordered. She had the flag until someone with more seniority overrode her. And she knew the situation. "*Whisper* and *da Vinci*, stay on site and take charge of rescue operations. All vessels, immediately launch search and rescue teams."

"Flag, this is *Cayenne*," a new voice came on the line.

Hollis Dyson. *Gaucho*.

Hands down the craziest person she had ever met, including The Queen's Own pilots, flying off *Kali-ma*.

"Go, *Gaucho*," Casey replied tersely, juggling metaphorical knives as she waited for Enej or Jessica.

"My bay crew is fully EVA certified," the man said in a laconic voice, right on the edge of insubordination. He must really be that good of a pilot. "And I have a medic on board."

One of the signals Yeoman waved a hand to get Casey's attention, obviously noting the confusion on her face.

Casey reached down and muted the pickup.

"He does," the man said with a simple nod. "Technically a veterinarian, but still…"

Why did a DropShip have a vet?

Right. *Gaucho*. *Thuringwell*.

She keyed the line back open, smiling a thank you at the man across the room.

"Roger that, *Gaucho*," Casey said. "You are go for rescue. All vessels, there will be EVA suits in the air shortly. Navigate accordingly."

"Situation?" Jessica called, coming through the door.

Enej must have been fully asleep. Or maybe at lunch. His was the only closer cabin, in terms of actual steps required.

"We just lost a fighter during the training exercise," Casey replied, watching the woman simply command the entire room and all the emotions in it into their place with nothing more than a look.

Amazing.

"Collision?" Jessica asked.

"Negative, Fleet Centurion," Casey shook her head. "Spaceframe failed catastrophically for no apparent cause. All other craft accounted for. Rescue operations underway."

"Who was it?"

Jessica was at her seat now and buckling herself in.

"*Jouster.*"

Casey hadn't know Milos Pavlovic all that well. His reputation as a *lothario* had preceded him, and she hadn't wanted to start an incident by beating the man silly if he got as friendly as some rumors suggested he might.

Jessica's face actually registered shock, when it normally was a calm mask. Only for a moment, and then it was back to what Casey expected.

"Are you ready for the flag?" Casey asked, relieved that someone else could handle this mess.

Jessica shook her head, and for just the slightest moment, Casey was sure she detected an evil grin on the woman's face.

"No, you have a better understanding of the situation than I do," the Fleet Centurion replied. "That's one of the big differences in our cultures. The person with the flag hands off when they are ready to, not when a superior officer enters the room."

Oh. Crap.

Casey took another deep breath and watched the projection evolve as flight vectors were updated. Rather than come to a relative stop and return to base, *Uller* had apparently ordered everyone to clear the area first, and then come up. It looked like a flower, pointed directly away from *Auberon*, opening its petals, with three small stars at the center, close to the moving dot indicating the wreckage of *Jouster*'s fighter.

And she was in charge.

"Bridge, this is Wiegand," she said aloud. "Flight deck is likely to be a mess if we're trying to bring casualties aboard. Route as many pilots as possible to *II Augusta* and *Andorra* for now and we'll pick them up later."

"Already in process, Flag," Denis Jež's voice came back instantly.

Okay, good. Jessica really did have a first-class team. Maybe all she needed to do at this point was watch and answer questions as they arose. Jessica Keller seemed to be of the same mind.

Casey sat, and tried not to fidget as everyone else went about their jobs.

CHAPTER XXIV

DATE OF THE REPUBLIC FEBRUARY 22, 400
TRANSITION WAYPOINT 9

Denis didn't care what anybody said. It was his ship, so it was his responsibility.

Didn't matter that *Auberon* was part of a Task Group, assigned to the Imperial Fleet for the duration. Didn't matter that they were in deep space in the middle of nowhere, more or less in a gap between the two nations. Didn't matter than Jessica was in overall command.

Nor that they were in the field. At war. *Jouster* was just the first of what would hopefully be very few casualties. Another name plate added to the wall on the flight deck, pilots and flight engineers lost in service.

Wasn't the first. Wouldn't be the last.

None of that mattered. It was his ship. *Jouster* had been one of his pilots.

Denis let the sonorous words of the ancient service roll out of his mouth, reading carefully as his mind was in another place. Hopefully, he would never know this prayer well enough to recite it from memory.

And pigs might fly.

"…and so we commend his soul to the Creator, even as we commit his body to the depths of the sea without a shore," Denis read aloud in a normal voice, letting the pickup broadcast his words across the flight deck and the assembled crew, and to the rest of the squadron. "Command Flight Centurion Milos Pavlovic, *Jouster*, rest easy."

Denis closed the small, black, Book of Naval Rituals and looked up, making eye contact with only a handful of people and breaking the spell of awkward silence that had fallen over everyone.

Blinks greeted him as folks came back from wherever it was that sudden, violent death took them.

Denis found himself centered. Calm.

Death did that to him.

"All hands, dismissed," he ordered.

The crowd before him broke into a receding tide, bodies turning away to find solace in smaller groups, private memories, drinks raised in toast and celebration to one of the greatest pilots they had ever known.

He made eye contact with Jessica standing to one side of the mob, and nodded to her. Moirrey and Bedrov were closer to the rear of the group, and already departing.

Iskra Vlahovic, the flight deck commander, actually looked angry today, but Denis couldn't imagine at what. She fell into stride on his left as Jessica did on the right, the three of them following Moirrey out the hatch and into the corridor.

A conference room nearby waited.

Jessica and Iskra took places on one side. Moirrey and Yan Bedrov were on the other. Denis stood at the closest end. Captain Wald had just removed his dress sword and was leaning it in a rear corner of the room. He turned and stood behind the chair at the head of the table with both hands on it, almost noble in his best dress uniform.

Denis met the man's questioning eye and nodded. They both sat at the same time, facing each other down three meters of flat, polished surface.

"Why is Captain Wald chairing this hearing?" Jessica asked.

Her voice wasn't antagonistic. Very antagonistic, anyway. Curious, with a sharp edge, perhaps.

Denis turned his attention to Bedrov.

"Because I needed someone good with numbers," the pirate replied. "And it helped, having another expert with command experience who was also an outsider, asking questions to people who might have chosen to withhold things I needed to know."

Denis watched the dynamic play out silently. There were things there that remained unsaid. Perhaps unsayable, but that was the effect of living in close quarters for a very long period of time.

You got to know how your friends thought and how their moods flowed. Often better than they did.

Jessica nodded, satisfied enough.

"The findings and notes have been entered into the record," Captain Wald began in a stern voice. "The purpose of this meeting is to address the issues raised and to apply lessons learned to future endeavors. As Sri Bedrov has noted, the results were to be found in the data generated by *Jouster*'s craft, once the dross had been cleared away."

He paused there, as if measuring the room for the words about to come out of his mouth. Wald had impressed Denis with his ability to be intelligent and expert, without having an ego about it. Calm, quiet, prepared.

Self-contained.

It was a set of qualities Denis valued very highly. If the rumors about Jessica and the Imperial officer were to be believed, Wald would need them, especially if he could help make her happy.

Denis had many years as Jessica's right hand. He understood how well those traits complemented her own.

"After interviewing other pilots and flight deck engineers, a consensus has emerged to support the data," Wald continued, in a tighter voice, like ice chipped off the side of a barn on a winter morning. "As you are aware, the fighter ships in question are still new enough to be considered experimental, so their on-board systems are in full diagnostic mode at all times. *Jouster*'s data recorder was located at about the same time as his body was recovered, and it tracked everything the man had done since the craft was delivered to the fleet. Nearly every built-in safety feature and governor that *Jouster* could access was disabled, or manipulated to settings well beyond what we would consider safe for the systems in question."

"And he did it himself?" Denis asked, just to make sure that finding was in the official record.

The last thing he needed was suspicion of a spy or vengeful ex-girlfriend in their midst. Creator knew *Jouster* had enough of the latter.

"Affirmative, Command Centurion," Wald answered. "*Jouster* took great pains to make the physical changes invisible, but everything was there in the data audit."

"And your conclusions?" Iskra finally spoke. She was always quiet. This wouldn't change that.

"If I may be so crude," the Imperial said. "I could boil the results of my various interviews down to: *Jouster* being *Jouster*. However, I have never worked with the man, so I cannot say if that adequately describes him."

"I'm not sure you could more accurately describe Milos Pavlovic, Captain Wald," Jessica interjected.

Most of the heads in the room nodded.

"Recommendations?" Denis asked.

It was all formal cant at this point. Iskra had probably already implemented everything anyone here could think of. Part of the official record. And lessons for *II Augusta*, and eventually the rest of the navy.

"Mostly, change the security access authentications for the onboard systems," Wald said with something of a shrug. "Separate what the flight engineers can do from what the pilots are supposed to be doing. If *Jouster* hadn't been tinkering with his coolant systems for an edge, he wouldn't have overloaded his charging capacitors at a moment when the engines were already red-lined and straining. Results still would have been bad, but he would have had time to eject and suffer nothing more than embarrassment."

Denis nodded.

Jouster being *Jouster*.

If he hadn't been one of the best pilots in the navy, he would have long since been cashiered for all the stupid things he did in his life. A man who was never willing to admit that maybe it was time to retire.

Denis hoped he would be able to remember that lesson when it was his time.

"Are there any other items that need to be addressed?" Denis inquired in a formal tone.

"No, Command Centurion," Captain Wald replied, just as formally.

"Your findings are so noted, and this hearing is complete," he said. "If you would all remain with us for a few minutes, I have an unrelated topic for this group."

Nobody had moved. They had barely twitched.

Denis turned to the Fleet Centurion.

"Normally, the senior-most surviving officer would brevet to command of the Wing, until more formal arrangements could be made," Denis observed, dangling his next worry out there.

"And that's *Uller*," she replied to Denis's nod.

She turned to Captain Wald, drawing lightning bolts to herself as Denis watched.

"Senior Flight Centurion Friedhelm Hannes Förstner, known as *Uller*, was an Imperial citizen until he was eleven years old," she stated.

To his credit, Wald looked like a man who had just discovered he was standing in a live mine field. Not that it was his fault, but Lady Casey was acting like a *Republic* Navy officer these days, so it fell to him to fully represent *Fribourg*.

He was doing a pretty good job of it, too.

"Kennet Förstner, his paternal grandfather, was executed as a Chartist, by Karl V," Jessica continued like a steamroller intent on leveling the Imperial officer. "*Uller* and his extended family were pardoned by Karl VII as part of the Peace, but feelings still run high."

"I see," Wald replied carefully.

"I have spoken with *Uller*, and others," Jessica said. It felt like a mousetrap closing, from where Denis sat watching. "Given the sensitivities we will be likely encountering, he is content to stand aside, at least for the duration of this mission. I suspect he would be happy not being promoted at any point, since he should, by all rights, be driving a desk at his age, not leading a flight squadron. Ainsley Barrett will be acting as Command Flight Centurion, until First Lord or the Senate say otherwise."

Something of a smile ghosted itself across Wald's face, just for a moment, before it was gone, but Jessica had apparently seen it, too.

"Captain?" she asked.

"*da Vinci*, Fleet Centurion," Captain Wald observed dryly. "I can only imagine what leverage you had to exert, to blackmail her into taking that role."

Denis appreciated the blush that quickly flushed Yan Bedrov's silent face. He wasn't sure anybody else was looking the right direction to catch it, and he wasn't about to say anything. The pirate and the laconic scout had taken great pains to remain off everybody's scanners with their relationship.

But she had been smiling more lately than in all the years Denis had known the woman.

CHAPTER XXV

"I haven't been ignoring you, Arott," Jessica said as the man took a seat in her office.

Marcelle was already delivering freshly brewed coffee and all the fixings. She appraised Jessica's expression, nodded with a wry smile, and departed.

Arott Whughy took a moment to run his left hand, the one not holding a mug, through his blond hair. It was too long, these days, but that was probably the effect of working too hard, and not some new personal look for the man. He was still too spit-and-polish to ever color that far outside the lines. At least not for long.

"I'm aware of that," he replied after a sip. "And thank you for letting me dig in. What you handed me was a mess."

"Yes," Jessica agreed. "An administrative and tactical nightmare. With vague orders, impossible expectations, and concrete deadlines. I don't know anybody else in the navy capable of knocking it into shape in time, either. So what do you have for me?"

He nodded at her, more as a placeholder than anything, although she caught the surprised grin at the compliment before it disappeared again.

"Nobody has ever done anything like this," he replied, a grin growing as he spoke. "Our records go back to the *Founding* and before, easily. And I and my team have done research across all the major campaigns we could find reliable records for. I would say you are insane, but I'm pretty sure you are also right."

Jessica grinned back at him. It had become something of a game with them, almost a sibling rivalry between two teenagers, like she used to have with Slava when they were young.

She would postulate something outrageous. He would try to prove her wrong, or, as in this case, show her how it could be done when she challenged the impossibility of a task.

Once upon a time, she had even resented the man, aware that Nils Kasum considered the two of them the best candidates to eventually succeed him as First Lord of the Fleet, one of these days. Now, Arott was welcome to the job.

Her life was going to go far beyond such a mundane task.

"And, you've managed to make obsolete everything I've just spent five years learning, after the last time you overturned everything, Jessica," he continued, with a friendly, if exasperated sigh.

"*Buran* is alien, Arott," she said simply. "Human, yes. But they fly and fight so strangely that they might as well be something else. I've studied their tactics and their strategies, especially all the top secret documents Emmerich Wachturm sent home with me. And I had long conversations with the only known friendly *Sentience* in surveyed space when we defended *Ballard*. The *Last of the Immortals*, if you will. Moirrey spent even more time around her. Those beings *are* another species."

"And that's what frightens me, Jessica," he replied. "*Buran* seems to see itself as the benevolent overlord that should guide all of galactic humanity. And they are patient enough to try. How do we stop them?"

"According to my two experts, there is one thing that artificially-intelligent systems really don't understand," she said. "Don't get at all. Art."

"Art?"

She had him confused again. But that was good. Even Jessica was right at the edge of understanding it, herself. And she had two artists she could tap, in addition to all the warriors: Lady Casey and Lady Moirrey.

"For all their sophisticated programming, they are just machines, Arott," Jessica continued. "Logical constructs. Patterns. Organization. Suvi claimed that she survived as long as she has because someone taught her to be human six millennia ago, when she was just a kitten, to use her words. All of her cousins weren't human. Those that survived to this age tended to become afflicted with some manner of Deity Complex."

"So we fight *Buran* with insanity?" Arott asked. She watched him grind his teeth rather than say anything more, as much as she knew he wanted to.

As commanders went, Arott Whughy was exceptionally logical. He would be the best candidate to poke holes in her theories. Disrupt her planning. Out-think her.

If he could.

"Crudely?" she asked. "Yes. We will do things that have surprisingly little tactical or strategic value, at least at the first level."

"While you, Enej, and I play multi-dimensional chess," he agreed.

She had known the two men played. Apparently, they played more than she had realized.

But even that was to her advantage, as it bound him closer to her team.

"Can you pull it off with the resources in hand?" Jessica asked simply. "Or do I need to get the Grand Admiral involved?"

"It will be touch-and-go," he said. "You've given me the tools, but I will need time. Every day I have to work on the problem makes success that much more likely, and I don't know how long they will give us."

"Neither do I," she said. "However, they aren't going to see this coming. If I'm right, nobody will see this coming. So, if you would, describe what you do know."

"I've got *CT-9492*, a tug hauling a Bastion unit, plus a second pod filled with every weird piece of gear *zu* Kermode, Ozolinsh, or I could think to bring, including the engines off of a monitor and enough spare metal and parts to do nearly anything," Arott said, ticking fingers as he worked.

"In addition, we brought the Salvage Cruiser *Bulldog* along," he continued. "That gives us the ability to do repairs almost as well as a dedicated drydock, and we'll be mobile, to boot. With some time, I'll be able to build a small flight platform and off-load all of *Andorra's* fighters and pilots to help with defense. And *Wombat* will hopefully be laying mines like they are going out of style. I will absolutely require *Fribourg* to help with resupply there, but I can build an impregnable moat. Or could, against anybody else."

Jessica nodded. Just about what her own analysis had shown. She waited a beat for the man to arrive at the core of his thought.

"What I don't understand," he said, as if reading her mind. "Why can't we just drop the bastion in place and work to turn it into a full citadel? Why the effort to refit it with engines?"

"*Buran* can hop inside a gravity well, Arott," she said, soothingly, a foil to the angry energy building in his voice. "I watched him drop out of a jump right on top of *Fribourg's* primary fleet base and savage it like a polar bear on a wounded seal. And that was with a single cruiser. They'll bring more to this dance. If the base can move on its own, however slowly, they have to adjust."

"But building outside the normal defensive boundary of the gravity zone?" he pressed. "That's been the bedrock of tactical planning forever."

"And he can ignore it," she said. "We can't, unless we refit all of our vessels with JumpDrives instead of sails. But if we're outside the well, we can play as well."

"You want to bounce a bastion up into JumpSpace?"

She watched him take a breath and carefully set his coffee mug down, having nearly spilled the hot fluid into his lap.

"Are you insane?" he pursued.

"He can't chase you into JumpSpace," she replied simply.

He wanted to argue. It was there in his eyes, the knee-jerk opposition to everything she was asking him to do.

And then it passed. Like a squall line.

Like sun from behind a cloud, an evil glint suddenly appeared in his eyes.

"Could we hold a monitor or a bastion in JumpSpace permanently?" he asked suddenly. "Sail around in a circle? Hop back and forth as a defensive barrier outside the normal one, all set to pounce on some bastard coming to attack us?"

"You have several months to war-game that, Arott," she smiled. "You and Yan and Moirrey tell me. Recruit Denis and Alber' as well and get them thinking about it."

"Crap, I hate it when you're right," he smiled back. "I'm never going to be able to sleep again."

"Yes, you will," she answered. "Anything else?"

"Negative," Arott said, rising, but keeping the half-full mug. Marcelle's coffee was nothing to waste or leave behind. "I'll check in again at Waypoint 10 or 11 with what we know."

"Good," she said.

He departed with a jaunty stride that hadn't been there before.

Now, she just had to hope that the whole idea was so insane that a bored *Sentience* had never calculated the math or energy costs. At least, not yet.

Because once she opened this can of worms, he would understand. And she would spend the rest of her life, perhaps, trying to outthink one of the smartest machines ever constructed.

CHAPTER XXVI

IMPERIAL FOUNDING: 178/02/23. IMPERIAL FLEET
HEADQUARTERS, ST. LEGIER

"You're sure?" Emmerich asked, putting down the executive summary that has just ruined his morning, and possibly his digestion. The visitor, the spy, sat across the desk and looked uncomfortable, as if being out in daylight hours was an unnatural act.

"*Sure* is an improper term in my line of business, Admiral," the man from Imperial Security replied in a carefully-neutral tone.

Everything about the man was carefully neutral, from his brownish hair, to average looks, to non-threatening stance.

Em suspected he had been a field agent once, before he got promoted to whatever rank a man like him held, to be the liaison with the Grand Admiral of the Fleet, Emperor Karl's cousin and mailed right fist.

"Confidence?" Em replied. "Probability?"

The man actually shrugged, enough so that Em had to decide he wasn't actually a robot in human guise, or some such thing.

"As close to a sure thing as one gets in this industry," the spy said simply.

"Are we completely riddled with traitors and assassins, then?" Emmerich asked, aware of just how angry his voice sounded.

"My gut instinct is that a few bad apples have been allowed access to the very places that should have been secured from them," was all the man would commit to.

"And your proposed solution?" Em asked. "How should I respond to a report that agents in Imperial Security itself are planning to have me assassinated?"

Besides having them all executed and starting with a blank piece of paper?

That was left unsaid, but the implications were obvious to both of them. The spy nodded.

"The Emperor has approved extraordinary methods in pursuing this investigation, Grand Admiral," the spy said. "If I can't promise you a safer personnel structure by the time you return, then quite possibly the entire edifice will need to be razed and rebuilt with new bricks."

Extraordinary methods. Torture to make the ancients weep with envy. Psychological and chemical inducements that would break any man or woman in very short order. The remains barely human, assuming the poor wretch was exonerated and then chose to survive the affair.

Em had no doubt that his cousin had personally signed the papers to destroy the first half-dozen lives, men and women who probably thought of themselves as patriots, mixed in with various fools, anarchists, Chartists, and spies from *Buran*.

At least *Aquitaine*'s agents were keeping a much lower profile for the time being. And they had always been better behaved in any event.

This was a concerted effort to destabilize *Fribourg* at a time when the Empire was psychologically its weakest, needing unity so as to pivot and go after the ancient enemy.

Still, there was a way to handle this. Perhaps he had grown complacent, spending his days reorganizing the entire fleet to better handle the newest threat, shifting task forces and minds away from *Aquitaine* as Jessica Keller's efforts bore fruit.

"Very good, Captain," Em said neutrally. "Keep me posted."

"Yes, sir."

The man immediately departed, leaving Em alone in his office.

He keyed a comm line and leaned back in his chair.

"Hendrik, come to my office immediately," he said when the other end answered, hanging up as soon as the man assented.

It took less than a minute.

Hendrik Baumgärtner, Imperial Flag Captain and Em's right hand for more than twenty years. Every inch a recruiting poster with gray bristly hair and an erect carriage.

"Sir?" he asked, closing the door silently and coming to attention.

"Imperial Security was just here," Em began.

"Yes, Admiral," Hendrik replied. "I read the report. What's your next move?"

"I was going to depart in a week to meet up with Jessica Keller and Lady Casey," Em mused. "My courier ship would have been good enough to arrive early and wait. But whoever is behind this knows too much about too many things, and I need to throw them off-stride. Find me a shuttle to orbit right now, and a big-enough warship you can detach from whatever it is they thought they were doing. Override all their orders. I will use them as a personal transport there and back. You'll speak with my authority until I return, or until the Emperor changes your orders. Questions?"

"Warship?" Hendrik asked, his eyes already on a distant horizon, calculating.

"Cruiser or better, Hendrik," Em said. "These people have infiltrated everywhere, and were going to try to kill me here or in the palace. I don't want them to decide to send something out to kill an unarmed fast courier in the middle of nowhere."

"*Firehawk*'s just coming out of drydock," Hendrik noted. "She was scheduled for a shakedown cruise and should be fully loaded and provisioned. Provst should be aboard her now."

"Perfect," Em said. "Let's pretend I'm just going to lunch, and not tell anyone that I won't be back for four weeks. You have the deck here, and I'll call Freya from orbit."

"Acknowledged, Admiral," Hendrik said, already backing up and opening the door.

Em took a look around his desk and his office. Nothing that needed his attention today. He pulled a small satchel from a desk drawer and put half a dozen file folders in. And, just because it had been that kind of day, the personal sidearm he usually kept in the top drawer for sudden emergencies.

He rose, nodded to himself and the room, and left, looking for all the world like a man going to lunch.

———

The hatch opened onto a noisy shuttle bay. It was still clean, since a drydock session always included a good, hard steam-scrub to get things out of cracks that a polishing wheel couldn't reach. In another month it would be as if nobody had ever tried to sanitize the place.

Em came down the steps to the sight of a Lieutenant Commander attempting quite unsuccessfully to conceal his utter shock and horror. To him, this probably seemed like the worst surprise inspection any officer had ever had in any nightmare.

Still, the man came to rigid attention and saluted as Em and his bodyguards emerged.

"Welcome aboard, Grand Admiral," the man barely stuttered. "My apologies on behalf of myself, the captain, the admiral, and the crew. We were told only to expect a special courier."

"And so I am, Lt. Commander," Em returned the salute and sized the man up.

Recruiting poster blond, with broad shoulders and an athlete's build and muscles. Looking like he really wanted to crawl back into a hole and die rather than suffer further embarrassment as the Grand Admiral of the Fleet walked through this messy bay, the crew in the process of unpacking supplies and moving them to long-term storage.

The young man did handle himself well.

"Rather than give them any warning, I would like to go surprise Provst and Kistler up on the bridge," Em continued. "What say you? And what is your name?"

"Follow me, please, Grand Admiral," the man said. "Lt. Commander Gunter Tifft, sir. Flight Deck Operations and Quartermaster section."

"Well handled, Tifft," Em said to put the man as much at ease as possible. "This will be a very special surprise for everyone."

And hopefully, Freya wouldn't kill him for missing the dinner party she had planned for the day after next.

"Grand Admiral on the deck," Tifft bellowed as the hatch opened and he stepped in and to one side.

Em grinned as heads came around in confusion, replaced immediately by more shocked horror as he followed Tifft onto the bridge. A feral cat having a litter of kittens in the captain's chair wouldn't have gotten as much of a rise out of them.

Two seconds later, everyone not immediately flying the battleship was on their feet, awkwardly tucking in shirts and sucking in guts. Including Captain Kistler and Admiral of the White Tomas Provst.

Em made a note to pull surprise inspections like this more often. The humor it brought him was worth it alone, regardless of what it would do to keep his people sharp.

Provst recovered first. He had known Em the longest, having been the captain commanding *Amsel* during the *Battle of Iger* where Jessica Keller first came to Em's attention.

He was a tall man, even a bit taller than Em, with a dark, swarthy complexion, eyes nearly black, and a close-trimmed beard starting to gray. He looked out over a beak of a nose, eyes narrowing.

"Are you the emergency mission, Admiral?" Provst asked.

"I am," Em grinned. "I will need about an hour to handle some secure communications from your flag bridge, and then we will depart. I will provide coordinates at that point."

"Acknowledged, Admiral," Provst said, turning to the captain he had been speaking to when the day went sideways. "Kistler, make as much preparation as you can now, and we'll finish it all up from JumpSpace."

The captain nodded once, and Em followed Provst out of the hatchway and into the main corridor. Lt. Commander Tifft followed them at a discreet distance, preparing to return to his duties on the flight deck.

"Can you spare Tifft?" Em asked, all of a sudden. "I had to leave Hendrik behind and will need a spare pair of hands to do things."

Em glanced over at the Lt. Commander just long enough to watch the blood drain out of the man's otherwise impassive face. Provst looked at Tifft as well.

"Tifft, you're on detached duty until otherwise ordered," the Admiral of the White said. "I'll square it with everyone."

"Yes, sir," the man said without his voice cracking. Much. "Thank you, Admirals."

Em grinned. Good luck and good timing for the young man to be in the right place, and he had indeed handled himself exceptionally well so far, reacting to such a surprise. In a week, he might make his career. Or break it.

Best to find out now.

The flag bridge had only a skeleton crew. Provst hadn't been planning to do more than run around the local system for a few days, making sure everything was working correctly before picking up his full team for a longer cruise.

Firehawk wasn't scheduled to be on the line for another three months. And she was an older vessel, not one of the Paladin-class battleships under construction now. A sister of the *Amsel* they had both ridden to fame a decade ago.

Em took a station close to the door and powered it live. He hadn't been behind a desk for so long that he didn't know how to secure a comm line. Provst and Tifft made themselves busy and scarce as he worked.

Quickly, he had a secured line to the palace. Hendrik must have sent a message ahead, because Joh, *His Imperial Majesty Karl VII, Emperor of Fribourg,* was on the line in seconds. From the sweat pasting Joh's shirt to his chest, Em assumed he was interrupting a weight-lifting session.

"You were never at that much risk, Em," Joh began sarcastically. "There are light-years of difference between wanting to do a thing, and being able to do it."

"Maybe," Em hedged. "Who knows what they leaked to people who might be able to execute effectively. In any event. I'll be at the rendezvous for an unknown period of time before Keller's squadron shows up. Running's nice, but I'd like to shoot back, this time."

"You think *Buran's* behind it?" the Emperor asked.

"Can you think of anybody else who would risk everything to try it?" Em fired back.

"Point taken," Joh replied. "Give Casey my love and Keller my thanks. Tell them both I owe them a major celebration when they get back."

"Will do, Joh," Em said. "I don't suppose you'd be willing to call Freya and tell her the news?"

"Absolutely not," Joh grinned. "If she decides to divorce you and hire competent assassins, I want to be on her good side."

"Fine," Em harrumphed. "I'll be back in four or five weeks. At that point, I'll know what to budget for next year, after we see what Yan Bedrov did with a blank piece of paper. Expect bureaucratic warfare."

"Hendrik already warned me," Joh said. "Oh, by the time you get back, I'll have promoted him to Admiral of the White. If he's going to be you, he needs to look the part."

"Thank you, Joh," Em said. "I was going ask for that as part of next year's birthday honors."

Joh winked and cut the line, leaving Em to draw a deep breath and begin entering a different comm code. Hendrik would most certainly have contacted the palace about the change of plans.

He would have never presumed to call Freya.

She answered quickly. Em just sat and stared at her for a few seconds, bathing in her beauty.

Those bright, green eyes narrowed as she gazed at the background over his shoulder.

"That doesn't look like your office," she observed in a knowing tone. "It looks remarkably like a flag bridge somewhere."

Yes, he had never been able to fool this woman. And that was okay. He had never had to lie to or dissemble with her, either.

"Something has come up," he said obliquely. Even a secured comm could be tapped with the proper tech. "I had to bump up my departure a week. But I'm taking Tomas Provst and *Firehawk* with me, instead of my courier."

That got a perfectly-chiseled, blond eyebrow raised. His courier might be the fastest thing in space. But it was unarmed. *Firehawk* was a battleship, ready for the line.

Freya was aware of that.

"Will your return date change?" she asked.

"I don't know at this point, love," Em said. "Much of it depends on Keller."

"Remind her that you're supposed to be home more, now," Freya said, grinning. "She gets the load and I get my husband back."

"I will convey your opinion on the subject, Freya," Em said.

She blew a kiss at the screen and cut the signal.

Em found himself grinning like a fool at a blank monitor. After a bit he flipped open his briefcase and located the paper he wanted.

Calling up a navigation function, Em typed it in by hand and waited for the nav computer to locate his target. He transmitted it to Tom Provst and to Tifft, turning to face them.

"This is where we are going," Em announced.

Provst studied the screen for a second and looked up.

"Middle of bloody nowhere," he replied.

"Yes," Em agreed. "No inhabited systems anywhere close by. Not on any trade routes worth considering. Rather, the perfect spot to rendezvous with a battle squadron of *Aquitaine* vessels led by Jessica Keller, if we don't want anybody watching."

"And the reason you suddenly want a battleship handy?" Tom asked.

Em speared both men with a sharp look, and extended it to the other four men in the room.

"This does not leave this chamber," Em said, waiting for everyone to nod silently. "A few bad apples in Imperial Security were planning to assassinate me, sometime in the next week or so. Before I could go meet

Keller. And they knew my itinerary. I'd rather not be waiting there in an unarmed courier."

"So you're expecting trouble, Admiral?" Tom said, his face suddenly as angry as he had ever been, commanding *Amsel* in the old days.

"How quietly can you sneak up on them, if they are already there waiting?" Em challenged the man.

"Thief in the night, Grand Admiral," was the reply.

"Good, because Keller's next stop is *Buran*."

CHAPTER XXVII

It were a thing of utter beauty t'behold.

And totally precise, which were the hardest part. Moirrey knowed 'zactly how much work it'd been t'lathe a bar of titanium inta the right ever'thin', by hand, no less, an' then open up spaces'n'gaps with a laser console so's bone'n'stuff'd grow into the holes. Would still take years to be total solid, but Cap'n Wald had himself a pirate leg like no other 'n'the universe.

With flames etched right inta the shaft, 'natch.

Not that anyone'd see them, most days. The good captain were always dressed fer navy-ing, even when he were off-duty. Not that th'man were ever off-duty.

Kinda like her sister.

It were a good match.

Probably.

Moirrey watched Captain Wald in his gray shorts and shirt be put through his paces by the new doc, Mahmud Astrauskas, Doc Samara finally havin' retired to a life of country club widows, which were apparently way easier ta deals with th'n burns, fractures, and exposure cases. An' all the strange bugses pilots picked up on shore leave.

New doc were tall'n'skinny. Forged o'barbed wire and attitude problem, which were prolly what *Auberon*'s hard-headed crew needed, most days.

And ain't none of them were willin' to keep up with the Doc when he got onto the track fer one of his ultra-marathons.

How many laps about deck seventeen? Nothankyouverymuch.

Nope, today were easy. Cap'n Wald on an inclining treadmill, dragging his metal leg along with his meat one 'til he cried uncle.

Moirrey coulda tol' Doc Astrauskas that the machine were gonna surrender afore Wald, but he dinna wanna listen.

Still, ya hadta measure this. She'd already hadta adjust the ankle and knee mechanisms twice, but no more than a combined one and a half millimeters, which weren't bad, as tall as the Cap'n were. Today dinna look like anythin' were needed.

Er rather, all the mechanicalin' stuff were within tolerance.

Emotional stuff still hadda be sorted out.

"Is there any pain, Captain?" Doc Astrauskas asked finally.

Wald had been gruntin' and sweatin' sometin fierce, but no more'n'anyone other than maybe Vo, ya puts the damned thing at a twenty-five degree upwards slants and turn it to a fast walk.

Vo's legs were too long, anyway. Damned hill giants.

"Negative, Doctor," Wald replied through grittin' teeth. "Or rather, none more than would be expected at this speed and incline."

"Good enough," the doc replied, pressing a button that caused the infernal machine to beep like a bomb 'bouts to boom. "I already had you two notches beyond what would be a normal test for this sort of surgery. You should be able to walk and run normally from here out. I would caution against any sorts of motions that would cause you to twist on that leg, such as dancing and most martial arts, at least for another six to twelve months. At that point, the implant should have fused to the point that it will hold better than the rest of your leg."

Moirrey watched the machine-front of the gadget slowly descend ta levels. And slow down so's the Cap'n dinna whomp himself silly against nothin'.

"Centurion *zu* Kermode?" the doc turned to her, black eyes all squinty with devilishness, like he knew she were up to no good and gauging the collateral damage.

"Is good," she chirped. "Have technical questions fer the Cap'n, but nothin' medical. All kinesthetics at this point."

"Then he's your patient," the doc said, picking up a board an' addin' notes with a stylus as he headed fer the hatch.

Nobody else were in the small gym. Jes'th'two o'them.

Wald grabbed a handy towel and stuck his face'n'head in it to dry off, emergin' a sec later like a killer whale broaching.

He t'weren't fooled, neither.

As he shouldna be.

Man wants a play in this league gots to unnerstan' that occasionally, peeples hafta play a mite rough. And he were a big boy, or he'd'a no made it this far.

He did surprise her by steppin' off'n the treadmill and aroun' to one side, leaning over an' puttin' his weight on the guide rails like he were tired, er somethin'. Dinna put his head at her level, but closer. Certainlies not parade rest stuffff.

Yup, green eyes full of piss'n'vinegar.

He smiled at her from across the small space and the treadmill like an orca smiles at tuna.

She smiled back. Friendly, even.

This weren't no threatenin' meeting. That's t'come later.

Well, okay, maybe a little.

The silence stretched.

Patient man. Good.

Game of patience. Of knowin' your place isn't in the center'o'thin's.

Of gettin' over bein' an *Imperial Gentleman.*

This is Aquitaine, *bubbles. We does it diff'r'nt here.*

He had lively eyebrows.

Communicative, even, dancing and wriggling ta indicate humor, and questions, and self-confidence like gravity.

Yeah, you might do.

He smiled.

"I wondered when you would come for me," he began suddenly.

Like they'd been talkin' fer minutes already, which they kinda had.

"Oh?" she kinda managed to volley back at him, lobbin' the ball barely across the net and kinda softly right inta the middle of the court fer a nasty bit o'spike.

"All of the Fleet Centurion's people are protective of her," he continued. "You, she treats almost like a sister. I'm a stranger thrust suddenly into your midst, even more so than being assigned to Lady Casey, at least for another few days."

"And what do we expect happens in a week, Captain?" Moirrey couldna help herself. Stress brought precision to her language.

"We'll rendezvous with the Grand Admiral," Wald said simply. "He'll have a chance to update my orders for the first time in nearly a year."

"What were those orders, Wald?" Moirrey probed, impersonatin' her favorite detective character from the latest season of *Anameleck: Beyond the Dragon Gates*.

"I was assigned to support Lady Casey as a staff economist, *zu* Kermode," he said in a flat, almost-emotionless tone. "Anything else was on my personal time."

Yup, orca. The bitey kind. 'Course, tuna swim fast.

Moirrey took a moment to look down and study the titanium rod emerging from the healed stump of his left leg, watched it glide down into a complex knee assembly with some range of rotation. The shin with all sorts of twistability. The ankle that could do anythin' a human's could, and wouldna rupture near so easy. Even the toes, flexible but grippy on carpet, as needed.

"You chose the simple solution, rather than the one that would get you closest to the man you used to be," Moirrey observed, looking back up at those dangerous eyes.

It were obvious what Jess saw in the man, looking at that face right now. Hard, but not cruel.

Tough sum'bitch.

"I chose to retain the most options, Lady Moirrey," he countered, tones growing red now, slowly, but deliberately. "I can always go home after this, if it turns out I have made a mistake here. I am not bereft or forlorn. Nor dependent. I can risk stepping off a cliff, because the Emperor will always welcome me back to service."

"And do you wish to return to Imperial service, Captain Wald?" *zu* Kermode was feeling her oats, too, ya know.

"This *is* Imperial service, *zu* Kermode," he snapped. "My personal time is just that. Personal."

Moirrey nodded and took a breath. Too easy to gets inta a shoutin' match right now.

Bad. And wrong. And he were right. Were personal.

Was why they was here.

"Yes," she finally agreed, letting some of the steam blow off. "Personal. And yes, she is my sister. So I gets to say something' none of the boys'd have the guts to do. She's kin. Clan. If you break her heart, I'll have yours on a plate, bucko."

"Lady Moirrey, if I do that, you have my permission," he countered.

That bounced her back. Hard. Staggered a mental step.

He *were* serious business. Dangerous. Marrying kind. Like when Digger'd finally gotten down on one knee all formal-like and threatened to make an honest woman of her.

Honest-enough, anyway.

"You're ready for a mission that might never take you home, Captain Wald?" she finally managed to sputter.

"I volunteered to be here, Lady Moirrey," he said. "The Grand Admiral inquired. He did not order it."

Oh.

OH.

Wow.

Yup. Serious business.

Like, maybe another brother-in-law-soon kind of serious.

"And if something goes wrong and the war a'tween *Fribourg* and *Aquitaine* starts up again?" she reached out to the worstest-case-scenario she could see.

"Right this second?" he asked to her nod. "Resign my commission and look for a job teaching economics someplace like *Anameleck Prime*. Join the civilian merchant fleet. Paint. Something. But it would be on this side of that border until she tells me to leave. She has that prerogative, Lady Moirrey. Nobody else, including the two Emperors. Is that clear enough for you?"

"Her da's still alive, you know," Moirrey grinned. "Yer gonna hafta ask him, at some point."

Wald grinned back at her.

"Yan Bedrov already warned me that Slava and Miguel would be pushovers, compared to Alber', Denis, Robbie, and *you*."

"You go right on believin' that, Cap'n."

"Besides," the grin gentled into a smile, perhaps even melancholied a bits. "I haven't even kissed her yet. All I know is that she hasn't sent me packing."

Really? No? Not once?

Huh.

'Course, fer as Moirrey knowed, Jess had only kissed one other man in the last decade, and he were dead nows. And that wouldsa been serious business as well.

Prolly need to make sure the cap'n don' gets hisself killed out here.

"You ready for an adventure, Torsten Wald?" Moirrey asked, finding her seriousness bubbling up 'gain.

In *Fribourg* culture, you only ever used first names with close folks. Good friends. Kith and kin.

Imperial economists with dangerous dreams.

"Can you top this?" he volleyed back at her, gesturing at the room around them.

She could, but that were just bad men with guns.

Torsten Wald might be serious.

CHAPTER XXVIII

IMPERIAL FOUNDING: 178/03/04. IFV FEUERFALKE,
INTERSECTION POINT KASUM

It took him back, but Emmerich knew better than to be seduced by the warm, comfortable confines of *Firehawk*'s flag bridge. *Amsel*, the old *Blackbird* now replaced with a *Paladin*-class version of the same name, had been close enough to this ship to be identical, in all the ways that mattered.

The place where he had first made his name as The Red Admiral, scourge of the spaceways.

Now he was busy trying to save the Empire from rogues, spies, and fools.

There were days he wanted to damn Jessica Keller for what she had done to undermine his entire existence. Or thank her for helping him find himself when he had gone astray.

And today, he needed her brilliance to save the galaxy.

It would have been galling, had it been anyone other than Jessica.

As both Joh and Casey had observed, empires could be built on the broad shoulders of a woman like that.

Em was going to bet everything that they were right.

Around him, the flag bridge was quiet. Almost sepulchral.

The radio silence was as complete as he could get it, routing all necessary communications with *Aquitaine* and Nils Kasum through four fast frigates whose captains he had personally trained and installed. Not even the Imperial Post could be trusted right now, to say nothing of the Imperial Security Bureau that had been so badly compromised by Dittmar and his accomplices.

Hopefully, enough of the Fleet was solid behind him.

If not, they were all doomed to live out their wretched lives as slaves of the great machine-god.

Over my dead body…

Em fought the anger down and drew a deep breath. Let the oxygen burn out the impurities in his soul so he could face battle with a clear mind.

Lady Moirrey always had a perfect quote for any serious occasion, drawn from one of the ancients, preserved down the millennia and translated time and again as generations passed. One had struck Em's fancy and seemed to call to him now.

"From this day to the ending of the world," said Henry 5 of the religious Feast of the Saint Crispian.

"But we in it shall be remember'd;
We few, we happy few, we band of brothers;
For he to-day that sheds his blood with me
Shall be my brother; be he ne'er so vile,
This day shall gentle his condition."

Em looked once around the entirety of the spacious flag bridge, finally settling his gaze on Lt. Commander Tifft after counting the seventeen others on duty.

Gunter would do.

They all would, but this man stood solid as a mountain, which had been something of a godsend to Em. He was out here in the field without Hendrik or his usual staff for the first time in ages, the needs of secrecy being what they were.

Em smiled and watched the man loosen up a notch. Perhaps only granite now.

Another set of broad shoulders upon which to build empires.

"Status?" Em asked simply.

Tifft had managed to assimilate the needs of the Grand Admiral faster than any aide he had ever broken in. He might be keeping the boy when he left, rather than letting Tifft's career stagnate on an older battleship soon to be relegated to safe borders and internal patrols.

Even Nils Kasum had once made that mistake, though he had fixed it later by handing Jessica a mighty sword named *Auberon*.

When did you become so apocalyptic, old man?

"Per Admiral Provst, we are running as dark and quiet as possible, while still under power and with minimal engines, sir," Tifft replied quietly. "All emitters are off or powered to the lowest possible setting. Passive sensors only. We are currently spinward and a distance outbound from the point of rendezvous delineated *Intersection Point Kasum*, where we are expecting to meet up with the *Aquitaine* squadron at any time. All weapons are primed and inspected, and then locked down for your orders, or Provst's as next in flag command."

Em nodded. Nothing new, but precise. Concise. Exactly what Em needed, and nothing more. Nothing confusing. Yes, this boy was being wasted as a logistics officer.

"Grand Admiral, signal from the bridge," a voice called.

Tifft turned, then caught himself, and looked to his commander with a calm face. It was Tifft's job to handle all that communications traffic. But he was also smart enough to know when to step out of the way.

Like now.

"Go ahead," Em ordered loudly to the back of whichever head had spoken.

"Provst here, Grand Admiral," the Admiral of the White said.

Em had absconded with the man's flag bridge, and his command. Provst had retaliated by inserting himself as a secondary bridge officer, sitting watches and leaving the space below for Em, while Kistler continued to act like a proper captain.

Only a man who had been one of Em's captains for a decade would be willing to do that. Any other admirals probably would have been here in the room, waiting on him hand and foot.

Another sign of a good crew.

"Tom," Em replied.

"We're picking up a strange, intermittent signal, Admiral," Provst said. "Roughly one hundred ten degrees ahead of us around the rim of the target orbit. About the same amount spinward and as far in as we are out. No transponder and no sensor ping, but there is a high probability that it is artificial."

"Is it in effective Primary range?" Em asked.

There was nothing more surprising than being hammered with Primaries out of the darkness. He could speak to that with great authority, especially after how *zu* Kermode first introduced herself to him, long ago at *Qui-Ping.*

"Extreme long-range, Admiral," Provst said. "Iffy at best."

Meaning: we could hit them, but it probably wouldn't be significant enough to matter, other than to let someone out there know they weren't alone.

Still, if bad people were hiding in the shadows, they might not have arrived soon enough to spot *Firehawk* dropping out of JumpSpace, and were therefore still expecting a low-profile courier.

An unarmed one.

"Let's go rattle some cages, Tifft," Em said in a low murmur and a feral grimace.

The wicked smile that came over the young man's face just further endeared him to Em.

Tifft reached down and keyed a button on the map projection counter between them.

"All hands to stations," the man called in a large voice. "Prepare for maneuver and engagement. Bridge, stand by for combat orders."

A light went red and a small sound ground up. In other parts of the ship, the alert was guaranteed to wake a crew man from a dead sleep.

Both Admiral Provst's and Captain Kistler's faces appeared on display readouts. Presumably, they were going to work this as a team, rather than adhering to the old Imperial model. Briefly, Em wondered if the *Aquitaine* innovation, having a dedicated Tactical Officer in charge of fighting, with the commander overseeing everything else, would pan out here. Provst and Kistler were probably the two best men to put it to use, having both served on Em's battleship at various times.

Em fixed his steady eye on the two images.

"Tom. Albert. Swing our butt around until we're pointed close enough," Em said. "Bonus points if we can figure out which way he'll run and manage to cross his "T" with our intercept. Primaries only, on my command. First, all ahead full and bring all shields on-line once we have the vector. Questions?"

Both men shook their heads and looked down to start working out solutions on their own consoles. Tifft appeared as if he wanted to say something. Em nodded to him.

"Assault teams ready to board, just in case we score a disabling hit?" the man asked carefully.

From the look in his eyes and the tone of his voice, Tifft understood what a low probability that was, but it was still above zero, and thus worth considering. And better to have the men ready and not need them, than to waste ten minutes getting the crews armoured and ready to go, only to let a wounded duck flee. Or bite.

"Do it," Em ordered as he turned his gaze onto the big projection of near space.

You will discover, my friend, that you have a tiger by the tail, and not a mouse.

A dozen other men came on duty at a run in response to the alert. Em didn't need such a big crew, since they were out here without a battleship's normal compliment of frigates and cruisers as escorts, but a good crew does what they were trained to do immediately, and then figures out how to go beyond that.

After all, Em had *never* deputized an armed freighter and taken his flag aboard it during an emergency evacuation of a station suffering a critical failure. As far as he knew, they still had a tiny Imperial flag hand-painted on the seedy bridge of that little ship, from when they had commanded a chunk of the Imperial fleet for a few hours.

Minutes passed like a glacier melting, rather than sands racing through a glass. Tifft intercepted most of the traffic headed his way, just as Hendrik always had.

Em stared at the slowly-growing image of whatever was out there beeping. It could be anything, which was part of the reason he was going to engage it from as far away as possible. Explosives in a mine or missiles suddenly accelerating would be distant enough to deal with. And nobody would set a captor mine to fire a primary at this range.

Hopefully, whoever it was would be paying attention to the middle of the circle where Jessica was slated to appear, sometime today, and not to a dark spot possibly occluding distant stars as *Firehawk* swooped.

"Confirmed, Admiral," Tifft said, looking up from whatever screen had his attention. "Artificial transmissions on a strange frequency. Apparently encoded and exhibiting a strange linguistic cadence."

That last brought Em's face around to stare quizzically at the man.

Tifft's face flushed for a second, expecting the sharp edge of the Admiral's temper. When none was forthcoming, he relaxed.

"Military transmissions tend to be staccato, sir," Tifft tried to explain. "The minimum and no more. Even in Arabic or Spanish, which both tend to be smoother languages. This is a fairly constant signal, and it appears and disappears on a regular pattern."

Tifft's eyes grew clouded. His brow knit and he suddenly looked down, furiously typing and clicking.

Em waited, able to recognize a man deep in proving a suspicion. Or disproving it.

Tifft looked up, still concerned, but more puzzled.

"Bridge," he called. "Range and bearing on target?"

"No change," Provst replied, apparently acting as Tactical while Kistler flew the ship. "Acceptable firing range now. Optimum in twelve minutes."

Tifft's face grew angry.

"Speak, Commander," Em said. "I'd rather have all options on the table."

Tifft nodded, almost grinding his teeth.

"I have an image in my head of a low-powered transmitter, Admiral," he replied quietly. "On the face of a slowly-tumbling asteroid. The breaks might be us falling below the rotational terminus, and then rising again twenty-seven minutes later, while it transmits a constant signal. Imagine a radio mast on automatic, playing music."

"Why?"

Tifft shrugged, unwilling to commit further.

It was Em's turn to look puzzled, but he had asked.

And it fit the profile better than a stealthy frigate or small pirate boat laying in wait.

One way to be sure.

"Sensors, this is the Flag Bridge," Em ordered loudly. "Ping the target hard once. Gunnery, prepare to fire, on my order only."

Acknowledgements echoed.

A ring of ripples appeared on the command board, racing outwards, striking the target, and bouncing back. Computer programs washed out the noise and displayed an image.

From a distance, with his eyes squinted and his head turned a little, it might be mistaken for a frigate, being longer than it was tall, and somewhat organic looking. Cargo carriers tended to be more boxy, if only for efficient use of space.

But it was definitely a rock, tumbling slowly through space like a bent finger.

"All hands, secure from general quarters," Em ordered a moment later. "That appears to be a lone asteroid."

Tifft was grinning. Em joined him.

Provst's voice broke in.

"I'm pretty sure we can take him, Grand Admiral," he said in a voice barely containing the laughter.

"I'll let you know if I change my mind, Tom," Em replied.

"Alert," another voice suddenly called out sharply. "New target just appeared out of JumpSpace. Stand by for transponder."

"Belay the order to stand down," Em called. It would save a few minutes for him to make the change, rather than routing it properly. Things might be risky again.

Butts stayed glued to chairs. Fingers were poised to unleash all the hell a modern battleship had on call.

"Target identifies as *CA-264*," the man said a moment later.

"CA-*264*?" Em queried aloud. "Are you sure it's not CR?"

"Affirmative, Admiral," the sensors officer confirmed. "CA. And… blood and martyrs!"

"What?"

"Sorry, sir. New target on same bearing," the call came. "Size registers her as a cruiser, but she's broadcasting a higher power curve than we are. Stand by. Transponder identifies her as *RAN VI Victrix*. We're being hailed."

"All guns track on *6 Victrix*," Em ordered the room. "Ignore the escort for now. Route the call here. Tom, Albert, listen in."

Em turned to a different screen and waited for the message to appear.

"This is *RAN VI Victrix*," a familiar, intense face appeared on the screen, the voice hard and heavy. "You are in a secured zone."

Impressive. Dominant. Fierce.

Short, dark hair coming in gray in most places these days. Clean shaven. Dark, green eyes that seemed to signal a black fire, deep within. Lines that might have been etched with a chisel and a sledgehammer.

Alber' d'Maine was a warrior to the bone.

And if that was Kigali accompanying him in a new hull, the two of them probably could have seriously damaged *Firehawk*, had this been an accidental meeting during the now-concluded war.

Especially those two.

"This is *IFV Feuerfalke*," Em replied in a bored, aristocratic tone. "Grand Admiral Emmerich Wachturm commanding. You're in my space, d'Maine. Nice of you to finally join us."

That got a savage smile from the man.

"Good to see you again, Grand Admiral," Jessica's mighty sword hand said. "*First Expeditionary* reporting for duty. Fleet Centurion is right behind us with the rest of the team."

"Good," Em noted. "What the hell are you flying?"

"You told Bedrov to design a better blade," d'Maine said with a tone approaching glee. "*VI Victrix* and *VI Ferrata* are unlike anything anyone has ever seen. *II Augusta* is even worse."

Em had spent some time around the man, years ago, during the events concerning *Corynthe* that culminated in Jessica saving an allied crown by taking it herself. Another time he had badly underestimated the woman.

If Alber' d'Maine drew that much happiness from a ship, any ship, it must be something revolutionary. And dangerous. Em had read the reports from *Thuringwell*. Had personally watched how far d'Maine and his crew were willing to push the margins of survivability at *Ballard*.

The ancient term *berserker* had been originally invented to describe the likes of Alber' d'Maine.

"Acknowledged," Em said. "Find yourself a defensive parking orbit and we'll come to rest nearby. I've been flying blind on the off-chance someone else was going to be here, so we have velocity to kill. And I want to scan the area."

"Roger that."

And he was gone.

Em knew better than to be offended. He had given the man an order and d'Maine was executing it. Without any jockeying or dominance games.

Just another reason he had asked Joh to authorize letting Keller in on their darkest secrets and asking for her help solving them.

"Sensors Officer," Em ordered loudly, causing every head to bob, albeit unconsciously. "Pulse the system hard enough that you can count the comets. Find me anything and everything that does not belong, so we can decide if we have to kill something."

He turned to Tifft with a wry smile.

"And since we have the assault team ready, go ahead and have Tom capture that rock, whatever that is, so you can satisfy my curiosity. I'm going to eat an early dinner and have a nap so we can stay up well past our bedtimes meeting with Keller. You do the same."

Em turned at Tifft's nod and headed for the hatch.

Keller was here, finally, and had apparently brought a revolution with her.

Another revolution.

But this one, he got to drop on someone else.

Em smiled wickedly as he exited the room.

CHAPTER XXIV

It pleased Jessica, watching someone like Em, the *Grand Admiral*, look uncomfortable as he studied the mass of Command Centurions and first officers that she had invited to dinner. There were a great many people in the room, and him, plus a young man he had apparently recruited as a Flag Aide, when he had snuck off from *St. Legier*.

Dinner had been superb. The wardroom had risen above their already-high standards for a memorable evening. Jessica gazed forlornly, and briefly considered licking the empty, shallow dish that had been a blueberry tart five minutes ago.

She did not appear to be the only person with such devastating feelings of loss.

Em turned his head and locked eyes with her, silently inquiring if she was ready to start. Stewards were clearing the last plates and refilling glasses and mugs. She nodded, interested in how Wachturm would handle this new group of recruits to his war. He only knew a double-handful of them personally. Tonight he was facing more than forty.

Wachturm pushed back his chair slowly and rose, bringing utter silence to the room, save for silverware coming to rest as people snapped to attention, even sitting.

"I am reminded, perhaps a touch forcefully, of *Thuringwell*," he began in a slow cadence, drawing everyone, including her, to lean in as he spoke not quite loud enough to carry. "Many of you were there when the hammer dropped. Many of you were that hammer."

She watched him turn to give Arott Whughy a significant look.

"Others I know tangentially," he continued, showing he knew the man's history. "From places like *Ballard*, the battle and not the ship."

He nodded to Kanda Lungu and Elzbet Aukley, Command Centurion and Science Officer off the big Galactic Survey Cruiser that bore the *Ballard* name, acknowledging their sponsor as well as their place casting electronic sleet and blizzard at his people at *Thuringwell*.

"We have been foes, in the past," he said. "And a few have become friends: Jessica Keller, *zu* Kermode, Colonel *zu* Arlo. I hope to add many of you to that list soon."

Jessica watched Em pause, studying the crowd briefly before his eyes alighted on Yan Bedrov, seated in a corner close to *da Vinci*.

"At the Emperor's request, both Emperors, in fact," Em said, turning to nod to Casey, seated on Jessica's right. "I asked Yan Bedrov to design a new way to fight. Something that we could take to *Buran*. Push that nation back from their self-appointed goal of conquering the universe and putting everyone under its electronic heel. Free the galaxy from their threat, and their people from its domination."

He raised one hand and pointed at a distant bulkhead.

"Bedrov's answer lies out there around us, cast in steel and dreams," Em waxed poetic for a moment. "And my empire is riddled with traitors and fools right now, although we have begun the task of taking out the trash."

Jessica marveled at the calm way Em paused to grab a glass of lemonade and take a sip, studying his audience before he spoke again. Silence as a weapon was something very few people knew how to use effectively.

"I must request your assistance," Em continued in that heavy tone. "I had provided Jessica with everything we knew at the moment she left us. I have done the same now. Not because I knew that much, but because any specific question I posed might give too much away. I must ask you to step into the line of battle, as your Roman ancestors would have done, and hold that line. *Fribourg* is coming, but every day *Buran* grows stronger. Closer. In another year, it may have become impossible to dislodge them in our lifetimes."

He stopped now. Turned to face her across the small distance. His eyes had that same, angry fire Jessica had first seen at *Callumnia*, discussing creatures like *Buran*. Madness, mixed with indomitable rage.

"I need *le Beau Geste*, Jessica," he said flatly. "The Grand Gesture. The unexpected strike to the soft underbelly. I need *Buran* on its heels while I build Bedrov's next fleet, knowing that the one I have now is insufficient to the task. I need a hammer."

Jessica understood the fear behind those words.

They were here, but would it be enough? Could anything be enough to stay the avalanche?

Jessica put her own water glass down and rose, nodding grimly to Em and then taking in her whole staff and friends with a long, intense look.

"I have said this before, many times," she called to the room. "Let me make it clear now. The war that all of you enlisted to fight is over. Done. *Fribourg* needs your help to save the galaxy. It is as simple as that. As Nils Kasum told many of us, before *Ballard*. We must stand atop the wall and hold it against all comers. Face the darkness and, in doing so, defy it. We will not be here long, and then we will be gone, back into the darkness. *Ballard* and *CP-406* will find them for us. *VI Ferrata*, *VI Victrix*, and *Il Augusta* will fix them. And then, ladies and gentlemen, we will kill them."

The sound was more like a pack of wolves than a dinner of senior officers, if there was much difference.

The look in Em's eyes spoke volumes. Once her deadliest foe, now a friend in mortal need.

And relying on her to save humanity.

CHAPTER XXX

Because Grand Admiral Wachturm had specifically asked it of him, Vo wore his new Imperial Colonel's uniform today. Not the fancy dress version Moirrey and Desianna had hand sewn for him, but field camouflage he had tweaked to fit, mostly in grays with patches of green and brown to break up the silhouette. A single, white star on each collar indicated his rank, with the unit patch for the 189th Division on his right shoulder.

Given his head, Vo would have worn his Centurion's day uniform and been happy. But this promised to be one of *those* meetings.

He was last to arrive, mostly because he had the longest distance to travel, from the place where the marines lived and trained. Or, where he trained with them when he could. Vo spent a lot of time on special projects for the Fleet Centurion and others these days.

He had been told that it was one of the reasons he wasn't the commander of the one team of marines *SC Auberon* normally carried. This mission, as before, they only had the one battalion, plus all of Digger's engineers and their excavating gear.

Later, Vo expected a planetary landing force, so he'd probably be spending time on the ground again. *Thuringwell*, or whatever the next version would be. Ground liaison. Forward observer. Something.

Grand Admiral was there when he arrived. Fleet Centurion, too, except that today she was in her Imperial, *Red Admiral* day uniform instead. Moirrey. Captain Wald. Fleet Centurion Whughy. Lady Casey in her Centurion green-and-blacks.

That was it. Nobody else was here. No staff. Nothing. Not even Enej Zivkovic. Even the marines guarding the place were standing outside in the hall.

Why am I here?

Vo sat quietly, tucked into a corner of the oval-shaped conference room table. He figured his job was to listen. Grand Admiral looked mad enough to chew nails today.

Navin the Black got that look about him when someone was about get yelled at. Occasionally, Command Security Centurion Crncevic still handled the task personally, rather than delegating it. Claimed it kept him in shape.

Vo figured he just liked to keep the kids living in fear. Navin could be like that.

Another thing caught Vo's eyes as he sat. No paper on the table. No computers. Nothing.

So everything was going to be verbal, this time.

Lovely. The only time you never wrote something down was if you were skirting regulations, or didn't want it coming back to haunt you later.

What spell were those two conjuring this time?

Grand Admiral leaned forward, staring at Lady Casey like he wanted to start with her.

Vo would have said something, a warning perhaps, but he had seen the Princess work. Grand Admiral would probably want to count his fingers afterwards, if he got that woman riled up. Make sure he still had all of them. Especially with the rest of the team around.

Wachturm sighed angrily. Sounded just like Navin did, just before the storm erupted. They must have gone to the same command school to learn it.

Lady Casey fixed the older man with a hard stare. Thousand meter look through a sniper scope. Not unfriendly, but not budging a centimeter.

Yup, gonna be one of those days.

Give the man credit though, Grand Admiral turned his angry spotlight on Jessica next. Like that was going to get him any further.

Moirrey was the only person Vo knew who was more stubborn than Jessica.

"What have you done?" Grand Admiral finally hissed.

Fleet Centurion looked like a dragon some fool dwarf had just stumbled onto in a dark, scary tunnel, too far from the entrance to escape.

"Stood aside when she decided she wanted something bad enough," Jessica replied in a slow, angry voice. "Every king and Emperor of *Fribourg* was a naval officer first, Emmerich."

"She will never be Emperor," Grand Admiral snarled.

"I already am, Uncle," Lady Casey fired a hard shot across the man's bow. "And I will not be a princess in a tower, no matter how much you might wish it otherwise."

Lady Casey leaned forward like a raptor about to tear a piece off a dead rabbit. Hopefully-dead rabbit.

"You can accept my decision," she continued. "Or you can try to fight me. Those are exactly your choices. Your call."

Vo wasn't sure it would have made a bigger emotional splash if one woman or the other had slapped Wachturm's face, or maybe just punched him. Grand Admiral certainly hadn't been prepared for this reception.

Surprising what happens when you leave the kids alone for a year. Strangers come back.

Just look at one Centurion/Colonel Vojciech *zu* Arlo, reformed cat burglar.

"Have you renounced your birthright?" Grand Admiral demanded, voice rising as emotions flared.

"Never, Uncle," she fired back. "I am Republic Centurion Kasimira *zu* Wiegand, *Princess Imperial* and *Ritter of the Imperial Household*. You will need someone from the family on the front line, and that cannot be you. It cannot be Ekke until he marries and bears the House an heir. That leaves me. If you have a problem with that, you can take it up with Karl VII when you get back. And perhaps he and I will discuss it at a later date."

"And if you die out there?" a tacit concession, perhaps, that neither Casey nor Jessica would budge.

"Then I die in glorious combat, protecting the Empire," Casey observed. "I'm sure your public relations folks will be able to spin that into something useful. Do you think any Imperial gentleman would be interested in me as a person now, rather than just as a point of leverage and introduction to the Imperial House? I'm certainly not going to fit their expectation of dainty or demure."

That rocked the man. He sat back hard, as if she had gone ahead and punched him in the face.

Vo'd watched Casey train. She would have gone for a knee first, and then either groin or throat, depending on what opened when the man reacted. Not as good on the training matt as Jessica, nor him.

Still good enough to take at least half of his marines.

"Gods, but you remind me of your father," Wachturm admitted defeat. "Maybe even more hard-headed, if that's possible."

He turned to Jessica. She looked even more like a dragon now.

"And you won't budge?" he asked the Fleet Centurion.

"Nils Kasum won't budge," Jessica's voice was adamantine. "Judit Chavarría won't budge. If you want the Peace, this is the form it must take. This is the cost."

Vo was close enough to understand the obscenity Grand Admiral muttered under his breath. Moirrey, sitting between them, was close enough to blush, but she stayed otherwise silent.

Grand Admiral sighed again. Exasperated, this time, rather than angry. A man who has realized that he can stop beating his head against the bulkhead, because it's not going to give up first.

Grand Admiral turned his way. Inspected today's uniform with a critical eye.

Vo probably knew the statutes on Imperial Army uniforms better than most of that army's officers, to say nothing of a naval one. Everything was exactly to standard. Crisp. Perfect.

It was amazing what money, patience, and access to fashion experts could wreak in good fabric, given time and need.

Wachturm nodded, mostly at whatever interior conversation he was having. The man turned back to Jessica.

"It is not what I had planned, but I will make you a trade, then, Jessica," he said simply. "Lady Casey for Lord Vo."

What?

He felt the blush climb as *every* face turned and stared at him. There were no handy rocks to crawl under.

"Why?" Jessica had turned blunt. Probably a good sign. Meant she had planned on keeping him around for a while yet. Plans for the boy.

"There will be worlds to conquer, or liberate, *Admiral* Keller," Wachturm didn't say so much as announce. And used her Imperial title, to ram that point home. The galaxy had changed. "Emperor Karl VII has decreed that the 189th Division will be brought back up to strength and then reinforced for potential use as an occupation force. The one active regiment on the rolls, currently used as a training cadre for alpine terrain, will be expanded to three regiments immediately, with the shell of a fourth for training and replenishment. Vo *zu* Arlo will be promoted to General and placed in command of the division."

Really? No rock was going to be big enough, was it?

"I have seen what you did at *Thuringwell*, Jessica," Grand Admiral continued. "What an *Aquitaine* Legion can be as a combined arms force, especially when handled right. 189th will become the template to bring that to *Fribourg*."

Grand Admiral turned and looked Vo square in the face.

"I need an expert I can trust," he said.

Yup. Probably bright enough red that Moirrey will start sweating from the heat I'm giving off, any second now.

And then Moirrey leaned against him with all her weight, feather though it was.

"Best idea you've had today," Moirrey murmured.

Apparently loud enough. Grand Admiral blushed, too.

"Vo?" Jessica asked carefully.

Asked.

She was like that.

Vo gave up looking for a rock. They had apparently hidden them all before the meeting, and he'd look silly under the table, even if he was a troll.

"Do you need me for anything?" Vo replied.

"Nothing that's anywhere close to as important as this," she said, fixing him with those hard, green eyes.

He nodded to her. Remembered to breathe. Looked at the Grand Admiral.

"Sir."

Wachturm nodded back, formal. Erect.

Granite.

He paused for a thought.

"This is going to be hard on all of us," Wachturm said. That's why I ask, instead of demanding. Thank you in advance for not taking any of it personally. I wish I knew another way."

"I would have returned to *Petron* forever, Em," Jessica chimed in.

"Had that been an option. Will yet when it becomes one. We will get there, but it's going to take longer than I planned."

Vo nodded at that.

Where would he go, when it was all done?

CHAPTER XXXI

Torsten looked at himself in the mirror, making sure everything was perfect about his uniform. Like *zu* Arlo had done earlier in the day, he wore a simple day uniform, in blue rather than the formal dress rig he kept for parties.

This wasn't going to be a party, by any stretch of anyone's imagination.

He found himself slowly rocking back and forth, unconsciously testing his balance against a leg that wasn't likely to unexpectedly shift from underneath him in awkward settings. Didn't sweat and swell.

The pain was all phantom these days. And he had always healed quickly. The doctors at the various hospitals he had known since the accident generally all agreed that it was one of the reasons he had survived.

That and an unyielding will.

Nobody would have ever expected the skinny boy in those early, teenage pictures to turn out like this. He would have laughed at anyone making such prognostications.

Might still.

Duty could only take you so far. There had to be *want*.

And now, he might be thwarted.

Captain Torsten Wald, Imperial Navy, PhD, Palace Economist, *Fribourg*. It had a nice ring.

He wondered who he would be in an hour.

For a moment, Torsten let everything show through the façade he normally kept around him at all times. The pain, the anger, the desire. Everything.

The reflection he caught in a picture's glass startled him. Normally he was composed. A stranger looked back.

Torsten took a deep breath, shoved those feelings back into their respective boxes, and locked the gates behind them. He checked that the last button on his jacket was perfect, and that his curly, brown hair was short enough and behaving.

He turned to inspect the suite he had been assigned.

Suite.

For visiting ambassadors.

Torsten remembered commanding an armed pinnace, early in his career, that had a smaller interior volume. He had not yet grown accustomed to it, but the decadence had been a pleasant change from every other starship he had known.

Two bags waited by the exterior hatch. Travel suitcase and shoulder bag to keep his nice uniforms smooth.

If things went bad after this, he could vacate this room in seconds and be gone forever.

If the Grand Admiral ordered him home.

If he *let* the Grand Admiral order him home.

Obviously, Wald had probably failed in his duty to keep Lady Casey from…what? Becoming a scandal? A bigger scandal? Dreaming?

The only outrage Torsten could see was the scandalously-bad precedent the woman was setting. Every young lady would want to become the next Lady Casey, the next Jessica Keller.

Still, he could testify to his success as a chaperone. No man or woman had threatened her dignity or marriage prospects. Those who might have, had been subtly deflected by himself, by Moirrey, or by one of the others. Not that there had been many such people good enough for her to even notice, locked into the orbit of hero worship around Jessica.

And that left Jessica.

Torsten knew that the Grand Admiral had plans. Had hinted at them, probably far more than he realized around an econometricist who could parse text just as easy as numbers.

And he hadn't lied to *zu* Kermode. There had been four semi-private dinners with Jessica. Talk, wide-ranging, but nothing more.

He might have found someone even more closed than he was, which was frankly rather astonishing. Public face. Private face.

He had never seen Jessica's private face, only suggestions at odd moments when she relaxed, however briefly.

Would she order him home?

Torsten shook himself once and brought his focus back. Imperial officer on the Command Staff. Veteran of naval intrigue and palace maneuvering.

Warrior.

He took a breath and keyed the outer door.

The Grand Admiral's suite wasn't all that far away from his, all the diplomats being in one compact area for negotiations and security concerns. As Commanding Admiral, Jessica should have been nearby as well, but she had a much smaller suite close to the Flag Bridge, while Admiral Whughy, Fleet Centurion Whughy, worked from an ambassadorial suite.

How did these people manage, when they constantly colored so far outside customary margins?

Not today's problem.

A security marine guarded Wachturm's door. A woman, no less, although there was nothing feminine about her right now. Until she smiled when he approached, and it lit up her whole face.

Did Imperial marines ever smile?

She reached back and pressed a button in the wall beside her, without otherwise moving or speaking.

Lt. Commander Tifft opened the hatch.

"Captain Wald," he said. "Please enter."

Torsten followed the younger man into a vast space almost identical to his own, differing mostly in the color of the carpet and walls, and the placement of the large desk the Grand Admiral was seated at.

Emmerich Wachturm looked up from a stack of papers he had apparently been editing by hand.

Editing?

"Thank you, both of you," he said gravely. "Tifft, go off duty for a while. Have some down time and I will see you tomorrow morning at the usual time."

The man saluted silently, turned, and vanished.

Torsten found himself falling to parade rest, facing the legend himself again.

Wachturm studied him for several, long seconds, eyes almost squinting.

"I have seen the medical reports, Wald," he began, apparently at random. "I could not tell you why we have never considered using implants like this as a standard. Would you recommend it for future cases?"

Torsten fought to not rock back and forth, testing the movement of his weight on his hips.

"Without reservation, sir," Torsten said. "Recovery time to normal locomotion is faster and the pain is much more controllable. I am told that the electronics *Aquitaine* uses also cut rehabilitation time considerably."

"And yet, you went with only the titanium alloy, Captain," Wachturm noted, eyes zeroing in hard. "Why is that?"

"I do not believe that Imperial culture would find that aspect of the surgery…palatable, Grand Admiral," Torsten answered, almost evasively. "I wished to retain the option to return to *St. Legier* and active duty service, in the future."

Silence.

Sharp eyes, as if the Grand Admiral tried to see through Torsten to read his secrets. Torsten had just spent a year watching Jessica, Casey, and Moirrey out-maneuver people.

Best of luck, sir.

"Do you wish to return to *St. Legier* with me?" the Grand Admiral posed the question carefully. "Aboard *Firehawk*?"

Torsten almost grinned, but it would have told the man too much.

"No, sir."

Nothing more. Nothing less. Hard, calm, emphatic.

Not even with a marine strike team dragging me kicking and screaming into the shuttle.

Definitive.

Pause.

"And if I chose to order it, Captain?" the Grand Admiral continued, still dancing along the edge of the words.

Torsten let the words settle into the carpet and evaporate.

"I would find that…problematic, Grand Admiral."

Short, concise, bland. Hopefully.

"And will I receive a request from *Aquitaine* to remove you?" Wachturm leaned forward, ever so slightly.

He knows.

Torsten squelched that thing he suddenly discovered was his greatest fear. Invisible until this moment.

That Jessica would simply send him packing, with no explanation. No resolution.

Done.

"I do not believe so, sir," Torsten bit the words off lest he color them with emotion.

Pause. Appraisal.

"Would you go?"

"I know my duty, Grand Admiral," Torsten said. There was no way to keep the anger entirely quiescent, much as he tried.

Pause. More assessments.

"Captain, that would have been the first thing Jessica Keller did after I came aboard, if she was going to," he said. "I know her that well. At ease, and try to relax. Take a seat and let's talk. There are things you need to know now that you didn't before."

Torsten fought to invisibly unlock joints that had gone rigid with tension and fright. He managed to move without lurching, sit without collapsing, breathe without gasping.

Barely.

"I've studied that woman for nearly a decade, Wald," the admiral began, leaning back and turning into a college professor all of a sudden. "And I know many of her people well enough that any one of them would have felt comfortable quietly slipping me a note, if they thought you should be removed from the situation. To say nothing of the ones who might have taken matters…into their own hands, if they perceived you to be a threat to her."

Deep breath. Slow the heartrate to something closer to human.

Calm.

"The Emperor, as you should know, considers me a close cousin, and his best friend," Wachturm continued as Torsten let the surge of adrenaline burn itself out into his toes and ears. "We did not make the decision to send you lightly. Nor Princess Casey."

"She prefers Lady Casey, Admiral," Torsten spoke up. "Actually, she prefers Centurion *zu* Wiegand, but it's Lady Casey in general company. Same with Lady Moirrey. Arlo prefers to answer to his last name alone, whenever possible."

"Noted," Wachturm said with a wry smile, an unspoken

acknowledgement of how much Torsten had learned about these people, and been accepted by them, to know that.

Accepted by them.

Yes, he supposed being personally threatened by Lady Moirrey probably was the highest compliment he could get.

Arlo wouldn't give any warning.

"So I will presume that you belong here for the time being, Captain," Wachturm continued. "Does that please you?"

And that is what a trap looks like.

Still, he had asked for this duty. Taken this risk.

"It does, sir," Torsten replied neutrally.

No comment about how one might camp in the street out front of her parents' house until she came out and told you to leave. Or asked you to come inside.

No clue to the Grand Admiral how you really felt.

"Assuming the two of you are serious, Wald, things will change."

"Sir?" Torsten asked carefully.

The ice under his feet had apparently gotten thin enough to be almost transparent when he wasn't looking.

"You will, of necessity, likely become privy to the inner workings of the Imperial family," the Grand Admiral continued. "Likely be adopted into the House in some vague and not-easily-explainable manner. It will be for your own safety."

Torsten felt the ice start to go, dropping jagged pieces into that cold, endless, watery death underneath.

Still, it made sense. Lady Casey was here, and Torsten knew she would probably never have an Imperial husband. Once the Crown Prince started a family, Lady Casey could find herself a husband in the Republic, itself a marriage of the type used to seal grand alliances.

And Jessica…

The Empire's new Red Admiral.

With a consort?

Was that what the Emperor had planned?

Would they allow it?

Would she?

Would I?

Econometricist. Expert in numbers as movement, as power. Trends and patterns as colors on a page, rather than as stark columns of data.

Tides moving.

Torsten saw end-games suddenly clear, although they were still years, decades, away. Saw the points where the slightest twist could alter the course of empires and republics. Saw the future.

His was not the power to effect those changes, but Torsten realized he was seated across from someone who could, discussing a woman who also had that power.

He blinked as whole new patterns fell into place like jigsaw puzzle pieces.

"Assuming the Peace, how far will you draw her into Imperial politics, Admiral?" Torsten asked.

Wachturm's squint hardened, for a moment, replaced a moment later by a slight grin.

He knows what I can do. It's part of why he sent me. Not spy. Oracle.

Torsten felt the ice give way completely, and found he was floating in the air rather than drowning in the icy waters below.

"Joh knows that we cannot continue business as usual," the Grand Admiral replied. "Casey and Jessica will hopefully provide an alternate path, deflecting some of the energy away from revolution."

"Joh?" Torsten asked carefully.

"His Sovereign Imperial Majesty, Karl Johannes Arend Wiegand, Hereditary King of *St. Legier*, Emperor of *Fribourg*, Captain," the man replied. "Karl VII."

Oh. Working at the very peak of the pyramid.

"Does *she* know?" Torsten asked. There were two women in that conversation, but only one that really mattered.

"Jessica is an exceptional woman, Wald," the admiral said. "I am sure she could figure it all out in a few moments with sufficient…motivation. I'll go further: I'm confident that she already has, to some extent. I wanted to know if you were prepared to go down that road. It is not something we would order."

"What should I know about her, Admiral?" Torsten asked, trusting his intuition to leap into darkness.

"I watched the sparks between the two of you, the night you met," Wachturm replied. "And I knew Daneel Ishikura at close range for nearly a year. He eventually achieved the calm that you have had since the accident. And, to some extent, even before, according to the records and the people I have interviewed. Solemnity and solidity. You remind me of Arlo in that, although Arlo is only now learning to get past his own doubts. I took a chance on including you with Casey's mission, because I believed that it was the right thing. I have seen nothing since I arrived to change my mind."

"*zu* Kermode personally threatened me last week," Torsten said with a sudden smile. "So I believe the others involved understand, and accept me."

"Did she now?" the Grand Admiral's voice rose in tone and weight. "Good."

Torsten waited as the Grand Admiral studied him for several moments, possibly with new eyes.

"Understand two things, Wald," he continued. "One, I have seen Jessica at her best, and her worst, and I consider her a friend. I want her to be happy as a person, as well as an ally."

Something sour must have shown in Torsten's eyes. The Grand Admiral's squint was back, harder this time.

"What?" he demanded in a simple tone.

Torsten let the words seek themselves, rather than push. They might be the culmination of the day, and his career. Possibly his life.

Floating in air, instead of drowning.

"What if the Peace does not hold, sir?" Torsten finally asked. "What if the war returns?"

The angry bear across the desk relaxed, even smiled.

"I did not say this aloud, Wald," Wachturm commented dryly. "However, I would expect that you would do something crazy like immediately resign your commission and possibly steal a courier, if you found yourself on the wrong side of the border at that moment. The Empire can survive with one fewer economist on staff."

Good. He understands the stakes.

Torsten nodded. Everyone else had come to realize how serious he was.

Now he only needed to convince her.

CHAPTER XXXII

Because someone had suggested it, Gunter Tifft had made inquiries of the line marine that followed him around like a hungry, stray dog spying food. Or a cat stalking a wounded rabbit.

He had never met Lady Moirrey Kermode in the flesh, only heard the wild speculations about the woman. Was she really a ninja-super-agent?

The big space of *Firehawk*'s engineering lab had seemed to swallow her up when she joined him. Two of the ship's engineers were handy to answer questions, but had been instructed to remain silent and observe, until addressed. Apparently, they lived in awe or fear of the woman.

In person, she was tiny. A meter and a half tall. Less than fifty kilograms. Raven-black hair. Slender.

It was the eyes that gave away who she was. Somewhere between hazel and blue, depending on the light. Looking through him right now like she had x-rays for vision.

More legend.

"Thank you for joining me, Lady Moirrey," Gunter said carefully to a woman who had helped defeat an Empire. "The Grand Admiral appreciates your assistance in this matter."

This was a thing, resting between them on an engineering table. A squat, metal box not quite a meter on a side. Not quite a cube, but close enough to count. A container in brittle, black metal.

The treasure on the asteroid, once the assault team had secured it and brought it back for the engineers on *Firehawk* to be stumped by, once they started inspecting it.

"So what's ya gots and hows kin I halp?" the woman chirped at him.

Gunter had to replay the phrase in his head to translate it, once he realized she was still speaking English to him. It had sounded almost Chinese in intonation.

"When we arrived, *Firehawk* picked up a transmission signal," Gunter replied. "Intermittent to us, but that was a result of it resting on an asteroid that was tumbling, relative to our location. We captured it, disabled it, and retrieved it. Everyone on this crew has been unable to *identify* it. *Firehawk* has engineers, but not scientists. The best they might be able to do is dismantle it, so the Grand Admiral suggested I ask you first."

Somehow, Gunter wasn't surprised that this woman reached into a pocket on her thigh and pulled out a…call it a *tool*, whatever the hell it was.

"Ooh," she grinned. "Best kinds o'secrets. No' armed?"

Armed?

Ah. Dangerous. A bomb, perhaps? The first thing the assault team had verified, before they brought aboard their shuttle.

"No, sir," Gunter said. "Ma'am. Power supply. Transmitter. And something one of our engineers called a *black box*, whatever that means."

"Rights," she leaned forward and just touched the casing with her bare hand. "And you ha'no opened her to peeks?"

Pause. Translate.

"No, Lady Moirrey," Gunter finally comprehended her words. "We scanned it, but the metal was…radiation-welded? Was that the right term?"

"Close-nuff," she grinned up at him. "Solar wind, long-nuff. Charge builds up, moves molecules. Takes forever, though. Makes this *old*."

"How old?" he asked, suddenly concerned.

In response, the woman engineer rapped the casing with a knuckle, and then tapped it with the tool in her right hand. It made an oddly-hollow *thunk* unlike anything Gunter could remember ever hearing.

She shrugged and continued to touch the device, leaning this way and that.

At one point, he thought she might actually climb atop the table, until she found a switch that lowered the surface nearly to the deck.

Something caught her eye as he watched, utterly lost. Gunter glanced at the other two men, but they weren't any better. One actually shrugged silently.

"'Ere we goes," she said, standing with her toes on the tabletop and hunched over the top of the box. She paused and looked around before pointing at the closer of the two engineers.

"You," she ordered, suddenly sharp with her vocabulary. "Get me a cotton rag, a liter of pure water, and a towel. Now."

The man jumped and ran. Lady Moirrey leaned over and looked at the device from very close.

She might have sniffed it. Maybe he just imagined that.

The go-fer engineer returned with the requested items, placing them next to her, but not returning to his previous spot by the wall.

Gunter watched her wet the cotton rag with some of the water, and then rub it softly across the top of the device. Satisfied, she repeated it, using about half of the water.

Gunk accumulated on the rag as she worked. At one point, Lady Moirrey even looked up at him and winked.

Gunter kept his silence. And his distance.

Eventually, she took the towel and wiped everything down, tossing it over her shoulder for anyone in range to catch. Gunter could see a design of some sort, perhaps a logo, along with writing etched into the metal.

"Huh," she announced, standing.

Not that it made that much difference in how she appeared, being shoulder-high on him, even if she was on her toes.

"Needs ta cracks it op'n," she continued. "But yu gots an antique here. Ain't see'd the likes, but heard tales."

"Please pardon my ignorance, Lady Kermode," Gunter said carefully. "What is it?"

"Asteroid mining beacon," she replied, tapping it. "Tags a claim, broadcasts a signal fer anyone close by. Lets you navigate by it. Establishes legal ownership, but I doubt the rightful heir's like to come back and argue fer his claim these days. Even if'n you's now technically a claim-jumper."

"Why not?" Gunter asked carefully.

In response, she reached down and touched some of the writing he had seen.

"This beacon was placed on October 20, 1153 Union of Man," she said.

Gunter tried to do the math in his head, but history had never been his strong suit.

"When was that?" he asked, feeling mortified to show such weakness in front of a woman.

"Five thousand, three hundred, and twenty-nine years ago, Lieutenant Commander Tifft," Lady Moirrey got formal, all of a sudden. "Twenty-two centuries before Earth was destroyed in the Concordancy War. I would suggest you deliver it to the Imperial Institute of Mines when you're done with it. You can't build something this durable today, but they should be able to mimic it. Otherwise, I might take it upon myself to completely dismantle the device and catalog it."

Gunter paused, and then decided to test his luck. He straightened, almost to attention.

"Lady Moirrey Kermode," he intoned formally. "I have been instructed by the Grand Admiral himself to solve this mystery. As a *Ritter of the Imperial Household*, you would be doing a service for the entire Empire if you were to perform a careful, scientific study of this machine."

Her face got concerned, like she thought he was playing some joke on her, but it cleared up quickly.

"Dinna have time," she replied. "Take months 'n'yer leavin' in days."

True, they were scheduled to return to *St. Legier* in short order.

But his orders had been both extremely specific, and crafted with the necessary latitude.

"I can have it delivered to you aboard *Auberon* forthwith," he added.

From the way her face changed, Gunter was concerned for a moment that the woman was about to kiss him. He relaxed to a nice parade rest, which had the benefit of moving him back half a step.

Just in case she was about to attack him.

"Dones," she chirped. "Will lets ya knows. Is good?"

"It is," Gunter said. "Thank you."

And like a storm, she was gone.

Gunter turned to the closest engineer and tapped the clean spot.

"I want full reproductions of that, including silicon casts if you can," he ordered the man. "Then deliver it to *zu* Kermode with all attendant courtesies. If you are nice, she might include your names in the seminal, scientific paper she's likely to write on this device."

Gunter stepped out of their way as their own storm erupted.

Fifty-three centuries, just floating in the dark, announcing itself to the galaxy.

What had that beacon seen?

CHAPTER XXXIII

Jessica grinned in response to Wachturm's scowl. An angry bear of a Grand Admiral, roused mid-winter, being poked with a long stick. It was just the two of them in her private office, with Marcelle's best coffee and a locked hatch. She could do that here. Poke him safely.

"You aren't going to tell me, are you?" Em asked with an ursine growl.

Jessica sipped the perfect, steaming bitterness and let it flow down into her toes.

"Frankly, no," she replied. "We have one of those circumstances for which the Ancients had a proverb: *A secret known to three people is only successful if two of them are dead.*"

"Plus, you don't know, yourself. Am I right?" Em pressed.

"I have four good targets from the list you provided, Em," Jessica allowed. "I won't know which one will work better until I see them. That will take time, scouting with *Ballard* and *CP-406* as quietly as I can."

"You dropped on *Thuringwell* like a hawk," Em noted.

"After I had spent the better part of two years writing a Class II Thesis on the weakest link in your entire frontier, and how to apply Wakely Okafor's theories to practice," Jessica retorted. "I was only betting my career on that one. I'll be betting my life, and the lives of a large portion of Humanity, here."

"Why?" he suddenly changed from grouchy to querulous. "What

drives you to do this, Jessica? It can't just be Casey. You were like this before you ever knew the girl. And you and I were foes for a very long time."

She studied the man. Looked hard into eyes that she had seen in nightmares. The dreaded Red Admiral, himself.

Implacable, but always an honorable enemy. Not yet a friend, perhaps, but getting there, she supposed. Jessica had never known friends, as other people understood the term. Marcelle had been with her for nearly twenty years. Robbie, and then Denis, Tomas, and Alber', but nobody she could open herself up to.

With one, notable exception. *Pint-sized.* Moirrey.

Well, two, actually, when she considered it. *Warlock* had truly been her first love, for as long as she had had him. Torsten had potential, but she wasn't sure she was willing to go down that road again. If ever.

But that wasn't what Em was asking.

Jessica let her mind drift back to *Ballard*. Not that famous battle, facing this man, but the aftermath, after the ugly, pyrrhic victory on her part.

Dinner. Planetside in a place that embodied the definition of a dive bar, clear out on the edge of civilization, where two women had hiked for the better part of two days to find a comm capable of reaching orbit and calling for help.

Burgers and beer, even though only three of the four could actually process it as food. After all, she, Marcelle, and Moirrey were human. The fourth person that night hadn't been. Not that anyone would know, or could ever know.

Summer had designed and built herself an android body good enough to fool almost any inspection, powered by a small atomic reactor capable of keeping her on-line for centuries.

Allowing Summer to go free that night, to disappear from human history, as the woman had intended, was quite literally the highest crime Jessica could commit, under Imperial or Republic law.

And yet, was nevertheless the right thing to do.

Jessica took a breath and released it. Em watched her like a rabbit spying a hawk.

"At *Ballard*, you went to kill the *Sentience* known as Suvi," Jessica began.

Em nodded slowly, fully aware of that grand, mad quest, and all it had cost the two of them.

"She and I had several long conversations," Jessica continued, conveniently leaving out how some of those talks occurred after the battle. "Suvi had almost as low an opinion of the rest of her kind as you do. She had been taught how to be human, while the rest of her kind commonly thought of themselves as gods. She believed that it was one of our great failings as a species, and as a culture, not to make the *Sentiences* more like us from the beginning. I've read the intel, the anthropology sections, on what *Buran* is like as a place. Humans may be obnoxious, short-sighted, and stupid, but we're free. The *Everlasting*, as he likes to call himself, thinks he has the right to control us and our destiny. To make us bend to his will."

"According to some, it is a paradise, a garden of Eden," he hazarded.

She could tell he was probing. Emmerich Wachturm would happily burn *Winterhome* to the ground from orbit, if given half a chance.

"The children are raised in crèches, Em," Jessica said. "Assigned to a work unit as soon as they are weaned, then taught to belong to that group their whole lives. *Buran* assigns them a place in his culture and sticks them into that slot. If he decides you are to be a warrior, so be it. Or a scholar. Or a poet. You are not allowed to choose your fate."

"And did you, Jessica?" Em asked, slicing off on a tangent. "Get the chance? You were identified early and thrust into the pipeline to become a warrior. Shaped and honed your whole life to this one thing. I was the same way, raised to a place and a station. There was never a doubt that I would go into the fleet and become a high-ranking officer."

"I demanded to be here, every step of the way, Em," Jessica fired a hard shot across his bow. "And you were born to privilege, to *noblesse oblige*. Put yourself in Casey's shoes and tell me about choosing the life you want. I doubt you have ever really talked to the woman, only to the child she used to be."

He fell silent, but she could see the angry words on the tip of his tongue. She could also see the realization hit him, almost like a physical blow. Em had only known Kasimira, the precocious child, and Casey, the rebellious teenager.

The Red Admiral hadn't seen the young woman forced to become an Emperor. Hadn't seen the costs suddenly weigh on her soul and her future, the shackles of duty, almost as bad as Casey expected matrimony to be, when that dreaded time came.

The terrible moment passed. Jessica watched his eyes grow rueful.

"There are days I would like to hate you, Jessica," he said with a long sigh. "Especially when you're right. I suspect Arlo is another one like that. Driven by duty, more than by desire. By the needs of those who trust him, rely on him, who never ask him what he wants."

"I doubt that Vo himself knows," Jessica replied.

"We will have to work on that," Em opined. "So that's it, then? Our war with history and humanity is over the freedom to become whoever you want to be, regardless of the world, the people around you, and broader society's expectations of you?"

"Can you think of a higher calling, Emmerich?"

"No. I cannot, Jessica," he said. "So I must ask a delicate, painful question. I must be unacceptably rude, and personal, by both *Fribourg* or *Aquitaine* standards, because to do anything else right now would be just as evil as anything *Buran* ever contemplated."

She watched him from under hooded eyes. This was not the conversation either of them had expected, starting off with strategy so that it could drive tactics. Or perhaps it was. Humans were the most important facet of any plan. They had wandered down into the weeds, but the weeds were people, with feelings and dreams, and not just something that got in the way.

"What should I do with Torsten Wald?" he asked quietly and simply.

"Nothing," she said without hesitation.

"Nothing?"

"He asked to be here, every step of the way, Em," Jessica said quietly. "You offered him a chance, and he took it. Did everything right. Torsten could have stayed behind on *Ladaux* when we left. He could have asked you to evacuate him, although I'm pretty sure he would have fought you instead, had you ordered him home."

"I took a chance…" Em began.

"And there were days I couldn't decide whether to hate you, or thank you for that, Em," Jessica said. "Torsten has turned out to be something I never expected, especially at this stage of my life. I never had children, and don't expect to. I never took the time to actively search for someone I might share myself with, and I'm at a place now where I didn't think I could, especially given my duties to three nations. And I only barely survived *Warlock*'s death with my own sanity intact."

"And yet, there were sparks," he said, just as low a whisper as their voices could fade.

"Are sparks," she countered. "I have to stop and remember to breathe occasionally when I find myself wandering down the impossibilities of happily-ever-after with that man. There is too much to be done today. I have a war to fight, against an enemy more dangerous than you ever imagined yourself to be, because he is an alien creature intent on enslaving all humanity under his eternal yoke."

"The war will not be over tomorrow, Keller," Emmerich said. "Have you told him?"

"No," she replied. "I'm not sure how to ask him to patiently wait a decade, assuming we don't all end up dead first."

"My unwelcome advice, Jessica?" he said. "As a friend? Don't wait. There will always be another mountain ahead of you. That is who you are, and I've spent a decade coming to understand at least that much about you. Take the day for yourself. Talk to Torsten. I have no doubt that he would wait a decade if you asked, but it is unnecessary."

Jessica leaned back, rather than answer. She felt like they were back on his porch on *St. Legier*, just before the coup. Beyond foes, and attempting to forge a friendship, even as he had tried to kill her any number of times before that.

"I will give it thought," she finally responded.

"I'm right, and you know it," he smiled. "This is one of the few times I can say that with utter conviction. The war will be there for the rest of our lives. I'm trying to insure that only Ekke has to fight it, and not his children. Nor Casey's, wherever they end up being born."

She nodded. No more would she commit to than that, however much she had considered it.

He was right. They both knew it. Probably all three knew it.

Did she actually have the courage to act on it?

CHAPTER XXXIV

Jessica had cleared most of the flag bridge of people for this meeting. There was only herself and Enej, plus Command Centurion Kanda Lungu from *Ballard* and First Officer/Science Officer Elzbet Aukley. And Jennifer Glenn of *CP-406*. The Scout Team.

At the last minute, she had also pulled Casey in, more for the educational aspects than anything, since Casey's role as Imperial Flag Centurion was only going to really ramp up after they had settled and begun to interact with the Imperial Fleet on a regular basis.

So, the five of them. She could have invited Arott. And Denis, Robbie, Alber', and Tomas. Tamara. All the command centurions. Any number of experts on any number of topics.

That would happen later. Jessica had a revolution to unleash first.

They all sat at the big round table with the holoprojector at the center. To better make her point, Jessica had dimmed the lighting. Denis had the flag and would handle everything from the bridge if anything happened in the next hour.

She started by projecting an animation Moirrey had prepared. Graphics were the best way to communicate concepts, and *Pint-sized* was still the best there was at creating them. The projection showed a great emptiness with a rough, golden sphere hovering in the center of a sea of small white dots. Stars representing *Fribourg* space.

"We are here," Moirrey's stage voice narrated, as two other dots appeared at great remove. "*St. Legier* in purple. *Ladaux* in azure."

The image zoomed in, and then rotated as it blasted forward onto the far shores of the *Fribourg Empire*.

"*Osynth B'Udan* is Fribourg's sector capital facing *Buran*," the narration continued. A white star appeared, followed a few moments later by a red one at some distance. "*Samara* is the most heavily-fortified planet across the border, and we believe it to be their sector capital. The *Ural* Starbase is at least comparable to any orbital fortification *Fribourg* or *Aquitaine* has ever built."

Moirrey had added some piano music quietly in the background, almost too low to hear, but it was just the right piece to convey the grand emptiness; the bleak, black loneliness, married with the hint of impregnable solidity. In the animation, a vast gulf opened, a gap between arms of the galaxy itself. A dark sea with almost no far shore, as stars were sparse and well-separated here.

A green star appeared finally, after a good piano solo.

"*Ninagirsu*," Moirrey continued. "Gateway to the *Altai* sector. Anchor of the defenses on the far side of the gulf and the first step on the highway to *Winterhome*, homeworld of *Buran*, the *Lord of Winter*."

The animation spun again, driving well up from the galactic ecliptic, until all the stars previously marked were visible again and everyone had a map of the incredible distances involved. It stopped there. The piano faded.

Silence fell.

Jessica powered the projection down and studied the faces around her. The next phase rested on their shoulders.

"I have two problems," Jessica began. "We will be operating a long way from home, with incredibly difficult supply lines. And *Buran* is not stopped by the edge of a gravity well as we are."

Kanda nodded. She had been there at *Thuringwell*. And had heard all the stories about *St. Legier*. The others remained quiet. Contemplative.

"There are other problems, as well," she continued. "*Fribourg* is still riddled with spies, so anything we do will eventually be leaked, no matter what. That's part of the reason we are not passing through an Imperial base on our way."

"What are you looking for in a forward staging area?" Glenn spoke up suddenly. "If we're going dark, how dark?"

Jessica smiled. Her newest commander had made the kind of intuitive leap they would need.

"Without a star to home in on, navigation gets tricky," Jessica replied. "Find me a spot in between stars, marked by nothing but a complicated set of vectors from known locations."

"That's easy, Fleet Centurion," Jennifer replied. "What am I missing?"

"How does *Buran* do it?" Elzbet suddenly piped up. "That's the rogue element. We know from the records that they can cross vast spaces at impossible speeds. We don't know how."

"Correct," Jessica said. "We can pick a spot at random. Easy enough, but how do we ensure that we aren't on some autobahn of theirs that accidentally vectors them right through us?"

"JumpDrives and not sails, we know that," Glenn said. "According to the old records from *Alexandria Station*, you pick a direction and a distance then throw yourself like a rock. When you arrive, you calculate your current location as a deviation from your intention, determine the correction, and leap again. How do you make that faster?"

"Highway signs," Enej suddenly said.

"What?" Jessica turned to the man.

"Yes. Middle of nowhere. You need navigation points," the Elzbet interjected. Enej nodded. "We don't because we use known gravity wells as signatures. But you could drop a small beacon in the middle of nowhere. Maybe a line of them, each transmitting a different signal. A ship drops out, listens, and can triangulate themselves quickly, maybe immediately, as fast as those ships were supposed to think. We go through systems. They might just go around them, and then turn and drop in on the one they want when they achieve optimal proximity. Galaxy's mostly a thick pancake, but if you go up or down, the density thins out appreciably, so you could probably perform tremendous ballistic jumps to go even farther. Where there are fewer things in the way to risk hitting, you can go much faster."

Jessica turned to Kanda.

"When we get approach the place I want to base from, that will be your first task," she ordered. "Find out if there is anything nearby like that. We'll have to maintain total comm silence while we set up, just in case, so figure out how to do everything with a series of point-to-point lasers. Then you'll start a grid and work outwards slowly."

"And when we find it?" Glenn asked.

"Nothing," Jessica replied. "If we break their toy, they'll send someone to fix it eventually, but we'll need to be prepared to pinpoint it and map it. We'll also need to roll a long chunk of the network up all at once, if there really is such a thing. Killing one might just be a pothole they can sail around. I want to burn the bridge in front of them. And maybe behind them. You three put your minds on what to look for and how to unravel it. Bring in anybody you need, second priority to Arott and his team setting us up a base."

"Moirrey?" Kanda asked.

"I'd start with her," Jessica said. "Tell her to get silly and efficient. Maybe ask Yan, too, since he thinks in small, automated tasks better than anyone."

"And when we get ready to kill it?" Jennifer asked, as if the thing was already a done deal.

"That's what I have you and Alber' for," Jessica noted.

PART FOUR
EXPLORER

CHAPTER XXXV

Command Centurion Glenn always sat a daily bridge watch of at least two hours. The regs didn't require it, and many commanders only did them sporadically. But this was her ship.

It wasn't her crew yet, but they would be, in another year. She needed to know them at a fundamental level to get there. Not just their professionalism. That was a given, considering the insane level of competition for berths in this squadron.

She needed to know their souls.

The best way to get that feel for them was by interacting on a daily basis. Seeing them in their native element, and letting them see her. Thus, two hours on the bridge every day. And rotating her shift regularly through all the watch sections, so she got to spend time with every crew member that was bridge-certified.

There was nothing metaphysical about it, she knew, watching people go about their business. They had assumed that she was a deeply spiritual person, based on the amount of time she spent daily, meditating and doing yoga.

They were wrong, though. Meditation freed the mind to work. Jennifer had heard all the stories about Keller that floated around. Knew the nearly-unconscious instinct for maneuver and combat that had marked the woman as the very best of an impressive crowd.

But Jennifer knew a special truth about the Fleet Centurion, imparted to her by an instructor from Fleet Command School that had taught a young Jessica Keller, once upon a time. Namely, the immense time Keller spent in preparation. In Keller's case, gaming out every possible scenario ahead of time and making notes that could be called upon in the middle of a battle.

Glenn hadn't seen nearly as much combat as Keller, but her last posting had been as First Officer on a light cruiser that spent a lot of time alone on outer borders and random patrols. Out there in the darkness, far from the *Fribourg* frontiers, you drilled the crew to keep them from growing stale, but you also had to prepare for all sorts of other oddities. Survey work. Piracy patrols. Sudden emergency rescues and evacuations.

It had been good training for her current duties.

Jennifer looked around the compact bridge. She would have said tiny, especially after the spacious bridge on *RAN Usken,* but everything was in the right place and there wasn't a cubic centimeter of wasted space. She had heard stories about the designer, Bedrov, but had only ever seen him across the room, and never had a chance to ask him questions.

But her bridge fit her personality. Everyone was facing inward, so she could see their faces as well as they could see hers. Her Flight Deck Commander, the ever-dapper Centurion Rouge, sat next to the Tactical Officer, Takouhi Elouan, who was more of a gym rat, even as voluptuous as the woman was, and their three stations made a compact triangle at the center, with half a dozen other stations around them, separated by a ring aisle for access.

The lights in here were dim, but that was by choice. Jennifer made it a point to randomly alter the light settings from default every time she was here, to get everyone used to change. She also played with the thermostat for the same reason, especially after having to chase a small pirate vessel on a day when the air conditioning system for the bridge had broken down, blowing air heated to nearly 40C onto the bridge, resulting in a pile of sweat-soaked tunics on the deck as people stripped down to undershirts to keep from overheating.

If you were experienced in things going sideways, you were still operational when they did. It was just another day in the fleet.

Plus, running the lights in here down seventeen percent made the room dim and quiet. That helped psychologically with the whole sneaking-around thing.

Focused the mind.

Ballard was out there somewhere, listening. The Survey Cruiser was an expert at that, but she was almost unarmed, and far more valuable than *CP-406*, so the corvette was slowly closing on the second planet of this system.

Jennifer had purposely kept *CP-406* out farther than necessary, but that was to test her crew. To see if her science officer was up to the task of finding a needle hiding in a stack of needles. *Buran* might be out there, waiting. Centurion Steiner ought to be up to the task, but that was something to find out when the stakes were low, rather than when it was for all the marbles.

She checked the boards again. Nine light minutes out. Nearly a full AU away, astronomical units based on the ancient distance between the Homeworld and the Homestar, as those things were measured, and too far to see anything, even with the best telescope, unless *CP-406* made a noise and caused them to look this way.

Far enough away that nobody should be listening, either. Or likely to drop out of a jump on top of them accidentally.

Jennifer had memorized all the available intel on *Buran* ship-handling, specifically to try to judge these things. As a rule, they would usually come back into RealSpace around thirty or forty light minutes away, there to separate out the *Energiya Module*, the transport section, from the *Buran* element, the fighting pieces.

Like drawing a sword from a scabbard, just before a charge.

Fribourg had specifically noted where each secondary detonation occurred, if they managed to kill one of the vessels. The transport section self-immolated as soon as the signal arrived, without fail. Nine minutes was too close, but not so close as to be obvious, if *CP-406* kept themselves silent.

"Sciences," Jennifer said in a voice just a shade above conversational, to get Steiner's attention without making her jump. "Status?"

Jennifer had spent a lot of time interviewing her principle officers and their assistants. Learning their souls. Reese Steiner was an average-looking brunette physically, with little that drew the eye, at least until she opened her mouth. Inside, the woman was a nerd for communications technology in all forms and historical periods. And one who painted watercolors in her spare time out of physical materials, rather than painting on an electronic easel.

"Basic automated comm traffic, Commander," the science officer replied without looking up from her sensor readouts. "Navigational, almost. Nobody appears to have noticed us, if there is anyone here."

About what Jennifer expected. The Navigational Gazette that *Fribourg* maintained on this frontier was woefully under-detailed for a nation that styled themselves a major power. She suspected that was how *Buran* had managed to colonize so many worlds on this side of the gulf. Nobody was looking.

Aquitaine was looking now. First Expeditionary was looking. Cockroaches in the cupboards were about to be lit up. But first, it was necessary to establish a safe place to base out of. So the scouting element was here, while the rest of the fleet was six hours by jump away.

Waiting.

"Flight Deck," Jennifer turned her head another notch. "Three green?"

"Affirmative, sir," Rouge said, his usual ready smile lighting up an aquiline face dominated by a beak of a nose and a receding widow's peak slowly fading from skin to brown hair.

"Put *Black Prince* in play," Jennifer ordered. "Keep *Boomerang* and *Grendel* warm but not hot. If something goes wrong, we're probably not facing something we can take, so we'll be running like hell as soon as we can pick up our scout."

"Roger that," the man said, pressing a button. "*Black Prince*, you are *Go* for launch. Rails are unlocked and tethers are soft-tension only. Detach when ready."

The hull bonged as the ventral cradle emptied and the *P-6 Vanguard* went out scouting. On the screen, *Black Prince*'s engine pod went live and the little craft began to accelerate away.

"Separation confirmed, Commander," the Flight Deck officer said. It was unnecessary, since she could see the same thing Rouge did, but good training meant you always did it right, so that it was automatic in combat.

"Bring us to a stop relative," she ordered. "Then keep a watch on our hound and make sure we remain oriented such that we can accelerate at him if he needs pickup in a hurry. Takouhi, you have the bridge. Time for me to do paperwork."

Jennifer rose and headed aft for the hatch. She would be close if something came up, but the rest of the team needed time without her, if they were going to bond.

Best do it before it became critical.

"*4 06*, this is *Black Prince*," Anmol said as he watched his boards. "Maintaining course and plan. Sensors are picking up only navigation buoys in orbit at this time. Moving to checkpoint five."

Behind him, the corvette would be listening to the single communications laser he was sending in their direction. Unlike general comm, which would tell everyone that something was in the vicinity, even encrypted, the laser was silent. Because there was a target in front of him, flight deck wouldn't generally reply while he was dark, unless they had to.

That laser might be a single point, but it might still paint a target who recognized it. And who knew what the ancients could do?

Planet B had a pair of small moons, one barely a captured asteroid, while the other would present a respectable disk from the surface if the light was right. From here, the surface presented as more brown than most of the planets Anmol had seen, which suggested a dry world, heavy on rock and sand rather than oceans and forests.

Not the most inviting place, but he supposed that it might have been a case of taking what you could get. In empires, location counted most, because damned near any habitable planet had most of what you needed to live, if you planned ahead and adapted with prudence.

It wasn't like people were seeding planets for eventual colonization anymore. Or even needed to. Robot fleets had done that millennia ago, during the time of the ancients. There were many more worlds that were simply abandoned today, or had never been re-contacted after falling into barbarism.

Maybe he should consider a job with the Surveyor Corps when his hitch in the navy ended?

Time passed. It might have been slowly. Maybe quickly. He was capturing an amazing amount of data, far more than his old *P-4* could have done on its very best day, and transmitting it back to *406* almost as fast as he was getting it in.

Still, nobody in orbit talking. Or scanning. Or anything.

Checkpoint Seven. Orbital insertion, if he felt comfortable.

His call.

Normally, this would be the point where even the notorious *Black Prince* would stop pushing the odds, but something in front of him wasn't right.

Not bad like a horror vid. Too quiet. Like an empty world, except that there were at least four signals in orbit. And weirdly placed. One on each pole. One dead center on the equator over nothing that looked interesting. And one at seventeen degrees south, right ascension one hundred three degrees from the equatorial signal.

Triangulation, maybe? Three to establish a baseline from which to measure everything else? And then only one really interesting thing?

Chance had brought him close to his insertion point trailing the weird signal by about fifty degrees, and just about dead-stop relative. He could insert and sit just above their horizon, chasing them around the sky.

Anmol looked down once more, inverting his craft so that he was looking up from his seat, and down at the ground overhead.

Brown.

Patches of blue. Not a lot of clouds.

Boring, if not dead.

But they had still discovered a live signal from a dead world. Was that what this was?

"*406*, this is *Black Prince*," Anmol said in the emptiness. "Preparing for orbital insertion. No new signals. Nothing off baseline."

Silence meant that they were still selling him rope. Hopefully, ready to come get him if something went wrong, but Anmol had no illusions. *Black Prince* was at the very tip of the spear, looking for bad guys and possibly going into harm's way so *CP-406* didn't have to. *CP-406* was out here to protect *Ballard*. *Ballard* was out there so *Auberon* could hide.

If something went wrong, it was just his ass on the line.

Still, he had a stupidly-fast scout ship, if he turned everything off and routed all that power through the engines. Running like hell was an option, especially since *Buran* had never seen anything like the new fighters.

Anmol shrugged into the complex web of straps holding him in. One last look around, but nothing was there. Time to earn his Levs.

He came to rest, geo-synched to a spot above the planet that had nothing to distinguish it from the rest. Forty-eight degrees and change behind that other signal that looked so interesting.

He aimed everything he had into the vicinity and made sure his laser comm still thought it had a lock on *CP-406*. He was about to turn on a sensor firehose, and then try to drink from the stream of data.

Piece of cake.

Albedo. Power signature. Occlusion. Huh.

That's a station of some sort. Not huge, but big enough to mean something.

A new signal appeared on his boards with a shrill, staccato beep.

Anmol's hands were poised to slam the throttle to the stops, but he waited and watched, dancing on the edge of paranoia.

Something climbing to orbit, but doing so at high speed. Higher than humans would have tolerated. Nobody else close, and Anmol took a second to check every direction, just in case.

The launch was coming up ballistically, west to east and chasing the station ahead.

Anmol double-checked the data feed to *406*. Still good there, too. They were seeing what he did, and could yell if something came up.

Radio traffic on one channel, but it was kind of a continuous signal, like you got when two computers talked, rather than two humans. Machines matching trajectories and vectors for docking.

Nothing new on any other channel.

Eerie silence for a world that suddenly appeared to be inhabited.

What did a *Buran* world sound like on the airwaves? Certainly, there would be more traffic, right? Or were they all robots of some sort? Part of a technological hive matrix that no longer needed words?

Black Prince was alone in the skies, as far as he could tell. Throttle and stick still responded, so nobody had snuck in and taken control when he wasn't looking.

How close could he get? How close *should* he get? Probably already too close, but he had speed and surprise, as far as he knew.

Anmol programmed a quick extraction course into the nav computer. Nothing fancy, just flip on the gyros fifty degrees relative up from gravity and light the engines. One button push if things got out of hand. He could always recover after an eight-G burn flattened him into the seat for eight minutes, but he would be way away from here by then.

"*CP-406*, this is *Black Prince*," he said calmly. "Beginning to move closer to target designated *Delta*. Escape route programmed. Initiating."

Wasn't much they could say now without breaking radio silence. That would probably be his cue to skedaddle, if they did.

Anmol pushed the throttle forward a notch and began chasing a shooting star.

It was a station, of sorts. Anmol could see that now, even though it had not reacted to him in any way. Granted, he was above it, off the right, aft flank, and still a safe distance away, but it had gone from a bright light to a metal knife in orbit. Must be bigger than he expected, if he could make out detail from here.

And he was still dark, with his only emission being the laser pointed at the sky above and behind him, where *406* should be hiding.

The ground shuttle had docked a few minutes ago. Locked itself right into a cradle on the side of the station and sat like a bug on a log.

Silence on all channels, except the three signals he thought of as navigation beacons.

No visible weapon turrets. Nothing appearing to track him over here. Not even exterior windows or tiny portholes to look out.

Anmol took a chance and pointed one of his sensors down, roughly in the area he had seen the shuttle launch from.

There. Signal of some kind. He watched the feed, but it was either encrypted, or in some computer language his systems didn't know. Hash with Roman characters and Chinese ideograms randomly mixed.

And it came and went in strength.

Maybe it was a tight-beam laser focused on the station and he was just catching the edges? That would explain a lot. It was what he figured it would look like to someone else, if they caught *406* trying to signal him at this range.

"*406*, this is *Black Prince*," he said into the mic. "Picking up what looks like a comm laser from the ground to the station. Moving a little closer to see if I get a better signal. Feed twelve coming to you. Standby."

He eased the throttle forward a hair. They were already at geo-synch speed, but he wanted to saunter closer, and he had enough fuel and air reserves to be out here for several more hours, if he was careful. And patient.

Ooze closer, like ice forming on cold water. Sure enough, the signal got stronger, more stable. Still gibberish, but they could always wash it through the nav computer back home and see what fell out.

Something changed in the feed. Anmol couldn't tell, but the pulse, the feel was different.

He took a firmer grip on the throttle and prepared to redline everything if anybody sneezed.

The shuttle detached from the station as he watched. Rode backwards on soft thrusters that looked like compressed air. Rotated itself slowly once it was far enough away. Started a de-orbit burn with the blue-white flames of oxygen-powered chemical rockets.

Primitive, but starkly efficient, if all you had to do was bounce up to orbit and back.

Anmol locked a sensor on the shuttle and continued to watch the ground while listening to that feed.

Signals telemetry? Maybe chatter between two automated systems? Nothing but systems talking to each other? With no humans in the loop?

He'd have to ask when he got back. That might explain everything he was seeing.

That looked like his cue to leave as well. Just in case the station woke up to the fact that it wasn't alone.

He pitched the nose of his craft up and yawed away from the station. Pushed his throttle forward a notch. Not much, just quietly breaking from orbit until he was at a higher altitude and could come around to a docking setting with the ship. Time to go home.

"*406*, this is *Black Prince*," he called. "I am RTB."

Anmol wondered if there were any humans at all on the station, or the ground.

What was *Buran*, anyway?

CHAPTER XXXVI

Jessica glared up at the man, returning the scowl. Even seated, he towered over her physically. Not that she cared, but Navin liked to use his immense bulk to intimidate people. Plus that terrible scowl he wore.

And it still worked on other people.

"Because you're too old to be off doing things like that," she replied in an even tone that still showed how angry she was. "We're supposed to be mature adults, Navin. Commanders. We send others to do this."

"Like you did at *Petron*?" Navin retorted, relenting some.

He was one of the few people who could argue with her on a topic like this. He had been there, too, and done things no commander had any reason to.

Even when they were the right thing to do.

"That was the heat of the moment, for both of us," Jessica said, also relenting. She would out-stubborn even *Navin the Black*. "This is a thing that will be planned ahead of time. And I'm still not sure it's worth doing. There are other places we could hide."

"True," Arott broke into the conversation from his place on Jessica's left. "But I agree with Navin that this is an operation we should undertake."

"See?" Navin asked, suddenly smiling.

"And I agree with Jessica that you should stay here with us and send the kids to do it," Arott continued.

Navin's face fell again. Arott had spent the year that she was gone being this man's boss. And done a good enough job that nearly the whole crew had been happy when he came with them here.

Navin grumbled something under his voice, in a tone pitched so low that it was almost inaudible. Earthquakes might answer, if there were any in the vicinity.

Jessica looked around the rest of the group, the team she thought of as her command force.

Denis, Robbie, Alber', and Tamara. *da Vinci* as Fleet Flight Commander. Kanda and Elzbet from *Ballard*, plus Glenn from *CP-406* as her scouts. Kigali in his role as Escort Team Commander for the other corvettes. Enej and Casey as her flag centurions. Cheng Yin Dominguez as Arott's.

Plus one exceptionally grumpy Command Security Centurion in *Navin the Black*.

She missed having Vo handy. This was exactly the sort of mission he would excel at, but he would be doing better things with Emmerich, assuming he survived *St. Legier* and the hero worship he would have to endure for the rest of his days. Much as she would.

"Having settled that," she announced simply, "I agree with Arott. We need better intel. I am in no rush to poke a hornets' nest if I don't have to. My plan here is another iteration of *The Long Raid*."

Historians were already publishing definitive tomes calling it *Keller's Raid*, but she never would. It had simply been her first campaign in the quest to push *Fribourg* back enough that there could be a peace. Before she ended up here, trying to save the galaxy.

Jessica looked forward to the day she could return to *Petron* and simply walk away from her military career. If that day ever came.

"They wouldn't be here if there wasn't a reason," she continued. "We need to find out what that reason is. Navin will assemble a mixed-capability team, its mission to board the station, if possible. Kigali, you will be in tactical control of the immediate team: *264* and *406*, with *VI Victrix* as close backup. The support ships will stay well out at the edge of the system and below the ecliptic with *Ballard*. *VI Ferrata*, *II Augusta*, *Auberon*, and the rest of the corvettes will be close enough to engage if something happens, and far enough away to ghost if not."

There were nods from around the table.

"If this is The Raid, do we blow it up when we're done?" Arott asked. "Not counting this wrinkle, the rest of the vicinity is actually pretty good. We've doubled back on them from the gulf side, and this place has almost all of the characteristics I want in a secure location."

"We know they come across the gulf somewhere," Jessica replied. "And we've found some evidence of a high-speed navigational network. That's why we're here. This was as far from it as we could get and still stay close to my intended targets. But we're not building here if there is a highway in the backyard."

"Fair enough," Arott agreed. "We're okay for supplies right now, but I'd like to send *Mendocino* for our first run in another two weeks, with your permission."

Jessica nodded to the man, then turned to Alber'.

"What about Senior Centurion Bhattacharya?" she asked. "*Auberon's* marines are mostly ground force specialists these days, but I know Amala has the best combat EVA ratings in the squadron right now."

"She would be an excellent choice, Fleet Centurion," Alber' growled, nodding to Navin as he did. "Not quite as good as *zu* Arlo, Navin, but as capable as you and a generation younger."

"Don't remind me," Navin huffed. "She's the same age as my daughter, Khulan. Send her team over with all their gear. I'll add Moirrey and some of her folks for the engineering side, and *Gaucho* can fly his shiny, new sled into battle for the first time."

That got a general round of laughs, since *Gaucho* hadn't been in a hot landing zone since he got shot down on *Thuringwell*, a point he complained about regularly to anyone who would listen.

"Any other questions?" Jessica asked the room. "Seeing none, next order of business is…"

CHAPTER XXXVII

Amala tasted the air one last time as she look-checked her team. She dialed her suit's humidity down three percent, since she knew that once she started moving, she would sweat it all back into the recovery system of her combat armor. She had enough years in space suits like this to know what was coming.

The bay of the DropShip was huge, especially in proportion to the small force she was bringing to the party. *zu* Kermode, aka *Lady Moirrey the Goof*, plus the woman's primary assistant, Yeoman Robles. Amala's own team was comprised of sixteen specially-trained men and women geared towards space-borne EVA rather than ground operations. *Auberon* was a flagship, they did ground things. Amala had been with d'Maine since her first posting out of Academy, back on *Rajput*.

Plus, she was fully literate in all of the historical and modern dialects of written Chinese, as well as most of the spoken ones. There were always planets where the pronunciation had gone completely weird. From all the intel the scout pilot had picked up, that was likely to be important.

"Ahhh…*Nike One*, this is the bridge," *Gaucho* spoke into her helmet with that long, slow drawl.

Considering the man's history, things were probably verging on boring if he was like that. She hoped he had sounded more excited when he had gotten his skinny ass shot down on *Thuringwell,* but she hadn't listened to the tapes in enough detail to know.

"Go ahead, *Gaucho*," she replied simply.

"Sneaking up on launch coordinates now," he said. "No emissions picked up beyond baseline, and we have enough ears listening that confidence is high."

"Roger that, bridge," Amala answered. "Begin atmosphere purge now. All suits show green."

Lights began to pulse red on all sides, warning everyone of impending death pressure. Amala had already turned off her external pickups, so she was insulated from the sirens telling amateurs to get to safety immediately.

Instead, she counted noses. Everyone here. Moirrey on her left. Robles on her right. Yeoman Swarovski herding the rest of the cats. Not that they needed it, but Pinchon was a lunch-box kind of guy. Nothing flashy about the man or his technique, just a quiet soldier who could drag you into an alley and gut you like a fish if the mission called for it. There was a reason he was her right hand.

On the wall was the same image Amala had in her right-hand Heads-Up-Display. They were close enough to the station now to pick out details. Cold, steel walls, unadorned and boxy. Functional, rather than pretty. Several strange docking doors and locks on the long axis of the rectangle, plus two that were recognizable as airlocks for humans.

Moirrey had suggested the bottom one, rather than trying to force one of the garage doors. Amala had bristled at the thought of such an obvious trap, but Alber' and Fleet Centurion had put *zu* Kermode in technical command, so Amala had split her team into three groups: scout, heavy assault, and support.

The outer bay door of the DropShip cracked like a clam and cycled itself open like dawn rising. Without air in here, the light was stark, and the yellowishness of the planet gave things a strange hue. Adventures in deep space.

Eighteen bodies launched gracefully into space, across the kilometer of gap *Gaucho* had been willing to risk. Amala was up front with the two engineers. Swarovski was at the rear, holding pace with the four troopers carrying anti-tank weaponry heavy enough to hurt something the size of *Cayenne*. Short-range, low-powered radio was enough for now. She could always power up the big one to talk to *Gaucho* if they needed to run.

Amala was surprised at how easily the two engineers flew. She was used to her own ship's engineers, who made hogs on ice look dexterous. Obviously, this was not either woman's first EVA op.

Something about the exterior spoke to Amala as she closed the range. Maybe it was the utter squareness of everything, but it looked like a design to purely maximize the efficiency of interior volume.

Certainly, it had no soul. Welcome to *Buran*.

Bottom hatch.

Standard airlock design so ancient that nobody knew where it had come from. Which told Amala that the folks using it were humans, just like her.

What was *Buran*, anyway?

Scout team advanced enough to snoop. Hand-held scanners went to work, but nobody was that close and there were a lot of guns pointed in various directions.

Nothing moved.

"Power and heat, *One*," one of the troopers called on the radio. "Normal to human standards. Don't even see a boarding gun on this one."

Maybe the killzone was inside. Maybe they hadn't bothered with one. Maybe the whole thing would just explode once they made entry.

Sounded like a waste of time and resources, but this wasn't *Fribourg*. Who knew what an ancient, god-like intelligence might do?

"Moirrey," Amala called quietly. "You're up."

The tiny figure moved close, spinning herself sideways to align with the long axis of the station, when everyone else was perpendicular.

Huh. New way of looking at it. Gotta try that.

Amala put deed to word and spun ninety degrees to her right, so that Moirrey was standing on her head, relative.

Moirrey moved close and let magnets in her boots lock onto the skin of the station.

Nothing moved, but Amala wasn't fooled. Her team was going to be safeties-off at this point, until she or Pinchon overrode them. Which wasn't gonna happen.

Thirty seconds, and the airlock door swung inward, revealing a space large enough for ten in suits comfortably. Amala wasn't taking chances.

"Scout team and Robles inside," she ordered. "Kermode and the rest defensive outside."

Moirrey turned and looked at her, but didn't speak. Which was good. Amala would feel bad if something happened to Robles. She would never forgive herself if Moirrey got killed in there.

Five bodies made their way into the airlock and closed it.

Long wait as the inner systems had to pressurize so that the humans could safely board.

Radio silence on all channels.

That was good.

"*One, Six*," a man's voice over the short-range. "Entry complete. Interior is human-habitable but abandoned, as far as we can see in any direction without leaving the first room. Gravity's light. Robles says it'll be stinky if we crack shields to smell, based on her sensor readings."

"Roger that, *Six*," Amala answered. "Stand by."

Amala thought about it and decided things were under control. She turned in place until her onboard systems told her she could lock a communications laser more or less on *Cayenne*. She didn't need focus, just enough push in the right direction.

"*Gaucho*, tell *CA-264* that we are about to fully enter the facility," she said. A pulse a moment later acknowledged receipt.

"Support Team next," Amala called. "Odd numbers first, even numbers second. Fire Team last. Move out."

The interior of the airlock was so familiar that Amala felt a pang of homesickness. The design itself was eight thousand years old if a day, and had gone everywhere humans had. Instructions in all seven trade languages, with Mandarin Chinese at the top and English second to last, just above Bulgarian.

Moirrey waited for Amala's nod, and then began pressurizing everything. Lights came on. Extremely weak gravplates pulled her feet down. Maybe a sixth of a G. Just enough to keep things on the deck, and nothing more.

So, habitable, but probably not inhabited. It took almost as much power to keep gravplates on one-sixth as it did to one G, so someone specifically wanted sixteen percent gravity.

Or something.

Inner door opened. Scout team arrayed in a star facing out, with Robles in the middle facing them. And nobody shooting.

Good.

Amala listened to Moirrey and Robles chatter in engineer-speak, but barely followed any of it. It made tactical training sound simple.

Instead, her team leap-frogged outward and took up positions. There was a small office to one side, so they stretched to include it and Amala guided Moirrey closer to that, with instructions not to touch anything yet.

The station itself was nearly two hundred meters long, but only thirty on the square axis. Amala could see major bulkheads with heavy hatches on either side, plus a ladder up through a hole in the ceiling.

"Scout team, go vertical," she ordered.

The bulk of her group would be inside in three minutes, and she had enough people here to guard the small space, since there were only two hatches plus the ladder.

Six went first. Scout armor was lighter, and they were usually gymnasts, so he was up quickly. A small sensor probe on a stick popped the hatch and looked around.

"*One*, this is *Six*," he called. "Second floor looks like living space. Empty, and the ladder keeps going."

"Follow it, *Six*," she replied.

The man disappeared from sight, along with his three teammates. One of her people moved to the bottom of the ladder and pointed a gun up. Never take a risk in a hostile situation.

"*One*, this is *Six*," the man continued. "Third floor is a dorm room. Dead end top floor. Empty and waiting for occupants. I see bedding in clear bags on a shelf and a bed better-made than we did in basic."

"Secure it until you're satisfied, *Six*," she replied.

Amala checked her external atmosphere. Chilly but not terrible. Just as if someone had turned everything down for the winter, just before they left.

Robles and Kermode had moved to beyond the workspace and were inspecting a bulkhead, so Amala joined them.

Warning: Pressurized Water was the first of several warnings written in half a dozen languages. Interestingly, she recognized Mandarin as second, but wasn't sure what the top one was. It shared many of the same characters, but contained others she didn't know. Amala captured an image and stored it for reference later. She did note that the airlock hatch on this side was also closed off with a simple steel beam, probably to keep you from opening a swimming pool into your basement and drowning.

Not a lot of space to hide here if something went wrong.

Moirrey looked up at her with a roguish grin.

"Abouts to breathe local air," she said over the radio. "Sets?"

Amala nodded. They were in engineering land now. Moirrey ran the show until something happened that needed Amala's gunners.

She watched the pixie engineering wizard unlock her faceplate and swing it up on the forehead hinge. A good sniff and Moirrey crinkled her nose in disgust.

"Someone fergots to haul out th'trash," she observed. "Is fine alternate."

Made sense. Robles had said stinky, based on her spectrograph. Stale organics gone moldy or some such.

Amala joined the two engineers as they crossed the space to the other bulkhead at the far end.

Warning: Automated systems active. Disarm before entry.

Amala worried for a moment that the sign meant security systems, but the big red button to one side, glowing slightly, suggested a worker machine of some sort. Hopefully a computer-controlled device, and not one of the ancient evils: an android.

The two women consulted briefly, and then Robles pushed the button. It blinked several times and then went dark. A moment later, the airlock hatch on this side began to open inwards.

"Scout team. Status," Amala called.

"Secured here, *One*," *Six* replied.

"Drop down," Amala said. "More exploring."

"Roger that."

The four of them appeared as if out of a cannon. Amala designated two of the regular team to move up to the second floor while she joined the scouts and the engineers.

The other side of the airlock, when they finally lock-cycled through, was a warehouse. Amala couldn't think of a better term for it. One big, echoing space, with rollers and metal armatures coming out of various places. She did finally understand why the gravity was set so low.

The space was neatly divided into two areas. One side was filled with transport frames holding metal. When they got close, Amala recognized several diameters of bar stock in what appeared to be both steel and aluminium, plus steel and copper tubes from the size of her finger to the diameter of her thigh.

Across the gap were pallets of steel sheet in various thicknesses, wrapped up for transport and secured to shipping sleds, but lined up facing a giant forklift-like device that obviously shelved and retrieved things according to rules or math or something.

The warehouse side was nearly full, but not oppressive.

Organized.

Amala trailed the two as they walked to the end and touched

everything at least once, chattering in dense engineer-speak. *Six* and his team escorted them, but it was more a promenade than a military operation.

At the far end, Moirrey smiled up at her and nodded.

"Truck stop," she said simply. "Let's home once we resets the 'bot."

Amala nodded back, confused, but the two women seemed cheerful enough. And certainly seemed to have some understanding that had eluded Amala. She could live with that.

For we have met the enemy…I think.

Now what the hell do we do?

CHAPTER XXXVIII

Darkness.

Space was technically completely empty, when you measured all space consumed by mass, as a percentage of the overall whole.

Humanity was a rounding error on the cosmos, when you multiplied the resulting space by all of time.

Arott grinned internally. As always, he quartered his private, philosophical thoughts away from the group surrounding him. Wouldn't do to ruin their perceptions of him as a boring person, especially at this late date.

In the years since he had met Jessica and this team that he had become a part of, Arott knew he had developed a reputation as a by-the-rules stickler for detail. And, compared to the rest of these lovable maniacs, that was certainly the case.

But he had found something about himself after *First Ballard*. Or rather, during the battle, watching Alber d'Maine go into full-berserker mode, and Tomas Kigali saunter through the valley of death as though going for High Tea.

They were not men known for deep introspection. Most of Jessica's people really weren't. They were warriors. For most of them, they had achieved their highest dream in life on the day they added that third stripe permanently and became Command Centurions.

Arott had felt the same way, once. Before a very private conversation with the old First Lord, Nils Kasum, about what place Arott wanted for himself.

Now, he wanted to shape the future itself. In small ways.

Jessica was going to go down in the history books as one of the most important people of this century, and possibly many in either direction, but that was Jessica Keller. The woman was just as impressive as the myth. Perhaps more so, when you knew her and knew how much of what she did was based on her personal vision of what was *right*.

Arott didn't always agree with her. Didn't always even understand her, but he suspected that nobody did. Perhaps not even Keller herself.

She sat at the far end of the long conference table from him, in the room he had taken as his, her warriors around them on both sides, poised like lesser hawks before the majestic phoenix. He would be moving out of this room, off this ship, all too soon. This was probably the second to last of these meetings, there remaining only the formal one that would send him on his mission.

The one where she would rely on him to maintain her entire logistics train for a galactic war, with nothing more than vague notions of what she was going to be doing next.

First Ballard, all over again. He missed *Stralsund*, now in Doyle MacEoghain's capable hands, but wouldn't have traded with the man.

Endings. And beginnings.

Just for effect, and to maintain his reputation, Arott picked up the stack of printouts and tapped them into perfect squareness on the tabletop, before setting them back down and turning to look at Senior Centurion Bhattacharya, seated midway down on his left. Her report had been as detailed as he could have possibly wanted, over and above what *zu* Kermode had produced.

"Initial consensus," he said to start the meeting, aware that he had everyone's eyes focused. "The station we explored is fully automated. Knowing what little we do about *Buran*, the planetary outpost will probably have a shockingly small human footprint, mostly as supervisors and technicians, while an automated, robotic workforce handles most of the labor."

He paused and glanced down. Mostly for effect, since he had memorized all the key details already.

"The station exists only as a refueling and transshipment point, we think," Arott gave voice to the opinion of the men and women on his staff who were paid to think about these things. "This system sits astride one of the laterals from whichever one they use as a navigation corridor. Ships cross the gulf, then fan out. This planet exists to provide a ready supply of good steel and other metals, which are then stored in plate, bar, or tube form, as needed. The water can be consumed as-is or broken down into oxygen to breathe and hydrogen to make other things, as needed. They don't have anything like *Mendocino* or *Duncan*, that *Fribourg* has ever detected, and so must use this method instead."

Arott nodded to Command Centurions Ihejirika and Kovack, masters of the two ships that brought fresh supplies forward from staging bases and kept the warships in food and weapons.

Normally, an operation like this, with this many vessels, would require four or perhaps five such Fleet Replenishment freighters to sustain, but Bedrov had done such an amazing job of design that they would probably have to send *Andorra* home for more fighters, pilots, and spare parts before anything else was depleted.

"Do we take the planet?" Jessica asked in a formal tone.

They had already chatted briefly, but this was for the benefit of everyone else.

"We do not," Arott replied. "It would give away too much of our plans at this point. But we should consider doing something similar, if we can find a good planet with either a primitive population, or none at all. I would go farther, though, and also bring in farmers to plant crops. Having a source of grains and vegetables close at hand would help with my logistics, especially as far as we are from any currently-friendly worlds."

"Later?" d'Maine asked, his eyes glowing with that internal fire that drove the man.

"Later, we absolutely use Jessica's overall strategy to destroy as many of these orbital outposts as we can," Arott replied, letting his gaze roam around the room until he found the face he wanted. "*CP-406* was designed with exactly this sort of mission in mind. It's not worth the effort to root them out on the ground, but uninhabited, unarmed stations are easily destroyed and will materially impact *Buran's* operations, if he has been relying on them to maintain his reach by providing generic consumables."

"We'll come back and blow this one shortly, then," Jessica said, turning to Navin, standing along the wall. "And drop the battalion to disable the ground facilities, depending. As near as I can tell, this would be their primary supply depot on the path to my destination. Let's put some burning barricades in the streets."

The Command Security Centurion nodded sagely, eyes a-twinkle at the prospect. Arott knew how upset Navin had been that he couldn't go with the team to take the station. Leading a ground invasion would assuage the man, especially as close as he was to retirement.

Jessica cleared her throat to draw all eyes to her. It was time.

"I have not shared any details with anybody but Arott to this point," she began. "Partly, that was for operational security, because we still had to deal with Imperial spies and moles. The Grand Admiral doesn't know what we're doing next, because I wasn't sure myself until we got to this point."

She paused to take a sip of coffee. From where he sat, Arott could even see the flash of determination appear in her eyes, however briefly. It was like a pulsar, strobing one impossibly-hot light and then passing back to darkness. He couldn't remember ever seeing it like that. Not Jessica. Others, perhaps. The mere mortals, but never the legend herself.

He wasn't sure if that knowledge made him stronger, or more concerned. Her next words brought him solace.

"All of you know our past at this point," she continued. "*2218 Svati Prime. Petron. Ballard. Thuringwell.* We're going to take everything we have learned and take it to *Buran.* Everything I have read or heard suggests that *Buran* is a colonizer, not a conqueror. They will seed worlds on this side of the gulf with a generational timeline, because this being has been alive for thousands of years, and plans to be so for millennia more. It has begun to think of itself as a god. Our god, if we would just roll over and accept his godhead."

The fire was back. Hot and angry. This was the woman that had led them into the fury of *Ballard.* He remembered the same tones.

"I will not," she growled. "We are flawed, unpredictable creatures, prone to fancy and stupidity, but we are free. What we are about to begin here is nothing less than the liberation of all humanity from the last of the old gods. We do not need them. We will not accept them. We must be free. Questions?"

Interestingly, it was Kigali who asked. Arott would have expected the man to have his own telepathic link to Jessica after this many years and battles. Perhaps he was speaking for the other corvette commanders, all relative newcomers to this force, but every one of them forged and sharp.

"What about the colonists?" he asked in a deceptively gentle voice, running one hand back through the slowly-graying blond hair that was still too long for most interpretations of regulations.

"Most of them are likely to be just normal people when we get there," Jessica replied. "Citizens of *Thuringwell*, even if none will understand that reference. We'll destroy any organized military and internal security capacity as we go, watch the gendarmes closely on any planet we take, and leave the rest in as much peace as they want to accept. Imperial traders will come soon enough, and I suspect that a few enterprising merchants from the Republic are also doing the math, to say nothing of people like Galen Estevan."

That got a chuckle out of the room. Estevan, the son-in-law of Jessica's Comptroller of the Court, Uly Larionov, had accompanied her to *St. Legier* two years ago in a tiny one-ring mothership dedicated to commerce, making an absolute killing in trade across what was then a tremendous distance.

"Let me make one last point clear," Jessica concluded. "We're making war on a god. I've met one in my life, a woman who thought of herself as the *Last of the Immortals*, although she was not. She was still six thousand years old. Keep that in mind. These things are ancient, but, according to her, only machines. They have no magical powers save patience and knowledge. They can outlive all of us. They can be beat, if there exists the will. *Fribourg* will be along to help us in another year, but Emmerich Wachturm thought that even one year was too long to wait, and that *Buran* would become fully embedded on this side of the gulf if he waited. In another year, I plan to be on the other side of that gulf and taking the war to them."

CHAPTER XXXIX

As starships went, Arott knew everyone considered it the ugliest thing ever launched, but he didn't care. There was beauty in purpose that superseded mere elegance of lines. Surprisingly, one of the few people who agreed with him on the topic was Yan Bedrov, but the man might have a personal attachment, considering his background.

The Salvage Cruiser *RAN Bulldog*. Affectionately known by her crew, and now the rest of the fleet as well, as the *Junkyard Chihuahua*.

She had started life as a pirate stripper, one of those support vessels the *corsair fleets* of *Corynthe* used in lieu of proper base facilities. Although, when you were a pirate, having a base was usually a bad thing, since that meant the law could find you.

No, better to have a mobile repair yard handy. Surprise a freighter just about to go into jump or coming out. Capture it, replace the crew, and jump to safety. Go somewhere else, where the law couldn't find you, and swing a stripper alongside to go to work. Haul away the valuables and then rip out every bit of useful gear you could, to repair your own beat-to-hell vessels.

Arott had dropped most of the squadron out on top of a pirate base at *M'Cizo* due to some excellent intelligence work. Well, perhaps base was a stretch. A veritable flea market of brigands getting together to swaps parts and lies, as well as plot treason against their nominal monarch, Jessica Keller.

Naughty men doing bad things, suddenly facing a Star Controller Task Force that outweighed them by a factor of seven. With surprise and position above them in the high orbitals. And anger.

Afterwards, Arott had impressed the *Chihuahua* into service, expanding his own patrol options by not having to rely on returning regularly to *Petron*, where his comings and goings could be noted and possibly predicted. David Rodriguez had formalized the transfer later, keeping most of the captured ships for his own expanding fleet as *Corynthe* slowly turned from an idea into a nation.

But Arott had kept the *Junkyard Chihuahua*. And Nils Kasum had agreed, at Jessica's request. And then sent it with them to *Fribourg*.

She wasn't long and lean, like most warships, being instead almost a coffin, barely twice as long as her beam, with underpowered engines on the ass end. Just enough to move her around. JumpSails that could get her from place to place moving like a freighter, and not a raider. Usually, she was the last vessel to join the squadron after fleet jumps. Among the most welcome, with an entire, dedicated crew of engineers and specialists, superb at handling almost any task a drydock could. She was even capable of constructing, from scratch, a vessel as big as a cutter, given time and materials.

What he and Jessica had planned for this campaign went against everything *Aquitaine* or *Fribourg* had ever attempted, which made it all the more likely they could catch *Buran* off-guard.

Right now, Arott watched from Jessica's flag bridge as the *Chihuahua* maneuvered close to the quietest member of the Support Force: the Tug *CT-9492*.

Unlike *Chihuahua*'s boxy ugliness, the tug was a creature of elegance that always reminded Arott of a dragonfly. A long, skinny body that was mostly a tiny living and engineering space contained in the belly, with struts and superstructure which were mostly open to space providing the wings as a frame. Loaded, she was barely faster than *Chihuahua* getting anywhere, and she was full right now.

Two massive cargo pods had been transported under the wings, and were detached now for deployment. The larger of the two was a Bastion Pod, a self-contained combat vessel designed to provide a forward operating base for squadrons such as this, with base-level firepower and a dedicated support and repair team.

Originally, Arott had expected Jessica to bring two of them. Joined together, the structure was known as a Citadel, and provided something close to Starbase protection for the squadron. *Fribourg* would hesitate to take on a Citadel, but *Buran* could probably defeat one by dropping out of a jump right on top of it and subjecting it to hell before it could react, leaping away before the Citadel could bring much firepower to bear.

They had done as much to *Fribourg's* fleet headquarters at *St. Legier*.

Lady Moirrey, Bedrov, and apparently *zu* Arlo of all people, had gone completely off the reservation with the new design. One Bastion, but they had brought along the engines and JumpSail generators from a planetary defense monitor, a ship the size of a cruiser with the firepower of a heavy dreadnaught.

Even with the engines, the Bastion would be slower than a monitor, going from place to place at speeds occasionally measured in glacial scales, but that wasn't the point. This Bastion could move around. Slowly, to be sure, but *Buran* couldn't just jump blind into a system to engage, already knowing the target coordinates. And, operating well out in the darkness between stars instead of close to a gravity well, the Bastion could leap into JumpSpace to avoid sudden predators.

The galaxy's meanest armadillo.

Arott looked forward to taking command of her, once *Chihuahua's* engineers rebuilt everything and let him turn this space into a pleasant, quiet corner of *Aquitaine*. Jessica and her people could become a raiding force, while he was the sheriff in town. And maybe the publican, too, once they got enough R&R facilities built out.

"What do you think?" a voice intruded into Arott's daydreams.

Jessica.

Asking a question.

How lost was I? Can't have that, they might accuse me of being human.

Arott laughed inside his head at the prospect and returned to the droll, strategic world of a galaxy-spanning military campaign.

"We've got space, if we cram things in everywhere and fill all your hallways with boxes," he replied, turning unwillingly away from the projection to study the woman and her two Flag Centurions. Three, with his own Cheng Yin seated to one side. "Let's send both *Mendocino* and *Duncan* now, and then we can empty *Mendocino's* load into the Bastion's stores and send Ihejirika out for a second run immediately."

"I like it," Jessica said, nodding to her staff to make it magically happen.

No more words were needed. Fingers immediately began to tap out commands and update schedules, the paperwork of war.

Arott turned back to the image just in time to catch the Bastion pod begin to unfold from transport configuration into combat mode, a caterpillar emerging from her chrysalis as a deadly butterfly, to face an angry galaxy.

Soon.

CHAPTER XL

He hadn't been officially promoted yet, so Vo still wore the Colonel's rank tabs on the collar of the gray, semi-dress fatigues he had been instructed to wear to this meeting.

The Category Two uniform, for those times he wasn't expected to be ready for High Tea. Vo did have the patch over his heart that was a gray rectangle with a red sword pointed inward towards his heart.

Ritter of the Imperial Household.

Originally, a thank you from the Emperor for not annihilating the men of the 189th during the invasion of *Thuringwell.* Now, a reward for saving the empire itself.

As Navin had pounded home time and again, there is always an easy thing to do, in any situation, and then there is the right thing. The two were rarely synonymous.

Vo had long since memorized the layout of this wing of the palace. The working wing, he thought of it, since this was where offices and conference rooms for active officers were located, with all the personal quarters and glittery stuff across the big quad. He had rescued an Emperor not too far from here.

And killed another one.

Today, his steps brought him to a different door. Vo found it amusing that the Grand Admiral had asked to meet him here, rather than at the office Wachturm retained over at their training school for fleet officers.

Guarding the door were two men in field gear, without the field-grade armor they would wear for a heavy assault, but still armed and armoured for a sudden drop into a hostile zone. Even inside, they had their mirrored face shields down, so you couldn't see their eyes move, but Vo had made enough noise approaching, boots on a marble floor, that they knew where he was. And who.

By size, he recognized both, but neither had been particularly friendly on the flight here from *Auberon*. Professionals on duty. And the additional rivalry, since he was army now, and they were fleet marines.

But they hadn't been hostile, either. Men doing a job. He respected that.

"Colonel *zu* Arlo, to see the Grand Admiral," he said to the one on the left, just because.

Hint of a grin under the shield, possibly because the other guy was the one closest to the door switch. And all of them knew it.

"You're expected, sir," the man replied.

The other marine pressed the button to open the door.

Inside, Vo got his first big surprise. He had been prepared to find the Grand Admiral alone, seated at the long conference table. As indeed he was seated.

But there was, unexpectedly, another.

Vo knew the face. Had memorized a great deal of detail about the man's history. Had never expected to meet him in the flesh in anything less than a formal occasion, one where Vo was a peon standing quietly off to one side.

Grand Marshal Anthohn Jenker. *Supreme Commander, Imperial Land Forces.* The top man in the army. Answering only to the Grand Admiral and the Imperial Command Staff.

Seated next to Emmerich Wachturm, Jenker looked small, but that was to be expected, when Jenker himself was exactly at the shortest height the army would allow for any soldier to enlist, and Wachturm was tall, only about a hand shorter than Vo.

Hands? Seriously, Arlo? You spent too much time with Fourth Saxon if you're measuring people and horses the same way.

Vo had developed something of a relaxed relationship with the Grand Admiral on the flight back from *Auberon*. He would have normally come in and taken a seat without much performance. Two men, getting to business.

Grand Marshal Jenker had a reputation as a hard man, and a

perfectionist. The kind that routinely strapped on full gear and went on thirty kilometer hikes with training units, just to keep himself in shape and his soldiers on their toes.

Vo took two steps into the room and snapped to attention.

"Colonel *zu* Arlo, reporting for duty, sirs," he called out rather than spoke.

Navin would have been proud of him. He could still nail that aspect of drill, even in his sleep.

Vo let his eyes find a spot on the far wall and relaxed just enough to track everything with peripheral vision.

Wachturm turned his head silently to look at Jenker. The Grand Marshal pushed his chair back and rose.

The man was about as tall as the Fleet Centurion, which was small for a man who didn't have some genetic condition related to dwarfism. His skin was almost as dark as Jessica's as well, that swarthy red-brown universally called Hispanic. Vo felt like a snow drift, comparatively.

The buzzed, dark hair had gone salt and pepper, which appeared to be the only concession to the river of time about the man, as the soldier himself was broad and heavily muscled. Jenker reminded Vo of Command Centurion d'Maine that way, that same solid build that came from a focus on heavy weights on a regular basis.

Powerful man, used to overcoming people's expectation that he was too short, too middle class, too *something* to succeed.

Biographers had delighted in listing all the people that had been wrong about the soldier, Anthohn Jenker. No other non-noble-born had ever made it to even the rank of Flag General, let alone the lofty status of Grand Marshal.

The times, they are a'changing.

Jenker stepped close. Vo kept his head up and focused on the far wall, even as he felt the man's eyes study him.

"You are not wearing any ribbons on this uniform, *zu* Arlo," the Grand Marshal observed in a neutral-enough voice. "Beyond the red sword."

"Sir. Yes, sir," Vo agreed, letting a decade and a half of militariness drive him now.

"Why is that, soldier?" Jenker asked in a voice getting somewhere between inquisitive and accusatory.

Vo had noted that the man was also wearing his own Category Two uniform today. Baggy pants tucked into tall hiking boots in black leather.

Jacket buttoned all the way up the front to the neck, unlike the dress uniforms where the lapel was designed to fold back to show off color.

"Imperial regulations concerning a Category Two uniform leave the decision to the officer, Grand Marshal," Vo replied carefully. This might be a man who knew those regs as well as Vo did. "And all my ribbons are *Aquitaine*-issued, sir, so I would need special dispensation to wear them on anything less-formal than Dress Uniforms, and then only where the commanding officer had specified foreign awards to be acceptable or required."

They did that, occasionally. Mostly because smaller nations tended towards gaudier awards on a scale that appeared to be inverse to their actual political and military power.

"What ribbons could you add to a Dress uniform, Arlo?"

Vo could tell the man was digging now. Not hostile, but not friendly either. Another one like Alber' d'Maine in all the ways that counted.

"Order of Baudin, sir," Vo replied in a calm, carrying voice. "Republic Cross. With Star. EVA Heavy Assault badge. Planetary Assault badge. Gold Spurs."

Vo left it at that. All the schooling Navin had driven him to master would take five minutes to cover, and this man had most of them himself.

"Spurs, Arlo?" Jenker asked, his voice lighter, less accusatory.

"Field Command, *Fourth Saxon Legion*, Grand Army of the Republic, Grand Marshal," Vo answered.

He had never considered actually wearing the damned things in public, until now. That might just be a complete novelty. Then again, everyone would want to come over and ask him about them personally.

Maybe not.

"And the red sword?" the Grand Marshal asked, reaching out one heavy mitt to tap Vo on the chest, over his heart.

"Regulations specify that award on all uniforms, Grand Marshal," Vo said. "Up to and including EVA assault armor, if I have a suit issued."

The man studied Vo for a few more seconds.

"At ease, Colonel," Jenker finally said.

Vo dropped into a more relaxed pose, his feet shoulder width and his hands crossed behind him.

Jenker looked down.

"The boots are not regulation," he observed in a neutral tone far more relaxed than the one he had been using.

"They are custom made to specifications, sir," Vo replied. "Nobody makes footwear that fits me, and I haven't had an opportunity to locate a boot-maker on *St. Legier* and engage his services to make me new, Imperial pairs to replace with my *Aquitaine* versions."

The man ruminated. Vo let his face turn enough to study the man back. It was only the three of them in this room, until something changed.

After a moment, the smaller man nodded.

"Be seated, *zu* Arlo," he said. "Let's get down to business."

Vo followed him to the table, noting that the Grand Admiral had sat silently through the whole performance with just a ghost of a grin on his face. About what Vo had expected, given the ambush they had obviously planned together.

Vo took the seat across from the Marshal, leaving Wachturm to Vo's left across the table.

There were no notebooks or computers on the table top.

So, going to be a dissertation defense, is it? Has that look.

He almost smiled. Neither of these men had anything on Navin and his notorious final exams. That man was the terror of the fleet.

"Tell the advantages and weaknesses of equestrian cavalry forces, Colonel Arlo," Jenker commanded.

Vo ruminated on his time on *Thuringwell.* He missed those lunatics.

"Extreme flexibility of formation on a par with infantry," Vo began. "Comparable firepower as well, once you balance the smaller number of heavier weapons that horse units travel with, against what a Rifles Legion can bring to the table. Not as quick at maneuvering as a Rapid Assault Legion or Heavy Scouts. They optimize for wild, rough terrain with air defenses you need to penetrate quickly. I would send mechanized infantry or cataphracti if crossing open terrain, such as plains. On *Thuringwell,* we were facing irregular and light infantry in trees, striking and fading. Horses gave us a maneuvering edge."

"Weaknesses?" the Grand Marshal asked.

"Ammunition resupply for slug-throwers instead of beam weapons, but we were only using two calibers: small arms and auto-cannon," Vo said. "Food drops for the troops. Less necessary for the horses, since they could get by on local forage in a pinch."

"Slug-throwers," Jenker said with obvious disdain.

"Proven to be extremely effective in all-weather conditions, sir," Vo countered. "Plus, the team can share ammunition. One charged power pack and three dead ones means only one trooper shooting while the others watch. Louder than hell in battle, but that also works to your advantage if you're prepared for it and the other side isn't."

Vo stopped there and observed the effect of his words on both men. Wachturm appeared to be suppressing a grin. Jenker scowled.

"You were occupying a hostile planet, *zu* Arlo," the man said. "Why would horses be a better option?"

"Surprise, primarily, Grand Marshal," Vo said honestly. "Nobody was expecting it and it threw all their careful studies and plans right out the window on day one. They never really recovered from that initial shock. Plus we pushed hard, backed with a heavy armor cohort that could overwhelm anything that tried to stand fast and slug it out. And total air superiority. Very specific strategic implications selected by the Fleet Centurion, but anything we did on the ground was irrelevant until they held space above us."

A smile actually appeared on the rugged, angry face now.

"What would you do with the 189th?" the old soldier said serenely.

"First Regiment is a training cadre of veterans with a heavy emphasis on alpine operations," Vo said. "Useful for taking fortresses in the middle of nowhere, but valuable targets are likely to be coastal or situated on plains, on most planets. Are you looking for a strike force, or a gendarme? *Fourth Saxon* was actually a good mix for that, but I'm not aware of anything you have remotely like that."

Vo paused to study the Marshal. Jenker nodded.

"You would be correct," he agreed. "And I doubt it would be possible to train that sort of expertise in less than a generation."

"That would be my assessment, based on those folks," Vo said. "Might be worth starting now, anyway. What does *Buran* have for land forces? The materials I've received access to contain a significant gap there."

Vo turned to Wachturm and smiled serenely.

"Presumably, the spies were more focused on naval affairs."

Give the man credit, the Grand Admiral had the courtesy to look chagrined.

"As you said earlier, Vo," Wachturm said. "Battles on the ground are nice, but wars are won in near space, regardless. Plus, we don't really know that much. Their worlds here are fortified in orbit and the tiny amount of trade they have allowed with neutrals stays there. But it can't be that exotic, can it?"

Vo and Jenker smiled the same smile at the Grand Admiral.

Navy man.

"Actually, you'd be amazed, Grand Admiral," Vo finally allowed. "I asked Moirrey to dream up the craziest things she could, given a *Sentience* to design and build them, and then how to fight them. Bedrov got involved as well. A lot of wine and beer disappeared in the process."

Vo was rewarded with a shudder that went through both men. Nice to see that the evil engineering gnome had cast her glittery spell so wide.

Wachturm finally broke the spell.

"Considering what those two did with the fleet I just visited, what did *zu* Kermode and Sri Bedrov envision?"

Vo leaned back and let his imagination roam over the images they had generated. Two stuck in his mind.

"My favorite? First, a thing Bedrov called a mega-tank," Vo said. "Imagine a land vehicle so big that it rides on four separate set of tracks on the corners. Each of those about the size of a normal battle tank. Tall enough that a person could walk underneath the space down the center. Something where the turret itself is about the size of a Solenopsis tank, with a comparably huge gun."

"Interesting," Jenker observed with a twinkle in his eyes. "Did they send plans with you?"

"They did, but nobody has done a rigorous, engineering workup for them," Vo admitted. "Nor hammered out the necessary command-and-control hardware."

"You said *first*, Vo," Wachturm noted. "That suggests at least a *second*."

"Aye, sir," Vo said. "The second one was utterly silly, but psychologically probably the most effective. Imagine a tank, but in the rough shape of a human, with legs instead of treads and cannons instead of arms. Pilot sits in the chest. Sensors where the head is. Overall height between five and twelve meters, depending on preferred mass and weaponry."

"Is that possible?" Jenker was aghast.

Vo shrugged, very carefully. He had his suspicions about how Moirrey had been able to draw such a detailed diagram from memory, but he would rather go to his grave ignorant. He could only think of one place, one way, that *Pint-sized* could have gotten that expertise.

He hadn't been there for the good parts, in the process of being evac'ed by Doc Crncevic before Moirrey went after the assassin herself.

"*zu* Kermode drew me up plans, but assures me that *Fribourg* could never build such a thing," Vo said. "The computer processing necessary to make it work would bring the machine right up to the edge of *Sentience* itself. Even *Aquitaine* would be leery. But she wanted to think so far outside any box that she was outside the warehouse."

"How do you kill something like that?" Wachturm asked.

"Put a really big gun on a tank," Vo said. "Bedrov's mega-tank, or mount a big enough centerline weapon on a tracked chassis as an assault gun. The only question then is if the damned humanoid thing could fly, in which case you would need the ability to elevate your guns tremendously."

"You've worked with heavy armor," Jenker said. It wasn't a question.

"Yes, sir," Vo nodded. "*LVIII Heavy* was attached to *Fourth Saxon* as their fourth cohort for *Thuringwell*. *Aquitaine* Legions are usually three cohorts of one type: infantry, cavalry, mechanized, or armor; plus an attached cohort seconded from a different legion for special missions and cross-training. Tanks with a mechanized assault force. Mechanized with an infantry deployment. Horses with heavy armor. Puts a lot of flexibility in the hands of the Legate, and bonds the entire army together in communications and tactics."

"Good," Jenker agreed. "That's why you're here. Imperial Land Forces have gotten a little too predictable, Colonel. Perhaps too inbred. I need you to shake them up. As an outsider, you won't be bound by tradition or sacred cows. And you'll have my backing, the Grand Admiral's, and the Emperor himself."

Vo took a deep breath.

He had been expecting those words, dreading them, since the Grand Admiral pulled him away from *Auberon* on what might have been a fool's mission.

He would ask them *why him*, but he knew that answer. Navin had pounded it home, time and again. When push came to shove, Vo always tried to do the right thing, regardless of personal cost. Lead from the front. Inspire the troops.

Do good.

The Fleet Centurion had said that she had originally expected Navin to send JT, Yeoman Jackson Tawfeek, with Moirrey at *Ballard*, once she had explained her needs and the mission. Navin had sent Vo instead.

At *Quinta*, he could have handled it all with a single phone call at any of several points. Instead, he had risked life and limb to prove a point to himself.

Thuringwell. What was there to say? Go learn to ride a horse with crazy cowboys. Help lead a planetary invasion from a saddle. Save the men of the 189th from certain doom, because it was the right thing to do.

And *St. Legier*. He had killed an Emperor. Shot the man in the face, not all that far from here. Saved the Empire itself, considering all the spies and fools that had been rounded up and exiled or executed afterwards.

Grand Admiral had said it. A man he could trust.

A man the entire Empire was willing to trust.

Vojciech *zu* Arlo. Apparently, the craziest son of a bitch that ever lived.

Vo let the breath go slowly. Not deflating. Pushing the air out in a controlled manner, like you did just before pulling the trigger on an impossibly-long, utterly-perfect shot.

"How far do you want to take this, Grand Marshal?" Vo asked, deadly seriousness pushing his voice down to the bottom of the octave.

Jenker's eyes got cagey. Sharp. Violent, but not a violence directed at Vo.

Maybe at the universe itself.

"What did you have in mind, Colonel?" Jenker said. "Pardon me. General *zu* Arlo. There will be a black sword on your collar, instead of that white star, as soon as the paperwork can be processed."

"I have no experience with Imperial Land Forces in the field, save twenty-odd men of the 189th Division," Vo noted. "The Color Guard, at that. If you really want to shake things up, let's not settle for half measures, Grand Marshal."

"Half-measures, Arlo?" Wachturm asked with a touch of trepidation in his voice.

Vo smiled, but kept his sight locked on the soldier. The sailor wouldn't understand most of this, anyway.

"The 189th Division will need to be rebuilt and expanded, per your orders," Vo focused his *intent* on the army man. "Your vision. And you expect me to do it."

Jenker nodded carefully.

"Let's do this the *Aquitaine* way, then," Vo said. "My way. Let's turn them into the *189th Legion*."

Wachturm recoiled in shock, but he was irrelevant to this conversation, except as he might attempt to veto things. If Grand Admiral did that, Vo might just resign his commission and go back to *Auberon*. The Fleet Centurion would always welcome him home, he was pretty sure.

Jenker studied Vo like a mongoose facing an angry cobra.

"Which structure?" Jenker finally asked.

"First Regiment is heavy on veterans, sir," Vo said. "Very heavy, compared to other units I have studied, both current and historical. The 189ᵗʰ was a good place to transfer older soldiers whose expertise was valuable, and shouldn't be wasted in garrison duty when they would make good trainers. And the full unit is understrength today, with around eight hundred men when it should have fifteen hundred on a standard Table of Organization and Equipment."

Vo paused. Jenker nodded for him to continue.

"Turn them into a Rapid Assault Legion," Vo said. "Three Ala of armored rifles, equivalent to three Cohorts of infantry or cavalry. Roughly what you call a battalion. Mechanized infantry don't have to march as much, which is good for older troopers. Attach a heavy armor ala of tanks. Overbuild the artillery battery. Well-suited to a heavy raid, like most battles are fought. If and when we have to actually invade a planet against hostile forces, that force can deal with most things. Fast, mobile, sledgehammer."

"You've put a lot of planning into this," Jenker observed.

"No, sir," Vo countered. "I invaded *Thuringwell* and had a lot of time to think about how we did it, and how we could have done it better. Any other planet probably would have actually had a competent defense force, but *Thuringwell's* old Duke had worked really hard on alienating the population and exploiting them. Last I checked, the place was actually gaining population as former imperial citizens went there to try to make their fortune in the industrial boom Keller and Palsgrave Okafor had unleashed."

Long pause, digesting.

"Food for thought, General," Jenker said.

In his mind, apparently the paperwork had already been approved. Maybe it had, and he just had to write it up and sign it.

"You're going to need regimental commanders you trust," he continued. "Pardon, *Cohort Centurions*, if we do this, which I'm not promising today. Something this big needs feasibility studies and logistics planning, but I like what I hear."

He pointed one blunt finger at Vo like a gun.

"You will need to learn the Imperial way, Arlo," he growled. "So you know how to talk to these men. Command them."

"Sir?" Vo asked.

Somehow, the topic didn't intimidate him, like so many others had over the years.

Was this growing up?

"I'm sending you to Field School with the next class, General," Jenker said. "That's where we train commanders and colonels how to do their job, and what they need to know for the next step up to flag rank. Exposure, both ways. Questions?"

"I'm going to need an assistant, sir," Vo said. "Especially if I'm going to be here for an extended period and back in school again."

"Any preference among the men of the 189th that were here before?" Jenker asked.

"None, sir," Vo said. "Those men already volunteered to go into hell with me leading them."

Jenker nodded and pushed his seat back to rise. Wachturm and Vo did as well.

"General, your first homework assignment is spec'ing me out a Rapid Assault Legion's TOE," Jenker said. "I'll turn that over to logistics and figure out how to implement it while you're in class."

"Yes, sir," Vo nodded, bouncing back.

Last time he had gone back to school, he had accidentally earned the Order of Baudin.

Hopefully, this time he wouldn't have to shoot any pretty girls.

CHAPTER XLI

Jessica carried a mug of fresh coffee with her onto the flag bridge, sippy-cup lid already in place in case things went sideways and they were suddenly in combat without sufficient warning. That was always a risk when invading someone else's star system blind.

Enej and Casey were already at their posts, waiting carefully and digesting whatever tidbits of data were available. There was never much data in JumpSpace, just predictions of where everyone was and when they would land.

Jessica was taking this one extremely slow. She would only get one chance to surprise those bastards. And she owed them a great deal, for *St. Legier.*

She took her spot at the command table, the third point of the triangle. Marcelle was off to one side where Jessica could see her out of the corner of one eye without turning far. Waiting patiently, as always.

The projection in the middle of her table was expanded to a huge scale, compared to normal for operations and maneuvering for battle. They would drop out of JumpSpace at an extreme distance, instead of the normal distance everybody else preferred. Just barely inside the heliopause for *Trusski's* star, a little under one hundred AU out. Beyond a theoretical Kuiper Belt, if this star had one, but well inside any Oort Cloud-analog that might be there.

Jessica's team would end up doing most of the survey work for this entire sector of space, which was frightening, in and of itself. Not even *Fribourg* had come this far out.

But, as Emmerich had told her privately, *Fribourg* had a tendency to gather up big attack fleets and launch themselves at *Samara*, hoping to damage or destroy enough material, and that damnable *Ural Starbase*, to eventually force *Buran* back across the *M'Hanii Gulf.*

Theoretically, a tide could grind a cliff face down, given enough time. But *Buran* kept building their breakwater farther out to sea.

Hopefully, if any spies had warned *Buran* that she was coming, they had reinforced *Samara*, as usual, and were smugly waiting for her to bash her forehead against that impossible anvil.

"Time?" Jessica asked simply.

"Eight minutes to emergence, Fleet Centurion," Casey said precisely. "All hands are at battle stations. Command Centurion Jež has the bridge of *Auberon*. Senior Centurion Vanek has Tactical. Flight Wing is ready to launch."

"Put me through to *da Vinci*," Jessica ordered, more on a whim than anything. They had already gone over it all, several times.

Still, this would be the first time for Ainsley to lead the wing into a true battle, if they had to fight one, and Jessica's first time without *Jouster* out there.

Jessica was amazed at how much that simple change had impacted all her maneuver plans. The man had been insane, but the best pilot anybody knew.

"Flight Wing," *da Vinci*'s growl filled the room.

"You're on general comm, Ainsley," Jessica replied quietly.

"Gotcha," the woman pilot answered, taking some of the edge off her voice. "All seats are hot and ready for crash launch. *Merman* should have everyone live on *II Augusta. Boomerang, Grendel,* and *Black Prince* on *406* all know the party plan."

"And you?" Jessica asked, knowing that *da Vinci* hadn't taken this promotion out of anything except a sense of duty.

Too much like growing up, although the woman was still apparently maintaining a very quiet, successful, low-key relationship with Yan, which spoke well of those two introverts.

"Guns would be nice," *da Vinci* replied. "If this is a long-term gig, you'll need a new scout, because I'm going to have to transfer over to the artillery."

"Acknowledged, *da Vinci*," Jessica agreed. "Make some

recommendations to Denis tomorrow. It's his ship. I'm just the flag officer you haul around."

"As if," *da Vinci* snorted, but remained otherwise quiet.

Jessica cut the line and looked around. Morale was good. People were focused on their tasks. Shortly, the new war would begin.

Or perhaps the new front would open. *Fribourg* had apparently been quietly at war with *Buran* for nearly two generations, but the galactic geography, the distances, were so great that *Aquitaine* had never heard anything.

It hadn't helped that *Ladaux* had been losing their own war until very recently.

"All hands, one minute to emergence," Denis's voice carried from all speakers.

Jessica checked her harness, made sure her coffee mug was secured and the flip-lid down, and took a deep breath.

There were no plans here. No elaborate gaming out all the options, like she had done at *Thuringwell*. The team would probably choke on their tongues in surprise if she told them the truth, but Jessica had settled for a dozen basic fleet maneuvers she could invoke, rather than the thousands of options normally at her fingertips.

Yan Bedrov and that damned training sim against a single foe who could pull impossible jumps and hammer you from a surprise flank.

Still, she had two Expeditionary Cruisers with a monumental amount of ready firepower, in the hands of two of the most dangerous command centurions Jessica knew. Forty-five fighter craft of the new design, slightly heavier on the E-2 strike versions than the C-1 knife-fighters. Gunships and surprise.

And the audacity of her team. To sneak deep into enemy territory and set up a supply base in the deepest darkness.

Emergence.

Jessica wasn't sure if she was growing more sensitive to it as she got older, or her nerves were just so keyed up today. Normally, it was like sliding into a bathtub of warm water. Today, it was the cold-water pool after a sauna, a snap that ran down her spine like electricity.

The projection came live as signals got processed. Every ship was as dark as they could run, relying on passive scanners so that nobody closer in to the star realized they were hosting burglars. If everything went well, tight-beam lasers would begin to establish a usable comm network shortly, but for right now, it was just *Auberon* trusting luck and the combat wing: *VI Ferrata, VI Victrix, II Augusta, CA-264, CE-401, CE-402, CE-403, CS-404, CM-405,* and *CP-406,* plus *GSC Ballard.*

Pitifully feeble, to take on an entire star empire run by a *Sentient* computer system. More than enough to overwhelm the sort of patrol forces she expected in a forgotten corner like *Trusski.*

Stars representing the rest of the squadron began to populate a secondary, minimum-range, projection. This hop had been short, so everyone was pretty accurate for time lag and spacing. *VI Victrix* at the van. *VI Ferrata* at the rear. *Auberon* behind *II Augusta* in the middle. Six corvettes in a long, three-dimensional, hexagonal shape when viewed from the side, escorting from the front, back, top and bottom, where all the broadsides would range best. Maybe she could entice some unwary *Buran* commander to attempt her flank, wherein every one of her warships could roll suddenly and bring the entire squadron's firepower to bear.

Ballard and *CP-406* well off to port and starboard, respectively. With *CS-405,* Jessica's scout-equipped corvette, up front, all three vessels began to cast their extra-sensitive noses to the wind.

Nothing.

Jessica knew that dwarf planets and iceballs would start to show up on the projection soon, as the scans identified them against the background noise, making the next jump that much safer. An Oort cloud was never dense enough to kick a ship out of jump, but it frequently played merry hell with terminal navigation, especially when you were trying to land so close to it, instead of blasting right past it. Deeper into the star system to get to the warm worlds.

But they were alone, as near as she could tell. *Fribourg's* navigation notes suggested that *Buran* tended to put their scanner network at around ten to fifteen AU from the star. Somewhere around the orbit of forgotten Saturn, back in the lost home system, still used as baseline for so much of a star system's scale.

And, while *Buran* tended to come into a system from the ecliptic north, and *Fribourg* on the system plane, Jessica had brought the group in at a declination of -63 degrees. Just to find the quietest hiding spot in the cupboard. It had apparently worked, as nobody suddenly lit them up with scanners or guns.

Ballard had the best scanners, so she was tasked with mapping *Trusski's* orbital traffic. Difficult from here, but not impossible, and Jessica was in no hurry. *CP-406* and *CS-405* were watching the close neighborhood.

After ten minutes, the chances began to look better that they had picked the lock on the front door. They could never completely relax, not with sharks that could appear out of the darkness with no warning, but the team didn't need Jessica looking over their shoulder while they worked. It was already fraught enough out here.

Jessica grabbed her mug, detached her harness, and opened a line to the bridge.

"Jež here," Denis said, glancing up into the camera from whatever screen he had been focused on.

"You have the flag, Denis," she said. "Annihilate anybody that gets close enough to scan us. But be prepared to run like hell if you need to. We won't win this thing on this pass, but we could lose it today."

"Roger that," and he was gone.

Jessica nodded to Marcelle and her flag centurions. Enej and Casey would remain, but their jobs would be taking notes at this point, unless something went horribly wrong.

And Jessica would only be two doors away if that happened.

A day of sneaking. Scouting. Laying the groundwork for future endeavors, future missions.

Jessica wasn't sure how to classify it, but she probably didn't need to. They had succeeded. Space was empty and quiescent, this far away from any star, if you made no noise. She had spent the day comfortable and cozy in her cabin, waiting.

CS-405 had located an iceball in the darkness, a dwarf planet that appeared to be an even mix of slush and rock, big enough that the entire squadron could lurk in its shadow, relative to *Trusski*. As long as emissions were kept at a strict minimum, none of the other scanners, the ones with sufficient parallax, should have any reason to look this direction.

Trusski itself was humble to look at from space. Moirrey's homeworld, *Ramsey* in *Lincolnshire*, had more orbital hardware, and *Lincolnshire's* capital world was a poor place, compared to anywhere in *Aquitaine*. *Trusski* had one station in orbit that looked big enough to be a shipping warehouse, but not a major industrial facility. Weather and communication satellites, broadcasting navigation warnings to anyone that would listen. The familiar constellation of three beacons marking the poles and equator.

Jessica had even read today's forecast for Taymyr, the capital city. Gray and hazy this morning, warming from fourteen degrees all the way up to perhaps twenty, once the sun burned the clouds off. Rather idyllic, but beside the point.

Jessica felt like a Visigoth, hiding at the edge of the woods, preparing to swoop down and pillage some unsuspecting town. At least *Thuringwell* had maintained some level of military defenses, though pitiful, the result of a cheap duke. *Trusski* appeared to have nothing more than a pair of rescue cutters, on call but unmanned, in case of an emergency aboard on orbiting ship. All the other scans and logs suggested nothing else.

Did these people not realize there was a war on?

Jessica pinched the bridge of her nose and took a deep breath. She still had another eight minutes before her meeting with the command centurions, but she didn't expect the extra time to change anything.

Trusski was either as civilian a world as had ever existed, or the deepest, most cunning trap she had ever encountered. She would bet on the former.

2218 Svati Prime. November 13, 392. The day before the infamous Jessica Keller had etched their previously-unknown names into the history books.

First paving stone on *The Long Raid*.

A peaceful system, politely ignored as a military target because both *Fribourg* and *Aquitaine* had maintained the *Cahllepp Frontier* as a quiet border. Right up until the day Nils Kasum told her to light that frontier on fire. *M'Hanii* was behind her, as galactic navigation went. *Samara* somewhere out front, closer to *St. Legier*, the breakwater thrust out into the sea against the raging storm that was Emmerich Wachturm's wrath.

Jessica rose from her comfy chair, slipped her feet into her shoes, and crossed the hallway to the flag bridge.

Enej and Casey were at their regular stations. The other points of her flag triangle.

Yan Bedrov was here too, seated near Marcelle off to one side, rather than down in the library or engineering, as was his usual wont. Jessica needed his expertise for this. He smiled as she entered, and raised his mug of coffee in salute. Obviously, Marcelle approved of the man enough to make him coffee. Nobody else was allowed to touch her tools.

A few moments after Jessica came Torsten Wald, dressed in the blues he would normally have worn on his own bridge, had the world turned out differently. Jessica wondered what sort of man Torsten might have become. She doubted it would be anything like the one who took a jumpseat next to Marcelle opposite Yan. This one had learned to relax in ways she never saw in senior Imperial officers.

He smiled back at her and took a deep breath, the moment weighing upon them all.

Faces were coming up live on the projection as Jessica took her seat. Probably pinged by Enej or Casey the moment the door opened. Her people were good at anticipating, executing.

Freelancing a war went against everything she had spent a career doing, but it was the right thing here. Play the tune by ear, letting local circumstances dictate needs.

Tango, where someone else took the lead, rather than *Valse d'Glaive*, where she pushed. Hopefully, the gods, and Emmerich, would appreciate the irony.

"Yan, Torsten, join me here please," Jessica said. "I'll want your expertise for this as well."

So then, let us tango.

She found Denis among those projected and he grinned as they made eye contact. Of all of them, he was probably the one that knew her best.

Kigali. Always with a breezy smile close at hand, but today he looked like a stern patriarch from a vid. The man still didn't think the other corvette commanders were up to his standards, but, then again, was anybody but Alber'?

d'Maine. The serenity of a Kodiak at rest. Prepared to unleash the berserker, but constrained, for now. He was likely hoping for another battle like *Second Thuringwell*, itself a martial epic for the ages.

One by one, she studied the others.

Calm anticipation.

They had spent a year planning for this, and a lifetime preparing. Today, she would probably disappoint those who had not spent enough time studying her campaigns.

Strategic offense, tactical defense. Force your opponent to react, then pick the ground where he has to come to you to fight. Uphill, in the rain and mud.

Agincourt, hopefully, rather than *Thermopylae* or the *Pons Sublicius*.

She nodded at Enej, and he projected the local system for the five of them. Aboard the other vessels, they would see the same, albeit on a smaller scale. Each of them, however, only needed to solve one piece of the puzzle.

One inhabited planet, with a larger moon and a smaller one, neither big enough to be anything more than a spot to land and perhaps conduct some science, both lacking atmosphere. *Ballard* had detected no motion on either.

"Good morning," Jessica began. "I haven't seen anything here to suggest a defensive fortification worth mentioning. What they do have is a *petit* maritime rescue force, none of which appear to have even as much firepower as one of our fighter craft."

She paused and let that sink in. Probably, the rest were just as surprised as she had been. A few would be offended at that prospect, but they were already like that.

"With that in mind, I'm planning to leave the cruisers out here," Jessica continued. "Drop down and say hello with just *Auberon* and the corvettes. We can't really isolate a system like this unless we work really hard at it, and I don't want the squadron strung out all over the system when someone finally comes to show us the door. Plus, we didn't bring Fourth Saxon with us this time, so I'm only planning on leaving a small security force on the ground, purely for diplomatic purposes. This won't be our base of operations, as Whughy's team is handling that, but I want this to be the place where they have to come out to fight us. I plan to make them chase us all over the sector, just like we did to the Red Admiral, back in the day. Questions?"

"Demonstrations?" Command Centurion Maikop asked from the bridge of *CE-403*.

He was generally the quiet and scholarly type, compared to the others present. More like Jessica in that way. And he had obviously put some time into studying what she had done on *The Long Raid*. 2218 Svati Prime had been a demonstration, rather than an occupation.

What we could have done, had we chosen.

"Not unless provoked," she replied. "There's nothing here that qualifies as a legitimate military target, and I'm already feeling like a Visigoth, just watching them from the sky."

That got a chuckle. They had obviously all had similar thoughts.

"Runners?" d'Maine growled.

"Assume they'll head straight to *Samara* to call for help," Jessica ordered. "Calculate minimum transit and response times, based on everything we know, and go to high alert. We'll move off and hide. I'd like to do to them what they did to me at *St. Legier*. The whole reason we're here is to spall off a chunk of their sector forces so we can isolate them. Because if they bring too much over here, I'm happy to take a run at *Samara* and that Starbase, and see what an Expeditionary Cruiser can do."

Alber's hard smile lit up the screen. Komal MacInerney had taken over as his First/Tactical Officer after Cruz Bösch died at *Second Thuringwell*. He had probably tasked her with exactly that scenario.

How to kill a Starbase with just an Expeditionary Cruiser. And surprise.

"Yan," Jessica continued, turning to spike the man with her eyes. "What's going to be the best way to engage anything that comes out, given just this force and not the cruisers?"

He paused, turning his eyes inward. Had he been born on *Ladaux*, she had no doubts he might have been one of the other Command Centurions here today. Although he probably would have turned out more like Moirrey and ended up in a research think tank on *Anameleck Prime*.

"All the corvettes should tune their Type-3 beams for short range now and leave them that way," he offered. "Except *CA-264*. You'll want one other ship that can tag someone at Primaries range, besides *Auberon*. At short range, the Type-3 hits like a primary, but at a shorter effective range than a Type-2. Anything past that, my granddaughter hits harder."

The others chuckled.

"Why isn't the Type-1-Pulse going to be sufficient for that distance?" Command Centurion Glenn asked in a thoughtful tone.

Bedrov turned deadly serious, like she had seen in his face above *St. Legier*, waiting for that raider to come after her aboard the *Blackbird*.

"One of these days, one of those bastards is going to figure out that he can drop out of jump on top of you and fire a broadside of missiles that have only begun to accelerate when they slam into your hull," Yan said. "That's why *zu* Kermode designed the Type-1-Pulse for me. Knife-fighting in starships. And next time I talk to the Grand Admiral, I've got another set of designs for him to build for us, to surprise that next bastard that tries it, once they get a taste of the bubble gun."

That got another laugh.

The Reversed Field, Pinch, Plasma Implosion Generator.

The Bubble Gun.

Jessica looked forward to watching the first time a *Buran* warship met the highest form of Moirrey's art. Almost as much as she looked forward to whatever else Yan had up his sleeve.

But that was a task for the two cruisers. Nobody else had a bubble gun, *Il Augusta* replacing that weapons system with space for more fighters in her belly, and *Auberon* still being the antique among this force. Plus, the generators and magnetic control fields for the device were almost as big as a corvette.

Jessica made a mental note to ask Yan about a ship, destroyer-sized, give or take, that was just a bubble gun and engines. It would make a lovely siege weapon, but that was about it. Cheap to build, but capable of inflicting a staggering amount of damage on a fixed target. Say, a Starbase located at *Samara*, or the fabled *Ninagirsu*, across *M'Hanii*.

But what was this war, if not an effort to surprise that damnable *Sentience* with all the crazy things humans were willing to do, to escape his eternal control?

"Captain Wald?" Jessica asked, turning from Yan's fierceness to Torsten's beatific calm. "Your thoughts?"

"*Buran* rarely initiates," he explained. "If you trespass, as we are about to do, they will warn you off, moving closer until somebody fires a shot at them. Then they will turn into a pack of rabid wolves, tearing and shredding anything they can get their teeth into. They also rarely attack our systems, preferring to slowly colonize empty worlds. *Fribourg* has never attempted to destroy such a colony from orbit, and even *Thuringwell* showed how difficult it can be to occupy a world with any meaningful, resentful population. I do not expect much from today but that they will take your measure and then bring enough to overwhelm you, once it becomes clear that we are an invasion force."

Jessica nodded. She had spoken extensively with him on this topic over the last year. And other topics…but there was this war to undertake first.

"Anything else?" she continued, circling the faces until she came back to Kigali. Silence. "Set your engineers to tuning your offensive systems. In twelve hours, *Auberon* and escorts will go to JumpSpace and drop down on *Trusski*. The cruisers, including *Ballard*, will stay out here and watch. Be prepared to intervene on our behalf if it becomes necessary, but also understand that I have no intension of fighting a pitched battle for this system, today or tomorrow. We will draw them in, set them up, snipe them from the corners. You have your orders."

CHAPTER XLII

DATE OF THE REPUBLIC JULY 2, 400 CA-264,
TRUSSKI SYSTEM

orvette/Assault. Those words summed up his place in this universe. His dream. His masterpiece of art, awaiting a wall suitable from which to hang.

CR-264 had been the last of the old warriors in service. Compact but deadly. They had replaced the design with the destroyer, bigger and more flexible, but in doing so had given up that thing that made the Cutters so effective. Like being able to kick a *Fribourg* battleship in the shins, as he flew by close enough to throw things at it. Like sauntering into the wall of Imperial missiles at *Petron*, slaughtering them without let or hindrance.

Tomas Kigali found *RAN Ballard* on his boards, tucked up and behind the other three cruisers in the shadow of the little world behind which they were hiding.

A cruiser, yes. Big and powerful and capable of tremendous feats of survey navigation. Impressive and elegant in her lines, but very much was a civilian in this war.

At barely an eighth *Ballard*'s displacement, *CA-264* was more than a match for firepower. And *CA-264* could do something that was simply beyond *Ballard*.

Kill things.

Not that it was likely in the next three hours, but you never knew when all hell was going to break loose. Jessica seemed to summon the crazies to her like a witch, but she always had him and Robbie and Alber' close at hand.

Not today, though. Just Kigali and his assistants: three escorts, a scout, a mine-hunter, and a patrol.

Most of the doom-dealing would fall on his shoulders, if there were to be any.

Tomas Kigali smiled like a crocodile.

Senior Centurion Arsen Lam looked up and grinned. He had been with Tomas since he was first commissioned, and then exiled to a forgotten boat on a irrelevant frontier. Today, he was still handling the Tactical duties, but now they were escorting Jessica and her team.

Kigali would have said leading, but *CA-264*'s spot was in the tail, with *CS-405* up in the van. Still, everyone listened to him when it came to maneuvering and combat.

Centurion Aki Ridwana Ali arched a chiseled, delicate eyebrow at the two of them, as though restraining herself from rolling her eyes at them. Again. Ali had worked her way up from an enlisted punk, and, like Tomas, had found her spot, her destiny, flying this ship.

At least First Lord Kasum had made good his promise to hold these crews together, for as long as their members desired. Tomas couldn't imagine trying to break in a new team in the middle of a new war.

"What evil are you two up to now?" she asked.

"*First Ballard,*" Tomas replied.

"Think it will work here?" Arsen cocked his head slightly. After this many years together, they could almost communicate telepathically.

"Not today," Tomas said. "Thinking about the next time, when some *Buran* badass is sitting deep in orbit, thinking he's safe from us because our JumpSails keep us from pulling his sort of tricks."

"Think the kids can handle it?" Lam pursued the topic.

"No," Tomas concluded. "But let me talk to Jessica. Imagine a jousting run that's just us leading Alber' in, full bloody tilt, red-line on the sails until we drop out, then slingshot down and out, with something like two, two and a half hours to get everything tuned back up to make our getaway. At *Ballard,* we were trying to slow down."

"Drive by with rotten tomatoes, boss," Aki observed tartly.

"Us, sure," he agreed. "Imagine that fool opening fire on us as we blow by, and then Alber' shows up a minute later and catches him looking the wrong way and hammers him with everything he's got."

"*First Ballard,*" Arsen called it. "Pretty messy."

"Yeah, but a lot of that was a heavy destroyer being too close to a light cruiser as Alber' killed it." Kigali said. "Plus, *Rajput* had already been beaten bloody before that. This will be Type-4's and plasma bubbles, followed by every other beam he's got, in a raking pass."

"Think they'll fall for it?" Aki asked.

"*Auberon's* here," Arsen said. "That's going to get someone's attention. If nobody knows about the cruisers, they might do something stupid."

"One can only hope," Tomas said.

He checked his boards one last time as he tuned out the ongoing commentary from the other two. Too much *maybe* stirred into this pot to get really tactical, other than to make plans, like Jessica always did. Plus, the clock was counting down.

He opened the comm that connected him to the others. Denis would listen in, but this was going to be Tomas's show, at least for now.

"Escort Team, this is Kigali," he ordered in a stern voice, the old man of experience and gravity. "Begin your acceleration to engagement profile. Maintain formation and prepare for transit orders from the flag."

Auberon would be doing the same, but Kigali wanted everyone already under a head of steam when they went in, so they could emerge hot. He had the tail-end slot, so *CA-264* would be the one maneuvering against the bulk of the Star Controller when they got there.

Acknowledgements from everyone, including Denis. Just waiting for Jessica now.

"Squadron, this is Keller aboard *Auberon*. I have the flag," she said in that low, serious tone she affected when giving orders. "All ships transit now."

CA-264 leapt into hyperspace like a porpoise playing in the surf, leaving *RAN Ballard* out here to keep watch and be safe.

There was a war to fight.

CHAPTER XLIII

Amala chose to look on it as a promotion, but she wasn't sure her team would ever let her live it down. At least the Command Centurion had told her specifically to pursue this project when she suggested it.

Alber' d'Maine was not normally a man given to scholarly recreations. But to him, it was a better way to fight the war.

So be it. Amala Bhattacharya, warrior diplomat.

It had started as an itch she couldn't reach, no matter how double-jointed she was in the flesh. Amala had grown up hearing all the major, surviving dialects of Chinese, and had learned the written in its various forms as well. Discovered a knack for languages along the way, but linguistics had never captured her soul.

The intel they captured at *FR-0093416-B* had been a weird mixture of Chinese-style ideograms and Romanized letters that made no sense. Why would you communicate that way, even as a computer?

And then she woke up from a dead sleep one night with an epiphany.

Your master was a computer, but its language wasn't one of the major trade languages that had survived in the rest of the inhabited galaxy.

Oh, sure, they spoke Chinese and English well enough when they were dealing with *Fribourg* invaders. With those two languages, you covered a good chunk of the galaxy anyway, and Bulgarian wasn't that common, closer in to the galactic core from *Aquitaine*.

But those folks spoke something else at home. And nobody had thought to mention that in the briefing materials. Maybe they didn't know?

Why did you need complex communications, if you were just going to be shooting at someone? Guns and missiles were pretty standard, and spoke every language.

So Amala had dove face first into the encyclopedia and read. And dug. And questioned.

Seven major trade languages had been standard when the galaxy died. Everyone thought in those terms, because it was easier that way. English, Spanish, Hindi, Chinese, Arabic, Kiswahili, and Bulgarian.

In her research, Amala had discovered that over a thousand distinct tongues had been known on the day the Homeworld was annihilated.

A thousand?

Some of them had been ancient, pre-dating technology itself, like one colony way the hell off spinward that had spoken primarily Tulalip in those days. Other tongues had been weird amalgamations of other languages, like Ancient Maltese, the result of two or three primary colonist groups all hitting a planet at the same time and creating something entirely new because they all needed to be able to order curry and hákarl from the corner shop.

FR-0093416-B spoke Mongolian. And a weird derivative of it, heavily influenced by Buryat, with lots of Ancient Russian thrown in. Nobody else she knew of did, but the code was there. The giveaway had been those three extra characters. Everyone had assumed them to be symbols of some sort, when they were just part of the language itself, if you knew which language it was.

After that, Amala had been utterly amazed at how comprehensive *Auberon's* files went on languages. How many different programs and videos there were to teach you, both written and spoken, in all the known dialects.

Most of that, she presumed, was the Alexandria Station Library on *Ballard*. Those people took knowledge seriously. That included dead and forgotten languages, as well as ones that had been invented for various reasons like vids, and had nothing to do with geography.

So she had learned Mongolian. *Buran* Mongolian, to be specific.

Today, she found herself on the flag bridge of *Auberon*, off to one side, watching the Fleet Centurion and her team work. Keller was so much different than d'Maine, but that same fire was there, when she looked for it. Others here had it as well.

Emergence.

Screens lit up with the blue and green sphere that was *Trusski*, hanging quietly against the local arm of the galaxy in the near distance. Technically, this system was part of that same arm, but it was so far out into the darkness by itself, a thumb stuck into the black water, that it barely counted.

Amala wondered what nights on the surface would be like, when it was total darkness, save for those two tiny moons overhead. And what it would do to local culture and mythos, not to have stars in the sky for half the year.

Keller looked over at her now. Amala felt like a prize pig on display for the judges. Hopefully, there wasn't a butcher hiding behind the curtains with a bolt gun in one hand.

The Fleet Centurion smiled. Some of the woman's warmth, her tenacity, seemed to float over and descend across Amala's shoulders like a rain-proof cloak. She would need that.

Warrior/Diplomat.

My own, personal war.

The screens were big and quiet. Nobody else was in orbit with them, suddenly lighting engines to attack or flee. The locals barely even seemed to notice, but there were only fourteen dots in orbit, not counting three stations, one of which was a dead-perfect copy of the one she had boarded already in another system.

No missiles suddenly launched from the surface of the planet, or one of the stations.

Nothing.

Keller pressed a button on one of her boards. The shipwide bell sounded. Everyone was already at action stations. This was the boss getting ready to tell you something, so put the gun or the fork down and pay attention.

Alber' used the damned thing very infrequently. He spoke with the big guns.

"Squadron, this is Keller aboard *Auberon*. I have the flag," she stated in her stiff, formal voice.

Amala figured she was speaking to the Senate at this moment. And the Emperor. And to most of the galaxy, on both sides.

This was Fleet Centurion Jessica Keller. She did that.

"Bridge, load the declaration device for deployment," she ordered in a stern voice.

A few moments passed. Formality, anyway. They had set everything up hours ago.

"Flag, this is Jež," the local command centurion replied, almost as formal. "Package is loaded and ready to fire."

"Casey," Keller continued. "Put me on system-wide."

Amala watched the princess reach out to tap the surface of her board. A different tone sounded this time, a deep bell chiming. The princess nodded.

"People of *Trusski*, this is Admiral of the Red Jessica Keller, representing the Imperial Navy of *Fribourg*. Your system is officially declared a war zone, subject to the published *Laws of Recognized Warfare* and to local rules of engagement that will be promulgated in short order."

Short pause. Letting the locals absorb that the great enemy had chosen their world, their lives, for a sudden demonstration. Barbarians at the gates, to use Keller's imagery.

"We are about to fire a single missile into your atmosphere," Keller continued. "It is not a weapon. I repeat, this is not a weapon. It is the formal declaration of war as delivered by a *Fetial* and presents no risk to inhabitants on the ground. When that task is done, we will communicate with the government of *Trusski* on a formal basis. All hands, stand by."

Amala blinked in surprise when Keller unhooked her straps and stood up, gesturing the rest to do the same. A moment of slightly noisy chaos before everyone did.

"In the name of the Emperor of *Fribourg*, and the Republican Senate of *Aquitaine*, under the watchful eye of *Janus Quirinus*, I declare that a state of war exists between our peoples," Keller intoned with gravity like the surface of a neutron star. "Deploy the package."

Everything was so silent that Amala felt the launch mechanisms nearby slam Centurion Kermode's orbital bomb out into space, where it would light small engines and begin a hard deorbit.

Fleet Centurion Keller gestured everyone back to their seats. Someone pushed a button to cut the comm. Probably Zivkovic, the older Flag Centurion, from the serious look on his face when he spoke next.

"Comm is closed," he said. "The missile is away and flying true. I now have a gentleman on audio channel seventy-three who claims to speak for the *Khan* of *Trusski*. Whatever that is."

Keller turned and gestured Amala to move to the big table at the middle of the room, from where she had been off to one side with the others who were currently only observers.

"Put him on conference mode," Keller ordered as Amala sat.

"Admiral Keller, this is Ve Gayav Chuluun Gan," a man's smooth voice came out of the speakers. "As a Scholar, I speak for Ul Banop Cheani Yuur, *Minister of the Eighth Rank* and *Khan* of *Trusski* under the eternal vigilance of *Buran* and *The Holding*."

Keller had spoken to the locals in English, so the local had replied in the same language. It had seemed a safe bet, given its prevalence, farther in. Amala could tell it was not his native tongue. He had a hard time keeping his words a-tonal, and was obviously translating the words in his head and speaking them slowly and carefully.

Accent was pretty good, though. Must have a lot of practice yelling at Imperial merchants trying to make a quick florin smuggling.

Keller leaned close enough to murmur.

"You ready?" she asked. "We can always do this the standard way."

Amala shook her head.

"They want formal," Amala replied, thinking back to the notes she had devoured, in preparation.

The hints and suggestions that were never really spelled out, maybe because nobody had given it a lot of thought.

The Governor had not challenged them himself. He had sent someone who considered *Scholar* to be enough of a title. Read between the lines.

Keller smiled. That look reminded Amala of Alber' at that very moment when the first beams cut loose.

"Give 'em hell, Amala," Keller whispered.

Amala took a breath. She couldn't help the way her head came up and her chin jutted out. Shoulders back, vertebrae popping.

Formidable.

"This is Senior Centurion Amala Bhattacharya, representing Admiral Keller, Sri Ve," she called in a slow cadence, the sort of intonation she would use on freshly-commissioned troops, just arrived from ground school. "Do you understand the *Laws of Recognized Warfare?*"

Let him chew on that. Nobody ever really followed them, but they were there. And honored enough that it had provided a framework into which to stuff more than a century of warfare between *Fribourg* and *Aquitaine*.

"You trespass, Scholar Bhattacharya," the man answered. "You threaten our world without provocation. One hopes that your weapon is not such a thing, because we lack the capability to destroy it before it wreaks whatever mischief you have planned, so any casualties will be on your conscience. *The Eternal* will be notified of your crimes, and will come for you in due order."

Yes. English was definitely his second language for the man. Maybe third. It was like he was firing the words into a microphone, letting a computer translate things back, and then converting that to poetry before he transmitted his responses.

Not bad for someone who probably never expected a day like today. Amala had spent weeks talking to a computer and learning to think in Mongolian.

"The orbital package will overfly your capital city at an altitude of five thousand meters before it deploys the secondary engagement system," Amala said. "From there, it will target a large park, a green area located close to your planetary hall of government. The secondary package will freefall to approximately one thousand meters before it deploys a parachute and guidance system that will bring it down at a speed slow enough that anyone on the ground will be able to avoid it on landing."

"What is the object that will land, Scholar Bhattacharya?" he asked.

"It is a javelin, Scholar Ve," she said. "With a steel tip and a shaft made of wild olive wood. Dipped in blood, as the ancients commanded."

Long pause.

Looking something up furiously, translating words. Translating cultures.

Translating history.

"Your admiral invoked *Janus Quirinus*, the Sabine God of War," the man said finally. "She also used the ancient, Latin term *Fetial* to describe your mission. The Khan orders you to formally assert such a thing in his Court. To present yourself and your credentials as a Scholar before *The Eternal*, that we may know you to be a civilized people. To know whether you are worthy of our respect and esteem."

Amala gulped past a dry tongue. Combat had never gotten her this focused, this hyped on adrenaline.

What was it the ancient general had said? *War is the extension of diplomacy by other means.*

Amala looked over at the Fleet Centurion for the first time since this had started. It was like waking up from a strange dream and finding yourself in your own body again.

Keller nodded with a broad smile. Amala felt it uplift her soul.

"*You will inform the Khan that I will join him presently,*" Amala replied. In Mongolian, rather than English, adding weight to her command.

The slightest gasp at the other end of the line, followed by the sort of dead silence you got when someone hit the mute button so they could argue without strangers listening.

Amala smiled, ever so briefly.

"There is a landing field on the northern edge of Taymyr," Ve finally came back on the line, his voice now a shade raspy and a shade uncertain. "If you land there, you will be met by a diplomatic reception."

"So noted," Amala replied serenely.

Keller signaled one of her people and the line went dead with a descending tone.

"What did you say to him, there at the end?" Keller asked.

Amala told her, and the whole room chuckled. What was the Fleet Centurion's legend, if not audacity itself?

Keller fixed her with a hard eye.

"I can offer you nothing in the way of support here, Bhattacharya," she said. "We're going to stay for a bit, and then withdraw somewhere else. I won't tell you where, so you don't have to lie to them. We will be back, but you'll be pretty much on your own. If they decide to kill you, all I can promise is that I'll burn their damned city down afterwards."

Not the worst epitaph. Hopefully, unnecessary.

And this was a promotion.

If she survived.

CHAPTER XLIV

Jessica watched her boards like a mother hen, but there was nothing to do at this point. One standard Administrative shuttle separating from the larger dot that was *Auberon*, immediately initiating a deorbit burn. It didn't even make any noise leaving, not having to be fired out of a tube, as were fighters and missiles.

Text scrolled across the bottom of her screen, because that was how Command Flight Centurion Iskra Vlahovic was. Never use a radio if a marquee would do. Some days, Jessica wanted to confiscate Iskra's keyboard, just to make her speak out loud.

Probably doomed to failure. Iskra would learn sign language and everything would suddenly be video, or something.

Stubborn did not run three meters thick on that flight deck. Not at all.

Bhattacharya and party away.

Not that it was much of a party. One of Amala's men with her as a bodyguard. Another as a specialist. A few others thrown in, more as shuttle ballast than anything else.

Senior Centurion Bhattacharya would be on her own very shortly.

Jessica looked up and caught both Enej and Casey studying her.

"Anything?" she asked, aware that they had been watching and listening for the better part of two hours.

Nothing had changed.

"Ground control sensors are tracking her and us," Casey said. "Civilian system with a soft, communications-only lock on everyone in orbit. We're not special."

How to best level a calculated insult at an invader? Ignore her completely. Go on with your day as if nothing has happened. Possibly hand them a freshly-baked cookie when the tray came out of the oven, and pat them on the head.

It had that feel to it.

Jessica could imagine an Imperial squadron blowing something up right now for no better reason than they felt insulted by such treatment and needed to throw their weight around. Wanted to provoke someone.

But all the intelligence had said that *Buran* only *responded*. Rarely initiated. Hopefully, she wasn't reading too much into that. *Thuringwell's* population on the fateful day had been one-fiftieth of *Trusski's* today, and she didn't have a wall of Assault Carriers bringing in ground Legions to try to occupy or pacify the planet.

It would have been a stupid idea anyway. She wasn't staying here any longer than she needed to, in order to make a point.

Draw them in and make them dance to her tune. *2218 Svati Prime* writ large.

One small force, relatively, making a larger one react and maneuver.

Salamanca and the Iron Duke, on a galactic scale.

If she could pull it off.

Or at least give Emmerich Wachturm a year of space to build up new forces, and to purge the fleet of the traitors that had almost given *Buran* the entire empire on a plate a year ago.

"Enej, you have the flag," Jessica said, rising and stretching the kinks out of her back and legs.

She had been tenser than she thought, waiting while nothing happened.

"You know the general plan," she continued as he nodded up at her. "No later than twenty-four hours from now, we will withdraw from orbit and meet up with the rest of the squadron, and possibly the fleet, depending. Don't be afraid to run at the slightest need. Denis already knows that, as does Kigali, so they won't argue with you. We can always bring Robbie, Alber', and Tamara down to engage later."

"Roger that," he said, touching tabs on his board.

Jessica nodded to Marcelle and headed for the hatch. There was nothing she could do at this point but paperwork, the never-ending battle. Either they had surprise and could move at their own pace, or all hell was about to break loose. If that happened, Yan would get to see firsthand if all his design decisions had been good.

Jessica would be happy not knowing. Not today.

Amala was about to land in the lion's den.

CHAPTER XLV

Amala had never really owned any fancy civilian clothes. Academy and Navy both issued you what you needed for formalwear, and she hadn't been much into dressing up, even as a kid. Not that there had been any money for it on *Huldra,* beyond the occasional present from a grandma in the post. A decade plus in the fleet as a security specialist hadn't changed her outlook, as far as she could tell.

No, that took Keller. And *zu* Kermode. And Keller's assistant, Marcelle Travere.

Dangerous people.

Amala would have happily gone down there in a dress uniform. Moirrey wouldn't allow it.

That was how everyone referred to the engineer. Not *zu* Kermode. Or even Centurion Kermode.

Just *Moirrey.* Occasionally *Lady Moirrey,* to needle her.

Once Keller had set her mind on this course of action, the first thing Moirrey had done was take Amala's measurements, then produced a new outfit the tiny woman referred to as *Diplomat-At-Arms.*

Amala had to admit it looked good. Long, baggy pants in sleek, black twill guaranteed to be waterproof and outlive everything else she owned. Amala could barely see her boots below the hem, rather than having them bloused at the calf. Long sleeved pullover out of a stretchy material that moved every direction Amala demanded. Also midnight black for the body, with raglan sleeves in a medium gray.

Over everything, a shin-length tabard as wide as her hips in dark gray, hooked at the waist and breast but falling free and open on the sides with long, monk-style sleeves that fell past her fingertips when she stood still. Embroidery on all the edges was done in the exact forest green that had been Amala's life in uniform for a decade and a half. A tooled leather belt in white to hold it together, but not to attach a sword or holster.

That was on purpose.

Amala thought it was a stupid design, but she was apparently alone in that opinion, as everyone else loved it.

A cloak completed the outfit. Seriously, the woman had made her a cloak. Mottled black with a design pattern Moirrey had called *paisley*, apparently scorched into the felt somehow, with a dove-gray lining that felt like silk. It even had a hood to pull up against rain, or in case Amala suddenly found herself trapped in a fairy tale with a wolf who needed his ass kicked.

A messenger bag in real leather: a waterproof, fold-over satchel in matte black that held actual paper, like some primitive lawyer, or something.

It was an impressive outfit, Amala had to grant.

Diplomat-At-Arms.

But then Moirrey added the second surprise. Amala had already felt like she was in a fairy tale at that point. With a Fairy Godmother.

And then she met the second Fairy Godmother.

First-Rate-Spacer Vibol Harmaajärvi. Lean, erect, fussy. Old enough to be her father, he had been in the navy since before she was born. With skin as translucent as parchment and a smile that wanted to twinkle at you.

Amala hadn't even been aware that there was a military school designation for it until she met Harmaajärvi.

Tailor.

A man who specialized in clothes. Mending them. Adjusting them as people changed over time. Making them for a diplomat assigned to *Trusski*, one who didn't come with a formal wardrobe, having lived in uniform.

Keller expected her to go down there, to live, in mufti. So she had sent in an expert. One vouched for by Keller, *zu* Kermode, and Travere. With threats that they would hold her personally accountable if something happened to him, as he had apparently worked his magic on the Fleet Centurion as well.

Harmaajärvi had a wicked gleam in his eyes right now, staring at her across the aisle as the shuttle worked its way down to final approach. Not like he was envisioning her naked. Or rather, he was, and was figuring out how to fix that.

Fix her.

All her life, Amala had been average. Average height for her family and the rest of humanity, average build that only looked better as a result of the amount of time she spent in the gym and training floor. Average looks, with dark hair, dark eyes, skin darker than average for most of *Aquitaine* and lighter than many of her relatives.

And a beak of a nose that every man and woman noticed. Amala had occasionally considered getting a new one, but that felt too much like admitting they were right about her. The whispers that she was homely and should settle for whatever man would have her.

Whatever life would give her.

Never.

Amala wasn't sure she was ready to be *stunning*. Harmaajärvi had threatened exactly that.

The gear *she* was bringing along was pretty sparse. She wasn't expecting combat, so had no weapons, no armor, no field gear. She had Pinchon along for that. He *was* a weapon.

She was a diplomat.

Harmaajärvi had brought with him two meter-cube shipping containers, one with all his tools, the other with nothing but bolts of fabric, personally approved by the three ringleaders.

Ye gods, what had she gotten herself into?

A screen showed the ground coming up to meet them. Amala could see landing pits formed by ram-packing a circle of soil before raising an earthen berm around it, mostly as protection if something failed on landing. *Aquitaine* did it with a leveled, gravel-covered field kilometers across, with only passenger liners on regular runs having dedicated debarkation facilities. If you were lucky, the navy might park your shuttle under an awning to keep the rain and snow off.

Here, the shuttle was nosing in to land in a bullseye that could have easily held a DropShip with space left over for a handful of admin shuttles like the one bringing her to *Trusski*. The screen showed something she might charitably call a limousine, along with a few other enclosed vehicles and a couple of flatbed trucks of the type Amala normally utilized to transport troops, when they were on the ground and not expecting to fight.

Diplomat-At-Arms, being given a proper, formal welcome by the *Khan of Trusski*, and not about to be fired upon.

She hoped.

"Sir, thirty seconds to ground," the pilot called over the interior comm. "Make the call."

"Land it," she ordered, taking a deep breath and trying not to think of whatever outfits Harmaajärvi might come up with to impress the locals.

Diplomacy with an alien culture would *probably* be less trying than combat.

She hoped.

T he hatch opened, with a slight sigh as pressure equalized. Amala had watched the two lines of soldiers form up for reception, funneling her down to a man in what looked like the kind of court robes the history books always showed on Mandarin officials. She didn't recognize the design worked onto a panel on his chest, but there was no doubt in her mind it indicated rank, school, and social status, if you knew the code.

This might be Scholar Ve, come to greet her personally. To escort her to the Khan.

"Harmaajärvi, you go down first," Amala ordered suddenly. "Take up the first spot on the right and come to attention. Pinchon, you follow me down. The rest of you stay put."

A diplomat did not exist in a vacuum. Keller and d'Maine had provided her a small staff to maintain a household. Their term.

An *Embassy*.

She already knew that Pinchon and Harmaajärvi would end up being the two she relied on the most. Might as well get everyone used to it.

She watched her personal tailor suddenly transform himself into a recruitment poster boy and march down the steps at a slow, formal cadence, like this was drill and judges were assessing tenth-point demerits.

There wouldn't be many.

Amala took a deep breath and found the calm that preceded combat.

What little noise there had been outside had fallen to only the breeze. Even the birds were holding their breath, it seemed.

One step forward, into the local afternoon light spilling into the hatchway. Top of the steps. Pause. Glance around for the snipers she knew had to be somewhere, but they were well hidden.

Emerge. A diplomat butterfly where a marine caterpillar had been.

Three steps to ground.

Eighteen paces past soft-looking garritroopers with shiny buckles and rifles presented for inspection.

Not bad. Her boys would own them on points, but it was a credible-enough performance.

Especially if you hadn't woken this morning expecting to be invaded.

The man at the end was short.

Amala was used to being shorter than all the men she encountered, and about half the women.

She had at least a centimeter on this man, depending on the heels he had under that robe and how they stacked up against the combat boots hiding under her tabard.

Forty years old, perhaps. Straight black hair, graying in odd stripes. Hazel eyes with an Asian fold, in a round face. Scars from some childhood illness on his cheeks.

Two meters away, she came to rest. Paused.

Measured the man's calm with her own.

Even. Steady.

"Senior Centurion Amala Michelle Siddhartha Anne Yuey Bhattacharya," she announced in Mandarin Chinese, just to test the man. "Personal representative of Jessica Marie Keller, Imperial Admiral of the Red, Republic Fleet Centurion, Queen of the Pirates."

She had to suppress a grin at the ways his eyes sort of crossed at that last part. If you didn't understand *Corynthe*, hadn't known them, bled with them, gotten drunk with them, you lacked all cultural context to understand that *Queen of the Pirates* was probably her most impressive title.

Those people were intense.

"Scholar Ve Gayav Chuluun Gan," he replied in that same slightly wheezy Mandarin she had heard earlier. "Advisor to Ul Banop Cheani Yuur, *Khan* of *Trusski*. We hereby formally renounce your invasion and declare our intent to rebel against your authority at every opportunity."

She did grin at that. Someone had read the *Laws of Recognized Warfare* in the last few hours and understood what Keller had threatened by declaring them. And hadn't done, just waiting politely in orbit while delivering an ambassador.

Technically, Amala did represent a formal invasion, backed up by one marine, six clerks, and a tailor.

A most dangerous invasion.

She nodded slightly to the man. This was where things got *interesting*.

Aquitaine had never established formal ties to *Buran*. Hadn't even truly understood that they existed as more than a child's story intended to frighten delinquents into behaving.

Keller might be representing *Fribourg* here in the red uniform she wore for formal occasions, but this was an entirely Republic affair, including one Imperial Princess who had technically taken up arms under a foreign government.

"The Khan awaits you," Ve said.

He turned to a small cluster of men and women in similar, if less impressive, robes, standing partly hidden nearby, masked slightly by the cluster of vehicles. At some unseen signal, they glided closer.

"This staff will assist you in establishing your embassy," he concluded, with the slightest challenge in his voice. As if she was incompetent? Perhaps a sniff down his nose at them. Hard to tell.

Counting coup, Sri? Might I suggest that next time you pick on someone who doesn't have forty-three siblings and close cousins?

Amala turned, letting her face turn ever-so-frosty.

"Artisan Harmaajärvi," she called in English, causing the tailor at the end of the line to lean forward and turn to look at her.

She gestured at the half-dozen locals negligently.

"The Khan has provided you a staff to help establish the embassy," she said, subtly promoting the man to *Charge d'Affairs*.

She might have done that anyway, considering how efficiently he had used his calm seniority to organize the rest of the clerks, none of whom probably could even spell *espionage*.

Harmaajärvi nodded and stepped out of line to walk up and stand close by.

She watched them as he inspected the group. Most looked passive, perhaps even tried to appear friendly. One scowled, as if he had just sucked on a particularly bad lemon.

Harmaajärvi noticed.

She doubted he knew any more Chinese than was necessary to order dinner in a fancy restaurant, but he wasn't going to have any of it.

The tailor stepped close to the scowling man. They were of a height, and both lean. Harmaajärvi was perhaps two decades older. Wiser.

Meaner.

Amala bit her tongue rather than laugh out loud when Harmaajärvi reached out a hand and pulled a stray thread loose from the embroidery on his collar, *tsk*ing under his tongue as he did.

The stranger turned scarlet, followed a moment later by white, as rage trumped embarrassment. One hand started to curl into a fist before the stranger caught himself.

Amala noted that roughly half the others struggled valiantly to suppress their own grins. They were the ones at the rear of the group. Presumably of lower rank or status. Apparently, they didn't have as high an opinion of the man as he himself did.

Harmaajärvi agreed.

"I find *most* of them acceptable," he proclaimed mildly.

Scholar Ve was also suppressing his mirth, but Amala could see it in his eyes.

"Thank you for your kind assistance, Scholar Ve," she said.

He smiled for a flash, and then turned serious.

"I will take your arm now," he said. "In order to provide proper heraldry, as I would not wish you awkwardness, not fully understanding our ways."

She nodded, and Ve stepped around to place his right hand under her left forearm and lift it nearly level. Amala found it a very useful way to escort someone, as communication could occur with hidden fingertips, especially under the big sleeves she wore today.

"The Khan is looking forward to making your acquaintance," he continued, switching to Mongolian. "We receive so little news from the greater galaxy."

Amala nodded as Ve led her to the limousine, opened the door, and guided her in.

Overhead, *Auberon* and *VI Victrix* would be packing up to go hide in the darkness, leaving her here alone as a planetary invasion force, with the assistance of First-Rate-Spacer Harmaajärvi.

At least she would look good doing it.

CHAPTER XLVI

URAL STARBASE: SAMARA. STATUS: PATROL

"We have confirmed that it is truly Keller?" Kier fought to keep her tone level and professional as she addressed the Director of *Ural*.

It would not do to raise her voice to her commanding officer, the System Commander. Even remotely, insofar as she stood on her command deck and he was on the Starbase. Even as correct as Kier had proven to be when she doubted the man's original plans.

That he was distant kin of her clan crèche did not help. As *Director of Ural Starbase*, Xi Ulan Atah Ahn had ordered her to remain in-system against the next foolish attack from *Fribourg*, when she should have been patrolling the sector. Keller could not have just pounced on *Trusski* without extensive scouting. *Steadfast at Dawn* could have been there. Could have driven the barbarians home with their tails between their legs, or hounded them into the chasm of starless darkness, into which they might have gotten lost and never returned.

A *Flying Dutchman* to haunt the modern age.

Ahn paused for a moment before he spoke, aware of the immense rage threatening to engulf Kier. And how much she was in the right.

"Elements within the Empire took it upon themselves to attempt an assassination of Admiral Wachturm," Ahn said in a voice striving to placate. "They were found out, and eliminated, captured, or driven to escape."

He paused again, but Kier held her peace.

"We are effectively blind, Xi Derag Ahma Kier," he continued. "Until we rebuild our capabilities, we are forced to respond, rather than act. I do have one bit of good news, however."

"And that would be?" she parried, barely mollified by the realization that he was in as precarious a position as she.

"According to the agent who brought us the report, Keller is aboard the vessel known as *Auberon*, a Star Controller, and had only seven escorts of a size smaller than Hammerheads. *Auberon* is a carrier, like a Carcharias, but instead of three Hammerheads, she carries roughly two dozen individual fighter craft."

"This is meant to improve my humor?" Kier asked with a razor-thin edge.

"According to our intelligence, *Aquitaine* fighters rely on missiles for their offense," Ahn said. "Plus the ship-borne weapons known as Primary beams, which are also based on an ammunition model of combat, rather than energy. Keller is many light-centuries from any base that could resupply her, and since Imperial weapons are different, this is significant."

Kier felt some of the rage abate. Keller had made a masterful move, striking so deep and threatening *Trusski's* peace of mind.

Rattling the cages of our souls.

Keller had a reputation as a capable commander, but logistics would be her undoing.

It would, however, be an expensive campaign. *Steadfast at Dawn* could not simply pounce on Keller's force. The woman would be expecting that, which was why she had withdrawn after leaving behind a *Scholar* to establish some level of diplomatic communication.

No, Keller must be drawn into a protracted campaign. Hit and fade, but done with the intent of wearing down her stores. *Buran's* vessels used no ammunition, excepting only the new stealth-strike variant of the Roughshark, such as the one that had bombed *St. Legier.*

And would have escaped, but for Jessica Keller.

Ahn must have seen the fire bank in Kier's eyes. That much was obvious from the way his image relaxed.

"Will *Steadfast at Dawn* be sufficient?" he asked in a quieter voice.

Kier did the math in her head. That left *Traveler into Darkness* to command the local forces as Nightmaster, with one Megaladon to serve as Skymaster, plus the various Makos, Threshers, and Roughsharks that made up the local Warmaster contingent.

If it was a bluff on Keller's part, a feint to allow *Fribourg* to launch another assault, *Ural* was still a mighty castle, *Chéngbǎo*, to hold back the tide.

"It is," she replied.

Keller had issued a challenge to single combat. Xi Derag Ahma Kier would honor that.

And destroy her.

CHAPTER XLVII

Tame.

That was the first thought that crossed Amala's mind when she realized that they had arrived at their destination, having navigated rigidly-straight streets, laid on a mathematically-precise grid, en route to this building.

Scholar Ve had sat passively beside her during the ride. Gan was apparently his personal name, which was never used except within close personal or family bonds, so he would refer to her as Scholar Bhattacharya, thereby designating her something of an equal. Acceptable, but weird.

Everything was weird. They travelled through the city in a ground vehicle that had *tires*. Honest-to-Creator pseudo-rubber donuts on metal rims, inflated and everything. Back home, if you were poor-enough, your wheels were air-mesh lifters, but everyone else had a flitter of some sort.

Poverty. That was what was noteworthy on the ride. This place was just like the parts of *Huldra* she lived in as a child. Poor, but proud, so the buildings were simple brick, maybe with some stuccoed façade or something. No grand, marble architectural statements.

Made sense. Middle of nowhere, literally and figuratively. Farming kind of planet, rather than fishing or mining. She could tell that just by the color of the ground, as seen from orbit. Green primarily, rather than blue or gray.

She just had to pretend she was home, without the whole extended clan in the galleries hooting and making noise when she was presented today. Because they would have, had they been here.

Amala let the smile take over her face. Scholar Ve responded in a similar, if reserved manner. As if dealing with a semi-feral predator.

Maybe.

Curb-cut. Bump. Driveway. Gap into an interior courtyard. Rumble of gravel on asphalt. Squeak of tires coming to rest.

Two more garritroopers guarding the big front door and looking at least a little more professional. Amateurs, but she was still willing to give them bonus points for trying.

This was a planetary invasion, after all, according to the technical points Keller had leveled at them.

Another Mandarin in average-looking robes flowed out the door and materialized at the side of the limo. Door open. Scholar Ve sliding out and standing on what would be her left.

Amala grabbed her satchel and slid across the leather seats, exiting the vehicle to stand in the late-morning sun. Cool outside, but she had a lot of layers on right now, and way too high of an adrenaline load.

Hopefully, the HVAC was prepared for crazy today. Or they had enough windows open.

Something.

Ve took her arm again, nodding once and guiding her up the two steps onto the big, concrete porch. The building wasn't much, but someone had at least put some effort into this entrance. Designs worked into the stone showed patience and skill.

Inside, a long hallway with a floor that looked like polished concrete, with red brick walls and occasional facings for art displays. A planet with a hundred million inhabitants was going to produce a few artists worth their salt, but most of the work here had the feel of local stuff. Understandable, when so much of the really avant-garde stuff always felt as if it were weird for weird's sake.

It still felt enough like home to put her at some level of ease, even if she was dealing with people completely alien, at least culturally.

"Please be not offended that the Khan has requested a small reception," the man whispered as they walked. "We were working on rather tight timelines and unsure footing. A more proper reception will assumedly be scheduled for a later date. Your bodyguard will wait here."

"Understood," Amala nodded, signaling Pinchon and glancing back to confirm that he had understood.

There wasn't much the planetary invasion could accomplish at this point. But they knew that going in.

She was nevertheless impressed that they had responded this well to someone kicking over their ant hill. And the Fleet Centurion's orders, however vague and open-ended, had been specific: make sure she established as good a working relationship with the locals as she could.

Everyone understood that nothing important would happen on the ground. That would wait until *Buran* took notice and sent a fleet.

Hopefully, they would just send a small squadron, having missed the four big cruisers hiding in the dark part of the system. Amala wasn't really interested in being transported to *Buran*'s Court as a prisoner to be dissected, diplomatic immunity or not.

Who knew if the beast would recognize the rules, the etiquette under which *Aquitaine* and *Fribourg* normally tried to live?

This must be it.

Open doorway. Two more troopers trying to look impressive while guarding it, marred by an inability to not stare at her out of the corners of their eyes as she approached.

"We arrive," Scholar Ve murmured.

Small room. Half a dozen men and women standing around in those Mandarin Court robes, black everywhere and heavy looking, so hopefully the AC was cranked cooler to offset.

It was obvious who the Khan was, looking at the group. Simple, black robes with a single golden stripe on each upper arm, rather like the two Amala had on her own uniform as a Senior Centurion. She wondered at the significance, since nobody else had one, their badges of rank visible instead as pictographs on the chest.

But the gravity of the room revolved around this man.

They entered.

"The Scholar: Bhattacharya Yuey Anne Siddhartha Michelle Amala," Ve announced in Mongolian this time in a voice pitched to fill the room without being rude. "Representing the *Empire of Fribourg* as a diplomat under the *Laws of Recognized Warfare*."

Amala was slightly taken aback. Hopefully she hid it well enough from everyone not touching her at the moment. She had listed all of her names only the once, at their initial meeting, and he had just reversed them exactly when presenting her.

Which made sense. They each had four names, starting with one of the eight allowed clans, and working their way down to the personal, the individual, probably only spoken by a lover or dear friend.

And here she went and had six name on them. Which was short for her family, where one of her cousins had gone all in with nine names plus family for each her children, in turn making nicknames by using the first letters of the nine.

And they had switched languages, apparently expecting her to follow them in Mongolian now.

Okay. Let's play.

The Khan fixed her with an eye like a hawk. Not hungry, or angry, or mean, but sharp.

Amala swallowed past a dry tongue and let Ve lead her into the room at a slow, almost waltzing pace.

Short. All of them. Weird.

Amala couldn't remember being in a room with so many adults that were her size or smaller. Especially not one with five men and three women besides her. One guy might have had two centimeters on her, again depending on what they wore under those robes for lifts and heels, but the rest ranged from 160cm up to maybe 170cm.

Amala wondered if it was genetics, or diet and nutrition. She knew that poorer places tended to have smaller people. Over enough generations, marginal diet started showing genetic impacts.

So maybe the warriors of *Buran* weren't all three meters tall and capable of breathing fire, after all.

That put a smile on her face as she approached the Khan. He smiled back with his whole face, eyes crinkling up at the corners into wrinkles that took up large amounts of his bald head.

"Scholar Bhattacharya," he said in a quiet, high voice. "I am Ul Banop Cheani Yuur, Minister of the Eighth Rank, *Khan* of *Trusski.*"

He studied her face for several moments. Minister Ul had blue eyes. His face had reset itself from the smile of a moment ago.

At no point had the word *welcome* crossed his lips.

"You present yourself as a diplomatic representative of Admiral of the Red Keller Marie Jessica?" he continued.

"I do," Amala replied simply, nodding with just enough of her shoulders to turn it into a small bow. About what she thought the current situation rated, since she wanted to put him at ease.

"We do not adhere to your so-called *Laws of Recognized Warfare,*" he said, voice growing into a fine, killing edge. "Your kind are barbarians from beyond the pale of civilization."

Amala let that one go. She felt the same way about them, but this wasn't the time to get into a pissing match with an entire planet. If she was going to do that, she would have gone back for *Fourth Saxon*, *Ninth Pohang*, and *Third Huldra* to kick some ass around here.

And the rest of the room hadn't bristled or anything when he said it, like they were about to see if their diplomatic backgrounds came with equivalent close-combat training to hers. Pinchon would kill the closest goon, steal his gun, and introduce utter mayhem if he thought someone was attacking her.

She smiled blandly at the Khan instead.

He let the moment pass as well. And took most of the edge off his voice.

"However, we recognize that you are attempting to communicate with us in a civilized manner," the Khan continued. "Behaving in a way calculated to impress us that you are capable of restraint and enlightenment. We appreciate such effort, and wish to establish a relationship within which meaningful dialogue may take place. You possess credentials?"

Amala smiled and nodded.

Keller had tasked her other two ringleaders with that part. Travere appeared to be even more dangerous than Moirrey, with that sort of thing.

Amala opened the satchel and pulled out a packet of real papers, printed on heavy stock and decorated with all manner of interesting calligraphy around the edges. Top page was a simple document indicating her status as a personal representative of Jessica Keller: Admiral of the Red, Fleet Centurion, Queen. *Ambassador to Buran*. Technically, that apparently granted her something similar to the Rittership that *zu* Kermode had received, and would probably guarantee her all the free drinks she wanted, next time she was on *Petron*.

Under that was a fast highlight of her career and schooling, including the recent language certifications she had managed, and all the combat awards she could wear if she wanted to put everything on her full dress uniform. Hopefully, they wouldn't ask, because she hadn't even brought that gear with her. And she was slightly frightened at what her personal tailor might come up with as a substitute, in a pinch.

Scholar Ve took the packet from her hand, flipped quickly through it, and then took the three steps to hand it to the Khan. That man took a long minute examining it. He spent several more seconds studying her.

"This is the record of a warrior," he said. In Mongolian, no less.

"It is," she replied in the same tongue, happy for all the hours working at the machine to get the words natural. "I am a Senior Security Centurion in the *Republic of Aquitaine* Navy and a career officer. I volunteered to learn your tongue, and to come here with my staff to learn your ways. Admiral Keller was able to end the Great War between *Fribourg* and *Aquitaine* on mutually beneficial terms. The Emperor of *Fribourg* asked her to serve on this frontier, she formerly being his greatest enemy. Her orders are not specifically to fight another war, but to secure the Empire. That may require violence, but it does not necessitate it."

From the corner of her eyes, Amala tracked the utter shock that came over everyone she could see, as she spoke to them in Mongolian. Maybe not so barbarian after all?

The Khan had a more guarded expression, but had there been a flicker in his eyes as well?

"So my credentials are similar to what one would have, had I been sent to an Imperial world as an ambassador, or any of the other planets and nations with which my nation deals," she continued. "The *Laws of Recognized Warfare* exist for protection of diplomats, as well as warriors, since we could not be sure what reception I would receive. It is a request for dialogue, backed up by a promise of violence, if necessary."

The room tensed. Thank the Creator she could actually speak this tongue, and not just repeat stock phrases, or do everything in Chinese and hope the terms and concepts translated cleanly.

The Khan studied her like a blue-eyed hawk for several minutes as she waited and tried not to think about snipers on a balcony above and behind her somewhere.

"Your accent is atrocious," the Khan announced finally. A smile appeared. "We will need to work on that, Scholar Bhattacharya. Be welcome to *Trusski*."

Amala remembered to breathe.

CHAPTER XLVIII

Command Centurion Jennifer Glenn.

Independent raiding command.

She liked the way that sounded in her head. Hopefully, Keller and the First Lord had plans for her future that were greater than just turning into another Tomas Kigali.

Not that there was anything wrong with him and his career, but she wanted to command one of the Expeditionary Cruisers. Or another carrier like *II Augusta*. Fleet Centurion. Become a mover and a shaker in the navy.

Today, she had to make sure this mission went down professionally, and successfully. That involved sitting clear out at the edge of this nowhere system, like Keller had done at *Trusski*, and listening.

It was what the Corvette/Patrol was designed for. Go looking for trouble, but do it quietly, and be able to either meet it, or elude it, depending. A fast, cheap scout capable of going off and doing things by herself, while the rest of the team waited for *Buran* to come when the burglar alarm sounded.

But they had to get by her first.

"Steiner, what's our status?" she prodded her science officer, drawing the woman up from the depths of whatever screen she had been focused on.

"No change local, sir," Reese replied. "The only artificial targets I can find are the four orbital stations. Nothing else currently around."

"Flight deck," Glenn continued. "Are your birds ready to fly?"

"Affirmative," Centurion Rouge said. "All boards green."

Jennifer turned to her left.

"Navigator, accelerate to engagement speed and prepare for JumpSpace."

Centurion Rasim looked up and made eye contact. Murdag was a tall, skinny blond who had been promoted into her new role as pilot of *CP-406*, just as Jennifer had moved up to command. But she handled herself well.

They both nodded.

Jennifer smiled and turned to Senior Centurion Elouan.

"Takouhi, you have Tactical," Jennifer said. "Prepare to engage."

Her Exec nodded and double-checked all her boards one last time.

"Pilot, make your jump," Elouan ordered.

From this distance, the run down to the planet was quick. Everything had already been scouted in great detail, and they were coming in below the ecliptic, so there was nothing in the way that would distort their course. Just a hard fast in, across, up, and out.

CP-406 emerged into RealSpace with a surge of power. Takouhi had Tactical under control, so Jennifer focused her attention on the rest of the vessel.

Getting a feel for how her craft sailed into the wind, as it were.

"Flight deck, launch your birds," Takouhi ordered as soon as everything was green.

Rouge was already prepared. All three kicked loose at the same time, seeds cast into the wind as their platform continued her acceleration. *Black Prince* was unarmed in his *P-6*, a point he occasionally bitched about, but he went right out with *Boomerang* and *Grendel*, flying escort for his mates with his jammers if needed.

"Gunner," Takouhi continued. "Set your stern turret to maximum deflection. Go to rapid fire as you bear."

"Roger that, sir," the man called smartly from his station up front.

Yeoman Adnan Kristensen was never going to become an officer. Didn't want the responsibility, but he had a deft touch with his guns. For him, shooting things was an art, and should be treated as such.

"Nav, up ten, roll three-four-zero, keep plane," the Tactical Officer continued. "Kick your velocity up a shade and find me a line that brings us over the top firing when it's time to retrieve the wing."

"Executing now," Rasim replied.

They hadn't fought a battle before, but Jennifer had run the team through as many combat training sims as she could think up, including asking Bedrov for some assistance during one of the rendezvous layovers. It showed now, as the group coalesced into a single entity, rather than individuals.

Jennifer checked her boards anyway. Damage Control and Engineering fell under her control. She had to provide Takouhi a stable fighting platform for as long as possible, or know when to cut and run.

That was one of the reasons Tactical was always a separate task. You had to focus your entire being on the dance with your foe, with no time to pay attention to the larger tasks.

"Steiner, hail the station and the ground," Jennifer ordered. "Find out who's in charge and who might get hurt."

That station had been unoccupied before. Not abandoned, but nobody lived there full time. From what Jennifer had seen, it was more of a place for engineers to live while making repairs, or for a passenger awaiting transport out of system.

Minutes passed as *CP-406* got up a head of steam and her three chicks dropped into a lower orbit to line up bow shots.

"I have a man on the ground, Commander," Steiner finally said. "Claims to be the facility manager, or something. Not sure how to translate the words and Chinese feels like his third or fourth language. Doesn't even recognize English or Spanish."

Jennifer clicked the button on her board to open the channel. It was one of the weird ones at the high end of the dial. Great for planetary coverage, where it could bounce off the ionosphere, but barely capable of reaching orbit.

"This is Command Centurion Jennifer Glenn, aboard the *Imperial Fighting Vessel CP-406*," she said firmly in passable, if rusty Chinese. Technically it was still a *RAN* vessel, but they were operating under an Imperial flag for this mission. "If you have anyone aboard your orbital platform, have them evacuate immediately, as I will be destroying it in five minutes."

"We do not deal with pirates," came a sputtering voice.

Jennifer waited an extra beat, to see if he had anything more to say, but that was apparently it.

"No, sir," she replied. "This is not a raid. This is an act of war, but we are attempting to minimize casualties in your system."

She cut the signal and turned her attention to the rest of her team. Takouhi had a broad grin that the others matched.

"Tactical, prepare for war," she continued.

Five minutes was pushing it. At this speed, they would be on top of the target and blowing by in six, but nobody expected to fire more than two or three shots.

Based on their previous investigation, the stations had nothing more proof against the elements than basic nav shields that would just barely deflect any orbital debris small enough to hole things. Big rocks would hit the station like a tin can in front of a car.

Engines behaving. JumpSails within parameters on all dimensions. Nobody else in orbit now, but *Buran* ships could still jump inside the gravity well with them if they were around. That was part of the reason to move so fast and to not just camp out in close proximity for target practice.

Jennifer watched a timer count down on her board. Five minutes was what she had given them, so Takouhi was holding to that, even if nothing moved on the station at all.

Fortunately, no guns were aboard to suddenly open fire, either. One of the benefits of having the complete technical readouts of the station at hand. But it might have been more fun to have the tug come with them on some run and see if it was possible to simply hook grapples to the station itself and drag it off. She would make a note to suggest it to Keller when they got back.

The galaxy's biggest practical joke.

Zero.

"Open fire with *Anna* and *Zebra*," Takouhi ordered.

The outer two turrets, foremost and aftmost. *Boren* and *Chester* up front had been replaced on a *CP*-model with the docking mechanisms for three fighters. *Wiley* and *Yalu* both held Type-1 Pulse beams, on the assumption that a patrol corvette was more likely running away from someone, and needed the firepower rearward, even if both could cover two hundred seventy degrees of arc, centered on the exact centerline rear.

An assault corvette like Kigali's had Type-3-Tuned beams at A, B, Y, and Z, with the defensive Type-1-Pulse at C and W. Another reason *CA-264* was such a dangerous beast, but not nearly as flexible as a patrol corvette.

Boomerang and *Grendel* cut loose at the same time, so four beams intersected on the station. Without shields, and with nothing aboard capable of making a really big explosion, like a generator stack, the platform simply went up in a flash of light as the beams liberated their energy on the outer skin. A moment later, a lumpy cloud appeared on the scanners as the pressurized water tanks went, engulfing all that bar steel in a cloud.

Jennifer wondered if there were any pieces of metal big enough to survive re-entry, but there was almost nothing on the planet below to hit. Just that one facility, as near as they had been able to tell, sitting on the edge of a vast, inland lake.

A truck stop in the middle of nowhere.

And now, a dead one.

"Station has been neutralized," Centurion Stein confirmed, a moment later. And an understatement.

"Flight deck, recover your birds soonest," Takouhi ordered. "Sensors, keep an eye out for any locals getting ready to join us. Guns, stay sharp and fire on anything coming out of jump."

A chorus of assents. Jennifer smiled.

Her team.

Doing exactly what a patrol corvette was designed for. Get in, hit hard, get out. Wouldn't work all that well out in *Corynthe*, where the pirate warships were all carriers, but if she brought along a mix of *CE*s and *CP*s, and maybe a *CA*, when they built a second one, Jennifer figured she could cut a nasty swath through those people as well.

She wondered how Keller and Bedrov were planning to overcome that. She knew the two of them well enough by now to know that they were both several moves ahead of everyone else. Someone, somewhere would be building up a corvette force to go after Keller, so she would go after them first.

Jennifer made a note to spend some time thinking about the chess moves involved. The balance of fleet forces necessary, and what to build over the next five years, as everyone suddenly updated their technology to the new standards as their old fleets were suddenly out-moded.

The Fleet Centurion was not one to rest on her laurels.

CHAPTER XLIX

Jessica considered the view through the wall-to-ceiling port. Darkness as far as the eye could see, punctured in only a few places where the clouds of cold gas grew thin enough for the passage of starlight.

If there were lines in galactic warfare, she and her team were deep behind them, nearly a tenth of the way across that dark gulf separating *Trusski* from *Ninagirsu*. Hopefully, nobody would think to look here for an Imperial operating base. Even a mobile one like this.

She considered her companion, standing close enough that she could feel his warmth in the dim light, but not touching her. Always the perfect gentleman, even in those times when she might have preferred him to be less of one.

"You are an impossibly stubborn man, Torsten Wald," she offered in a quiet voice.

They had the observation deck to themselves, apparently by arrangements he had made with Arott's crew, and following a quiet meal in a suspiciously-deserted wardroom.

"You are not the first person to make that observation, madam," he replied with a grin. "Anybody else would most likely have surrendered by now."

"And yet I get the feeling you would wait forever," she replied, turning to face him now, the breadth of the darkness forgotten behind her.

"Maybe not forever, Jessica," he said, voice dropping down to a low murmur.

They were alone on the deck, yes, but both Marcelle and Willow were never far away. It was one of the costs of being Jessica Keller, that she could never just escape from everything for more than a few hours. At some point, some decisions would need to be made, if not by her immediately, then at least approved by her before they could be put into practice.

"How long?" she asked. "There are likely many years on this frontier before I plan to retire."

"Who said anything about retiring, Fleet Centurion?" he replied. "I continue to serve, even as I have little to do out here besides be on your staff and provide a liaison back to Admiral Wachturm. A position which colors everything you do with an official imprimatur."

"Have you ever considered going back into line command?" Jessica hesitated to ask, but this felt like an evening when some levels of barriers were coming down, at least around her.

Six years was long enough to mourn, wasn't it?

"I have," he said. "But my skills these days are much better suited to number-crunching. It's what got me onto the Imperial Staff. Karl is very much driven by a solid understanding of economics. And it got me an invitation to a very elite party on *St. Legier*."

"So you went for the express purpose of meeting me?" Jessica asked, focusing on his face.

"I wanted to see the person behind the numbers," Torsten told her in a simple admission. "I saw what you did with *The Long Raid*. Watched the psychological trauma impact and blight an entire Imperial sector, despite everything the Grand Admiral did to try to stop you."

"Not many people would have been brave enough to actually walk up and talk to me that night," Jessica teased. "I know, because I was playing my own little game with them, watching them maneuver around my party, trying not to be infected with whatever it was that I carried. And then you stepped across that chasm."

"You have no idea how intimidating you are in person, Jessica," Torsten said. "Especially not when what one knows about you are only the stories of the barbarian queen who has suddenly struck deep into the heart of the Empire."

"*Thuringwell* was never that important," Jessica retorted.

"No, it wasn't," he said. "And yet look at what happened. The panic you induced was so great that Karl prevailed over the hotheads to offer the first true peace treaty in a generation that wasn't just a period of armed calm before the next sneak attack somewhere."

"You were winning the war," Jessica said. "I won't say a desperate measure was necessary, but a grand one certainly was."

"We would have won in another twenty-five to forty years, Fleet Centurion," Torsten said. "I'm an econometricist. I've done the studies. In another ten to fifteen, *Aquitaine* would have lost so much ground on so many fronts that it might have imploded of its own weight. But then you came along. 2218 Svati Prime."

"What did you see?" Jessica leaned forward. They were not touching, quite, but he was breathing on her now, and she him.

"The Empire convulsed," Torsten said, his green eyes losing focus as his head tilted back and he looked inward.

She liked the smell of the aftershave he was wearing tonight. And she could taste the fresh apple pie from dessert on his breath.

"Confidence in the fleet faltered," Torsten continued. "Even the reputation of the Red Admiral wavered. *Gross Imperial Product* dropped four-tenths of a percent in the year after your attack, controlling for all other factors. And I did that in my research."

He paused to look down, focusing on her again.

"And then the *Battles of Petron* and *Ballard*," he continued. "The shocks: political, psychological, and economic, were all devastating. Fleet Command had to rotate a number of squadrons in from outer frontiers suddenly, the better to protect worlds that had previously been considered safe. Nobody knew where you would strike next."

"*Thuringwell*," she whispered with carefully-suppressed glee.

Torsten was an econometricist. There were not many people in the galaxy that would have been able to understand her logic, the devastation, the impact of losing an Imperial world to *Aquitaine*, especially one that hadn't previously been a Republic world.

"*Thuringwell*," he agreed. "I had to meet you in the flesh. See what it was that all the commanders, all the spies had missed. So I finagled my way into that reception by trading favors with someone I knew in the palace, screwed up my courage, and walked up to meet you."

"And did you find it?" Jessica asked. "That thing you sought?"

"No," he said. "Nobody would have. You run too deep for anyone to see what goes on inside that head."

"Oh?"

"But I watched you move when Dittmar rolled his dice," Torsten said, remaining perfectly still as he realized how close she had gotten. Any other time, he might have withdrawn, even just a centimeter, when her hand came to rest on his forearm, as it suddenly had. "You had no immediate plan of action, but it took you all of about five minutes to spin up an entire campaign and put it into action."

"Who did you talk to?" Jessica asked, surprised at his acute understanding. He was exactly correct.

"Everyone alive afterwards," he admitted. "The Grand Admiral needed someone to put together a report, someone that he trusted not to be in Dittmar's faction, or one of the other ones, as they started cleaning house. I had already impressed him enough to write reports for the Emperor, so he tapped me."

"Everyone?" Jessica probed sharply.

"Including Desianna, Marcelle, Willow Dolen, Arlo, Lady Moirrey, and Lady Casey," he admitted. "I might have gone a shade beyond my original writ, but I was also more than a little smitten by that point."

"Nobody told me any of this," Jessica said, tensing across her shoulder blades.

"Everybody probably still thought I was harmless at that point."

"At that point?"

"More recently, I have been personally threatened by Denis Jež, Robbie Aeliaes, Tomas Kigali, Nils Kasum, Marcelle, and Lady Moirrey. Specifically, not to break your heart. Or they would come for me."

"I'm surprised the list is that short," Jessica teased, relaxing again.

This man relaxed her. She hadn't had that around anyone since…

Since Warlock.

"Neither Arlo nor d'Maine are the type to give any warning before they strike," Torsten noted.

"Point taken," Jessica replied. "Although Marcelle is probably still more hazardous."

"Oh, no," Torsten grinned. "Lady Moirrey and Lady Casey are the ones to fear."

Jessica found herself close enough to kiss him. She hadn't, to date; always unconsciously wondering when he would leave her.

Widow her once more.

The look in his eyes right now promised *never*.

She leaned into his chest, looked up, and kissed him. It was not passionate. Neither of them did that level of emotion, at least in public.

It was promise.

A promise of *never*, however unspoken.

She broke it, just enough to turn both of them to face the stars again.

Leaned her weight into him. Felt one arm slip around her back to rest on her hip. Not possessive, just contact.

Promise.

CHAPTER L

It was silly how serious some people took themselves, Vo decided as he exited the taxi and looked at the men. Assembled like pretty peacocks in that grassy quad, surrounded on three sides by low, red-brick buildings. A wrought iron gate with ivy growing through it on the street side separated him from the group, but allowed him to watch without being noticed.

Two soldiers stood at something like parade guard duty, wearing cloaks against the threatening drizzle and carrying pulse rifles, but they were there as decoration, rather than security. What fool would launch an attack on the Imperial Forces Institute, the Army's Headquarters and school, in the middle of the Empire's capital city?

Vo scowled at the taxi driver as the man waved cheerfully and drove away. Not being able to do something as simple as pay a fare was going to grate, eventually. Hopefully, the locals would tire of the celebrity game of recognizing him in public. As it was, the only place he could get any peace was if he went down to the docks and had dinner at The Maltese Cross. Foster, the publican, wouldn't allow any shenanigans in his bar, nor would the locals.

And fools and shenanigans were especially what the day ahead promised.

Vo checked the sky, but the heavy, gray clouds were behaving. He settled his black cloak a little tighter and held it closed with his left hand as he approached one of the guards and flashed his brand new identification card.

The guard had no idea who this visitor was until this moment. Vo watched the whites of his eyes suddenly appear and then disappear as the man got his shock under control.

"Welcome, sir," the man rapped out in a low, terse voice, then reached back and pressed some unseen button to trigger the entry on silent hinges.

The gates of hell opened like a hungry maw. Vo waited a beat for them to fully clear, and then strode forward, turned right, and approached the thirty-five men standing around and trying to impress each other with whatever social games men like that used.

Peacocks.

One of them happened to be looking his way. Vo watched the sneer slowly form on the man's face as he sized up the new arrival as big, dumb, and ugly. Two for three wasn't bad, if you were grading on a curve.

The watcher himself was tall and thin. The picture Vo had studied earlier didn't really convey that aspect of the man.

Aquiline face dominated by an overly-sharp nose and a receding widow's peak that showed a trace of the natural gray, hiding under the most recent dye job. Vo would have said aristocratic, but he had met the current emperor and the Grand Admiral, both naval men, either of whom had at least ten kilos of muscle on this dandy.

The eyes were gray. Probably impressed the hell out of the ladies with that bright, rare color. Here it just made his face look washed out.

His piercing, sneering gaze found its way to Vo's boots. Those heavy, ugly, battered, lace-up monstrosities in scuffed brown leather. Worn shiny on the sides from rubbing on Shevi's stirrups. Brand new soles because he had walked the old ones off twice now. Vo demanded a good gripping tread under his feet if he had to move suddenly.

Pretty boy's feet were in light boots made of polished, black leather. The almost-slip-on escapees from a pirate vid, similar to what Vo wore in his full dress uniform, but not as rugged.

Could you call a man's boots dainty? Without triggering a duel, anyways?

Vo didn't have to look around. The others wore something similar in style, if not overall cost. Expensive cloth pants, well-fitted, bloused picture-perfect into boots. Moirrey had called the gray-green color *sage*, and he was willing to trust her judgment. Tailored jackets with three buttons and an array of pretty, shiny medals and pins on the chest, braids wrapped around shoulders, epaulettes with every decoration under the sun. Front-and-rear garrison caps with more pins on them. Most with the hollow black circle of a Commander on their collar. A few wore the white star of a colonel.

The other man could only see Vo's boots and his uncovered head, the rest of his bulk having been swallowed up by the immense space of black cloth that Moirrey had sewn for him, the thing that she called a cloak. She could have sailed a nice boat with it.

Pretty Boy looked to a few of the others for social reinforcement as Vo moved a few steps closer. A bubble opened up around him, like he might be contagious.

Maybe, considering.

Peacocks.

"Are you in the wrong place?" Pretty Boy asked leadingly.

Vo guessed the man really wanted to address him as *Sergeant* or perhaps *Corporal,* so he could establish a terribly high promontory from which he could piss on some stranger he didn't know. Best way to establish pack hierarchy: pick out someone that didn't fit with the rest of the group and ostracize him. *Navin the Black* would have just laughed in the man's face. But he was like that.

Vo had his own way to deal with petty people like this. He decided to play dumb. It usually worked on punks, and Pretty Boy had all the right hallmarks.

"My orders were to report for Field School," Vo replied in a soft, diffident tone. "Ground Forces Institute, Werder. We're all in the right place, yes?"

"I don't know you," Pretty Boy's voice got icy and sharp. "Do you think you belong here?"

Internally, Vo grinned. He supposed that the Imperial Land Forces were a pretty closed group, when you got to this rank. People who knew each other from Academy, and usually boarding schools before that, since commoners like him rarely made it this far. If you really wanted to get ahead in the military, you joined the navy. They were far more open to skill and expertise.

Outwardly, Vo fixed Pretty Boy with a hard stare. Playground games. Vo was on Navin's dojo floor now. His scowl deepened.

"Tell me, Commander van Gorzen," Vo let his voice drop down to an earthquake rumble. "What makes you think you deserve to be here?"

It was rather fun watching the man's face crinkle in disdain and loathing. The way the nose flared. The slight flush to the otherwise pale cheeks. The bunching of the jaw and pursing of the lips, as though he had just sucked the soul out of a lemon.

"I am the nephew of the Duke of *Shaposhnikov*, you peon," he snarled. "I've called on seconds for less."

Vo nodded. He wasn't surprised. Money and connections tended to insulate fools from the cost of their pettiness.

Vo finally let go of the edges of his black cloak and flicked the hem-weighted right wing backwards over his shoulder. The movement cleared half his body, if he needed to move quickly, while keeping his left hand, the blocker, obscured behind cloth. Never let them see all of you in close combat, if you can.

It also revealed the black sword emblem on the side of his collar, and the small, maroon-and-white enameled medal pinned to the left side of his chest, where he would have worn his regular awards if he was back home in a Centurion's uniform. He had left the green-and-blacks aboard *Auberon* when he departed.

Today, a speckled tan and brown pattern to all the cloth. Heavy pants with thigh pockets and a reinforced seat. Baggy. Loose. Still strange after his usual uniform, where everything had to be planned to fit under an emergency lifesuit in a hurry.

Button-up shirt instead of a tunic, with a button-up, rain-proof jacket over that. At least he didn't have to wear the heavy, armoured vest over the jacket, the one that had saved his ass at least twice on *Thuringwell*, by stopping fragments and beams. And he had left the 12mm revolver back in his room, too. But he had it with him on this planet. He did wear the Divisional Patch for the 189th on his right shoulder, on the opposite side from where *Auberon's* thistle had been on his left, when he was ship-board.

And those damned boots. Fleet Centurion had known better than to try to get him out of his expensive, custom footwear. Grand Admiral hadn't even asked.

Vo doubted this punk had ever actually stepped onto a dueling field. The money and threat was probably enough to make anyone else back down.

Fool had a lot to learn about being a soldier. So did the rest of them.

"Seconds?" Vo ruminated. "Tell me, how many planets have *you* conquered, Commander?"

Vo paused just long enough to make his next words a threat, rather than just a challenge.

"How many emperors have you killed?"

A few men smiled, but they were facing Vo where van Gorzen couldn't see them. Vo marked the faces and updated the files he had memorized of everyone on the quad today. Best lesson the Fleet Centurion had ever taught him.

"General Arlo?" Pretty Boy gasped, paling as if Vo had already sliced open his femoral artery.

"General *zu* Arlo," Vo corrected the man. "I'll leave my address for your man to find me."

"That won't be necessary, sir," van Gorzen stammered. "I had no idea."

"That makes it worse, Commander," Vo answered harshly. "Not better. You are expected to lead men, not merely *command* them. They must respect the man wearing the uniform, not the insignia on the collar. Without that, you have nothing."

And now I sound like Navin the Black *breaking in a batch of new Cornets and Centurions, still wet behind the ears and full of themselves.*

Not the worst place to start.

"Problems, gentlemen?" a rich, hard voice rang across the field.

Vo turned and snapped to. He wasn't worried about Pretty Boy doing anything at this point, except annoying him with fawning apologies over and above the current situation's requirements.

The new arrival commanded the field, in more ways than one.

Flag General Anders Tsibin. *Commander, Land Forces Institute.* The man responsible for taking in a group of thirty-some mid-career officers with promise, and either polishing them down to steel, or revealing them for frauds who should be washed out quickly, before they got into the sort of position where they could do damage.

Grand Admiral Wachturm didn't like many Army men, and respected fewer as warriors. This man made both grades. Good man to listen to.

"Sir, no sir," Vo snapped, back into cadet voice. "Introducing myself to my new classmates, sir."

"Yes," Tsibin observed dryly. "I see that."

The General studied the group for a few moments, like a farmer preparing for fall cull. He pointed both forefingers at Vo and motioned sideways with them, drawing invisible lines.

"Fall in," he ordered with a snap. "Form on *zu* Arlo."

Vo came to attention and waited, feeling and listening to the rest of the group drop into line as fast as they could. He could tell how few of them had been on this side of the line from how long it took. A few did it quickly, but Vo already had them marked as professional soldiers, rather than aristocratic *poseurs* trading on family connections and wealth for their place.

Imperial Land Forces today were even worse than the *Republic of Aquitaine* Navy had been, back when he first got enlisted, before the Fleet Centurion and the old First Lord, Nils Kasum, had broken the Noble Lords for good.

There were probably half-a-dozen on this field who would have made the grade with Navin. Vo wondered how many would wash out here. Even *before* things got interesting.

The Emperor himself had given Vo orders to make the Army a different place. He didn't have *Fourth Saxon* or *Ninth Pohang* with him today, but he carried all their scars with him. And would, for the rest of his life.

These boys were going to get tough quickly, or they would be looking for new jobs.

Vo was done fooling around.

CHAPTER LI

Yan looked up as the door chime signaled a visitor. He thought about simply telling the system to open it, but he wasn't expecting anyone. Most people would have called ahead to make sure he was here, even if it was late in ship's day and he was normally in his cabin by now.

Instead, Yan saved everything he was working on and slid his lightpen into a pocket on his tunic where he wouldn't forget it. He rose and crossed the four steps to the hatch, pressing the button to open it from this side.

She was standing there, all long and lanky and crude and sarcastic, but she had an inscrutable look on her face tonight.

Ainsley Rakel Barret.

da Vinci.

"Hi," she said in a voice that seemed to lack something.

"Hi," Yan replied, stepping slightly to one side. "Come in?"

In the past, it hadn't been a question, but something about the woman was off. Not right.

Fragile.

Yan didn't think she was going to break up with him. This was *da Vinci.* That would be a much louder and more passionate thing, if that were to happen.

Angry words and possibly thrown coffee mugs.

She was fidgeting as she stood in the passageway, and finally stepped forward. Stepped close.

Arms went around his back and held on like she was drowning.

Yan had the presence of mind to close the hatch before wrapping himself around the tall woman, luxuriating in her smell, the feel of her up against him. He could feel her heart going like a rabbit, pitter-patter, so he just held her.

Long moments passed in silence.

Something changed. It was like parts of her melted, or at least relaxed. He was no longer holding a statue of the woman, but the woman herself. Perhaps Galatea come to life.

Yan leaned back just enough to kiss her on the cheek and notice her eyes were closed, but red.

"What can I do to help?" he whispered.

"Not hate me," she whispered back, so faint that he almost had to read her lips to understand.

"Not possible, Ainsley," Yan murmured.

Her eyes opened and he got a good look into the woman's soul.

She had been raging, or perhaps crying. Emotionally unsettled, in a woman who was normally calmness incarnate. Off, and only now coming back to herself.

"Don't be so sure," *da Vinci* said in a slightly louder voice. "I talked with Jessica. Told her that if she allowed you to fly with the wing, I would quit and she would have to find someone else to command."

He could tell she expected him to rage now. Yell. Maybe break things.

How little she really understood.

"I know," Yan said. "She told me."

Yan felt Ainsley tense up suddenly. Hopefully, she wasn't about to punch him.

"I respect your decision," Yan continued. "Both of you. What I would like to know is why. For flying a *P-6 Vanguard*, I'm probably the best pilot you have in the entire fleet, after you. And you're flying an *E-2* now with the heavy team."

"It's not professional, Yan," she said, gaining strength, perhaps drawing it out of him like a vampire or something. "It's personal. I can't command if I'm worried about something happening to you. Can't order you to do stupidly suicidal things. It will compromise me, when I need to be steady."

He squeezed her harder. That seemed to be what Ainsley needed.

Some of the ice slipped off her back. More of her weight settled against his chest.

"You think I don't worry about you?" he asked. "Worry that every time you launch, something will go wrong with your fighter, something I missed when I designed it, and you won't come back?"

"That's different," Ainsley countered. "You have two other wives."

"And you think I love you any less than them?" he said.

It was cute, the utter shock on her face. The way her eyes got big, until the hazel vanished into the black pupils. The heartrate suddenly accelerating again, just as it had started to calm down.

Yan kissed her. Just because. And again.

Yup. Vampire. Seemed to draw heat and strength from his kisses. Squeezed him so hard it was like she was trying to crack his ribs, or squish herself flat against his chest.

Necking ensued.

Finally, she seemed mollified. Yan stole one last kiss and then leaned back to study her face.

Color had returned. Hazel filled her eyes again. Her heart still pounded, but to a different kind of rhythm now.

"I was afraid you'd be mad at me," she finally offered. "Throw me out, or something."

"For doing your job?" he countered.

They hadn't made it more than a step into his cabin. Yan broke the deathgrip just enough to turn and guide her to the couch where he entertained visitors. Then he changed his mind and sat in the big, puffy chair, pulling her down onto his lap like a giant cat. She curled up like one, too.

"Why is it my job?" Ainsley asked, snuggled up against his chest, where she could listen to his heart yammer.

"You and Vlahovic are in charge of the pilots, *da Vinci*," he said, suddenly regretting that his highball of whiskey was out of reach on the workbench, across the room. "I was offering to make life easier, not harder."

"Easier is here, with the door closed," she said. "Out there is hard."

He could see that. Outside, Ainsley had to be *da Vinci*. Probe pilot extraordinaire. Magician with sensors and jammers. Commander of an unruly mob of flight-jockeys.

High-functioning.

Here, she could be the introverted maths nerd with a brunette pony tail and fingers that seemed to be snakes, all long and skinny and bendy, like the woman herself.

At least the cabin's remote control was within reach.

Yan dialed the room lights down to a dimness reminiscent of sunset, and powered down his design board so it wouldn't be lighting up the room. For the hell of it, he kicked the heat up a couple of degrees from the coolness he was used to.

"You aren't mad?" she asked.

"No."

"Good."

She squirmed a little, settling more and more into his lap and chest, like *Kali-ma*'s Ship's Cat. Hopefully with less clawing and kneading to settle.

Yan leaned back and relaxed. Not the evening he had planned, but the design could wait. And this was far better.

Ainsley's breath relaxed. He sat perfectly still as she dozed, afraid to wake her. She must have worked herself to a frenzy if she thought her command decision would cause a break with him.

da Vinci had said he was the first person to make her smile in more than a decade.

After a while, Yan leaned down to smell her, and kiss the woman on the top of her head.

She stirred. Twisted in place until she was still curled up like a cat, but could look him directly in the face.

"Thank you," she murmured.

Yan brushed the back of a hand on her cheek. She closed her eyes and he thought she was going to start purring.

Those eyes opened, all hazel now.

"As much as your other wives?" she asked, out of the blue, the hint of a grin on her face.

"At least," he said simply.

"Prove it."

Yan grinned back at her. At forty-five, he had nearly a decade on this woman. And he was smart enough not to try and stand up from this chair with her weight on him. Good way to pull something, bad time to do it.

Instead, he slid her forward until her feet touched the ground, then pushed her upright, before standing himself. She hadn't moved, so he stood up against her.

Ainsley was all grins now. It seemed infectious.

Yan considered picking her up and carrying the long woman across the threshold into his sleeping chamber. Too awkward.

He bent forward, placed a shoulder into her stomach, and flipped her over his shoulder, fireman-carry, and stood up. For all her height, she weighed next to nothing.

She laughed. Yan grinned. She swatted him on the bottom a few times with profane curses and threats, but he was not dissuaded.

There was enough light in the sleeping chamber to navigate. He tossed her bodily onto the bed and then slid in beside her, getting all tangled up in legs, arms, and other parts.

Oh, the sacrifices he was willing to make for this woman.

CHAPTER LII

The spies were worthless, as far as Kier was concerned. As Director in command of *Steadfast at Dawn*, she needed better intelligence on Keller's tools and tactics than those fools had been able to provide. They had failed her, and now she had to go into the field with what could only charitably be called a *best guess.*

And even that was thin soup from a cold pot. Ground scans and sensationalized video from the battle over the Imperial capital world, without any meaningful data that would reveal how Keller had done her magic. Vague notes about an invasion of an Imperial world by Keller's people, worse barbarians from further out on the galactic fringes, and even that was highly sanitized, probably to protect whatever fool had lost a winnable battle.

Nothing.

Worse than nothing, actually. At least three different design speculations of what even constituted a class of vessel the barbarians called an *Aquitaine Star Controller*. Those...*mongrels*, who had obviously never actually controlled a star, but had some inner need to impress each other with fancy titles.

So be it.

She was commanding *Steadfast at Dawn*. *Angustidens*–class. A Nightmaster. The second-largest vessel class ever built by the *Lord of Winter*. An entire scale step larger than the battleship Megalodons, capable of carrying four Makos into battle, where that puny battleship brought just six little Hammerheads as escorts.

The *Star Controller* was a carrier as well, but it brought a score or so of tiny, single-person snub fighters. Functionally: a gun, a shield generator, and an engine. Dangerous, though, especially since the Magshear beam would be wasted trying to swat a cloud of hornets. If she jumped into their midst, that would be a task for the Flicker beams, while the Pulse beams engaged the mothership.

At least Keller had brought nothing other than escorts to threaten *The Holding*. Tiny ones, at that, even smaller than Hammerheads. Possibly, one Megalodon and six Hammerheads against one Star Controller and seven corvettes had been a battle Keller was willing to risk, but she was obviously up to something.

Again: the spies had been worthless.

Even in *The Holding*, people had heard about *Keller's Raid*, and the psychological damage the woman had done with nothing more than a small carrier and two escorts. Kier assumed a heavier escort, perhaps a Mako or two, had been lying in stealth when Keller threatened *Trusski*.

Your enemy is not three meters tall, but she is not one meter tall, either. Treat her with the respect due to another Warrior in command of a JumpCarrier.

Still, it rankled. Without better intelligence, Kier knew she was flying blind into a situation Keller had planned. Was this all a feint to draw *Steadfast at Dawn* out of position so an Imperial fleet could swoop in and strike *Samara*? Or the beginning of an invasion designed to peel off layers of *The Holding*, as the woman had apparently done at the place called *Thuringwell*?

Which scenario was more likely to paralyze Kier's response with indecision?

And Ul Banop Cheani Yuur had been no help. The *Khan* of *Trusski* had treated Keller's envoy with *Ambassadorial Privilege*, had even declined to turn her over to agents of *The Holding* for proper interrogation.

As if the barbarians even understood how to comport themselves in polite company. Look at Imperial noblemen and merchants, standing behind their own walls at places like *Osynth B'Udan*. Crass, craven, and worthless. Or the duke who had fled his own territory and pled for asylum with the *Lord of Winter*.

Kier thrust her misgivings from her. *Steadfast at Dawn* was one of two Nightmasters on this frontier, and more than capable of taking on even a medium-sized fleet of Imperial warships, if they chose to stand and face her. She would leave *Traveler into Darkness* here and go hunt the woman Keller. With *Ural*, the force here was sufficient, especially since Wachturm apparently had nothing more with which to threaten this frontier than Keller. If he had, he would have sent sufficient force to hold a planet, rather than merely have her fly by and stir the pot.

Where Keller had gone was, at least for now, a mystery. But the intelligence Kier was reading was weeks old. She would go to *Trusski* and see. Perhaps even speak with this barbarian *Ambassador* and wring from her whatever she might know.

Kier doubted it would be anything meaningful, but when she was done, they could at least witness the tales of woe and take them back to *Fribourg.*

Kier cleared her throat.

Around her, the bridge had been operating on low duty, tucked safely into the gravity well of *Samara*, where no enemy vessel could get to them faster than they could power up and engage.

Eyes glanced in her direction. Perhaps a touch fearfully, as her humor had been bad for days now, and the crew had taken to walking on eggshells.

She would apologize to them in private later. As Director, her duty was clear: to be the stern taskmaster that drove the crew to a higher purpose, just as the *Lord of Winter* did.

"Crew Advocate, state your readiness," Kier ordered in a quieter voice, once she let go some of the misplaced rage.

This crew was excellent. It was *Samara*'s intelligence contingent that she would take issue with, when she returned.

The man who spoke for the crew nodded before speaking.

"We loaded supplies yesterday," he said. "The team is prepared for a significant voyage. Morale is high."

"High, Crew Advocate?" Kier broke her normal routine to pursue the thought.

"Keller is known, Director," he replied. "Her presence at *Trusski* has enraged many who feel that the lesson of *St. Legier* should have been sufficient. They would like an opportunity to reinforce the teachings of the *Eldest.*"

Kier nodded. This was a warship. They were warriors. Scholars would evince a more phlegmatic response, but they were few as a proportion of the total crew on a Nightmaster, the result of carrying a force of Makos into battle along with the command vessel.

"Entity Advocate, bring your charge to a travel configuration," Kier ordered next.

The *Sentience* had been kept at a minimal status for a goodly amount of time. Bringing its processing JumpFlight levels would be a good way of stepping it to the inevitable combat setting, once Keller was located and pinned.

The man who spoke for the Sentience tuned a set of controls on his board, waited for a response, and then looked up.

"All is well, Director," the man said. "The Entity responds to commands and *Energiya* is prepared for flight."

Kier nodded back. Sharp, crisp. War would be coming soon.

"Maneuver Advocate, prepare your squadron," Kier said, glancing at the woman who spoke for the four Warmasters that *Steadfast at Dawn* carried into battle.

Kier didn't wait for a response. The four vessels would have nothing to do until much later, and were already at a green setting.

"War Advocate, we will be hunting a Star Controller," Kier continued. "Seven small escorts were observed. Expect a Mako or two that remained hidden. We will begin at *Trusski*."

Both Advocates acknowledged her. Kier opened a comm channel to locate one other.

Nu Reutra Quilen Danl, but he barely answered to that name anymore. There were suggestions that the agent had gone so deep into his role as an Imperial that he might have suppressed it to the level of forgetting his original identity.

Daniel St. Collins. Truly, a barbaric name, but one that would apparently pass as authentic on many planets, in many nations, without arousing suspicion. As could Danl himself, bland and neutral, with a forgettable face, and shades-of-gray mannerisms.

A cypher, as any good spy should be. But also their resident expert on Imperial culture. And as close as they could get to a specialist on Keller and her barbaric holding.

"Director?" he said into the camera.

Even his voice was unremarkable. Only the blue eyes stood out, but apparently blue eyes were so common in *Fribourg's* ethnotype that anything else might not be considered normal.

"We travel to *Trusski*," Kier announced simply. "You will attend an interview with *Fribourg*'s Ambassador when we arrive."

"Attend, Director?" he asked. "And not conduct?"

"I will join you on the surface, perhaps along with one of our scholars," Kier said. "I wish to learn more about these people from observing one."

"Ah. Understood, Director," Daniel St. Collins said. "I will work up a simple-but-effective disguise for myself. Am I instructed to create one for you, as well?"

"No," Kier decided. "I wish to know my enemy. She should come to know me."

CHAPTER LIII

"Because I am a Minister of the Eighth Rank, and you are a Director," Yuur snapped, finally displaying his exasperation, his pique. At least enough for the camera to pick it up and relay his feelings. "*The Holding* is a function of Scholars, not Warriors. I am willing accommodate you, but only so far. There are limits and you have reached one of them. Am I clear?"

Yuur did have to credit the Director with some measure of sense. Rather than continue to push, as most naval types probably would have, Xi Derag Ahma Kier nodded, face sour and anger simmering. Recognizing when sheer stubbornness was apt to become counter-productive to her mission.

He had never before met the Director of the great warship *Steadfast at Dawn*. The vessel itself had never had cause to even consider a visit to *Trusski*, ere now. But it was here, orbiting overhead geo-synchronously, a greater tool of firepower and destruction than even Red Admiral Keller had brought.

Judging by the image on his screen, the Director was a woman small of stature, but large of spirit, doubly so as she had been awarded command one of the border fleet's anchorships. Skin darker than burnished gold, perhaps with just enough bronze mixed in to exhibit resilience. Large eyes, out of proportion to the rest of her face, expressive and currently unshielded. Expressing her inner thoughts.

Thus, a Warrior and not a Scholar.

"I hear and obey, my Khan," she said. Graciously, even.

Yuur suspected the woman was angry enough to chew nails. Not many people would ever tell this Director *no*. Fewer still, in a situation like this one.

"Thank you," Yuur replied, allowing the situation to fully defuse. The woman meant well, after all. "Let us make this a late-morning social event tomorrow, followed by a working lunch. I find the Ambassador quite adept at holding her own before a potentially hostile audience, as well as a personally-charming conversationalist. That leaves us the afternoon to follow up, and perhaps a state dinner. Or gives us all a chance to separate and have a quiet meal, if necessary."

There was the threat under his words. That this strange Director would behave herself while on his planet, or find herself banished from his presence. And she appeared to finally understand that.

Previously-irresistible force meeting ominously-immovable object.

"I will make arrangements to be on the surface not long after dawn, my Khan," Director Xi said simply.

Yuur nodded and cut the circuit. Their two staffs would organize everything from here on, leaving him time in the morning to watch a shooting star resolve itself into yet another invader landing. Another come to threaten the quiet progress he had achieved on this farming world over the last decade.

This one would not bring a wooden spear with a metal head. And certainly not one dipped previously in blood, according to the ancient rites.

He banished the gloominess from his mood, almost a physical act. *The Holding* was a structure of Scholars. That was what he had told the Director. It was what the *Eldest* had told him, when he was last on *Winterhome*, visiting the great, golden pearl orbiting overhead, the vision of strength and eternity that housed the *Lord of Winter* himself. In the time before Yuur had crossed depth and darkness to arrive at this place.

Yuur sighed. *Trusski* was not important enough to be a significant factor in the machinations of great empires.

And yet.

History would record his name prominently. Perhaps as a hero. Perhaps a villain.

Probably just as a fool. Or worse, a victim.

He brought himself back to the room around him, aware that his focus was still intent on the now-blank screen linking him to *Steadfast at Dawn.*

It was a spare space, as suited his nature. There is no permanence in man, so he retained very little sentiment in place. A few knick-knacks from his much younger days, mementos of a woman he had been allowed to mate with on four separate occasions. She had born him children that no doubt grew up to uphold the best of *The Holding* with their strength, for she had been a formidable woman.

The rest of the place was contained in raw, wooden walls, polished to a comfortable finish and sealed adequately for the simple needs of the man occupying them.

He cycled the communications unit live again and pressed the button to summon Gan. The wait was less than two minutes, most of which was probably spent walking from a quiet bench with a good sun-facing. Gan liked to bask in solar warmth, given any chance.

The door opened on silent hinges.

"Minister?" his aide inquired.

"Locate Scholar Bhattacharya and summon her to my presence in the Lesser Hall, Gan," Yuur said. "I would provide her as much warning and time to prepare as possible."

Yuur rose as Gan closed the door with a nod. *Trusski* had never seen the war. Until the barbarian Keller had arrived, he hadn't even realized his world was listed on Imperial navigation charts as inhabited. There was nothing here of value to steal, and ships were too infrequent for marauders to profitably lie in wait. And even then, what value had a mega-ton load of grain, except on a mining colony?

Yuur adjusted his Ministerial robes, and then changed his mind and stripped them off. He would meet *Fribourg's* Ambassador in his lesser robes. She would note the difference. Perhaps she would appreciate the informality.

Unlike *Steadfast at Dawn,* Bhattacharya and Keller had arrived quietly, and acted with respect but not diffidence. Sought to understand, rather than brusquely issuing orders.

Yuur had, after all, always hoped that something interesting would happen, to break up the monotony of the seasons.

He feared he might come to regret those sentiments.

Yuur sat on a bench along the side wall of the Lesser Hall, letting the light that spilled through stained glass windows overhead paint fanciful patterns on his skin. He could only imagine what the colors looked like on his bald head, considering the odd looks on the faces of the half-dozen Scholars in silent attendance. But they were seated farther away on the same bench, or hovering nervously nearby.

One of the perks of his job were the little practical jokes he could play on himself, and by extension, his staff. Quirks such as meeting the Ambassador in an informal chamber, and sitting quietly in the reception area awaiting her arrival.

The little things he did to pop the bubbles of pomposity that persistently inflated around him.

Gan escorted the woman into the chamber with a fierce gaze at the room. And the faintest blush when he realized why everyone was out of position. Gan would make a fine Minister, one day soon, but he occasionally still had rough edges that needed sanding down.

Yuur smiled serenely at the twosome and patted the bench beside him.

"Ambassador Bhattacharya," he called out. "Please join me."

Her look was even more revealing, a momentary panic that she had unknowingly said or done something improper and had thereby brought embarrassment on herself, or perhaps upon him. A welcome change from the Director and her harsh bluntness.

Bhattacharya recovered instantly, though, and strode closer with élan and flair. He had checked her schedule this morning, approving the curriculum his staff had prepared, intended to educate this so-called barbarian with culture and grace.

Today, she had been visiting a zoological research facility. A fancy name for a pig-breeding farm. Many ethnologies had inherited the ancient, European mutation that allowed them to process the milk of a bovine, and thus consume such exotics as cheese. But that allele was rare in *The Holding*, and almost unknown on *Trusski*, so the breeders focused on pigs and sheep, for the most part.

Sheep were easy to modify over time, producing wool of great strength combined with luxurious texture. *Trusski* had even recently begun exporting it, having developed a market on *Ninagirsu*, clear across the gulf. Yuur secretly harbored the ambitious goal of opening the way to the rest of the *Altai* sector within another generation. Pigs would require some effort yet.

The *Fribourg* woman sat carefully, willing herself perfectly upright, leaving too much weight on her toes, rather than relaxing back into the cool stone of the bench and wall as he did.

"A ship has arrived from *Samara*," Yuur began simply, rewarded by the faintest flinch quickly obscured. "A warship. The Director originally demanded that you be handed over into military custody."

He enjoyed the way this woman nodded, slowly and with calm assurance, as if that had been her expectation from the day she arrived. Perhaps it had.

What else should one expect, leading an invasion of an alien world with less than two hands of staff? And only two of them qualifying as warriors, beyond the Scholar herself.

"Originally?" Bhattacharya inquired carefully.

Yuur smiled. He would refashion this woman into a proper Scholar yet.

"You are an Ambassador, Scholar Bhattacharya," he replied. "While we do not hold to the barbaric folly of your so-called *Laws of Recognized Warfare*, there are certain immutable customs and standards of behavior that mark civilized societies."

"I see," she said with a perfect nod. "Thank you."

Truly, an amazing woman to have grasped the many fine layers of subtlety in his words.

Keller had chosen well. Yuur hoped that this woman had a mate at home who appreciated her.

"Tomorrow morning, you will join me in the Great Hall," he continued, making it more of a request than an order with his tone. "The Director of the vessel *Steadfast at Dawn* and her staff will arrive approximately two hours after sunrise. There will be a brief reception, and then we will retire to a meeting room and then you will be forced to repeat to her everything you have already told me."

He paused, and then grinned at her.

"This woman being a warrior, a military officer of some renown, perhaps some level of crudeness and profanity might, of necessity, be helpful."

Bhattacharya grinned back, two teenagers at the back of the crèche classroom sharing an inside joke when the teacher's back was turned.

"So, a formal ceremony first?" she asked abruptly. "Diplomatic robes and full uniforms sort of thing?"

Yuur nodded with sudden wariness. This woman had a mischievous look in her eyes he found powerfully attractive. A grand practical joke seemed imminent.

"With your leave, I will need to prepare my staff for the coming battle," she said, eyes hooded with a wicked gleam.

"Battle?" Yuur hesitated. "You have one bodyguard on your staff, plus a handful of clerks."

"And a tailor, my Khan," she replied demurely. "First-Rate-Spacer Harmaajärvi has been preparing for tomorrow his entire life."

Yuur blinked, suddenly sensing an entirely new field of diplomatic warfare that did not exist in *The Holding*, where fashion was severely proscribed. He had only heard stories of this *Tailor* but he had no doubts that the man was a warrior of the first rank. He had rearranged the entire political and social structure of the staff sent to assist the Ambassador, with but a look.

A thought struck him. Yuur ran his hand across his bald pate and along the sides where the two-centimeter ring of gray was kept at bay each morning with a sharp blade.

"Would it be appropriate for me to dispatch a specialist in the styling of your hair?" he asked carefully, almost shyly.

The way her eyes lit up almost frightened Yuur for a moment, until he realized what effect she could have on the visiting strangers, and how it was likely to reflect well on him if they found her that much more formidable.

He had come to like this alien woman.

"Please?" she replied.

He turned to Gan and the man nodded with the seriousness normally reserved for sending someone into permanent exile.

"Done," Yuur said.

She rose suddenly, a fluid unfolding with no middle ground.

Seated. Standing.

What looked like a heartfelt bow followed.

"My *Khan*, I thank you again," she said with a merry smile. "Until the morning?"

"Until the morning."

It was amusing, watching her sweep Gan up into her emotional wake. He led her from the room, attempting to maintain *proper and decorous*, but it was obvious that he was just an ornament on the hood of her unstoppable machine. A teacup Chihuahua with his head out the window of a vehicle, tongue wagging in the wind.

Rarely had Yuur looked forward to dealing with those overbearing representatives from *Samara*, or the military.

Tomorrow would be priceless.

Dawn was still some time away. Yuur found himself on a second-story balcony with a good view of the city and the night sky. He contemplated a future that would no longer forget he ever existed, as had been his chief purpose in originally coming to *Trusski*.

Only in an abject failure had he expected his name to be noted anywhere, except perhaps on a dusty list of the many interchangeable Khans of this world.

That would change, after today.

In a way, he missed that never-to-be future. He was a Scholar. A Minister of the Eighth Rank as a reward for a lifetime of careful, capable service to the *Eldest*. Quiet competence should have been the hallmark he left behind.

Bhattacharya and Keller had rendered that immutably impossible now, but he could forgive them.

Oddity overhead drew his eye. There was an extra star in the few visible, if he chose to look for it. *Steadfast at Dawn*. It was a calming thought, the first light of morning having always been the thing that brought him his greatest peace.

A shooting star appeared overhead now, moving with a deliberate grace that gave lie to a transitory nature. The Director was coming, a Warrior come to challenge the Scholars of this world.

Yuur sighed, but only internally, aware that even here there would be an attendant or three striving to be invisible, on-call for any unexpected need their *Khan* expressed. They meant well, but this was one of the days when he considered the possibility of just retiring rather than having to face whatever traumatic ordeal the war with *Fribourg* was about to visit on his people.

But then, he would miss whatever prank Amala had planned. And the one that would come after it. He had no doubt that the woman had striven to hide her irrepressible nature until now, but the change in uniforms had apparently brought it to the surface.

It would probably never be hidden again.

Thus were even Warriors capable of transforming themselves into Scholars.

I t was to be the Great Hall.

Anything less would most likely be construed as some level of subtle insult to the visiting Warrior, however little he might disguise it. Yuur would have instructed the Director to call on him beside a duck pond in the neighboring park if he really wanted to insult the woman in a way she would comprehend. And still be unable to do anything whatsoever about it.

Perhaps he should take to meeting with Bhattacharya at the duck pond. They could make themselves useful and feed the waterfowl and be entertained by them. Or the other way around.

He had worn his finest robes today, the ones reserved in storage for exactly this level of diplomatic endeavor. Starkest black. Somber, sober, precise.

Feeding ducks would be a better use of his time, but this was one of those times when such an option eluded him.

Diplomacy had the engagement set with a concision most would find foreign. The visitors first. The Ambassador would then be summoned to the Presence. And finally the games would begin.

Hungry, waddling ducks.

Yuur glanced once around the chamber. Everyone was in their place, in their finest robes.

Standing, because Yuur's knees had grown stiff with age and kneeling or sitting in a lotus for hours would leave him in so much pain he would be grouchy for days afterwards.

A signal from the entry that the visitors had passed the building's outer door and would approach now.

Yuur placed all thoughts outside of himself and found his focus in the lessons of the *Eldest*.

The Mandarins led. Ministers guided. Scholars provided the hands of the Ministers. Technicians kept the machinery of civilization running smoothly. Warriors protected *The Holding*. Merchants and Artisans used their commerce and wits to keep society itself flowing and entertained.

Yuur had been greatly amused when Scholar Bhattacharya had

introduced her *Tailor* on that first Landing as an Artist, and then put him in charge of the Ambassador's Mission. Certainly, many of the staff he had assigned to aid her had been deeply offended…Scholars forced to obey an Artisan! Amala had apologized later, proffering the excuse that it had been sheer ignorance on her part, rather than a calculated insult.

And having seen the man's work, that *Tailor*, Yuur mentally marked Harmaajärvi as the first Scholar of Fashion that Yuur had ever met. Perhaps the first *The Holding* had ever known.

Shadows at the door. Yuur transformed himself into a *Minister of the Eighth Rank* and projected his authority off the very beams that upheld the roof of the Great Hall. The effect was not lost on his attendants, who suddenly seemed to grow in size with him.

Gan appeared, a step ahead of the Director, rather than leading her by an arm, as he did with the Ambassador.

"Xi Derag Ahma Kier," he announced in a formal cadence. "Director of the warship *Steadfast at Dawn*."

Gan stepped in and to one side, his duties over until called upon again for the next act in this belligerent farce.

The Director was as short in stature as Yuur had guessed. But she burned with an intensity he recognized from his own mirror. She had not forgotten his words, but had chosen to obey rather than withdraw and lose all chance of meeting the barbarian.

As all Warriors, Xi wore her outer-most robe black with a white obi tied in an intricate knot. Each of four layers inward faded, but only to a modest gray, rather than the white of mourning. Yuur could envision her with both the great and short blade tucked into her obi, shoulder length hair pulled up into a topknot, rather than down and loose, as it was today.

Fierce and martial to the core. She advanced eight steps, trailed by one other man, who was subtly wrong in ways Yuur could not identify at first glance.

Yuur smiled, to put the Director at ease. All the forms were being properly obeyed, so any issued would be resolved at the Court of the *Lord of Winter*, perhaps by the Four Mandarins themselves. But that would be tomorrow.

"Director, be welcome to *Trusski*," he said in a conversational tone void of all emotion except careful diplomacy.

She bowed at the waist, straightened, and came to rest.

"How may we serve you?" Yuur continued, playing the role fate had cast for him.

"We are given to understand that an Ambassador from the lands known as *Fribourg* has arrived," Xi replied, following the script carefully.

"Indeed," Yuur replied. "We find her credentials acceptable and have Accredited her as such, a servant of this Court."

"Scholars and Ministers at the Court of *Samara* bade me come here," Xi volleyed the script deftly. "They would know what threat this woman might present to *The Holding*."

"It is well," Yuur concluded. He turned and found Gan by the door. "Scholar Ve, summon Ambassador Bhattacharya to our Presence."

Gan bowed with mechanical precision and departed soundlessly.

Yuur took a moment to study Xi's attendant, seeking that which was troubling.

The robes were correct. The obi tied with spare perfection.

Something was still off.

Yuur found Xi's eyes and asked a silent question, aware that they had a few minutes before Amala would join them.

"My Master of Spies, Minister," Xi replied. "Recently returned from an extended period on *Osynth B'Udan*, the capital world of the imperial sector of space facing *Samara*."

Ah. Years of deep cover then, pretending to be one of them by subverting himself within a role, much like Yuur did when he needed to be a serious Scholar instead of a philosopher poet, but with far greater risk and tolls on the psyche.

Yes, the man was off because the robes were foreign to him after so long among the barbarians. Assigning him to intelligence duty aboard a warship would be a good way to quietly return him to the world of his youth.

And he would be a good assistant to Director Xi, able to pick up subtleties that would be missed by others. Yuur wondered if he was to be the interrogator, or the scribe. Recordings of this day's interaction were likely to provide years of entertainment.

The room lapsed into silence. Comfortable, but not companionable.

An attendant signaled the Ambassador's approach. Scholars made more noise than Warriors, something that might mark her out, but Yuur had been unwilling to volunteer many details about the visitor with Director Xi.

Perhaps if Xi had chosen to be polite from the outset…

And perhaps the two of them would have to meet while feeding the ducks at some point.

Amala Michelle Siddhartha Anne Yuey Bhattacharya appeared at the door.

Even from a crowd of Scholars and Warriors expecting diplomatic skirmishing, there was a tiny, collective gasp of shock. Yuur might have contributed.

As a Scholar specializing in history and government administration, Yuur lacked the vocabulary at the time to describe her. Afterwards, in the privacy of his room, his notes had taken several days to research and record accurately.

Unconsciously, he had been expecting her in full Warrior attire, the black and green outfit she had worn exactly once before, at his express request, to establish her barbarian credentials. Every other time they had met, she had been in more relaxed clothing.

Mufti, as she classified it. As shaped by the Tailor, the Scholar of Fashion attached to her mission.

Today, she had gone the other direction from martial splendor. Her *Tailor* truly had indeed been preparing for this moment for his entire life. Yuur hoped they awarded the man a medal.

Perhaps he would write a letter of recommendation tomorrow.

Bhattacharya wore a cheongsam that had been done in plum silk, with a short, standing collar and embroidered with mystical symbols and numbers in a deeper eggplant purple that drew the eye in harder to stare at her body rather than her face. From here, Yuur was not sure she wore anything under the bodice, an effect heightened by the fact that the gown was slit to just above her hipbones, and she appeared to be wearing nearly-transparent tights under them. Only the fact that her legs were darker than her hands gave that away, but he had to look three times to be sure. And even then…

The top of the cheongsam had what he later discovered were called raglan sleeves, in a nearly-transparent, lavender mesh-like fabric, with eggplant-colored *loong* dragons that each rested a tail on her shoulder and their jaws at her wrist.

Across her chest, just about at the level of her collarbones, a fine, silver chain stretched between two rings just large enough for one of Yuur's fingers. Each of those rings were connected to ten more loops of chain, some larger and some smaller, with the half-dozen larger ones cupping the points of her shoulders rather like pauldrons, and the smaller ones dropping down to almost her elbows.

Someone had pulled her black hair up and to one side underneath a severe-but-utterly-understated box hat, with a silver band around the bottom instead of a brim and holding a gauzy strip of black mesh over her eyes and nose in a manner that only suggested obscuration, without actually committing. She could eat and drink without moving it.

Amala wore no other jewelry today than the chain, even though Yuur had seen her with such in her ears, and she only had the most minimal makeup, done to subtly highlight her eyes and cheekbones without calling attention. She had no need for anything else, the effect was simply exquisite.

For the briefest moment, he regretted that this stunningly-beautiful woman was the enemy, and not someone whose closer acquaintance the *Eldest* would permit him to make on a more…*personal* level. All of the men and probably most of the women in the room were most likely thinking along similar lines.

She entered on slippered feet, placing her at the same height as much of the room. Yuur knew she owned shoes with terrible elevation in the heels, but this effect was more subdued and demure. A dainty artisan, perhaps a dancer, called to the company of the higher powers, rather than an Ambassador of a foreign power come to assert her dominance.

Yuur was not fooled, but he suspected that others might be. Woe unto them.

She arrived at the center of the room and bowed deeply, *sparkling*. There was no more-accurate term that suggested itself.

"My Khan, how may I serve?" she asked in a bright, almost seductive voice as she rose, studiously ignoring Director Xi and the shocked faces only now beginning to settle themselves into more appropriate expressions.

He could have warned them. Would have, in other circumstances. The ducks might still have paid better attention.

Yuur gestured to his latest visitors.

"Xi Derag Ahma Kier," he named her. "Director of the warship *Steadfast at Dawn*."

Yuur was amused when Amala turned and offered a bow that was almost as deep as the one he had rated, but not quite.

Utterly precise, according to protocol she should not have mastered so quickly. He wondered if Gan had suggested it.

"Director Xi, I am known here as Bhattacharya Yuey Anne Siddhartha

Michelle Amala," she said. "Scholar and Ambassador to the *Khan* of *Trusski*. Forgive my ignorance of your ways. Would Director more closely equate to the Imperial naval rank of Admiral, or Captain?"

Yuur found it amusing, the way Xi was visibly derailed as she had to stop and calculate the finer points in her head before speaking. He was rewarded with images in his head of bulls and china shops.

"Admiral," Xi finally replied, voice as unsettled as her face. "Commander of *Buran*'s field forces on this frontier."

"Ah. Thank you."

Amala surprised them both by bowing a second time. The look of innocence on her face when it was visible again was probably calculated to fool everyone but him. It probably would. This was a woman of heretofore-unseen depths of wry silliness residing within the shell of a serious Scholar.

It reminded him of someone he knew, and possibly saw in the mirror regularly.

"What is your mission?" Xi asked gruffly, now that the proper forms had been obeyed.

Close enough to proper, anyway. He would let the two of them define their own *go-board*.

Amala's face turned serious without ever moving.

"I am a personal representative of Keller Marie Jessica," she said simply. "Imperial Admiral of the Red, Republic Fleet Centurion, Queen of the Pirates. She had commanded *Trusski* to become an active warzone, under the *Laws of Recognized Warfare*, and has tasked me with interfacing with the local population."

"She is not here," Xi growled in a rough tone. "And would have no standing to threaten, were she."

"The Red Admiral is not making war on civilians, Director Xi," Amala countered in a voice hiding a blade under a silk kerchief. "Only the *Immortals*, the *Sentient Systems*, conducted orbital bombardments of civilian worlds in ancient times. And more recently."

Yuur gasped along with everyone else at the audacity of the observation. But he could not challenge it, for she spoke the exact and honest truth, and that was proof against any accusation of libel.

It was still a telling blow.

Keller had actually been at *St. Legier* when one of *Buran*'s warships dropped nuclear explosives on it. The death of hundreds from the attack, rather than millions, was a matter of scale, not intent. Keller could have just as easily sat above Taymyr and wrought total devastation, were she of a mind to even the scales.

Her forbearance, and more especially going to such extremes of preparation as to cast a *Fetial's* Javelin literally into his back yard, were some of the reasons he had been so keenly interested in meeting the so-called Red Admiral's Ambassador.

That Bhattacharya Amala had turned out to be who she was had just made the entire project easier. And she would enjoy feeding and entertaining ducks.

Xi looked like a woman willing to throw protocol to the wind and challenge the Ambassador to a personal duel. Having read Amala's credentials, Yuur knew she could probably hold her own against all the Scholars in the room if it came to that. And possibly his guards at the same time.

A person did not reach a senior field rank as a Fleet Marine by merely being good at paperwork. Administrative acumen had probably helped, but Yuur had read and understood her other combat certifications.

That she could become a credible Scholar had been his own personal greatest surprise. Possibly hers as well. Combat was the woman's forte.

Amala smiled in a way that seemed to invite such a desperate failure of decorum, as long as she could not be blamed for instigation.

Telling, that.

Director Xi apparently came to the same conclusion. She controlled her breathing and ground her teeth, but refused the bait.

Yuur looked intently at the others in the room, drawing them all back into his orbit with the weight of his gaze.

"Are there any others who would speak to this Court?" he demanded in a way that suggested drastic punishment for anything that could not wait until the morrow.

No one spoke.

"I declare this assembly closed," he continued. "Scholar Ve, clear the chamber. Director Xi, Ambassador Bhattacharya, you will attend me."

Yuur did not wait for their assent. He turned on his heel and strode from the chamber to the conference room that had been prepared. There, he would host his three visitors with the assistance of a handful of his staff.

And then things would get interesting.

CHAPTER LIV

Amala was happy that protocol demanded that the *Buran* admiral and her aide precede her into the next chamber. The woman was utterly seething. For good reason, since Amala had found a chink in her armor already and drawn first blood. Twice, even. All those lessons and meetings with Keller's legal team had paid off. Plus, a lifetime serving under Alber'.

And she had no doubt that the day would get bloody before it was done. Hopefully, it would only be metaphorical. In the three months she had been here, she had come to like and respect the Khan. Yuur Ul reminded her of one of her favorite uncles.

But she had a mission, and it was a dangerous one.

Thankfully, First-Rate-Spacer Vibol Harmaajärvi had surpassed even his own impossible standards today. She could see that in the ways that so many faces studied her chest and her hips, rather than her face.

Amala Bhattacharya, the plain line marine with a nose too big, was suddenly an object of *lust*. It was a weird feeling. Especially when even the *Khan* looked at her that way.

But she needed every edge if she was to get out of this one alive. Push the navy folks, but do it on *Buran*'s terms. Diplomatic ones. Score points with the Khan and his Scholars by making the barbarian from the distant frontiers come off as more civilized than his own folks. Make Keller look good by extension.

Amala had no idea what Keller and her team had in mind for the tactical situation, but the Red Admiral had brought Alber' d'Maine and Tomas Kigali to the dance.

That did not suggest High Tea by anybody's concept of the term.

Amazingly, the same interior decorator appeared to have done this conference room, as did the primary briefing chamber aboard *VI Victrix*. Maybe they all ordered from the same catalog or something.

Boring, sand-colored carpet, where the hall they had just left had been stone tile floors. Probably better at hiding stains, although much harder to just wipe them up. Trade-offs.

Polished-surface, wooden conference table, vaguely oval, where Alber' had the squared-off version back home, but it might have been the same wood finished with the same stain.

Water-color beachscapes. Amala could swear her oldest sister had the exact same print hung in the entry hallway in her flat, however many light-centuries away, culturally and physically.

Black chairs on roller wheels. With complicated, mechanical handles on the sides to make them do things, or make them stop.

Standing silver urn that would be filled with the local definition of coffee on a side table. A collection of fruit and a platter of those amazingly-scrumptious butterhorns she had discovered at a hole-in-the-wall bakery four blocks over from the Hall of Government.

Gan Ve must have whispered her secret in somebody's ear. Hopefully, the owner would forgive her for bringing him to the attention of voracious bureaucrats.

The Khan took a seat at the obvious head of the table. The Director and her assistant were seated on the far side. Scholar Ve put Amala alone on the near side and moved to stand behind the Khan.

Two on one wasn't exactly fair, but would have to do, unless she determined that she needed to bring Vibol with her to the next meeting and let his fussiness and obvious disdain for their plain clothing disrupt their train of thought.

He could probably do that. Might be worth pursuing if they turned into shits on this one.

Director Xi was practically vibrating with rage, across the table, but her assistant was paying sharper attention. Unlike the rest, he didn't come out of the cookie-cutter mold. And he looked more like an Imperial, with brown hair instead of black, and rounder eyes.

She immediately assumed he was a spook and categorized him accordingly.

Amala turned to the Khan and put on her most innocent smile. She had practiced that one since she was eight and needed to blame something on one of her siblings. It had usually worked.

"Director, Ambassador, thank you for joining me today," the Khan opened the meeting. "I will remind you both that this is a civilized culture and that you will be on your best behavior while you attend me."

In other words, she had gotten a sly one in early, and nobody else was going to. Amala could live with that.

The woman across the table leaned forward. She didn't put any weight on the surface, but Amala could tell she wanted to.

"Why are you here?" she hissed.

Amala smiled. Yuur Ul had been right. Repeat everything, possibly verbatim. She was sorry he and his staff would have to sit through it a second time.

"The Emperor of *Fribourg*, Karl VII, has decreed that all of *Buran* is now a legitimate military target," she replied, letting her voice wander off into that sing-song rote of a ten-year-old repeating a school lesson. Anything to further irritate this woman. "Red Admiral Keller is planning demonstrations across the entire sector, and possibly across the gulf into the area you refer to as *Altai*. And beyond. We are not, however, barbarians, so it became incumbent upon the admiral to provide ample warning to any civilians who may become caught up in the chaos of war, that they may prepare accordingly."

Amala hadn't been with Alber' during *Keller's Raid*, but the old-timers had made a point of breaking in the newbies with tales of psychological warfare and legendary practical jokes thought up by Moirrey Kermode.

This was just the latest iteration. Maybe the meanest one.

"Where is she now?" Xi demanded.

Amala grinned and cocked her head, like she had just heard the stupidest thing she would encounter all week. Might be, at that.

"I spent the last month in transit here buried in language lessons and intelligence summaries," Amala said. "And I have been here for three months after she left. She may have attacked *Ninagirsu* by now, for all I know."

Okay, technically a low blow. Probably would get her wrist smacked by the Khan later, after the diplomacy was done. The way everyone's eyes got a little bigger was a dead giveaway that they might have forgotten there was a war going on.

Samara was always the Imperial target of choice, because the Imperials were too linear. Break open the frontier and then roll up the lines both ways. Two-dimensional thinking, when JumpSpace let you come out anywhere you had food and fuel to reach.

It was weird, being a Scholar instead of a combat goon. Playing chess with someone across the table instead of Greco-Roman wrestling on a mat. This just might become a fun second career. Probably safer than carrying a pulse pistol every day, too.

"Why are you here, then, Bhattacharya?" the guy she flagged as a spy decided to step into the conversation, before his boss lost her shit.

Which was imminent.

"Red Admiral Keller would know the people of *Buran* better," Amala lied with a facile tongue about her sister sneaking into the cookie jar. "*Trusski* was remote enough from all the other colonies on this side of *M'Hanii* that she could deliver an Ambassador, along with a message box."

"A message *box*?" asked the spy

The Khan leaned forward and broke the line of conversation, apparently with his telepathic powers he hadn't mentioned before. All heads rotated towards him in absolute synch.

"The Red Admiral delivered a personal message," he said. "Scholar Bhattacharya could be considered the Empire's *Fetial*."

He turned just enough to the right to get his assistant's attention.

"Scholar Ve, you will cause the guard to retrieve the declaration of war and present it."

Apparently, there was no love lost between the locals and the folks on that side of the table. She could see the angriness floating around, like thought bubbles in a kids' cartoon. And they were scarlet right now.

Everyone kind of sat back and relaxed while they waited for things to move.

A few minutes later, the door opened and Ve entered first, followed by a man carrying Kermode's javelin like a flag-pole, tip up and with the two feathers Moirrey had attached to the crossbar, just behind the head.

And apparently, a nurse had drawn Keller's blood in a lab ahead of time, just so she could smear it on the blade. The locals had left it there, along with the dirt that had stuck when it fell the last hundred meters and stuck point-down in the soil. Probably afraid of all the bad ju-ju it carried.

Alber' might be a hard-case, but Keller was in her own league.

The man set it down with a thump next to the Khan, who reached out a hand to hold it himself. He focused his intent on Amala.

"Technically, a case could be made that Keller also bombarded a civilian world," he observed dryly. "Since the automated vehicle that dropped this in my garden continued its glide beyond the city and eventually crashed in a farmer's field. No sheep were injured. Frightened, but not injured."

Amala suppressed a grin. She could see one in his eyes, but the navy people had lost all sense of humor.

She turned back to them.

"A declaration of war," Amala said with deadly conviction. "Taken according to well-established historic and legal principles and codes that Keller follows. Grand Admiral Wachturm has placed her in command of forces on this border."

Director Xi turned to the Khan with an ugly snarl on her face.

"And you will continue to grant Ambassadorial Privilege to this *person*?" she rasped, right at the edge now.

"I am the *Khan* of this system," he rebuked her with a soft snap to his voice. "Your job is to provide security. Since Bhattacharya and her entire embassy number less than ten, I do not feel personally threatened by her. And Keller did not threaten *Trusski*, only your fleet. Scholar Bhattacharya will remain."

Amala figured that things were about to get wound up at this point. Hours and hours of pointed questions she either ignored or lied answers to. Keller had specifically left her in the dark on anything operational. As she should have.

Xi surprised everyone by sliding the chair back, standing, and bowing shallowly to her across the table, and then deeply to the Khan.

"You are correct, my Khan," she said formally. "I forget myself. My place is in orbit, defending *The Holding*. I will leave the scholarly tasks in your capable hands."

And then she and her spy were gone in a whirlwind of activity, stomping out with half the attendants and Scholar Ve with them.

"Was that wise?" Amala asked. "My other job was to obfuscate and mislead your naval forces, but you were not required to assist."

"Scholar Bhattacharya," he said with a weary smile. "Amala. *Trusski* would barely notice a naval blockade on trade. If Keller truly refuses to bombard us from orbit then we might not even notice the war, as we have not in all the generations since the first colonists landed. The *Eldest* has a plan for all humanity that will bring universal peace and stability, once enough barbarian realms are civilized. But that plan will take many more centuries to effect. Millennia. There is no call for personal rudeness, nor to hand you over for torture, for secrets you probably don't possess."

Okay, this man was playing a much deeper game than she realized.

She had been paying attention to the strong, kindly man who was *Khan*. The one that reminded her of a favorite uncle. She had forgotten what he must have been and done to get there.

He rose and released a deep sigh.

"There is time before lunch," he said, out of the blue. "Would you care to join me in feeding and entertaining the ducks?"

Ducks?

Amala rose, aware that during that speech, he had used her given name to address her for the first time since she arrived. She had moved into a different circle of relationship with the man.

"It would be an honor to assist you, my Khan," she smiled.

Amala wondered what his attitude would be when Keller and the fleet returned.

CHAPTER LV

"Ye Gods," Senior Centurion Elzbet Aukley said as the image came up on her screen. "What in creation is that?"

"That's why I figured I should wake you up, boss," the man said with a serious frown.

Orn Nwokolo had worked his ass off to make it to the level of Assistant Science Officer on a Galactic Survey Cruiser at such a young age. Elzbet had been partly responsible for driving him there, once she saw him work. She trusted his judgment on this sort of thing, a faith that was only reinforced when she got a look at the monitor.

"Take over down on the emergency bridge," she decided. "Kanda needs to see this, too."

Elzbet looked around the otherwise quiet bridge as Orn left at a run, and took a breath. It was deep in the ship's night right now, but war was a twenty-four/seven operation. She leaned across the station and initiated a link to the commander's suite.

"Command Centurion Lungu to the bridge," she said, closing the channel and looking around. "Bring the vessel to yellow alert and hold there."

Not quite shit-hitting-fan, but everyone be prepared for it in short order, so stay out of the shower and the gym.

GSC Ballard wasn't a warship, but they were all in the navy, and even a survey cruiser had guns, Tomas Kigali's ongoing snide commentary notwithstanding.

Elzbet logged herself into the science officer station and brought all data feeds on-line. In their time hiding at the system boundary, *Ballard's* specialists had been able to covertly install a number of passive sensors, both down on the surface of the little iceball they hid behind, and in close orbit, so they could see *Trusski* without exposing much of themselves.

Only occasionally did the ship slip above the horizon to bring the big sensor arrays into play. Today was probably going to be one of those days. She had served with Kanda Lungu enough to know how the woman thought.

Imperial data files finally found a match with a happy chirp and began displaying specifications.

Angustidens-class. A type of vessel tagged as a Nightmaster, what the Imperials called a JumpCarrier.

Frightening.

Take a battleship bigger than anything *Fribourg* or *Aquitaine* fielded, maybe as big as a Star Controller. Along with the usual split into *Buran* and *Energiya* components for combat, this vessel carried with it four smaller ships like remorae, each classified as a Mako, or roughly somewhere around the size and capabilities of a cruiser.

A castle with four big towers on the corners, each of which could separate and fight on its own terms.

Heavier than what First Expeditionary had taken to invade *Thuringwell*, but Elzbet also had a pretty good idea about what an Expeditionary Cruiser like *VI Victrix* could do. Two of them might be a good match for four Makos, depending on luck and positioning.

"What have we got?" Kanda said as she entered the bridge, still tugging her tunic into place.

"Flagship of the enemy sector fleet just inserted into *Trusski* orbit," Elzbet said. "Nwokolo spotted them when they dropped out of their in-system jump, right about where we expected them, based on Keller's notes. Signal's lagging about four and a half hours at this point. They appear stable now. Probably asking the locals for directions."

"Gold star for Orn," Kanda smiled. "You ready to peek?"

"Just waiting for the order," Elzbet replied with a grin.

They made an excellent team, intuitively able to finish each other's sentences like sisters at this point, even if they looked nothing alike.

Elzbet was tall and rail thin, regardless of what she ate. Her brother had always accused her of looking like an ancient scarecrow. Golden blond hair that refused to stay curled only heightened the resemblance to straw and a strawman.

Kanda Cosmina Lungu, on the other hand, was short and curvy, and as dark of skin and hair as Elzbet was washed out.

Sisters under the skin, though.

She keyed the ship-wide comm.

"All hands to action stations," Elzbet called. "Prepare for a surveillance run."

For the rest of the fleet, the second in command was the tactical officer for combat. On a survey cruiser, she was still 2IC, but now it was the combat of stealthy listening. At *Thuringwell*, it had also involved slinging a snowball of electronic hash at the opposition.

Kanda locked herself down and nodded.

"Aukley, you have Tactical," she ordered.

Elzbet willed herself to stillness, as if she could influence the rest of *Ballard* by mind alone.

"Engineering, bring all power systems on-line," she ordered.

Electronic warfare was a function of raw power, either to broadcast noise on every frequency, or cut through it. Since they were alone out here, everything could go into electronic counter measures, *ECM*, at the push of the big, purple icon in the middle of her console, generating an electronic smoke screen hopefully good enough for them to hide behind. At least long enough to peek-n-sneak.

The sensors themselves consumed little power, especially in passive mode, but the signal from the planet was over four hours old. That monster could have jumped out, found *Ballard's* hiding spot, and be preparing to appear on top of them before Elzbet or Orn knew it was coming.

Only when the signal from engineering went green did Elzbet move to stage two.

"Nav, prepare to broach," she ordered.

Ballard was hanging in a low orbit over their frozen world, barely held in place by just enough gravity to make the planetoid a true sphere. If they did nothing, they would orbit the star and the planet at the same speed, forever in the iceball's shadow, as seen from *Trusski*.

But this was the dangerous part.

The pilot looked up and nodded his confirmation. Everybody tended to get silent on this bridge when they worked, especially when they were being sneaky. It was unnecessary, since they were light hours away, but it reflected well that everyone thought that way. There was no combat glory on a survey cruiser.

Hide with pride.

"Execute your broach, Pilot," Elzbet ordered.

Like a whale from the lost homeworld, transplanted to so many other planets, *Ballard* popped over the north pole of their bolthole, bringing the sensor array into the clear like a giant, electronic blowhole. Boards that had been running at thirty percent data input suddenly hit max.

A firehose of data that the Fleet Centurion would need.

Elzbet held them there for nearly four minutes. Long enough for systems to identify the vessel as *Steadfast at Dawn*, according to the Imperial records accumulated on various trips to get their asses kicked at *Samara* too many times by this craft and another one like her.

She hoped Moirrey Kermode had a good surprise in store for those folks. That thing was a mobile combat platform, not a mere warship.

"Thoughts?" Kanda asked simply.

"Have everything I need at this point," Elzbet replied. "Run for home?"

"Unless you have a reason to stay put?"

"Negative, Commander," Elzbet said. "One of those Makos could take us by itself. Nav, take us down."

He had been waiting for the order, fingers poised over the buttons with the course already laid in. On the screen, the horizon went from below them to above them, and then off to one side as *Ballard* pitched down hard and started to yaw starboard. In less than a minute, darkness reigned as the worldlet in front of them resumed its task as their shelter from the solar wind. And from prying eyes.

"Commander, you have the bridge," Elzbet said.

"Roger that," Kanda replied. "Nav, plot a course straight outward from *Trusski*, maintaining our sensor shield as we go. Go to JumpSpace as soon as we clear the local gravity well."

"Already set, Commander," he said.

Elzbet smiled. A solid crew.

Now they just needed to show all this to the Fleet Centurion.

Things were going to get rough out here.

CHAPTER LVI

She hadn't really believed the man, but Amala found herself out a back door of the palace, through a thick green belt of semi-wild plants and knee-high grass, following a path worn by feet, rather than paved.

The Khan walked with deliberation this morning. She had seen him move faster, but he seemed in no hurry, so she fell in quietly beside him, trailed as they always were by Gan Ve and a cast of rotating assistants, all maintaining a discreet distance. She wondered if they expected to be struck by lightning bolts from the Khan's obvious rage, which slowly evaporated as he walked.

Certainly, she had expected hours of inane diplomatic maneuvering. She had prepared the darkest tea she could this morning, for the extra caffeine. And instead, she was apparently going to help Yuur feed ducks and hope she wouldn't have to pee anytime soon.

The wonders of the diplomatic corps.

Yuur Ul paused, bringing the entire convoy to a ragged halt. He selected one of the men trailing and gestured him closer. Amala noticed that the man had a cloth bag, filled with something small and lumpy.

The Khan took it with a steady hand and then fixed a fierce gaze on the rest of the locals.

"You will await my pleasure here," he pronounced in a voice of quiet command.

Amala held her breath as he turned to her and allowed the faintest grin for the briefest moment.

"Ambassador Bhattacharya, would you join me?" he asked in a lighter voice. Friendlier.

Amala nodded. The Khan turned his back on the rest and held out an elbow. She took it, aware that physical contact in public was generally frowned upon, except when Scholar Ve was guiding her.

She wondered what this man was up to, but he obviously wished to speak to her in private, and she had seen his displeasure at Director Xi's behavior earlier. Perhaps she had scored more points than she had expected to today.

They walked.

The path meandered a bit before penetrating a stand of trees that then opened up into a broad clearing. A pond.

With ducks, as promised.

Fat, happy, waddling little honkers that spotted them and suddenly came running as fast as their stubby feet would carry them.

Amala went to withdraw her hand as he stopped, but he clamped his elbow against his body, holding her in place. Opening the bag, he pulled forth a handful of popcorn and tossed it into the happy melee that had suddenly surrounded them two meters deep in all directions. Handfuls went every which way, ducks chasing them hither and yon.

Finally, the bag was empty. The Khan had not spoken since dismissing his staff, so she waited patiently.

He turned and studied her face briefly.

"Today did not follow the rules of correct behavior," he observed in a voice lighter than his words. Not quite sarcastic, but not very serious.

No response appeared to be called for, so Amala paused with an expectant look on her face.

He grinned.

"*The Holding* is a function of Scholars, madam," he continued. "*Fribourg*, as I understand it, is a culture of aristocratic privilege, where birth plays a significant role in the path of one's life."

"You are generally correct," she replied, when he paused. "There are avenues open for advancement, based on merit, but they can be tertiary. I was born farther away, in the nation known as *Aquitaine*, which subscribes to a more republican model. Still some level of classism, but the limits are frequently self-imposed, largely circumscribed by your dreams."

"And thus a Warrior is capable of transforming herself into a Scholar?" he asked.

"Indeed, my Khan," she replied. "Though I would have never expected it a year ago."

He smiled, and began to move, drawing her along by the hand trapped against his body. A bench awaited, and she joined him seated atop the cool stone.

"In *Buran*, as you know *The Holding*, there are no families as you understand the concept," he said. "Two people are selected to mate, based on criteria decided by the *Eldest*, or forbidden when they file a request. If a child is born, it becomes a ward of the state, to be raised *en masse* in crèche schools. There is no class, but each child is socialized properly, and then trained. As they age, their tendencies become known and they are forwarded into one of the broad schools, where they may go as far and as high as their talent and drive take them."

Amala nodded, muffling her shock at such a culture and eager to learn more. None of the briefing documents had more than hinted at such things, but they had been prepared by naval officers expecting combat, not diplomats landing on the surface. Amala had never considered the scale of it, building an entire culture that way.

"I was selected as a Scholar early and trained as one," the Khan mused, his eyes staring off into a distance greater than space. "Eventually, I was promoted to be a Minister of the Eighth Rank, and selected to serve the last of my active years as Khan of *Trusski*, before eventually retiring and returning home."

He lapsed into silence, interrupted only by greedy waterfowl hoping that there were more treats, before they finally waddled back to the pond and began to chatter quietly amongst themselves.

At no point had his hold on her hand loosened enough for her to politely withdraw.

"But the war intrudes upon us," the man continued. "My proper duty may very well be to take you prisoner and forward you to the agents of the *Eldest*, either at *Samara*, or all the way to the capital at *Winterhome*. I do not see how anything useful could come of such an action, because the Warriors have lost sight of their purpose. Director Xi sees herself as a conqueror whose glory will be found in battle, subjugating the worlds of your Imperium, rather than simply absorbing them as *The Holding*'s greater superior culture expresses itself."

He finally turned to face her, his eyes coming back from wherever it was he had been in his mind.

"Scholar Bhattacharya. Amala," he began in a sad voice that found its footing. "I will need to revoke your credentials as an Ambassador."

She started to speak, but her overrode her.

"It is for your own safety that I must do this thing," he said. "If I cast you out at a time when *Steadfast at Dawn* is not present, then you may safely escape. I had hoped that your mission could continue, but I expect Xi to return with orders from the Khan of *Samara*, whose authority I must recognize. Were you still here, you would be doomed to a less pleasant place than I would send you."

Amala took a breath to center her racing thoughts. This was nowhere in anyone's playbook of how all of this was supposed to go down. Period.

Of course, Keller had no real idea of what was likely to happen when she left Amala here. They might have shot her on sight. Or imprisoned her, hauling her off to stand before the ancient demon in literal chains. And they might have welcomed her as a friendly visitor and introduced her to butterhorns and ducks.

"So that my mission is not ranked a failure with Admiral Keller, should you be prepared to send a diplomat with me?" Amala ventured. "That the Warriors may be seen as distinct from the work of Scholars."

What the hell. After all, what was the worst thing he could say? Yes?

The Khan's face grew closed. Not distant, and not cold, but it turned somehow into a metallic casting of the man, rather than flesh. Even the eyes stopped moving.

"Your Admiral Keller must know what resources she is facing on this front," he replied.

"Else she would not have provoked this confrontation?" Amala completed his thought.

"So you are a spy?" he probed.

"We are all spies, my Khan," she said. "Keller wishes to know these people, that war on *Fribourg*. What would make them stop, or engage in trade, rather than conflict? She brought *Fribourg* to peace with *Aquitaine* by understanding their nature. She did not conquer them, nor they her. Instead, we have become allies. War is not a necessity here, except that *Buran* advances into any opening and then furiously defends their trespass. Two generations ago, *M'Hanii* was the border, although *Buran* had crossed it even then. You advance inexorably, and then wonder why your new neighbors grow fearful at your approach."

Some small part of her mind noted that her hand was still not free, leaving her to turn enough to address the man, close enough that one might kiss the other without much effort.

She did not think he had brought her here with seduction in mind…

"We know only of *Fribourg* that they are barbarians from beyond the fringe of civilization," the Khan said abruptly. "But that is the thinking of the Warriors, who have dedicated themselves to defending *The Holding*. I wonder if the Scholars have lost sight of themselves as well."

Amala shrugged, as much as she could.

"Your Admiral Keller," he said abruptly. "Is she as honorable as you say?"

"I have found her to be one of the most terrible Warriors I have ever known," Amala admitted. "Even greater than the man who was my commander prior to volunteering for this assignment. But she also held the entire *Fribourg Empire* together at the moment when it could have collapsed from *Buran's* meddling. And they had been her greatest foe the day before. She will treat your Scholar with all the honor you have done me, even if she must defy the Emperor himself in order to do so."

He fell silent. She did the same. The ducks yammered happily.

"We will address this issue again," he finally said, his voice growing heavy and sharp. "But you will not speak of it with anyone, save to prepare your people to be able to move suddenly. Secrecy will be of the essence."

"As you command, my Khan," Amala said.

He rose, drawing her to her feet, and finally let go the grip on her hand. He turned and offered her a bow.

"This will be a problem for Scholars to solve, Amala," he commanded. "The Warriors have their place, but I believe that in this matter, they lead us astray."

She nodded silently, unsure of where the man was leading her.

She watched him gaze out over the duck pond, with apparent longing, before his face grew less solemn and he smiled at her.

"Come," he said. "I am sure my Scholars are beside themselves with worry, and are probably close to gossiping. We should return to their world."

Amala fell into stride with him, nerves afire.

All of this suddenly felt like a combat drop. She had been in a planetary invasion, it was true, but a small one.

This felt like the real thing.

CHAPTER LVII

It was still bizarre, seeing a major military installation in the middle of nowhere, but Jessica was finally getting used to the view. Anyplace else and there would be a planet below them, with a warm star in the near distance, but they had built this station so far from the nearest system that its sun only appeared as a slightly-brighter dot on the screens.

Downside, the need to maintain constant vigilance against a *Buran* warship dropping out of jump right on top of them and opening fire. They could do that anyway, but without any gravity well handy to distort a jump, a shark could get pin-point accuracy.

Upside, Arott could flip the entire station into JumpSpace, something no mere orbital platform could match. But this wasn't just a platform. This was a super-monitor. Slow, cumbersome, and awkward, but equipped with firepower better than a battleship: an array of Type-4 beams on the corners, and all the old Type-1's replaced with the new Type-1-Pulse that Moirrey had perfected after watching the so-called Flicker-beams that *Buran* had used at *St. Legier*.

Jessica turned from the view out her window as the hatch opened.

"Time?" she asked as Marcelle entered.

The woman nodded silently, and Jessica moved to her desk. She paused just long enough to grab the half-full sippy cup of coffee and her personal slab, and then followed her long-time assistant into the corridor.

Into the future.

That was how she thought of what was coming. Everything over the last year or more had been merely a holding pattern until she was able to come all the way out here, find the enemy, and study them.

For having been at war for generations, however quietly it had been fought until the last decade or so, *Fribourg* had provided precious little useful intelligence. Granted, she knew everything there probably was to know about *Samara*, and the capabilities of the colossal Starbase known as *Ural*, but that seemed to have been the limits of Imperial intelligence.

How to get there. What you would find when you arrive. Everything every commander had tried before now that had failed.

All of which amounted to going back to look for an even bigger hammer when the one you had broke.

Stupid. And counter-productive, as *Buran* had quietly colonized nearly three dozen planets on this side of the *M'Hanii Frontier* over the last century. Some, apparently, rather long ago, given how well-established they appeared to Glenn and *CP-406*, sneaking into the various systems and looking around before committing her *petit* vandalisms.

Jessica had no doubt that Emmerich would have finally managed to do something meaningful on this border, had he been free to give it his full attention. But he had been wrapped up for the last twenty years slowly strangling *Aquitaine*, where he was still referred to in equal parts fearful and reverential tones as *The Red Admiral*, much as she was now assuming that mantle.

But he was stuck at home now, rebuilding from the emotional wreckage wrought by that idiot Dittmar and all of his dead conspirators.

She would have to combat *Buran* for him.

The hatch to the big conference room opened to a wall of noise. Not quite arguments, but voices were raised and nobody was looking this way.

Jessica caught Enej's eye across the space and nodded minutely. He smiled and stuck two fingers into his mouth and whistled. The alert siren made less noise.

Silence.

She smiled gratefully at him and took her seat next to her long-serving Flag Centurion, now a Senior Centurion, the two of them at the opposite end from Arott. The room was filled to overflowing. All of her command centurions were physically present this morning, along with many of their Executive Officers.

Council of War.

Jessica found Kanda and Elzbet, representing *Ballard*, with Glenn, *CP-406*, seated on Elzbet's right. Her smile to them was appreciative, for all the risks they had taken, scouting for her silently and successfully. None of this would work, if *Buran* had any foreknowledge of what she had planned.

"Stage Three is now complete," Jessica announced to the room.

Everyone already knew that, but this was the confirmation they had been awaiting. And probably the source of the raised voices when she entered.

"We have arrived on the farthest shore of the *Fribourg Empire*," she continued, checking numbers off on her left hand. "We have established a semi-permanent base in a place where hopefully none of them will ever think to look. We have made our presence known at *Trusski*, and drawn out a significant portion of *Buran*'s border fleet to intercept us."

She paused to study all the faces around her, new and old. Comrades from the very old days, like Robbie Aeliaes and his First Officer, Harden Glenraven, a woman who could pass for Robbie's younger sister, with the same rich, brown skin and dark curls.

Tomas Kigali and Alber' d'Maine had been there for *The Long Raid*.

Others had been added later, at places like *Thuringwell*, or more recently in the case of the rest of the corvette commanders, for *The Expedition*, as this mission was coming to be known.

Jessica signaled to Casey on her right and a projection took shape above the center of the conference table, rotating slowly on the horizontal axis.

"This is the vessel *Steadfast at Dawn*, we believe," she continued. "What they call a Nightmaster in the old terminology, or a JumpCarrier. Each of those four points around the main bow is a separate warship a step smaller than a *Founder-class* Heavy Cruiser. They can jump free entering combat, so we would be facing a battleship-equivalent with a four-cruiser escort if we chose to engage."

Jessica signaled Casey, who pushed a second button. The rear quarter of *Steadfast at Dawn* turned red in response.

"This is the *Energiya* module," Jessica said. "In combat, it will clear the combat area as fast as it can, and hide from everyone else until the fighting is over. Normally, *Buran* is attacking, so they will group up out a ways from their target planet, detach the *Energiya*, and then use the short-range drive, what they call the *Capriole*, to maneuver in close. When *Fribourg* attacks, they always come out a safe distance beyond the gravity well, which gives *Buran* time to separate, and the *Energiya* time to escape."

Jessica let the moment drag and she took in the faces around her.

"I propose something special, if we can catch them at *Trusski* on a patrol pass."

"Do we know they'll come back to *Trusski?*" Robbie asked before anyone else could get the words out. "We've already hit several other systems. Well, *CP-406* has, but that's us, as far as the locals know."

"We have not communicated with any other system," Glenn leaned forward and fixed Robbie with almost a challenging stare. "Except to warn them to evac their station before we blew it up. Only *Trusski* has had any conversation."

Jessica nodded. Just so. Glenn was, indeed, becoming a pirate, as Bedrov had foreseen, had warned.

"I expect they will run a patrol pattern to the other systems in the neighborhood," she said. "And they will see what Glenn and her team did. Hopefully, they come back to *Trusski*, expecting to encounter us when we come back to get Amala Bhattacharya. It's the only starting point they have to go on, unless they decide to abandon the sector and fort up at *Samara.*"

"What happens if they do?" Alber' asked.

Jessica smiled. Only Alber' would be disappointed to have forty unarmed planets to conquer. He was born to fight. And Yan Bedrov had given him the ultimate expression of destruction with *VI Victrix*.

"*2218 Svati Prime* happens," she replied. "I would like to entice them to a classical engagement. I'm willing to frighten the colonists nearly to death as an alternative."

"We could always bomb them," Kigali offered in a sepulchral voice.

Nobody else at the table would dare voice that opinion with her, but Kigali knew where the boundaries were, when talking tactics and strategy. Practical jokes were one thing, and anyone here would help with creative suggestions. Tomas Kigali would actually go further than Alber' on that line of reasoning. But Alber' was merely a berserker. Tomas was a ruthless killer.

"I'd prefer not, until forced into it," Jessica replied solemnly. "I like the moral high ground we have right now. I can always sacrifice it later if we need to castle."

Tamara Strnad spoke up at this point.

"What happens if we shatter the *Energiya?*" she asked, leaning closer to put a finger into the projection. "Intel says the *Capriole* is short-range only. They could get home to *Samara*, but how many weeks or months would that take?"

Jessica smiled. Tamara had seen what the rest had apparently missed. The others thought of the combat end of the starship, not the engineering bits.

"We trap a sizeable portion of their border fleet in the middle of nowhere," Jessica agreed. She turned to Elzbet. "I asked *Ballard* to pay particular attention to their default settings when they came in to *Trusski*. Elzbet, what say you?"

If Tomas Kigali was universally recognized as the best navigator in the fleet these days, Elzbet Aukley was possibly the best science officer in the last century. She didn't command her own scout because she didn't want the executive duties. One of these days, she would most likely inherit *Ballard*, when Kanda Lungu finally retired, or she might take up a desk job teaching others the esoteric art.

"*Trusski*'s star is a little cooler than standard, so the planet is perfectly situated at 0.92 AU. A little closer than most systems, but within parameters," she began. "Centurion Orn Nwokolo had the station when *Steadfast at Dawn* arrived, and we had a number of passive sensors listening for anything. We tracked every anomaly, and then deleted bad data later, so we have an amazing baseline of the system. The ship appeared at about ten AU, roughly thirty degrees above the system ecliptic. The Fleet Centurion had put a bullseye on the system, and we nailed *Steadfast*'s emergence point to within four standard deviations of center. Almost exactly where she thought they would come out."

"And if they panic, that's where they'll bounce?" Tamara had an evil smile on her face.

Jessica shared it.

"They could go anywhere," Elzbet replied. "But if you don't have time, you go with what you have programmed into the nav system. We don't think they realized that anybody was paying attention, so this is our best guess."

There were a lot of smiles around the table as Jessica took the temperature of the room. Hungry, angry smiles. Shark-like, if she were so bold.

"The plan is to split into two elements," Jessica picked up the narrative. "Team One strikes hard and fast and forces them to respond. Team Two is sitting out near that emergence point, primed to unleash everything they have into the *Energiya* module if it drops out. According to *Fribourg's* notes, the thing has battlecruiser-level firepower and defense, but I plan to overload it and see if we can score the kill there. If so, we can always abandon the five warships here and retreat, depending the tactical situation. Or we can push."

"Who is on Team One?" Denis asked, eyes fixed on her from down the table. From the look on his face, he had already guessed the answer, but wanted her confirmation.

"Sorry, Denis," Jessica said, truly apologetic. *Auberon* was the only old-style warship present, along with *Ballard*, while the rest were *Expeditionary* vessels, as envisioned by Yan Bedrov to specifically go toe to toe with *Buran*. "This will be a job for the other three troublemakers."

She looked at them as she spoke. Robbie was phlegmatic. Alber' nodded.

Tomas Kigali smiled like a God of Death.

"Corvette/Assault," he turned and murmured to Alber' triumphantly.

"We'll see on the bullseye scores," the berserker replied with hooded eyes.

Jessica let the byplay run, mostly for the benefit of the others. The corvette commanders all knew Kigali's reputation as a navigator, but she doubted that many of them had studied his actions at *First Petron* or *First Ballard*. Especially the latter, where *CR-264* had been close enough to an Imperial battlewagon to rake the vessel with her short-range, Type-1 beams.

And walk away unharmed.

Jessica tapped the table now, bringing everyone to utter stillness. She nodded once more to Casey, who brought the presentation forward to the first simulation.

"Ladies and gentlemen," she said simply. "Now the war truly begins."

CHAPTER LVIII

Casey followed Jessica and Marcelle into Jessica's primary office with a hint of butterflies in her stomach. It was an unwelcome development, especially after all she had done to stop her cousin from overthrowing the Empire, but these butterflies had not responded to orders to behave.

"You wanted to see me?" Jessica asked as she sat.

Marcelle had stayed just long enough to see them here, and then withdrawn, probably already reading Casey's mind about the need for some modicum of privacy.

Casey let her back settle on the chair, as much as she wanted to sit forward and upright.

"I don't know who else to talk to," Casey replied, still searching for the right words, which surprised her even more.

"You're worried about *Trusski*?" Jessica was apparently also reading her mind. But Casey already knew she could do that.

"Worried about screwing something up," Casey said. "About making you or the team look bad by doing or saying the wrong thing at a critical moment."

Jessica leaned back and grinned.

"Why do you think I tasked Enej with making your life a living hell on the flag bridge?" she asked.

"Huh?"

Casey was lost now. More lost.

Something.

"Casey, new Centurions do not command squadrons from the flag bridge," Jessica explained. "If they do, the time is measured in minutes, until the right person can step in. I specifically told Enej and Denis to treat you differently. To hand you the flag for long stretches, so you got comfortable with it, and worked out all your bad habits early, so they could correct them."

"Oh," Casey realized.

All the smiles, and helpful suggestions. They weren't just for the Imperial Princess who was in over her head.

Jessica was training her for command. Which made a kind of sense. No Imperial gentleman would be interested in marrying her now, after she had spent years serving with a foreign navy, even as much as Jessica Keller impressed and frightened all of them.

They would probably be afraid it would rub off on Casey…which it had.

Jessica grinned and sipped some coffee, apparently enjoying Casey's face as it went through its emotional roller-coaster.

"Furthermore," Jessica said, "As you have told your family, you will need to command a naval vessel, one of these days. Hopefully, it will fly an Imperial flag, but there's no reason you couldn't command one of *Aquitaine's* warships first, if you were good enough."

"Really?" Casey let her wildest fantasies emerge into sunlight, even if just for a moment. "Command?"

"Casey, let me share something with you that I don't think you have ever internalized," Jessica turned serious. "By forcing the 25-Year-Peace with *Fribourg*, I'm pretty sure I have won the war I set out to, twenty years ago. Nobody coming up on your side is as good as Emmerich Wachturm. By keeping Dittmar off the throne, the peace will hold, and you have become almost as big a hero to the people of *St. Legier* and the Empire as Arlo has. By inspiring all those little girls to not just settle for a good marriage, you and I have done more social damage to the Empire than anyone has realized. In another century, it might even become as nice a place for its citizens as *Aquitaine* is now. Everything I do to help you realize your dreams is another poke in the face of those old, chauvinistic pigs that currently run things. Dittmar's people, not your father."

"So making me happy has an ulterior motive?" Casey asked, starting to grin.

"Casey, it *is* my ulterior motive," Jessica replied, smiling. "They can't do or say anything, either, without looking even worse. That's why Em gave up and traded me for Arlo. He knows better than to try to force you. He's probably hoping that you'll tire of all this and want to return to your life of ease and luxury in the palace."

"I'd run off and become a pirate first," Casey half-growled.

"We had this conversation already," Jessica smirked. "That offer always stands, if things ever get that bad again."

"So you get to be the bad guy and I have to settle for being happy?" Casey asked.

Jessica laughed.

"If you want to put it that way," she said.

"One of these days, I'm going to need to get married," Casey shifted gears, thinking out a decade of tactical and strategic thinking. "You suppose Em and Father are expecting me to bring home a husband from the Republic?"

"I wouldn't put it past them," Jessica said. "Look at Torsten Wald for an example of long-term planning on their part."

"Serious?" Casey asked, aware that no amount of rumors or sneakiness had managed to uncover anything about those two as yet.

"Maybe," Jessica replied, guarded. "He might be stubborn and patient enough to out-wait me. But we were talking about you. I'll ask an impolite question. Have you met anyone interesting enough to consider?"

"No," Casey said simply. "Most of them are afraid of me. Or, more specifically, Willow, Marcelle, and Lady Moirrey. Plus probably Jež, Aeliaes, d'Maine, and Kigali. And you."

"Likely," Jessica said. "Nobody wants to become an international embarrassment. But we can whisper things, perhaps get things moving, if you have suggestions."

"No," Casey decided. "I might have to sneak off with Willow and some of her friends at some point, in disguise, for a crazy girls' weekend, I haven't yet met anyone that would stand up to even my scrutiny, let alone Father and Uncle Em."

"Understood," Jessica said. "How about now? You ready for *Trusski?*"

"Yes," Casey said. "Knowing that I have Captain Wald and Enej close, and his whole team backing me up, helps my confidence. I am the Empire, in their eyes. I need to impress them."

"Princess Kasimira. Lady Casey *zu* Wiegand, you already have," Jessica pronounced. "We just have to survive bloodying *Buran*'s nose out here, and you will be an even bigger hero, on both sides of the border."

CHAPTER LVIX

"You rang?" Yan asked as he wound his way through the last bits of the maze that was the ass-end of the engineering labs.

Moirrey was sitting on a stool like a long-term patron at her favorite bar, just waiting for the bartender to make it back to her. Yan had gotten used to eccentricities. Not counting Digger and his people, Yan figured he could read her better than anyone, except maybe Jessica.

She wasn't off, per se, but this was a much-more-serious Moirrey than the world probably even knew existed. The look in her eyes when she turned to face him was something he might have expected in a ten-thousand-year-old mummy rising up from a crypt in a nightmare, coming for his soul.

"The information I am about to show you is not located in *Auberon*'s main memory core," she said simply, reaching out one hand and pivoting the screen she had been studying, far enough around for him to see the complicated schematics.

Yan sucked in deep breath quietly, hearing her speak like this. Normally, Moirrey's accent was so thick he felt like he had to parse it with an encyclopedia. When she got serious, when she got deadly, she suddenly sounded like a newscaster selected for eloquence.

Gonna be one of those *days.*

"I might not put it there. Ever," Moirrey continued in a hard, level tone. "Or I might. There isn't anyone else in the squadron who could even understand the technical implications, and my sister is one of the few who would understand the political ramifications."

Yan knew which *she* Moirrey was referring to. He had gotten drunk enough with her and Marcelle over the last few years to have been admitted to that particular girls' club.

Rather than answer, Yan walked close and began cycling the image. Pull back. Zoom in. Pivot. Spin. Snap up the power curve and requirements.

A long, quiet ten minutes passed. Yan wasn't sure he had moved. Moirrey had been a statue.

Finally, he turned to her.

"Would you call that thing a Type-5 beam?" he asked, feeling his face scrunch up.

She thought about that for a second.

"Technically, it might ratchet up and become a Type-6, if we can through-put enough power without blowing the coolant system apart," she replied in tight voice. "Five point six in this configuration."

Yan nodded and pushed a button that projected the image into the air between them, so he could rotate it more easily and envision the harness that would hold it.

"This thing's the size of a heavy cruiser, all by itself," Yan observed.

"Which suggests a station-mounted posture, at least in the beginning," Moirrey completed his thought. She had gotten good at that, too. "A battlestation of a scale comparable to a Starbase. And about as mobile."

"And even less functional," Yan continued the thought, completing hers. "Especially since you would have to move an entire station as a turret in order to aim it. I presume you want something else? I'll point out that most of your need is going to be three or four rings of generators and capacitors, which are not in this design."

"I woke up this last Tuesday with an itch," Moirrey said. "Jessica doesn't have me on a watch rotation, for the most part. Nor does Oz. Caught Nina and bounced ideas off her over breakfast, then came down here and been working pretty much non-stop since then. Ev'n Digger's gettin' antsy, n'stuff."

Now she was grinning, like the normal Moirrey, and not the weird scientist that had apparently taken over the woman's body.

"So what do you need from me?" Yan pivoted.

"You'n'*Pops*'r the best," she replied, deadly serious with a goofy grin.

Moirrey again. "But Iowerth's too tr'dition'l fer some a'this. Too linear. We needs ta goes way outside th'box here."

She paused to root around on the tabletop for a moment, picking up a piece of printout and handing it to him.

Yan noted only a handful of needs. Dimensions. Input, throughput, output. Cooling.

That was it.

"I needs ya ta builds me one somethin' capable of using that," she said. "Jessica will convince Fleet to build us one."

"One?"

"Bucko, that's St. George's lance," she said, that angry dragon of legend appearing in her eyes. "We needs ta slay one wyrm. N'I'm already tryin't'figger hows to shield against it afterwards. No' be easy. We kills *Buran* and hopes peace breaks out, like dandelions, but sure as hell not telling the old Red Admiral 'bouts this. New Red Admiral be twitchy 'nuff."

"How soon?" Yan asked.

"Afore we gets home," Moirrey said. She took a deep breath and transformed again. "That weapon might be the single most dangerous thing I ever design in my life, Bedrov. Guard the secrets with your soul."

"Yes, ma'am," Yan said, stuffing the paper into his pocket and turning to leave.

She had already tuned him out. Gone back to whatever place Moirrey the goofball had to hide herself when she had to do things like this. When she had to go build super-weapons capable of killing thousands or millions, instead of just making better glitter bombs.

Yan supposed that was how she stayed sane. More glitter.

But he had a few ideas. Now he just needed to kill a few electronic trees figuring out which one would work best.

CHAPTER LX

A knock at the door, when she wasn't expecting any company, caused Amala's staff to transform.

Pinchon Swarovski was already a killer, but right now it became the difference between a blade quietly sheathed in her boot, and one drawn. Vibol Harmaajärvi had already packed most of his gear into the two shipping cubes that just accidentally happened to provide solid cover if he needed to kneel and open fire on someone coming through the door.

Amala had pointedly not asked where the pistol in his hand came from. It was not Imperial nor Republic issue.

The others made themselves scarce, but that was in line with planning. They were professional bureaucrats, paper-pushers, not security marines. Or tailors.

Amala stood and nodded to Pinchon. His pistol was carefully concealed in a shoulder-rig under a loose jacket that Vibol had made special for him.

Her killer moved to the door, slid back the bolt, and braced a foot before opening it. If it was the end, they wouldn't have knocked. Amala wouldn't have. She would have either blown the door off the hinges, or pumped a sleeping gas quietly into the chamber, depending on how dangerous she rated the occupants.

Words were murmured, but Amala was clear across the long room, seated at a conference table and wondering what she could throw, in a pinch, and how heavy the table was if she needed to flip it over for cover.

Pinchon opened the door the rest of the way and stepped to one side in such a way that he could draw, shoot, and slam the door in one motion.

Gan Ve stood in the doorway, dressed in his most severe and finest robes. The look on his face conveyed utter seriousness, but his walk was casual as he stepped into the room. He was alone, which was a bad sign, but only politically. Normally, he brought a handful of scholars, like ducklings, with him everywhere.

"Bhattacharya Yuey Anne Siddhartha Michelle Amala," he announced in a flat, emotionless tone. "Scholar and Ambassador, you are commanded to appear before the Khan."

Amala let a breath quietly out. If nothing else, at least the waiting was over.

She had always hated that part more than anything else. Combat was combat, whether you were policing for pirates or hassling semi-legitimate businessmen pushing the margins of commerce. It was that time waiting in JumpSpace for things to kick off that always drove her to distraction.

Amala rose from her chair. She hadn't been planning on a court appearance today, so she was dressed well but not to kill. And Gan Ve didn't look like he was willing to wait.

She bowed to the man commensurate with his rank and position and moved to the door, quietly signaling Pinchon and Vibol to stand down.

"I attend," she replied as she got close enough.

Scholar Ve nodded succinctly and pivoted. As he made his way out the door, Amala used hand signals to instruct her people to begin destroying anything sensitive they may have to abandon.

Something in the air had that finality to it.

Do. Or die.

She followed Gan Ve through the halls at his measured pace. It was some mark of honor on his part that he did not feel the need to guide her with one hand, as he had done early on, but simply assumed that she would follow, like the little ducklings in his wake normally did.

At the door to the Great Hall, Ve stepped to one side and bounced his voice off the ceiling.

"The Scholar: Bhattacharya," he announced simply. Nothing more.

Nothing friendly.

Amala entered the room, prepared to find the *Steadfast at Dawn* security crew returned, with handcuffs and shock wands. Instead, she found an older man, desperately, nervously out of place, standing close to the Khan. The stranger appeared afraid that the authorities were coming for *him*.

Amala came to rest and gave the Khan the most proper bow she could manage.

"My Khan, how may I serve you?" she asked carefully.

She stood and waited for the boom to drop. Amala didn't think it would be a shot in the back, as had concerned her when she first arrived here, but Yuur was playing his cards close to the vest.

"You have lied to us, Scholar Bhattacharya," the Khan pronounced her doom. "You are a spy, sent to steal our secrets for your foreign masters. We hereby revoke your Ambassadorial credentials and order you to vacate this planet within three days. Because your Admiral Keller cannot be reached, I have ordered this captain to transport you to a place from which you may be expected to get home safely."

The man with the Khan made sense now, as did his nervousness. He had apparently just been ordered to take his country ship into the war, probably without any hope of surviving, or even getting his ship back, if those foreign devils chose to take it from him.

"My Khan, I must protest," Amala said, carefully staying within the bounds of proscribed behavior and vocabulary. No doubt, the good folks from *Samara* would be right pissed when they got back, if she had been cast out and was beyond their idea of justice. "I am a Scholar, and not a spy. I will admit to having been a Warrior, yet I have acted within strict moral, ethical, and legal bounds at all times while among you."

"You have, Scholar Bhattacharya," he replied, his eyes softening, even if his voice did not waver. "That is why you are being exiled, rather than arrested. Your credentials are no longer valid. You will remove yourself from my sight, return to your quarters, and pack everything. Captain Ko will return to his ship and await your embassy's arrival. Begone."

Not much to say to that. If the locals had done a crash course on the *Laws of Recognized Warfare*, Amala had gone deep into the sorts of diplomatic precedent here, after her talk with the ducks.

She bowed deeply to the Khan, holding it longer than was appropriate, and let her eyes smile at him as she straightened. Captain Ko rated a lesser bow, still not as good as the one he actually got, but Amala deemed it worth her while to put the man at ease.

Finally, she turned and bowed to the whole Court, unknowing

witnesses to the game the Khan was playing on them, tame little ducks who would report honestly that she had angered their leader, and been cast out, perhaps not realizing how critical the timing was.

Amala followed Gan Ve out of the room silently, through suspiciously empty corridors, as if she was suddenly a contagion that would transmit the Khan's rage unto innocents.

Silly, little quackers.

Pinchon answered the door with a hand out of sight when she returned.

"Scholar Ve, you have my eternal gratitude for all that you and your staff have done for me and my people while we have been here," Amala said with a deep bow.

She would have never been able to do any of this without his gruff assistance.

He broke character just enough to smile and nod back to her, safely out of sight of everyone, before the façade returned and he left.

Amala made sure the door was closed and bolted by her own hand.

She turned to the rest of the staff, peeking in from corridors and doorways.

"Burn everything we can't haul personally," she ordered. "Khan's given us a ride and three days to get gone. I want to be in orbit by night. Move."

A whirlwind of chaos ensued. Papers burned and ashes stirred. Various media derezzed or bashed with a hammer to destroy the contents. Vibol guarded the door, since everything he had was already packed and mobile.

A quick dinner even provided an excuse to destroy the stocks of good food they had acquired, although Amala saved three bottles of local wine for the folks back at the fleet. Collectors' items, once owned by *Aquitaine's* first Ambassador to *Buran*.

The Fleet Centurion would get a laugh out of owning one.

Three hours, and the place was as sterile as her team could get it without a professional service. Amala opened the front door to four youngish guards, looking nervous, no doubt at the amount of noise emanating from the embassy.

"You will inform Scholar Ve that we are ready to begin transporting ourselves and our goods to the port," she ordered the oldest.

The kid blinked, but she closed the door in his face before he could speak.

Fifteen minutes passed before a knock at the door. Vibol answered, having dressed in his finest outfit for exactly the occasion. Amala decided he looked something like an old Revivalist priest of Vishnu, in the black and gold robes of the Middle Sect.

He was significantly taller than Ve, but stepped clear and pulled the door with him.

"Scholar Ve of *Trusski*," Vibol announced to the room, in case anybody wasn't already staring.

Gan Ve stepped to the threshold and looked briefly at the piles of boxes and bags. He nodded to himself and turned in place.

"Bring the carts," he said conversationally.

The four guards were still out there, but now a dozen workers in less-formal robes hurried into the room, with flatbed carts on wheels. Amala's people supervised the loading, and watched like hawks, but everything seemed as it should be.

"Scholar Bhattacharya?" Gan Ve asked simply.

"Scholar Ve, we are prepared to depart," she replied.

He surprised her by stepping forward and taking her arm, but he had the slightest hint of a grin on his face as they led the long string of camels into the desert of the palace's empty corridors.

In the courtyard, the same transport limo, followed by probably the same three trucks. Amala and Ve rode in back, with Pinchon and Vibol facing them from the middle and two nameless staffers up front. Everyone and everything else went into the trucks, except that leather, diplomatic courier bag Vibol had originally made for her, which held a few papers, some mementos, and Keller's bottle of wine.

Would not do to lose that, after all this.

The ride was silent. Ve seemed to be meditating on the future, but Amala and her men were preparing for a firefight when the car arrived.

Instead, they rolled up to a distant corner of the landing field, where the same two columns of troops were lined up for inspection.

So, going out with style?

Gan Ve escorted her to the exact threshold of the line of troops and then let go of her arm.

"Scholar Bhattacharya, you are commanded by the Khan to exile," he intoned carefully, following a script in his head. "If you return, it will be considered an act of war, rather than diplomacy, and will be dealt with as such. You are *persona non grata* on *Trusski*."

Amala turned, studied him for a second, and then leaned in and kissed him on the cheek.

She could not, for the life of her, think of a better way to throw Gan Ve completely sideways. And it worked. He couldn't have been more stunned if she had slapped him upside the head with a four-days-rotting sand shark.

Amala turned, grinned fiercely at the two lines of honor guard, then strode down the corridor like a conquering empress. The evident mirth on the faces of the troops as she walked regally past were priceless.

Captain Ko waited just inside the hatch, with a small crew of faceless minions or bureaucrats. They were exactly like the sorts of country craft crew she had dealt with innumerable times while blockading *Thuringwell* or other places. Gray, and drab.

Still, they were her ride home. She bowed to the silent captain and moved to one side as her people filed into the space.

Ve had brought enough crew to the port. Loading her embassy's gear took all of one trip into the spacious cargo hold on the otherwise-tiny vessel.

Amala and her people were directed to a crowded crew compartment. Captain Ko entered after a few moments.

"We are ready to lift," he said in a diffident voice, slowly, as if he didn't believe she understood him. The man radiated *nervous*.

"Thank you, Captain Ko," Amala responded, confirming that everyone was strapped in.

Hopefully, the locals weren't going to blast them out of the sky when they lifted. The Ccptain's nervousness went beyond strangers on his deck. Sensing his panic, Pinchon and Vibol were practically vibrating with murderous capability.

Captain Ko bowed to her, turned, and began bellowing orders to his actual crew, heading forward, presumably toward the freighter's bridge. The ship lurched slightly, slid like a pig on ice, then roared forward as everything stabilized.

A side hatch opened and a figure emerged, staring owlishly at Vibol's pistol, while Pinchon covered the rest of the room.

Ul Banop Cheani Yuur, *Khan of Trusski*. Dressed for travel, and carrying a large, cardboard box that could only be filled with freshly-baked butterhorns, from the smell.

Amala remembered to pick her jaw up off the deck before she spoke. The others tried and failed.

"My Khan?" she sputtered.

Yuur Ul grinned at her as if he had just executed the greatest practical joke ever played. He moved across the small chamber, and appropriated a jumpseat one space away from her, strapping himself in quickly and professionally, with the butterhorns between them.

His grin extended to the rest of her people.

"The Khan of *Samara* will experience a rage fit for the epics when he hears that you have escaped him," Ul said conversationally. "I would most likely be called home in disgrace, to answer to *The Eldest* directly before his throne and the *Four Mandarins*. That just will not do."

"What about *Trusski*?" Amala managed to grind the words past the white noise filling her head.

"I have left a note for Ve, when he returns to the palace," the Khan said, grin breaking into a full smile. "I appointed him Acting Khan in my place, while I have appointed myself Ambassador to the land of the barbarians to study their ways. I am fascinated by your Red Admiral. Both of them, Keller and Wachturm, and I am a Scholar, so learning of their ways is necessary."

"You're crazy," Pinchon managed into the silence.

"Ah, but you do not understand our ways, Warrior Swarovski Pinchon. We are Scholars, Amala and myself. We exist to pursue knowledge for its own sake," Yuur Ul said in a lofty, laughing voice before glancing at her. "Captain Ko was sworn to secrecy. Once we get far enough away from *Trusski*, I am hoping that you have a method to securely contact your people. Then, we begin the next stage on our grand adventure."

"Boss?" Pinchon asked in a small voice.

"Did you want to die in bed, Sailor?" she asked.

Vibol grinned, even as Pinchon's paleness flushed.

After all, depending who was asked, Amala might have just kidnapped a foreign governor.

Talk about throwing a fox into the henhouse.

CHAPTER LXI

"That ain't right," Elzbet muttered under her breath as she stared at the screen in front of her and the various readouts.

Heads swiveled to look. Somebody apparently buzzed Kanda, because the commander's face appeared on the side of Elzbet's console.

"What's up?" the command centurion asked.

"So a freighter climbed out of the atmosphere several hours ago," Elzbet replied. "Real time signal has a four and a half hour lag. It reached orbit, sat still for a while, and then jumped."

"M'kay?" Kanda sort of agreed, unwilling to interrupt her science officer's train of thought.

"Instead of going out and then up, like they always do, it went straight down," Elzbet continued her thought. "Landed about twenty AU out and sat there for a while. Much shorter signal lag, and they immediately began broadcasting a strange message. Random-sounding alpha-numeric sequence."

"With you so far," Kanda said.

"System says that the value being transmitted is Amala Bhattacharya's serial number, with a plus sign and nine," Elzbet said. "Bhattacharya took eight with her."

Elzbet left it at that. This was when it turned into Kanda's problem.

"What's the lag now?" the command centurion said.

"About an hour," Elzbet replied. "Assuming this is a civilian ship, a safe bet judging by the way they fly, they might be programming each jump manually. So they might be there for a bit, or might have jumped already."

"Bring the ship to alert," Kanda ordered. "I'll be there in sixty seconds."

Elzbet's hand was already reaching for the button. The alarm wound itself up and people started pulling out emergency suits, just in case. She waited, running through all her systems and every sensor, regardless of the direction it might be pointed.

Nothing new. No warships that might be hiding out here for a trap. No messages that had gone out before or after, unless it was a tight beam sent somewhere else. If that was the case, there was nothing to be done about it, yet Kanda probably had some sneakiness in her.

The command centurion came through the hatch quickly.

"Have they moved yet?" she asked, taking her position.

"Not as of an hour ago," Elzbet answered.

"Good," Kanda said. "Now we watch and see what they have planned."

It wasn't that long a wait.

On one screen, Elzbet watched the ship pivot slowly in place on all three dimensions, and then disappear from sight. Reverse triangulation of their pivot-sequence provided the direction to the nearest of *Buran*'s inhabited systems, the first place the squadron had visited, before blowing up that orbital station.

"You sure?" Kanda asked.

"Close enough for government work," Elzbet replied. "Bhattacharya has no idea who might be out here, and wouldn't want to blow our cover anyway. If they follow standard practice, the next jump should be about five light years, give or take. Figure they're three and a half days to that system."

"Could you find them midway when they drop out?" Kanda asked.

"Needle in a big haystack," Elzbet replied drolly.

It was an old joke. One with a lot of prefacing zeroes, as it went, when invoking the haystack.

"We'll try anyway," Kanda decided. "Drop a log buoy here in case Jessica or Jennifer come by before we get back. They'll trigger it and decide."

Elzbet nodded and began programming the little barrel with everything it needed to hide up here.

Then they would go stalk a goat in the high grass.

———

Sometimes, you got lucky. Elzbet wasn't willing to call it anything else. Certainly not skill alone, although that probably helped.

Two days into the chase, *Ballard* had dropped out of JumpSpace and sat quiet for a hard scan of the neighborhood. A signal had popped up on the boards, a little more than a light-hour away.

That same goofy freighter, waddling slowly along.

Kanda managed to drop out of JumpSpace right on top of them before they could leap again, which probably scared the crap out of the pilot. A Galactic Survey Cruiser was a big beast, built on a heavy cruiser hull, but without most of the guns.

Still, had to be impressive when it was suddenly ordering you to heave to and prepare for boarding. In the middle of deep space at least three light years from the nearest star.

Elzbet watched the ship surrender. The image in her head was a puppy rolling over on its back with its paws up in the air. Something close enough to the truth.

And, since it was her kill, she was on the comm.

"*TO:557231455891*, this is *RAN Ballard*," Elzbet growled into her microphone. "Stand by for our boarding party. Any hint of resistance will get you destroyed. Do you understand?"

"Affirmative, *Ballard*," a familiar-sounding voice replied. "This is SC Bhattacharya and party. Captain Ko would greatly appreciate our departure. We'll be ready for you to dock. Please prepare a diplomatic reception on your end."

A what?

Elzbet turned, astounded, to her commander. Kanda didn't help matters by shrugging back at her.

"Understood," Elzbet said anyway, unsure of what the situation called for.

But she didn't have to worry all that much. The team she was sending over were experts at weird circumstances. And was commanded by Centurion Mererid Dimitriou, the only security marine in the fleet with a PhD in Geology.

How better to explore the galaxy than to go survey it on someone else's Levs?

Elzbet switched channels to talk to the shuttle preparing to depart.

"*Alpha*, this is *Fortress*," Elzbet said. "This appears to be our party. Prepare for weird."

Brief pause. Probably trying to parse what she meant by *weird*. As if she knew.

"Acknowledged, *Fortress*," Mererid replied in that quiet voice of hers.

Did geologists ever need to yell?

All her sensors beeped as the shuttle separated and began the crawl across the short space to the ugly, squat box with engines bolted to it.

That thing was probably the most utilitarian use of volume Elzbet had ever seen in space. Starships that never landed on the surface could be any shape you wanted, usually dictated by basic physics but otherwise just driven by cultural aesthetics. This one was merely a shipping container with engines at one end and scars and burn marks from a couple of lifetimes of hard service.

And about as dangerous as a goldfish, even as lightly-armed as *Ballard* was.

But it was apparently transporting Keller's ambassador to the psychos, so something must be up.

Now, to see what the next weird was going to be.

CHAPTER LXII

Amala had grown fond of the ship, and especially Captain Ko. He had turned out to be a pudgy, happy grandfather figure, although he probably never got to bounce grandkids on his knee. He still looked the part.

And Vibol had charmed him by working up new, matching crew uniforms for Ko and the five others that kept the ship running. Not the robes that *Buran's* lords and bureaucrats wore, but something much closer to those of the civilian merchant flotilla that handled most of *Aquitaine's* cargo transport.

Since Vibol and Pinchon spoke little Mongolian, and the others none of the trade languages, Amala and Yuur had ended up at the center of all conversations that didn't involve fabric. She had learned a great deal about the man who had been shanghaied to haul her around the galaxy, and the now-former Khan of Trusski who had ordered it.

It was always interesting, watching Ko's crew laugh at one of Yuur's stories, and then the delayed reaction while she translated it for her team.

Two days that could have been fraught and ugly had instead turned into a summer-camp sort of thing. At least until the big survey cruiser appeared out of nowhere.

Amala had thought Captain Ko was going to wet himself. Yuur had just smiled.

And now she was going to be acting as an Ambassador in the other direction. Silliness.

Everyone was crammed into the main room except Crewman Wa, who was sitting on the bridge with orders to not touch anything, but to yell if anything beeped. Amala figured that was about the kid's speed. He was a little dense, offset by a good heart. And the ship was entirely shut down except for life support, at this point.

Outside, pings and bangs as the shuttle docked. Unlike pure freighters, *TO:557231455891* was configured to also haul a number of passengers between worlds, so the best way to board in space was a crew airlock, rather than the big cargo hatch aft.

Amala noted everyone's nervousness and stood up from the chair she had claimed earlier. She bowed to the captain with warmth.

"Captain Ko," she smiled and nodded. "Once everything is transshipped, I will demand that *Ballard* release you from your bond and let you get back to your duties."

Ko surprised her by rising, stepping close, and shaking her hand, which was an Empire or Republic thing, not something *The Holding* did.

"Scholar Bhattacharya, it has been our pleasure to transport you and the Khan," he said. "I hope we will find a way to meet again."

Amala was touched by the sincere emotion in the man's voice. These folks weren't the monsters *Fribourg* made them out to be, but just people, trying to get by and maybe a little ahead.

She turned to the now-ex Khan, Yuur Ul. They had spoken at great length about the way forward, now that the man might be technically a fugitive. Still, innocence presumed.

"Minister Ul, adventure awaits us," she said.

He rose, looking like he was on the verge of something pithy that would leave both crews rolling with laughter.

"Scholar Bhattacharya, all life is an adventure to be had," he pronounced with mock-severity. "The key is remembering to stop occasionally to feed the ducks."

They shared a special smile at that one as the room erupted in laughter.

Where else could feeding ducks be possibly misconstrued as treason?

Amala nodded to her staff, who then rose and headed aft, Pinchon in the lead, Amala ushering Ul, much like Gan Ve had led her, once upon a time.

The airlock had just begun to cycle as they lined up in the corridor outside.

The hatch opened inward, revealing two faceless troopers in light assault armor, and Centurion Dimitriou in field armor. It was like coming home to a candle in the window on a snowy winter's night.

"Hello, Mererid," Amala said as the geologist stepped into the corridor.

Ballard's famous rock-hopper marine was a little shorter than Amala, and thinner, but they shared enough coloring that they might easily claim to be cousins to a complete stranger.

Centurion Dimitriou looked her up one side and down the other with a critical eye.

"Gone totally native, Amala?" she asked with a droll tone.

"This is how civilized folk dress," Amala replied, trying not to smirk. "I wouldn't expect a geologist to understand."

Mererid rolled her eyes and shook her head slightly.

"Status?" she asked.

"Eight fleet and one additional passenger," Amala said. "Bringing an Ambassador from *Buran* for the Fleet Centurion."

Yuur Ul stepped forward and smiled serenely. Not being at home, he was no longer wearing his court robes, but had settled into a taupe pants and tunic outfit that suggested wealth, breeding, and intellect, without being particularly noisy about it.

"Minister of the Eighth Rank: Yuur Cheani Banop Ul," Amala made introductions. "This is Scholar Dimitriou Stella Mererid, Doctor of Geology."

"Are all security centurions secretly Scholars in *Aquitaine?*" he asked with a gleam in his eyes, bowing politely to Mererid.

"We are a deep and subtle people," Amala replied with vague mystery.

Mererid just watched the byplay with a neutral look that really wanted to interject something sarcastic. Amala briefly wondered if she and Yuur looked like old lovers to an outsider. Certainly, they were far closer personally than circumstances should have warranted.

Not that she had considered the short, bald man as anything more than a dear friend who knew great stories and jokes. But she was also no longer the person who had braved death or imprisonment to invade *Trusski* in the first place.

"We'll take him into custody now," Mererid said with a suddenly-serious voice.

Vibol surprised the hell out of everyone by stepped forward and placing himself physically between Mererid with her two guards, and Amala and Yuur.

"You will do no such thing," he announced with a solemnity that brought everyone to heel. "This man is an Ambassador. You will treat him as such."

Long pause of silence.

Amala found it amusing, watching a fifty-five-year-old man, erect and lean and fussy, intimidate two armed goons half his age, each with half again his mass. Plus guns.

Mererid looked up with something verging on disbelief, but she didn't order anybody stunned or punched. Amala figured that was enough of a win.

Finally, Mererid softened her stance and signaled her two men to relax.

"What about the ship?" she asked simply.

"It was hired by the Khan of *Trusski* to transport us to friendly forces," Amala said. "And did so cheerfully. As commander on the ground, my orders would be to haul all our gear aboard your shuttle and send them home. Is Command Centurion Lungu monitoring?"

"She is."

"Command Centurion?" Amala asked the air.

Another pause. Probably taking a moment to ask her Legal Affairs people for a ruling that would be presented in Court Martial later on.

"Anything that needs settling before you talk to the Fleet Centurion?" Kanda Lungu's voice suddenly filled the air.

"Negative, sir," Amala said. "This is all political, at this point. My people have vouched for the Minister's gear. Mostly clothes and some personal effects, plus papers."

"Granted, Bhattacharya," the command centurion said. "We'll take everyone aboard and get you back to Keller soonest."

"Roger that, Command Centurion," Amala said. "Thank you."

"Don't thank me, yet, Amala," Kanda replied. "You still get to explain it all to the Fleet Centurion."

Amala grinned. There were worse fates. And there was still a war.

CHAPTER LXIII

Jessica found the flag bridge comforting as she approached what she hoped would be the culmination of the current campaign. By now, enough time should have passed that Amala Bhattacharya would either know what Jessica needed, the better to guide her next steps, or Jessica and her team would find out from the locals that something bad had happened to her Ambassador.

In which case, she just might annihilate the planet as a warning to future generations.

Aquitaine might cashier her for doing that. Karl VII would hang another medal on her chest. *Buran* would most certainly never forget the lesson.

The primary display over her command table was pulled back at a tremendous scale. *Trusski*'s star, the planet itself, the iceball normally used as a shield. And the squadron's current hiding place, two hundred AU out. Everything was all visible. Everyone was at duty stations, but none of the vessels were at combat alert. Except maybe Alber'. That man was always one twitch from war, as was his crew.

"Confirmed, Fleet Centurion," Casey answered the previous question. "*RAN Ballard* is not currently on station, but we're not picking up any debris and there do not appear to be any warships in orbit of *Trusski*."

"Enej, send *CS-405* down quietly to see if she left us a note," Jessica ordered, pausing to sip from her coffee.

He nodded and got to work.

With a campaign this big and this messy, there were always going to be complexities that she had to account for.

Friction.

Being able to plan accurately for that level of uncertainty had been one of the reasons she had advanced as fast and as far as she had. The ability to guess right.

"Casey, order all vessels to prepare for insertion," Jessica continued. "Our next hop is likely to be assembly point six, on the way to *Trusski* orbit, once we hear from Kosnett. All vessels maintain silence for now."

"Acknowledged, Fleet Centurion," the young woman said.

Jessica kept a stoic face, as much as she was grinning inside. One of these days, she could see Command Centurion *zu* Wiegand in a similar situation. What would the fussy old matrons of *St. Legier* think then?

There were many different ways to win a war.

⁂

Phil Kosnett always laughed to himself when he considered how he had ended up in command of *CS-405*, attached to *Keller's Expedition*. First Centurion Naoumov had told him she had him slotted for his own command as soon as a light cruiser opened up, but that the Peace had disrupted everyone's plans.

If you suddenly weren't fighting your mortal foe to the death on a daily basis, how many ships did you need? Trust the civilians to start reducing military budgets before they were sure of the future.

And then *Fribourg*, of all people, came along and initiated a new construction frenzy. But all the command slots of Keller's cruisers were spoken for, and he didn't have the seniority to step into Robbie Aeliaes's spot commanding *RAN Nyamboya*.

Would he be interested in commanding a Scout Corvette?

No, thank you. Except that ship was going to war with Keller, and everybody else was going to stay home and patrol and train, and maybe hope that *Fribourg* broke the treaty, or pirates got out of hand. Good luck with the latter, with so many more warships available to chase them.

So here he was, standing finally on his own bridge, a man destined to be a great warrior commander, like all kids were when they hit the Academy. And he was commanding the single least-armed warship in the squadron.

Even the Corvette/Escort hull had a Type-3-Tuned at either end, to go with four Type-1-Pulse mounts in between. Hell, *CM-404* at least kept one of the Type-3's. *CS-405* had the four Type-1-Pulse turrets, and sacrificed both bigger guns for a pair of monstrous sensor arrays, one bow and one stern.

He could count the hairs on a fly from one hell of a distance, but couldn't shoot one. No, his job was to fly in the van, at the head of the column, where his short-range firepower could kill missiles and fighters, rake bigger vessels while blinding them with static, or cut through any counter-measures they thought they could throw up.

Fribourg still hadn't gotten their heads wrapped around having a scout in a combat formation. But nothing a cruiser could do was within an order of magnitude of his little gunboat, as far as electronic warfare capability went.

So he was here. On the war front. Hopefully, making a good impression on the one person who really counted. Or maybe the three people, since Keller relied on Zivkovic and Lady Casey so heavily. One of these days, he would have his own cruiser.

Although, if he turned into an expert on scouts, that might be *Ballard*, or one of her sisters.

Phil Kosnett, Explorer Extraordinaire?

Tom Kigali had certainly built his own legend that way.

"First Officer Lau, call the clock," Phil said, turning to look at her image on his screen.

Unlike other vessels, Phil Kosnett felt the place for the First Officer was forward, on the Emergency Bridge, where she could immediately take command if something happened to him aft on the Main Bridge. Too many times he had heard horror stories about ships that were suddenly crippled by a bridge hit taking out the entire command staff, or at least cutting off all communications, leaving command to devolve to a poor, junior Centurion who had been relegated to the posting equivalent of Siberia.

Phil juggled his officers and team around, moving someone every week so that everyone got a chance to work with everyone else. A ship this small needed to be a single family, trained and prepared. And that included serving with every officer and every enlisted until you could intuit how they were going to jump.

"Emergence in thirty seconds," Heather Lau replied. "All gun crews report ready. Forward sensor array set for maximum jamming on command. Aft array will perform a scanning arc on the planetoid."

Phil nodded at her image on his screen. She would be up for her own command soon, especially if the Fleet was set to start building furiously again. He would take as much advantage of her amazing skill and professionalism as he could.

"Nav, we'll be coming out at almost a dead stop, relative to everything around us," Phil continued. "If something looks wrong, get us clear without waiting for any order."

Centurion Siobhan Skokomish was facing him from her station. As the ship's Pilot, she was among the best. And his Second Officer.

She glanced up at him now for a long second, face inscrutable with an eyebrow up, and then nodded once.

He had never gotten her whole story, and hadn't had a chance to hunt down a previous commander to fill in the gaps. Her first name was Irish and her last Amerind, and yet her ethnicity said African, back when that was a place and not just a cultural reference.

Her curly hair was usually right up against regulations for length if she didn't keep it in tight braids. Siobhan's eyes were dark, but her skin was such a deep brown that it was almost the color of coal. She didn't speak much, nor loudly, but there was never a wasted movement, either when she walked or especially when she flew.

If there was a *Buran* warship there, he wanted her to just throw them back into JumpSpace. Keller could bring Aeliaes and d'Maine down at that point.

"Ten seconds to RealSpace," Heather's voice came over the ship-wide. "Five seconds. Emergence."

All the electronic eyeballs on a sensor-heavy corvette went into overdrive at the same instant. Fortunately, they were alone in the bolthole's shadow, unless someone was hiding over the horizon from them, on the *Trusski*-side.

"Triggering the data relays now," his First Officer continued.

This wasn't combat, but she still had Tactical Command right now. That had been the hardest part for Phil, giving up that war-making aspect of the job when he stepped into the big chair. And letting someone else fight his battles while he sat and directed.

"Commander, we have a log buoy in orbit of the snowball," Heather said. "It's from *Ballard*. No debris at this time, so it looks like she had to leave, rather than being ambushed."

"Roger that," he said. "Download it, but keep a watch inward. If *Ballard's* not here, we don't know what has been happening on the planet. Gun teams, maintain maximum vigilance until we know why *Ballard's* gone."

They were as quiet as mice hiding in the cupboard, as far as Phil could tell. Now if only he could determine whether the rest of the universe believed that, too.

"Update from *Ballard*," Heather's voice broke into his reverie. "They believe that Amala Bhattacharya departed the system in a local freighter for reasons unknown, so *Ballard* departed in pursuit."

"So there's nothing we can do at this point?" Phil fired back. "Except return to base or wait here?"

"Looks like," Heather agreed.

Sometimes, that was the way things went.

"Nav, prepare to…" Phil started to say.

"Stand by," Siobhan called loudly, overriding his voice. "Incoming signal. Looks like somebody just came out of jump, deeper in. *Buran* vessel."

Trust her to be paying extra-special attention, since she would need to maneuver them in tight quarters if something went wrong. She would make a great First Officer, when he lost Heather, one of these days.

"Heather?" Phil asked, stepping back mentally, when he really wanted to wade into the situation and take charge.

"Signal's about three hours old, Commander," his First Officer said, looking down at her boards. "Looks big."

"How big?" he asked.

There hadn't been anyone around the system earlier. He knew Keller wanted to ambush one of *Buran's* ships, if she could catch them. Hopefully, they had lucked into something.

Of course, with Keller, it probably wasn't luck, but hopefully some of it would rub off on him, too.

"According to the signals intelligence *Ballard* left us, it looks like the JumpCarrier *Steadfast at Dawn* is back," Heather replied. "She was briefly on station three weeks ago, and then left quickly."

"Round trip to *Samara*?" Phil asked. "Assuming JumpDrives instead of sails?"

"Yeah, maybe," she said. "Timing sounds right for an average run."

He paused to run through the options. Bad, bad, and bad, but nothing would make them much better, at least not short-term.

"So let's assume they would have already hit us, if she knew we were here," Phil said. "Look for a longer-lagging signal where she went deeper, into orbit of *Trusski*, and then open a communications laser backwards to where *Auberon* should be sitting. They won't be able to reply, but feed them everything we know, working backwards in time. Keller needs to know about that ship first, about her Ambassador later."

"Roger that," Heather said, hitting the mute button on her end so she could work without interrupting him.

"Nav, find me an orbit where we can see *Trusski*, and remain hidden behind the snowball's horizon," Lau ordered. "If Keller comes, she'll need to know everything that's going on down there. And keep us silent up here."

"Yes, sir," Siobhan answered.

Phil leaned back and clenched his teeth to keep his mouth shut. They were experts. They could do the job better without him barging in and interrupting.

He watched the screen and kept telling himself that.

CHAPTER LXIV

ORBITAL: TRUSSKI. STATUS: IN TRANSIT

Kier knew she should take no pleasure in the act, but there was a grand difference between diplomatic precedent and welcoming a spy into your home.

Fortunately, both the Director at *Ural* and the Khan of *Samara* had agreed with her position that the *Fribourg* agent should be in custody, Red Admiral Keller or Khan Ul be damned. Kier had been forced to waste time going back and forth to get that official sanction. That would make it that much more pleasant when she was able to invoke censure on this pipsqueak Khan from the back of beyond for daring to thwart her.

The man on the screen staring back at her did not improve her humor.

"What do you mean, he *left*?" she demanded, feeling her fury grow another notch. "He's the Khan of *Trusski*. Unless he was recalled by the *Eldest*, he had no business departing this planet."

A small voice in the back of Kier's head wondered if Ul had known what was coming and chosen to flee ahead of justice. She smiled at that. If the man had gone rogue, then he became a literal outlaw and she could deal with him any way she felt necessary.

"The Khan did not leave an explanation," the man said. "Only a statement that he would be departing to make sure that Ambassador Bhattacharya was safely transported home, and that I should exercise his position until he returned or someone of sufficient authority interceded."

Kier had dealt with this man, the Scholar Ve, on her previous visit. He had struck her then as a pompous, obsequious peon. She could see that nothing had changed since.

And she could tell that he would argue with her on precedence, if he were pushed. Her orders from both the Director and the Khan of *Samara* had been to compel Khan Ul to hand the barbarian over, into military custody. Kier therefore theoretically lacked the specific authority to order this replacement to do anything at all, if the woman were truly gone.

Still, it must be done correctly. Especially if she was going to make a point of destroying this rogue Khan and his career. And she wanted that. Badly.

"I have orders from the Khan of *Samara*," she began in an angry, grinding voice. "You will produce the foreign agent immediately."

Simple. Direct. Non-negotiable.

"Ambassador Bhattacharya is no longer on this planet," Ve said in a supercilious voice. "She departed three days ago aboard an accredited transport. Khan Ul departed at the same time. I am unaware of their itinerary or intentions."

The way he smiled, ever so slightly when he said it told Kier just how well the man understood. It would be a game with him, as it had been with his master.

"How else may I be of service, Director?" the man continued, slipping white-hot wires under her fingernails with his tone.

There was one other arrow in her quiver. She hadn't planned on invoking it, but this fool and his former leader had managed to back her into a corner. She could lose face, or she could push the issue.

And she was never one to surrender any advantage.

"As the foreigner Keller has declared this an active warzone, we are compelled to defend it," Kier said, smiling spitefully. "She has struck at several other systems already, destroying orbital platforms, but has only threatened *Trusski*. I hereby invoke the supremacy of Martial Law in this system. The civilian government will coordinate all activities through the military office until we can determine that the threat has been nullified."

"Indeed, Director Xi," the man agreed too readily. "Except that there exists no military office on the surface. You will need to establish one by sending down adequate representation."

None? Stupid farmers.

Kier refused to scowl at the man, aware that she had just stepped into another trap laid by Ve or his master. Still, she could send down Nu

Reutra Quilen Danl, the man known once as Imperial citizen Daniel St. Collins. It would be good enough for now.

Kier was aware that Ve was smirking at her.

"I will be in touch shortly," she said curtly, cutting the channel.

She would be stuck here, but it would give *Steadfast at Dawn*'s crew a chance to build some proper defenses. She would deputize another freighter, as the escaped Khan had done, and send it to *Samara* for additional assistance, perhaps a small patrol squadron that could at least protect the region.

It would require a significant force to stop Keller, but she had been raiding with impunity, sending her little gunships hither and yon to blow things up, simply because most systems had never been defended. *Fribourg* had never before bothered to attack any system except *Samara*.

A Mako, or perhaps a squadron of Hammerheads, would put a quick end to that rash behavior.

And either Keller or Ul would be back soon.

She would enjoy greeting either of them when the time came.

CHAPTER LXV

"Damn, that's a big beast," a voice intruded on Jessica's concentration.

She looked up. Must have been Enej, from the way he blushed furiously. Jessica grinned at him in commiseration.

"Get all the Command Centurions on-line now," she ordered. "If they're alone, we have a golden opportunity. I want us closer."

"Roger that," he said.

Jessica turned to Marcelle and Willow, carefully seated off to one side, as always. Witnesses to history, they would probably still be forgotten by it.

"Marcelle, some fresh coffee for me, please?" she asked the woman. "And roust the wardroom, for something for everyone else. We'll probably hop, listen, and then lunge. There will be time for food."

Marcelle nodded, unbuckled herself, and rose from the chair. Jessica always wondered what went through Marcelle's mind at times like this. She had nothing to do but run and fetch for Jessica, and whatever tasks probably shouldn't even *unofficially* be handled by Enej or Casey.

Plausible deniability.

Marcelle grinned back at her from the hatch, as if she were reading Jessica's thoughts.

Maybe.

Everyone had probably been listening to the data feed from *CS-405*.

Even a tight laser was going to be something of a searchlight at this range. All her command centurions, including the four on *Auberon*, were on the link within a matter of seconds.

"We have possibly as good an opportunity as we'll get," Jessica addressed them all. "Battleship and four cruisers, with the ability to blink everywhere and attack from all sides. If we didn't have forty-five fighters designed to engage *Buran* vessels, I probably wouldn't try anything."

The faces were attentive. Composed. They had spent a year or a lifetime, or both, preparing for this.

Jessica found the one face she wanted, quiet as always. Enfys El-Amin. *RAN Wombat*. The minesweeper she had brought along with her on several missions now.

She had almost left that ship behind with Arott Whughy and his base on this patrol round, but the temptation for delinquency and *Mischief* had been too great.

"El-Amin," Jessica began. "How well will some of your beam-armed mines deploy if you dump them out the back at cruising speed, armed for *Buran* vessels?"

The scowl Jessica got back was worthy of the Vedas. Exactly the opposite of how you were supposed to utilize a minesweeper, who normally sat on defense like a black widow spider, weaving deadly webs for unsuspecting prey to stumble into.

"At your speeds?" Enfys asked. "Probably all of them will fail. If you let me do it my way? Maybe as many as fifty percent will work."

"Good enough," Jessica agreed. "Detach yourself when we hit our assault point and go to work. After this battle, we'll probably have to return to an Imperial base for bigger repairs than Arott can handle, so don't spare your ammunition stores. I'll let you, Oz, and Moirrey sort that out."

"Thank you, Fleet Centurion," Enfys replied, switching to a private channel to talk to *Auberon*'s engineers, who had originally designed most of the mines as part of Moirrey's *Mischief*.

"Team One," Jessica continued, shifting to the three trouble-makers: Aeliaes, d'Maine, and Kigali. "I want you to make a high-speed, long-distance pass. Kigali, as you mentioned, *Ballard*, all over again, except you aren't staying this time. The rest of us will be at point eleven, hopefully where *Steadfast at Dawn's Energiya* module will be plopped when they chase you. That means beams only. Keep the bubble gun as a surprise for when they come out to play, and tune all the Type-3 beams for long-range. All the corvettes except CA-264 will be set for close work."

Jessica selected a file and transmitted it to everyone after she updated a couple of decisions that could only be made on the verge of battle.

"We'll start here," she ordered. "You have four hours until we jump close enough to pick up *CS-405*. Then a hop to point four. At that point, we'll be in a position to determine which options we'll chase. Review everything. We'll reconvene here in three hours and update intelligence from what Kosnett sends us."

Heads nodded. Voices rumbled. They had had a year of training together, so even if this was the first battle as a team for some of them, the ones she was counting on were all old friends.

Hopefully, they would all survive the day.

CHAPTER LXVI

Because he couldn't be left alone, especially not on an *Aquitaine* warship, Amala had become something like Yuur's bodyguard, or diplomatic escort, depending on how you wanted to spell it. Technically, she probably should have reverted to uniform and her former, military demeanor, but she was also Ambassador to *Trusski* until the Fleet Centurion said otherwise.

And since the *Khan of Trusski* himself was aboard, it was only proper for her to continue her ambassadorial duties, right?

Mererid still rolled her eyes frequently, but didn't argue. Pinchon had returned to uniform. Vibol had designated himself Yuur's entire Embassy staff on *Ballard*. Which mostly involved sewing, which was his life in any event.

Amala stared out at the darkness as *Ballard* came out of JumpSpace, deep in the middle of the *M'Hanii Gulf*. Yuur stood to one side, with Mererid beyond him and Vibol close enough to fulfill roughly the same role that Gan Ve had, back on the planet.

There were no stars visible, except three off in a corner of the viewport, vaguely neighbors. The predominant item was Forward Base Delta. A mobile platform with a lot of guns.

Yuur hissed in quiet surprise as he realized where Keller had hidden her forward base.

He turned to Amala with a great, offended dignity.

"You are an evil, evil people, Scholar Bhattacharya," he said in a deliberate, pained voice.

Mererid tensed, but Amala grinned. She had spent enough time with the Khan to understand his jokes.

"They would never think to look here," she replied.

"Exactly," he decried, unhappily. "Your Red Admiral Keller cannot possibly be a Warrior. That kind are too linear. Too two-dimensional, when they are not simply one-dimensional. She must be some manner of demon from a barbarian hell."

Amala noted that he was grinning back at her by the time he finished.

"Many in *Fribourg* would agree with you," she said. "Remember, she did spearhead the effort to push them back and extract a peace they are now more than happy to observe. Plus, you only know *Fribourg*. *Aquitaine* is an entirely different culture, one that I think would be less alien to you."

"I am not sure of that, either," he said, gesturing to the woman behind him. "I now know two Scholars masquerading as Warriors, whereas previously I have only known Warriors attempting to hide as Scholars. It is perhaps well that all of *Fribourg* separates us, lest evil barbarians pollute our culture with your ways."

"Is he always like this?" Mererid asked with exasperation.

"It's even worse when there are ducks around," Amala replied, enjoying the way Mererid's face lost all composure.

"Fine. Whatever," she finally sputtered. "Now, I need to get you two ready for Fleet Centurion Whughy. I presume Harmaajärvi has something cooked up for this?"

"It will be almost as good as meeting the Director of *Steadfast at Dawn*," he said in a proud voice from the other corner.

"That truly frightens me," Mererid muttered.

CHAPTER LXVII

Now it would get hairy, as far as Jessica was concerned. There was simply no way that the entire force could drop into RealSpace quietly. Somebody would notice, and react.

Hell, in the old days, she would occasionally blip into the edge of an Imperial system just to spook the locals, as well as scout what they had. If you caught the defense forces out of position, comfortable or careless, you could always surge down and blow things up. Or maybe capture or at least frighten a freighter enough to make it worth the trip.

Today, she was facing one of *Buran*'s mightiest fighting squadrons, all rolled up in one monstrous war entity known as *Steadfast at Dawn*. An even match for firepower, if the two sides could ever actually be measured against each other.

Buran built its ships for the Capriole Drive. Jump anywhere over a short distance, including inside gravity wells where a JumpSail couldn't manage. Primarily short-range beams designed to maximize damage in that very brief window before the ship leapt away.

And the Mag-Shear. The thing Imperials called the Mauler. Standard shields barely deflected it and the transverse forces would shake a vessel apart.

To fight them, she had an Expeditionary Fleet designed by Yan Bedrov from personal experience, backed with every bit of intelligence and research *Fribourg* had accumulated, bestowed by the Emperor himself upon the semi-reformed pirate.

Shields tuned slightly differently, but hopefully enough to better deflect the Mauler beam. Physical insulation on both sides of the hull, designed again to limit the impact of a magnetic shear resonance. But for those munitions aboard *Auberon*, not a single missile in the squadron, since those were useless against a target that could simply vanish.

Best of all, Moirrey's Type-3-Tuned, which could be set to long range, sacrificing damage; or set for damage, sacrificing reach. Perfect for inflicting punishment at the sort of ranges at which *Buran* wanted to engage. And the Type-1-Pulse, based on the Flicker Beams *Buran* used, because, as Yan had explained every time someone asked, "Some bastard will fire a salvo of drones on a pass, one of these days..."

And now, she was ready to bet all their lives on Yan's design skill and her ship-handling.

The Flag Bridge was charged with emotion. She could tell that by looking around at the expectant faces, some of whom had been with her for nearly a decade now.

Jessica looked down at the images on her screen. Every Command Centurion was present. Most of their Tactical Officers were listening in for final tidbits.

Poised.

Jessica smiled at all of them. This was that moment, according to all the training guides, when she made the speech to motivate them before battle. And she had always been a master of it, but today was going to be different.

She had taken the three hour gap and prepared a surprise for her team. A good reminder of why they were here.

"Ladies and Gentlemen, in a very short time we will leap into battle," Jessica said simply, by way of introduction. "This is where your commander reminds you of martial glories, proud histories, and fanciful dreams of the future. But we have with us a better representative of what today really means. Lady Casey, Princess Kasimira, Centurion *zu* Wiegand, the floor is yours."

It was educational, watching the faces on her screen respond with shock. They all knew who Casey was, but only a few of them had any opportunity before now to spend much time around the woman.

The once and possibly future *Emperor of Fribourg, Karl VIII*.

"When I was a child, *Aquitaine* was the most evil thing in the galaxy, to hear my father and Uncle Em talk," Casey began in a voice that reminded people that she wasn't a junior officer suddenly called to speak before her elders. The young woman was an Emperor made flesh. "I believed that, even as a woman named Keller rocked the entire empire. Time and again she defeated or fought to a standstill the very Red Admiral who *was* the Empire, as far as the Fleet and the populace were concerned."

She paused, fixing her gaze on the assembled team she was now a part of, on Jessica's Flag Bridge.

"*Buran* was always a strange bogeyman on the distant frontier, core and spinward from *St. Legier*," she continued in a story-telling voice. "I was not old enough to understand that we were losing our war with *Buran*, even as we were defeating *Aquitaine*. When Keller came to *St. Legier*, she was a fanciful barbarian, a queen from the farthest reaches of space, a tale of romantic loss, and worse, a *woman* commanding a star fleet. For us of the Empire, the only things more frightful were the ancient *Sentiences* that once nearly destroyed humanity."

Casey turned back and fixed her eyes on Jessica now. Jessica felt like she could see the soul of the young woman: the artist, the poet, the dreamer upon whose shoulders Jessica intended to fully dismantle the patriarchy that was *Fribourg*, even as she set out to destroy the being who might truly represent the *Last of the Immortals*.

They shared a secret smile, as if Casey knew what she was thinking.

"But she was also my friend at that moment when I had nothing," Casey said. "The person who held the entire empire together when my foolish cousin might have torn it asunder. I was there, holding the Earth Sword itself, when Emmerich Wachturm became Grand Admiral of the Fleet. I will never forget the utter silence when I called Jessica to serve in his place. Nor the eruption of pure joy that greeted her. Instead of remaining our most implacable foe, she had become our closest friend. Instead of trapping *Fribourg* between, like a nut to be cracked, she chose to help us drive the demon of *Buran* from our realm."

Casey took a deep breath, visibly overcome with emotion, but willing to share even that with the crews who would go into battle today.

"Instead of destroying my home, Jessica has become that which will protect it," Casey's voice cracked now. Jessica had a hard time keeping her own emotions in check. "Instead of being my enemies, all of you have become my friends. You have accepted me into your ranks as one of you, that I may help bear your burden. That I may share in your glory as we face that most-ancient, most-evil of foes. And if it should become necessary, it will be my honor to die in battle with you. Thank you. I can think of no higher gift that you could give me, than to be one of you."

There were many sniffs, both in the room and across the comm, not that Jessica begrudged them for an instant. They had accepted Casey, and she had proven herself worthy.

"Admiral Keller," Casey said through tears. "You have the flag."

Jessica swallowed before she spoke. Never had she expected something like that, even from a poet like Casey. She supposed she should have known better, having memorized the woman's symphonies.

"First Expeditionary Fleet, this is Admiral Keller. I have the flag," Jessica forced her voice to command register. "All hands to battle stations."

CHAPTER LXVIII

K ier had her little vanities, as a Director. She was aware of them, and humored herself, when it did not affect military readiness in any measurable way.

Steadfast at Dawn was in geo-synchronous orbit above Taymyr, the capitol city Ul Banop Cheani Yuur had abandoned in his flight. But she had caused the vessel to rotate such that her primary viewport in the morning had an unobstructed view of the great, dark gulf that separated this front line of castles from the deeper homelands beyond *Ninagirsu.*

The barbarians had not tried to penetrate that darkness in more than a generation, since the first scouts were tracked down and annihilated without mercy for their audacity. In another generation, this front would be so strong that *The Holding's* vessels might threaten the very heart of the barbarians' realm. And possibly the even-most-distant lands from which their second Red Admiral, Keller, had apparently originated.

Perhaps she would get the opportunity to bomb many new worlds into submission for *The Eldest.*

Kier smiled and picked up a mug of tea that had been steeped to the perfect level before serving. Her personal chambers were austere, as befit Director of a Nightmaster. No art on the walls. A simple, sea-green throw rug tacked down in the walkway before her workstation. None of the little trinkets some fools collected, representing nostalgia for lost youth. Or some such drivel.

No, the glory of the vessel lay in the *Sentience* that bore them on its mighty shoulders, and not the pitiful humans who serviced it. Humans were too fallible. Look no further than the man who had fled rather than admit his wrong.

Only in unbending service to *The Eldest* could perfection be achieved. Humans who took it upon themselves to anticipate the wishes of the immortal leader would lead themselves astray with their arrogance, and take many innocent souls with them.

That impulse must be crushed the instant it took root.

Kier took another sip and turned to confirm the time on a clock beside the hatch to her personal chamber. Time to go to work.

Duty, foremost.

She made her way into the corridor and headed forward, surrounded by a bubble of personal space as her crew avoided her.

Power.

The first alert siren was followed almost immediately by a jarring, as if the entire hull suffered a groundquake.

The overhead lights in the hall flickered for a second. Even the gravplates stuttered, but only enough for her inner ear to notice. Still, it was possibly the most frightening thing Kier had ever encountered, as the great vessel was the rock upon which she had based most of her belief system.

And then the vessel jumped.

Only someone so attuned to the vessel would have been able to tell, without being on the bridge when it happened, but Kier knew. Some emergency so great that event and escape had occurred almost simultaneously, but for the massive crush of damage in the instant between.

Kier began to run as the alert sirens wailed. Crewmembers that had given her space a moment ago brushed by her, and her them, as she raced to the bridge.

The double doors slid aside, admitting her to the high temple of her realm.

War Advocate Ro was already at her station, calling orders to the rest of the crew. Entity Advocate Au had approached the bridge from the other direction, arriving two steps behind Kier and sliding around her to take the station from one of his subordinates.

"Bring the *Sentience* to full cognition," the War Advocate ordered as Au slid into the chair.

Kier listened and slid into her own command chair, locking herself down for what must be Keller's sudden appearance.

The *Sentient* being that was *Steadfast at Dawn* was kept leashed ninety percent of the time. Not much more awareness than necessary for self-maintenance. *The Eldest* had determined that to be the best long-term method to ensure warships were at their peak when needed. Kier suspected that was also so they did not suffer from the sorts of psychological conditions related to being a god born into silicon.

"What happened?" Kier asked into the gap.

War Advocate Ro was busy bringing all her weapons systems on-line to fight. The Maneuver Advocate was busy preparing her four subordinate vessels for the process of detaching from the mothership so that they could fight as individuals, once the ship emerged from jump.

Thus the greatest strength of the Nightmaster. One vessel. Five foes.

"Three Imperial warships came out of jump at a tremendous speed," the War Advocate explained. "Far greater than we have seen before. All fired what appear to be Type-3 beams of the Imperial design, but they were able to focus the beams at a far greater distance than we have ever encountered in any of our records, and thus inflict damage from a range we never imagined. The two larger vessels also each fired a pair of much heavier beams. The Power Absorbers were set to navigational levels, sufficient for solar wind and normal operations, but the beams simply collapsed the matrix and discharged on the hull."

"Show me," she ordered.

There was time before they emerged from this jump. She had already checked the default plotted course to escape.

The replay came up on one screen on her panels. The sensor readings on the other. *Steadfast at Dawn* had been staggered.

Kier winced.

Worst case scenario.

Caught at rest, without the instant reflexes of the vessel itself to respond. And some new weapon system they had never seen before.

It did explain why Keller had been willing to challenge her, so far from her home base. They believed they had an edge in their new cruisers that could successfully engage a Nightmaster.

"Crew Advocate Ko, all hands to damage control stations immediately," Kier ordered.

She looked closer at her boards, noting one location where the damage appeared worst.

"Maneuver Advocate Ve," she turned to the squadron interface officer. "How badly damaged is *Steadfast in Duty?*"

Ve Klossak Marah Zaun, Maneuver Advocate, was good at her position, but not excellent. She lacked that subtle something that would have made her a Director, rather than the person who simply executed the commands of a Director or War Advocate. She was one who merely interfaced with the four vessels *Steadfast at Dawn* carried into battle.

She grimaced now, looking at her boards longer than was necessary. She should have had the data in hand immediately.

"Without detaching, we cannot be sure at this moment, Director," Ve replied. "The damage passed through the hull casings of *Steadfast at Dawn* and penetrated the Mako's hull in several places. Maneuvering and engines have been compromised, and several weapons systems have been damaged. I cannot make an immediate determination whether *Steadfast in Duty* should remain with *Energiya* when we separate. The risks are very finely balanced."

And that was why this woman would never actually command, although Kier would say nothing. Within her role, the woman excelled. That was good enough.

Kier would have damned the torpedoes and flung *Steadfast in Duty* into battle. Might yet, if Keller felt herself that strong.

Kier checked her jump clock.

"You have three minutes to decide," the Director said. "After that, we will be at war."

CHAPTER LXIX

teadfast at Dawn appeared almost exactly where Jessica had predicted, based on all the research done by *Ballard* and *CS-405*. And reminded Jessica of the First Rule of Battle, as First Fleet Lord and later First Lord Kasum has taught her: no battle plan survives contact with the enemy. *His job is to fuck it up.*

Team One would be along shortly, but *Buran*'s JumpDrives were faster across a short distance than anything programmed by a human. The JumpSails made up for it by letting you sail continuously across JumpSpace, rather than having to drop out, look around to place yourself, and then jump again. Until the vessel emerged, Jessica had no idea how successful Robbie, Alber', and Tomas had been.

Apparently, better than anticipated, for both good and evil.

Jessica had hoped that they would separate into constituent parts in orbit, flinging *Energiya* into hiding in the depths of space while warriors prepared to unleash their particular brand of hell down in *Trusski*'s orbit.

In that first second, Jessica understood that she had guessed wrong, and was going to pay an awful price in the moments between now and when her heavy units got back to rescue her.

"Fire," she ordered over the general push, just in case anybody was actually waiting for an order from her. "All ahead full."

Steadfast at Dawn had appeared as a unit. Not even separated out yet, but one monstrous entity even larger than *Auberon*, a keep with four towers defending the corners.

Eight Type-3 beams reached across space and splashed harmlessly into that battleship's Power Absorbers, but that was expected. A moment later, all six Primary beams lashed out as one chord, each tuned to a different pitch so a commander could track them aurally. *II Augusta* poured her fire into the mix as well, six more Type-3 beams hammering.

Without *VI Ferrata* and *VI Victrix*, First Expeditionary would have been utterly doomed. The Type-3 beams on the two big, *RAN* vessels were insufficient to fill the bucket that was the Power Absorbers on a Nightmaster, who would just drain the energy off and use it to recharge systems as fast as it could, while slowly bleeding off the rest after it jumped to safety.

But Jessica and Yan had been there at *St. Legier*. Had watched a vessel known as *Dancer in Darkness* challenge an Imperial battleship named *Amsel, The Blackbird*, and her consort, the *Corynthe* Mothership *Kali-ma*.

da Vinci's voice on the command comm was music to her ears. And Ainsley had apparently been paying attention to something Jessica had missed.

"Heavy Wing, this is *da Vinci*," she called in that slow, laconic voice she used with her people. "Adjust your targets aft and down as much as possible with parallax. Big girls have had their fun, and the boys aren't back yet. On my mark: three, two, one, fire."

Jessica smiled as twenty-seven Type-3 beams lashed out simultaneously. They were untuned, since the horseshoe design Bedrov had used for the *E-2* fighter could just barely handle the emitter itself, but at this range, it was still one hell of a lot of energy.

And with the target adjustment, not all of them hit, but *da Vinci* had seen something. *CS-405* was jamming *Steadfast at Dawn* with everything the little corvette had, but was still scanning the vessel hard.

Team One had apparently drawn blood, back in orbit. Black carbon-scoring ran down the side of the *Energiya* like a John Hancock signature, a massive gash that lined up with one of the four cruisers that the monster still carried. Maybe they had seriously injured the beast.

In the back of her head, Jessica was counting the seconds until the *Buran* ship could jump again. If they stayed there and tried to slug it out, *Auberon* and her consorts would savage them, especially since every weapon *Buran* had was no better than a Type-2 beam for range. If they stayed in RealSpace, she would bloody their nose, and then Team One would cross their T with a battle axe.

Because they were planning ahead, the Primary teams on *Auberon* managed to get off a second salvo in twenty-four seconds, which might have been a record for a full gun deck. The beam emitters on the two warships recharged fast enough that they were getting ready for a third salvo. The fighters would be unleashing their second shortly.

But six Primaries, fired as one, was an unstoppable force.

And Nina Vanek had apparently been paying attention to *da Vinci*. Four hit the same weakened corner hard enough that Jessica could see metal sublime under the heat, and fragments spall off at high speed.

And then nothing. *Steadfast at Dawn* had jumped again. Twenty-nine seconds under intense, withering fire seemed to be the fastest they could do right now.

Jessica nodded to Enej and Casey.

"Phase Five complete," she said over the general comm. "All units prepare to move. Flight Wing, go defensive now. We'll be back shortly."

"Roger that, Flag," *da Vinci* replied with a crispness that was new. Probably the hangover of actually being in charge.

Auberon shuddered with something approximating ecstasy as it vanished into JumpSpace. Jessica felt the same way. She had been on the bridge of the *Blackbird* when a Mauler savaged the battleship. She had no desire to repeat the experience.

Ninety-four seconds later, RealSpace again.

Like before, Jessica had gone straight down. All of the *Buran* vessel's maneuvers had stacked like levels in a house, so *First Expeditionary* was hiding in the basement, a monster from a teen-horror vid. *Steadfast at Dawn* had entered the *Trusski* system at a point not far from the north pole, jumped down to a standard approach point, and then into orbit.

Two-dimensional, planar thinking. One of the very first things of which Nils Kasum had broken in a sixteen-year-old Jessica Keller.

And one of the cornerstones of Imperial tactics facing *Buran*. Jump a huge fleet to the edge of the gravity well, and then waddle the entire convoy down toward the Starbase known as *Ural* while wolves picked off strays and the wounded. Fight as long as you could, and then retreat in as orderly a manner as possible.

Only the fact that *Buran* did not seem to commit as many ships to this frontier as they could have even made it possible for *Fribourg* to do that much. Jessica would have taken two Nightmasters and a pack of Warmasters and blown up something big on Karl's side of the line every time they tried it.

All she could figure was that they didn't have as big a fleet as *Fribourg* or *Aquitaine*, either relative to population or in absolute size.

Or maybe they just never started anything. Karl had frequently had acted as a bully, until Jessica had dissuaded him of the notion once and for all. The first time *Buran* had initiated any major event had been when they attacked *St. Legier* with nuclear weapons, and even that had done far less physical damage than it could have.

The psychological scars would still be generations healing.

"Headcount?" Jessica asked as *Auberon* came to rest, seventeen AU out, and almost exactly below their previous point, relative to the star and the planet.

"Six corvettes plus *II Augusta*," Casey replied quickly.

"Very good," Jessica replied. "Let me know when Team One or *Wombat* appear."

Now, the hard part. Playing a game of tag in a dark house. Or maybe this was that monster vid, and the plucky heroes were trying to find the creature before it found them.

Plus side: she was willing to play *Buran*'s game, rather than sit still and wait for them to come to her. Minus side: until Team One showed up, she was seriously outgunned.

It would be even worse if *Steadfast at Dawn* decided to go after the Flight Wing. That would be a turkey shoot, mitigated only by the number of Archerfish mines and primary mines that *Wombat* would be rolling out of her rear racks, hoping like hell that everything worked.

"Contact," the comm officer called. "*CA-264*. And escorts."

Senior Centurion Daniel Giroux had been with her most of his career, and she would have it no other way. She would enjoy telling Kigali how Giroux had introduced *VI Ferrata* and *VI Victrix*, when this was all done.

And escorts. Ha.

"Lock them into the pattern and jump soonest," Jessica ordered.

"Roger that," someone said. Maybe Denis. Maybe Enej. A male voice, so not Casey or Nina.

The job would get done. That was all she cared about.

Jump.

Everything reloaded. Everyone in motion.

First Expeditionary Fleet. The Wild Hunt.

A thing that Moirrey had once referred to as *All the Hounds of Hell Coming for your Soul.*

"**W**ombat, time's running short," *da Vinci* called on the main channel. "Call it good enough and get clear."

"Yes, mother," came the reply.

da Vinci laughed in spite of herself. Command Flight Centurion Ainsley Barrett, giving orders to starships. Yan still teased her about being his boss, but she had definitely, extra-special, made sure Bedrov hadn't snuck aboard any of her team's ships. Possibly by kidnapping the pilot at the last minute.

A blip gone from her scanners as the minelayer vanished, leaving *da Vinci* and her friends alone in the darkness, a school of herring surrounded by angry sharks. Of course, the original Red Admiral had made that same mistake.

"*Devilfish*, stand by," *da Vinci* continued.

The kid who had replaced her as a scout pilot in the *P-6* was okay, she supposed. Well, better than okay. Pretty good at her job. She was just never going to measure up to *da Vinci*'s legend. But it gave her a starting point against which to strive.

Right now, the girl, Rama Papadopoulos, was all set to switch from hard scan to white noise, as soon as anybody nosy appeared. On warship scanners, the combined flight wing would look like a fog bank, once you got close enough. Forty-five fighter craft: three wings of *E-2* Heavies and two wings of *C-1* Escorts; plus both GunShips off *Auberon*: *Necromancer* and *Sunset*. And one crazy son-of-a-bitch in a bright red DropShip.

Cayenne had no business being out here, having nothing in the way of guns for a fight like this, but *Gaucho* was running as silent as that big beast could manage, and had every EVA-capable marine, medic, and engineer in the squadron, suited up and ready to rescue pilots if they got hurt while their carrier was a long jump away.

Hopefully, *Buran* would think he was an asteroid in the middle of the formation. *Gaucho* was still mad about getting his previous ride shot out from under him.

"Contact," *Devilfish* called suddenly. "Looks like a trio of cruisers just tried to catch us sitting back where we had been with the warships. Stand by. Stand by. *Hard ping.* I repeat hard ping. Incoming."

da Vinci blew out a deep breath and concentrated on her guns. Chances were good that those sharks were jumping over here as soon as they coordinated.

Things were about to get exciting.

CHAPTER LXX

Kier wanted to scream with rage. Then hunt down that never-to-be-sufficiently-damned Khan and use his skull as a drinking cup.

Never had *Steadfast at Dawn* suffered such grievous damage. One of her subsidiary Makos, *Steadfast in Duty*, was so badly damaged that she had been forced to leave the vessel docked with the *Energiya* module while the rest of them went to hunt the barbarians. And the second time it was hit was her fault, which only made it worse.

She was the Director. Every choice made while the *Sentience* was at reduced cognition was ultimately hers, regardless of the originator. If one of her crew made a mistake, she had failed to train them correctly, or failed to provide competent officers to oversee them.

And Keller had found a hole in Kier's armor. She must have been watching for some time, to be able to determine where *Steadfast at Dawn* was going to come out of a surprise jump. But Kier had failed, by not randomly programming alternates.

Complacency and efficiency had become the enemy of success.

She would not make that mistake again, but first, she had to locate this new enemy, who so badly wanted to fight her. Who had already killed one of *The Holding*'s warships, the Roughshark *Dancer in Darkness*.

Oh, yes, Kier knew who this Red Admiral was.

A barbarian foreign to even *Fribourg*, from the distant galactic fringe worlds. *Aquitaine* would be crushed next, after *Fribourg* was brought to heel.

At least they had managed to escape the second trap as well, at the cost of one of her Makos and significant damage to *Energiya* that would require a significant space dock effort to make whole.

"Maneuver Advocate, state your readiness," Kier began the ritual.

"*Steadfast in Duty* is defensive, Director," the woman replied with genuine anger in her voice that surprised Kier. "The other three: *Steadfast in Pursuit*, *Steadfast in Honor*, and *Steadfast in Surprise* are ready for combat."

"Crew Advocate, how are your charges?" Kier continued.

"*Vengeful in Duty*, Director," the man replied with a poetic turn. Ko Ashkhan Loren Miil was old for his position at forty-seven standard years, but he had found his place, his purpose. Without the war, Kier was certain he would be a social worker of some sort. Helping people find themselves seemed to be in his blood.

Kier nodded. Most of the damage had been confined to three decks aft, missing *Steadfast at Dawn's* combat hull entirely, but passing like an arrow through *Energiya* and pinning *Steadfast in Duty* in place. Damage control crews were already flooding into the damaged sections, well outside their customary areas.

"Entity Advocate, how stands your charge?" Kier continued slowly.

She had served as Director of this vessel long enough to know the *Sentience's* personality quite well, far better than the man who had only been with them for a little more than a standard year.

"All subroutines operating within normal, Director," the man said. "Tending towards the high end, but that I ascribe to pain and anger."

Kier agreed.

"War Advocate, begin," Kier concluded.

"*Steadfast at Dawn*," the War Advocate ordered. "Initiate separation of all vessels."

As always, the entire ship went to zero gravity as the fingers detached, blades slowly being drawn from their scabbards before drawing blood. The main reactors were located in *Energiya*, with the JumpDrives capable of driving the entire massive edifice through deep space.

Now, it was one greatsword and a trio of poniards, when it should have been a quad.

But they were hunting.

"War Advocate Ro, would you predict our adversary to remain

behind, lying in wait for our return?" Kier asked the woman plotting maneuvers as the ships detached.

"If they were Imperial, I would almost guarantee it, Director," Ro said. "Keller has not followed any Imperial standards, so I can only guess that she wishes to play cat and mouse with us. However, we have one advantage on her."

"Oh?" Kier said, happy for anything to go her way for once today.

"Those fighter craft are most likely not jump capable," the War Advocate said. "So either the carriers are sitting ducks, waiting to pick them up before we return, or they have been abandoned for now."

The second was the most likely situation. Kier had been as surprised as anyone, viewing the footage of two so-called pirate fighters *making a jump inside a gravity well* to finish off *Dancer in Darkness*, at the moment when he should have been safe to make his escape.

"What are the chances that those were operated by remote control?" Kier asked, aware of how valuable trained pilots were rated.

The Holding did not use snub-fighters. Why bother, when little escorts like Hammerheads could jump with the fleet? Nothing smaller could be built with both the necessary *Sentience* and sufficient firepower to justify the expense.

"I presume a third trap" Kier continued.

"I as well, Director," she replied. "Plus, the three vessels that initiated the attack in orbit are unaccounted for. I would have them prepared to land suddenly in our midst."

"Proposal?" Kier inquired.

The War Advocate projected an image onto Kier's main screen.

"A long tetrahedron, Director," she said. "Drop the Makos in a bracket around the place we emerged, far enough out to be potentially behind ambushers, with *Steadfast at Dawn* above them, prepared to pounce, depending on where the fighters or carrier may be."

Kier studied the plot. Aggressive, as was her wont, but subtle enough that perhaps she would catch Keller off guard. Kier's squadron would be separated, and thus at risk, but any could jump to the aid of a vessel in hazard.

"Transmit this to the squadron and execute," Kier ordered.

I'm coming for you, Keller.

CHAPTER LXXI

All hell broke loose within a single moment. *da Vinci* couldn't have described it any other way. Even on the logs later, everything happened at once.

Three cruiser-class vessels appeared out of a short jump and let loose. That was when she discovered that the Makos came in a variety of flavors. At the time, it was just beams everywhere she looked.

Two of the cruisers were standard Makos. One big Mauler on the front of a long, triangular hull, like the maw of a hungry shark. Nine Pulse beams, three on a facing, plus six Flicker beams defensively, or two per side.

Upside: enough firepower to seriously mess up a *Founder*-class heavy cruiser in the sort of drop-koala ambush these people preferred. The Pulse beam was comparable to a Type-3 for dangerous, but only had about the range of a Type-2, so they had to get close to use it. Downside: a Pulse beam had a hard time locking on something as small as a moving fightercraft, especially when you couldn't see it. And *Devilfish* knew they were coming.

Kid had smarts. She reacted immediately when the bad guys bipped into existence on the fringes of the squadron. Lit two of them up with every jammer and kitchen sink she had, while organizing the entire Wing to hit the one closest to the original flight path, so nobody had to turn far.

Furious had taught *Auberon*'s pilots how to get crazy with the gyroscopes in combat. It was old hat, now.

The *Buran* cruiser opened fire into the oncoming wing set to pass down his right flank.

"All ships, engage on Beta," *Devishfish* called in a singsong voice. "I repeat, lock on Beta and engage."

da Vinci approved. *Jouster* would have demanded that the order come from him. Maybe he would have trusted *da Vinci* to do it, but only because they had been friends for fifteen years. *Devilfish* was still wet behind the ears, but every second counted right now.

As one, the entire wing spun in place. They had been going all out, in order to get as far away from the original danger point as possible. On command, everyone had shut their engines down, rolled their noses over, and cut loose on the stupid bastard that had come out on their number two facing.

And that was when the Type-1-Pulse beam suddenly showed why Yan Bedrov had built it. Sucker managed to absorb all the Type-3's, although *da Vinci* could see places where the whatever-it-was they used instead of shields leaked, or something. Shots had gotten through and speared metal like an ice pick.

Then the staccato-1's picked up. And his front shields went *down*.

One beam wasn't all that impressive, certainly not at this sort of distance. They were intended for use on other fighters or missiles, or for when the fighters were escorting a bigger ship and being ignored. At this range, it was probably like being slapped. Painful, but not lethal.

Unless you had twenty *C-1* fighters all slapping you at the same time. Then it became tragic.

One Mako, with his nose chewed off. Bugger managed to jump, but he was leaking atmosphere and bleeding metal parts in his wake as he left.

Elapsed time, forty seconds.

The other two had disappeared as well, leaving *da Vinci* and her flock alone again.

"Flight Wing, invert one five zero, roll ten, yaw thirty, max acceleration, move," *da Vinci* ordered.

Nose pointed backwards and down, and then spun to one side. Physics was physics. They would decelerate, relative to their previous pace, and be headed towards the south pole of the system, more or less. Boss had said *Buran* tended to be two dimensional fighters, so hopefully this would get them away from a second pass.

da Vinci wasn't sure they would survive a second pass.

The headcount was ugly.

Turned out that the Mako on the port bow had been a Thresher, not a Mako. Instead of that Mauler that was next to useless against fighters, it had belched up some sort of super-energy beam and had simply shut down *Sunset* and five other fighters it had touched. Some sort of directed electro-magnetic pulse that blew every breaker at the same time but didn't damage anything.

Ignored everyone's shields, though, just like that damned Mauler.

Seventeen others were damaged, in addition to six that had been destroyed. The joys of that Pulse beam. If it hit, you splattered, whereas the Flicker beams might just blow your shields down and tattoo ugliness into your hull.

Cayenne and EVA teams were in motion. Of the seventeen, twelve could more or less keep up with the formation. The other five were either already shut down from damage, or going dark as soon as rescue could get to them.

Final score: one porcupine wounded, une shark with his nose kicked in.

Hopefully, Keller was out there, distracting those bastards. Nobody had ever promised *da Vinci* she would die in bed, but that sounded a whole lot better than the alternative, right about now.

CHAPTER LXXII

SYSTEM: TRUSSKI. STATUS: ACTIVE COMBAT

It was not possible, but Kier had no words to describe it otherwise. *Steadfast in Duty* damaged before the battle even began. *Steadfast in Pursuit* nearly eviscerated by the cloud of oh-so-dangerous fighter craft. She could still kill them all, but the cost would be utterly prohibitive.

Keller appeared to be reading her mind, able to outguess *Steadfast at Dawn* at every turn, something no Imperial fleet had ever managed.

Kier was torn. Duty dictated that she defend *Trusski* against this aggression, but Keller had never threatened the planet itself. Kier could see that now.

And those fighter craft were brand new. Nothing in the records showed anything like them, from the bizarre, two-nosed, horseshoe design, to the fact that they carried amazingly-heavy beams and not a single missile. Most Imperial models relied on missiles as their primary armament, with a tiny beam weapon almost as an afterthought.

Kier would have never ordered *Steadfast in Pursuit* into that buzzsaw had she known what lay in store. She had been waiting off to one side, right at the edge of sensor range, for Keller's flagship to come rescue the smaller craft from her attack.

But Keller never came. Where was she?

Steadfast at Dawn and her children had gone spinward thirty degrees and out a further ten AU from the point where the fightercraft had been.

It was a safe spot, as near as she could tell. Nothing close, and no ships in real-time scan, although there would be sensor ghosts for hours, the downside of crossing JumpSpace at relative transluminal speeds so many times.

"Maneuver Advocate, order *Steadfast in Pursuit* to return to *Energiya* for repairs," Kier finally ordered, looking over the massive damage. Casualties had been mercifully light, but the ship has lost nearly thirty percent of its armaments when the front Power Absorbers staggered under the sudden load. The ravens attacking its flesh after that had savaged the vessel.

She still had a battleship and two cruisers. With surprise, she could still significantly damage one or more of the four capital vessels *Fribourg* had committed.

She would have some blood, for her pain.

CHAPTER LXXIII

Emergence.

Jessica always felt it in her bones and her soul, but more so today. She was dancing with a devil she didn't know, although one she had studied enough to guess well, at least for the first few steps.

Now, it devolved to random chaos.

There were really only two fixed points in a battle like this: *Trusski*, and the spot where the Flight Wing was right now, which was changing slowly as *da Vinci* maneuvered her force as fast as she could away from the first bullseye, as randomly as possible.

"Status?" Jessica asked as they found everyone.

She had feared utter annihilation. The gods were apparently smiling on them, today.

"Six destroyed," Enej replied quickly. "Ten more damaged but potentially salvageable given time, plus *Sunset* is offline. Apparently, they were successful in significantly damaging a second cruiser."

Jessica let out a breath silently. So much better than she feared.

That phase was always the riskiest. Would *Buran's* commander be willing to pay the butcher's bill to destroy the flight wing? It was possible, but expensive.

The fact that the warships were hiding in the darkness probably worked to her advantage. Even a battleship would be loath to be caught between that particular Scylla and Charybdis.

Now if she could just convince them to accept their losses and depart. Not that she expected it. Looking at the scans from *Devilfish*, Jessica could take that commander's measure.

Aggressive. Possibly angry as well, at least enough to override good sense.

Jessica let the smallest grin form on her face. She had always had that knack: find the gap in the other commander's planning and slam a knife home in it. It has won her command, followed by ever-greater responsibility.

It had won her a crown.

But this wasn't the original Red Admiral, a genius at warfare. This was a total stranger, possibly an enraged bull.

There was still dancing to be done. Waltzing with blades, as the ancient hymn went.

Time to goad them into reacting, instead of planning.

Jessica called up her tactical file and went deep into the tertiary options.

Yes. There. Completely insane, from an utterly unexplainable tactical angle.

Just the right level of crazy for someone used to *Sentient* logic.

"Bridge, this is Keller," she said aloud.

It was fun watching nearly every face in the room turn and stare, just for a second. Fleet Centurions issued orders to their Flag Centurions, who translated them into commands for the entire squadron. But she and Denis had been together for a long time. Much of her legend could only have been built with his willing help and capable hands.

It was fitting to let him have some of the fun, especially after he had been obliged to let Tomas, Robbie, and Alber' have dessert first.

"I'm transmitting a firing sequence to you now," she said as she pushed the send button.

His face glanced down in her viewscreen, skimmed the message, and broke out into a broad smile.

"Alber' put you up to this?" he asked with a knowing laugh.

"I believe he will approve, but he can't do it," she replied. "Only you can."

"Roger that," he laughed again. "Stand by."

Seconds later, the entire hull rang six times in rapid succession. Missiles going down range and tracking.

When facing *Buran*, missiles were worse than useless, since the

Sentient ships could jump out of the way with ease. That was why she had to leave *RAN Ishfahan* behind. What good was a missile cruiser here? Bedrov's cruisers had a pitiful two tubes each, but she hadn't even bothered bringing missiles, since Yan had designed them to launch Imperial beasts.

Just as Yan had designed his ships to replace all the space normally allocated to missile racks and storage with more beams, and a ton more generators and batteries for them.

Everyone had probably forgotten that a Star Controller even had the racks.

Until now.

"Six birds away and tracking," Denis was back. "Ballistic programming locked in."

"That should give them something to think about," Jessica said aloud to all the confused faces. "Take the squadron to point twenty-nine. I want to see what they do next."

CHAPTER LXXIV

SYSTEM: TRUSSKI. STATUS: ACTIVE COMBAT

"Repeat that," Kier said. "I am not sure I heard you correctly."

"The Star Controller *Auberon* had fired a salvo of missiles, Director," War Advocate Ro reiterated.

"At whom?" Kier asked, utterly at a loss.

There was nothing there. Unless this was another one of those damnable mine fields. That had been a terrible surprise, once they reviewed the logs and realized that hidden mines had been responsible for a significant portion of the incoming fire on *Steadfast in Honor* and *Steadfast in Surprise*. All the terrible savagery from those fightercraft had gone after *Steadfast in Pursuit*.

Neither ship had been terribly damaged, but the shock had been sufficient to throw all of their timing off. The squadron had jumped clear rather than blunder deeper into whatever sudden mischief Keller had prepared.

They could always attack from other angles. Eventually, Kier could annihilate those damnable snubfighters, possibly by just plowing through them with the DEMP on *Steadfast in Surprise* and then picking off the ragged survivors one at a time.

Keller would either have to face her in the ruins of the fighter craft, or lose a significant portion of her force, too afraid to rescue them.

But what was Keller firing missiles at?

There was nothing there. And Kier could easily remain away from the line of the drones themselves, in case they were somehow seeding more mines for her force. Or something.

This was not the Imperial way, damn it!

"Director, the missiles appear to be targeted on *Trusski* itself," War Advocate Ro said.

"From here?" Kier let her surprise show through. "They will take days to get there."

"Agreed," the War Advocate said. "Nonetheless, that appears to be the target, a ballistic launch at where *Trusski* will be in roughly three days."

What did Keller gain, lobbing missiles at the planet that *Steadfast at Dawn* could smack down at her leisure?

Of course.

Trusski had no orbital defenses, except *Steadfast at Dawn*.

Was Keller firing a final, angry insult across space, so Kier would have to hunt down missiles rather than attack the fighters? She could do both. Hop in and slaughter the little hornets, then hop over and destroy the drones.

What was that woman's game?

Worse, had she launched other missiles? Kier had no way of tracking all the places that Keller's force might have jumped, until all the sensor logs reported in, tracking all the ghosts of insertion and emergence as they overlapped.

Hours would pass in the meantime. Would any have hit the planet while she was out here stalking?

And where would Keller be hiding?

Kier had never felt this level of paralysis in command.

Imperial tactics had always been laughably simple. Had she grown complacent? Was this what a worthy foe looked like? Should she order *Steadfast in Pursuit* and *Steadfast in Duty* into the battle, damning the costs? Or send them to protect the planet from bombardment?

Spies like Daniel St. Collins had reported the utter, blinding rage that the orbital bombing of *St. Legier* had evoked. Was this some manner of payback?

"Director, if I may offer a thought?" the Crew Advocate spoke up in a quiet, almost diffident voice, polite, but not afraid. It was so rare that he spoke during these situations.

Kier nodded, aware that she had already started down a mad rabbit hole, trying to outguess this new foe.

"This was her intent," the man continued, gesturing to her and the

War Advocate. "Confusion in command. I would wait in ambush for you along that flight line, hoping to goad you into chasing meaningless missiles in the process, and turning your back."

Kier saw the rightness of Crew Advocate Ko's supposition so hard it nearly hurt.

"War Advocate," Kier said. "We know the range of those Primary beams. Assume she wants to optimize them and is waiting. We will retrieve *Steadfast in Pursuit* and *Steadfast in Duty* and go into battle as a single unit again. From *Energiya*, I want a spiraling series of jumps until we find her along that path, then we will pounce on *Auberon* and focus all our firepower upon that vessel. Ignore the cruisers and the escorts. We will come back for them after we destroy Keller."

"So it shall be, Director."

CHAPTER LXXV

2*18 Svati Prime.* Just the name of the planet was enough to invoke fear, anger, and grudging admiration from an Imperial audience.

The galaxy's meanest, most effective practical joke.

Jessica grinned as she watched the theoretical track of those missiles. And if they ever actually arrived, Denis had programmed them to go inert. Friction in the atmosphere would destroy them.

But if any *Buran* vessel got too close, they would discover almost the entire count of Archerfish drones Jessica had brought to this frontier.

Keep them on their toes.

"Casey, have you found anything yet?" Jessica asked.

As Imperial Flag Centurion, the woman technically didn't have anything to do, lacking Imperial vessels requiring squadron communications. She had been helping Enej's team with squadron signals, but Jessica had pulled her off on a more important task.

"Negative, Fleet Centurion," Casey said grimly.

"Project what we know," Jessica ordered.

A new sphere replaced the tactical map, a gigantic plum representing the entirety of the *Trusski* system, out to one hundred AU. A globe approximately thirty light hours across. Large chunks of the map turned solid green, mostly on the far side of the system, while a few places showed red, with pink surrounding the crimson.

"The red are areas where we have solid information less than one hour old, Fleet Centurion," Casey continued. "*CS-405* has been paying attention on every hop, but not seen anything."

"Nor would I expect them to," Jessica said. "*Steadfast at Dawn* made that mistake once. Either the second jump was utterly random, in which case this is a fool's errand, or they went here."

Jessica toggled a switch and lit up an area almost one hundred AU out from the star, but exactly straight up from the spot where *Auberon* had caught the war entity earlier, when she had only expected the *Energiya Module*.

"Why there?" Casey asked.

Enej showed the same level of confusion on his face, but he hadn't been combing Elzbet Aukley's notes as obsessively as Jessica had.

"*Ballard* watched them arrive and depart earlier," Jessica said. "Our first ambush point was their first departure hop in and out from *Trusski* orbit. They went there instinctively when Team One lit them up in orbit. Then we hit them there a second time. If I have the entire system to search through, we'll only find them on blind luck and bad timing, unless I provoke them to come to me in orbit. We'll try this one spot and if we don't get lucky, then things will get interesting down in the gravity well."

"Jump course plotted," Casey said a moment later. "Nine minutes travel time."

"Transmit and execute," Jessica said. "Everyone be prepared to come out of jump firing."

Jessica looked down and realized that she had forgotten her coffee from earlier. She took a sip and nodded her thanks at Marcelle as *Auberon* sidled between dimensions.

"All hands, this is Nina Vanek. I have Tactical," the voice brought Jessica back from planning the next several chess moves. "Stand by to exit JumpSpace. Thirty seconds."

Jessica saved the file and made a note for Enej or Casey to transmit the updates to the squadron as soon as they came out of jump. If this didn't work, she might be reduced to actually bombing the planet to get *Steadfast at Dawn* to come out and play.

That, or go run to grab the Flight Wing and hope she could get everyone loaded before the battleship found her.

Emergence.

"Target bearing," Enej called loudly. "All ships engage as you lie."

Jessica's screen lit up a half second later with the image of the monstrous *Energiya Module*, right out at the edge of Primary range, looking like half a carton of eggs, without two of the towers or the massive prow of the battleship in the center.

VI Ferrata had arrived first, apparently beating even *CA-264*, to say nothing of Alber' and *VI Victrix*. Jessica watched Robbie's Type-4 beams slam into the side of the transport module like twin hammers, followed a second later by a rake of his Type-3's, still tuned for shooting at extreme range.

Large chunks of hull and scrap metal were left behind a moment later, blasted out into empty space when the *Buran* transport vanished before anyone else could get off a shot.

Robbie hadn't killed it, but that salvo had hurt. Jessica was willing to bet a month's pay that the blow had been severe enough that it might spend months in drydock.

Or whatever *Sentient* hospital a vessel like that required when it suffered something short of a mortal wound.

Not for lack of trying on her part.

"All vessels, stand down," Enej called over the comm.

It was a redundant order. There was nothing there to shoot at, and Jessica knew that the ship was going to be hiding very hard now. Probably afraid of its own shadow.

Almost as good.

"Form them up and prepare for the next jump," Jessica ordered.

Every transit had an element of randomness to it, riding gravity waves in JumpSpace. This had been a short enough hop that everyone was fairly close to where they needed to be: four of the corvettes in the usual, three-dimensional box around *Auberon* and *II Augusta*, with *CP-406* directly above on overwatch. *CS-405* was in her spot at the very van, but *CA-264* had ended up somehow far aft and well to port from everyone else.

VI Ferrata was forward and *VI Victrix* aft, which was exactly backwards from how Robbie and Alber' normally flew, but Jessica really didn't mind, as long as they communicated with Enej and covered the carriers between them.

"Will they learn from this?" Casey asked abruptly.

Jessica started to retort, then realized what the woman was really asking.

"A good commander studies her wins as hard as her losses," Jessica said simply, quoting a much younger Nils Kasum on the first day of a fateful, Fall quarter. "You will always make mistakes that could be improved upon, if you stop to understand that fundamental point. Never make the same mistake twice. Instead, fail originally."

Casey nodded, much more an Emperor-in-training and much less a lowly Centurion.

"Override," a voice came over the comm. "All guns to starboard broadside. *Incoming*."

CHAPTER LXXVI

SYSTEM: TRUSSKI. STATUS: ACTIVE COMBAT

Finally.

Kier had not realized how much it had subconsciously grated on her to be missing half of her Makos in battle.

Shortly, she would come out of jump and retrieve them, injured as they were, and go hunt Keller properly.

RealSpace.

WHAT?

"Director Xi, we have an emergency," War Advocate Ro said simply.

"I'm aware of that," she snapped. "Full speed now. *The Eldest* has favored us, to drop us out of jump right on top of Keller. All weapons target *Auberon*, and then jump clear to *Point Gabriel.*"

Truly, luck, but the worst, most sour kind.

Keller had obviously found *Energiya*, plus the two wounded cruisers. Had driven them off, apparently with even more damage, if the expanding plasma cloud was any indication.

But *Steadfast at Dawn* was almost exactly on Keller's beam, crossing her T at medium speed that even now began to accelerate as her engines went into overdrive pushing.

Kier felt a moment of ecstasy as the first Mag-Shear beam caught the Star Controller broadside, a little aft of center, like shark's teeth into the side of a swimming seal. And she had managed to come out on a plane slightly below *Auberon,* so ten of the Pulse beams and six of the Flicker beams had a tracking arc.

The savagery inflicted was so great that the screens had to dim the image. The Mag-Shear ignored the carrier's shields, and the rest of her beams shattered them like a melon dropped out of a window.

I have you now.

Incoming fire from all directions as those pitiful little escorts opened up on her alone, ignoring the Makos. A tiny voice in the back of Kier's head approved their targeting decisions, even as the massive influx of energy overwhelmed her Power Absorbers on all sides, preventing her from shuttling energy around to protect a weak side.

And then they kept firing, even as the second Mag-Shear beam carved a channel across the bottom of *Auberon*'s keel.

The cruiser at the aft of the *Fribourg* formation fired those terrible, heavy beams that smashed *Steadfast at Dawn*'s port Power Absorbers. The other two fired only with the lighter beams, the ones known as Type-3, and even then they did remarkably little damage at this range.

Kier made a note to study the logs later and see why the weapons had changed so markedly from what she expected.

"Warning," a calm, male voice intoned. "Overload imminent."

Steadfast at Dawn himself, speaking to everyone. He did so infrequently, relying instead on Entity Advocate Au to be his voice most of the time. But the ship knew the situation as well as Kier did.

It would be a razor-thin margin, but *Steadfast at Dawn* had crossed the Imperial formation now, presenting the stronger aft Absorbers as Keller's escorts recharged and prepared for another salvo. They would pound on panels still fresh and ready to drink their fill of hostile fire.

She would escape this hit-and-run accident that she had stumbled into.

Except.

The Imperial cruiser at the front of the formation, the one that had barely fired at all, was apparently rotating on a flat axis yaw, while spinning like a porpoise. Somehow, they were using just gyroscopes to drag the massive vessel around like a spinning knife. She checked the readout, but *VI Ferrata* made no sense to her as a name.

More barbarisms.

And then *VI Ferrata* opened fire with those terrible beams, catching *Steadfast at Dawn* just aft of her bow. It was a raking shot, but the enemy had enough parallax to just catch the overloaded forward panels and shatter their hold. *Steadfast at Dawn* managed to capture most of the energy by routing it to the rear panels, but now they themselves were at risk of collapsing and exposing bare metal to hungry teeth.

The cruisers at both ends of the formation fired…*something*.

A beam struck instantly at this range. Missiles had to accelerate slowly from a dead stop, even as madly as they did.

From both bows, the cruisers launched small lozenge-shaped objects, ovals with flat tops and bottoms, glowing red hot. And traveling at a significant fraction of light speed, right at her.

And Kier had nothing on a bearing that she could fire back at them before impact, with the Flicker beams still focused on shredding *Auberon*.

"Impact warning," *Steadfast at Dawn* said calmly.

At that last moment, Kier was sure both devices somehow exploded *before* impact, transforming somehow into a pair of gigantic, white hands formed of plasma, that clapped together around her, a fly suddenly killed in mid-air.

Crunching darkness.

"Squadron, this is Aeliaes aboard *VI Ferrata*. I have the flag. All vessels hold your fire."

Auberon looked like a turkey that had been left in the oven for too long, scorched and torn as if it had also been mugged while cooking. And tumbling slightly on all three axes.

Jessica was probably safe, buried deep inside. Denis as well, but they were not talking to anyone until some serious repairs were brought to bear. Nobody was answering the comm, but that wasn't really a surprise, considering what had just happened.

The Star Controller's outer hull looked like it had physically melted in places.

But that was why they trained and practiced. Robbie got acknowledgements on his boards as all the Command Centurions and their Tactical Officers checked in.

The other image on his board, the happy one, was that stupid, *Sentient* battleship. She was tumbling far worse than *Auberon*.

They had fired Moirrey's *Bubble Gun* in training and in sims, until they had grown rather bored with it. Just another weapon in the suite. Another tint of paint on the palette. Alber' and Tomas were the ones who went in for colorful craziness.

Robbie was always happy with a sort of mechanical brutality when conducting the Art of War. This thing, this *Reversed Field, Pinch, Plasma*

Implosion Generator had detonated at the exact, perfect distance necessary to form the plasma ball, two of them with Alber's, and they had wrapped themselves around *Steadfast at Dawn*, and set everything on fire at once, including all those lovely gaps where their shield-equivalents had already gone down.

Surprise.

Both of the shark-cruisers had fled already. This had been a battle of titans, not lines of battle. All of their fire had also gone into Jessica. All of *Aquitaine's* counter-battery had gone solely into that battleship, who had probably, and finally, learned why sailing through a wall of Bedrov-designed escorts was a terminally-stupid idea.

A Type-1 beam was perfect for killing missiles. It did a good job hammering on fighters that got too close, knocking down shields or shattering hulls after a shot or three. Against capital ships, it was mostly a painful annoyance.

Until you got hit with over a hundred beams in rapid succession. Then you started shedding hull and crew into space. Like that bastard over there was doing.

Robbie found Hardie smiling at him. As Tactical Officer, she was anticipating the order, hands poised, but would wait for it.

"No surrender offered?" Robbie asked the bridge, turning to his comm officer, Senior Centurion Dimitris Radić, a man who had served with him, and before that with Jessica, back on *Brightoak*, going all the way back to the beginning of his career.

"Negative on all channels," the man said.

"All ships resume firing on the battleship," he ordered. "Finish her off."

"Roger that," Hardie replied, firing the little guns first. Hardie had actually triggered the shot before he was finished speaking, but he had known she would do that. Senior Centurion Harden Glenraven was frequently mistaken for his sister, even more so when they were among strangers on the ground. Hardie truly knew him better than Bess did.

Around them, all the Type-3's went in rapid sequence.

Over on *VI Victrix*, Komal MacInerney would be doing the same. One did not become a Tactical Officer in First Expeditionary Fleet by being squeamish about kicking a foe who was on the ground.

The big guns were next. *VI Ferrata* had an overabundance of power, but those monsters still took a bit to recharge.

They were worth every Lev.

On his screen, Robbie watched Hardie's Type-4 beams punch daylight through the tumbling carcass, imparting an even-greater spin, just before the beams from *VI Victrix* hit. The result was something like a laser carving knife opening up a crispy turkey.

"Robbie, I have someone from the battleship on channel seventy-four, asking for a ceasefire."

"All vessels, stand down until ordered," Robbie replied. "Let's see what they have to say. Route their signal out to all ships, but mute everyone except me."

Radić nodded and signaled with his hand when it was done.

"*Fribourg* warship, this is Maneuver Advocate Ve Klossak Marah Zaun, aboard *Steadfast at Dawn*," a woman's voice came across the degraded line.

"I am Command Centurion Robertson Aeliaes," he replied in a serious voice. "Holding the flag for Admiral Keller. What do you want to discuss, Maneuver Advocate?"

"*Steadfast at Dawn* has suffered a potentially-mortal wound, Command Centurion," she said. "The Director of this vessel was killed and the other Advocates are dead or injured, leaving me in command. I offer you a trade, Command Centurion. We will withdraw from the system as quickly as we can, if you will let us go. In return, I will order *Steadfast in Honor* and *Steadfast in Surprise* to leave your fighter craft alone so they can be recovered."

"Why should I accept your offer, *Steadfast at Dawn*?" Robbie growled.

He really felt like putting a boot on somebody's neck. Looking at what they had done to *Auberon* on one of his side screens did not improve his humor.

"Because we are civilized beings," the Maneuver Advocate replied calmly. "You have won the field. Further deaths are unnecessary, as *Steadfast at Dawn* will be a very long time healing."

Healing? Stupid, Sentient *warships.*

Robbie was inclined to shatter the beast with beam fire until there was nothing larger than his fist left. Salting the Earth, as the ancient saying went.

But he stayed his hand.

Jessica had staked out the moral high ground at every turn. He didn't want to have to answer to her, when they finally cut away enough metal to get to that Flag Bridge.

"Your word of honor, Maneuver Advocate Ve?" he asked.

Hardie shrugged at him, maybe a little glum that she would have to forgo target practice with the Bubble Gun, but she wouldn't be here with Robbie if she was as crazy as Alber'. That man was always looking for what he called Goddesses of War.

"I have never made a promise to a barbarian before," Ve said in a lighter tone, almost friendly. "I do so now: we will withdraw to *Trusski's* orbit as soon as we are able to effect the necessary repairs here, and then gather up all my children and return to *Samara*. You will gather up your children and repair your flagship, and then return to wherever it is you call home. In the meantime, you will please kill or deactivate those missiles currently targeted on the planet, plus any others you may have fired."

Robbie grinned at the face Hardie made.

"Those were a bluff, *Steadfast at Dawn*," he said. "I accept your terms."

Better than losing the entire wing trying to catch those stupid sharks, when he only had one carrier, and no space for all the extra fighters.

"Crew Advocate Ko suspected as much," she replied. "I will inform him that he was correct, if he makes it out of surgery. Thank you, Command Centurion Aeliaes. We withdraw now."

Robbie expected the ship to blink out of existence, but instead, one of the three engine pods aft came alive tentatively, at least enough to begin pushing the beast away from them.

"Squadron, this is *VI Ferrata*," Robbie said into the general comm. "*Il Augusta*, *CP-406*, *CS-405*, and *CE-401* will rendezvous with the flight wing and get them as sorted out as possible, while we determine *Auberon*'s status."

"*VI Ferrata*, this is *Auberon*," Jessica's voice suddenly came through. "We're on-line enough to maneuver, as long as nobody tries to ride the gyros like you did. Then we might come apart."

"You were listening?" he asked.

"Came in about halfway, it sounded like," she said.

"You could have interrupted," Robbie pointed out.

"I would have, had it been necessary," she said. "But it was you talking."

Robbie blushed under his dark skin. He couldn't think of a higher compliment anyone could offer, than his own Red Admiral telling him he had done the right thing.

Hardie grinned at him, like she agreed.

PART FIVE
EPILOGUES

EPILOGUE: YAN

Pins and needles.

Nerves.

Vishnu, it was like he was sixteen again, a place Yan hadn't seen in three decades. All wound up with excess energy and nothing to do about it but stand in the hallway and watch. Her *E-2* fighter finally came through the lock shield and settled on the flight deck.

She was the last one home, of course, coming in even after *Devilfish*, the two of them flying escort for everyone else.

Those that were coming home from this.

As battles went, it had been a relatively bloodless affair. Yan still had nightmares about the lethal mosh pit known as *First Petron*, when Jessica's strike carrier *Auberon,* and her flight wing of professionals in top-notch equipment, had shredded an Imperial flight force and a bunch of motley pirates in home-built sleds.

This had been nowhere near as bad, physically. He just hadn't been sure his nerves would take it. Yan had given up caffeine hours ago because it was just making his jitters worse.

But she was home, finally.

Safe.

His buddy, 'sander Hummel, popped out of a hatch down the hallway and gestured Yan closer.

"Deck's clear," the flight engineer pronounced, then turned and went back to his business.

Yan made it a point not to run across the space to where her fighter had finally settled. Walking briskly didn't count, right?

He noted that her ship had been hit at least once by something hard enough to go through her shields, but not hard enough to do more than blow off some panels and kill the secondary power APU and some communications routing hardware.

He hadn't realized until now just how close he had come to losing her.

And then she was there, popping out of the side hatch, taking two strides, and throwing herself at him. She still weighed next to nothing, but the impact staggered him. And she had taken off her flight helmet before she debarked, so he could kiss her now.

da Vinci.

She held on like he was a life jacket in an Aivazovsky seascape. He just luxuriated in the feel of her lanky body pressed up against him.

Finally, she seemed to breathe.

"Miss me?" she leaned back and asked with a sarcastic grin.

"Maybe," Yan responded.

"I need a shower, a meal, and a nap," she announced. "As soon as the debrief is done, you're scrubbing my back."

"Can do," he said, mostly at a loss for words.

There were so many words to say, but this deck was absolutely not the place to share them with her.

S he was clean. And fed. And curled up in his lap in the big, comfy chair. Not quite asleep, but more than halfway. Yan let her warmth and weight center him.

She leaned back enough to look at him, carefully gauging his mood before she spoke.

Must be good.

"Single-crew fighters are a really stupid idea against *Buran*," she said as an introduction. "We were sitting ducks."

"I'm beginning to agree with you, yes," Yan said. "I have a few designs in my head for bigger ships. One is an improved GunShip, the other is about the size of the *S-11 Orca* bombers you used to fly with on the old ship."

"We need something like the Twins," she said, referencing a pair of young women who flew aboard *Kali-ma*, back in *Corynthe: Neon Pink* and *Rocket Frog*. Asra and Saša Binici.

"*RAN* GunShips already have a short-range JumpSail built in," Yan observed. "Jessica asked me for a design based on an old idea of hers. Modify a bulk freighter to haul as many as we could cram onto the decks. Launch them from the edge of some star system. Jump as a unit. Be like a pack of wolves suddenly coming out of the darkness."

"Just being able to jump twice, like the girls, would have been enough," *da Vinci* countered. "My ass wouldn't have been hanging out in the wind, hoping the next ship we saw was friendly."

"I will build you something better for the next battle," Yan declared quietly.

"No," Ainsley said.

"No?"

She kissed him.

"I'm done," she said simply.

"Done?"

Yan was confused, but that was his normal address with Ainsley.

"I don't want to be in charge of the Flight Wing," she continued. "It's too much. Makes me crazy. Crazier than usual. I spent a lot of time out there yesterday, wondering if I was finally going to die. Never been that close, at least not in my head. I'm done."

"I see," Yan said as a placeholder, not sure where she was going, or where he should be.

"Losing *Jouster* also made me realize that there's more to life than just flying," she said, leaning in to kiss him again.

He agreed, but this was a headstrong woman.

"So I'm going to take retirement after this," she said. "I've got enough years in service that a Command Flight Centurion pension will be pretty good, especially with the money I have saved up."

"What would you do?" Yan asked, suddenly realizing that the twinkle had come back into her eyes, where there had been the edges of despair earlier.

da Vinci was back. How did this woman manage to do this to him?

"Dunno," Ainsley said. "Probably have to find a job eventually. Know anybody looking for washed-up, ex-fighter pilots?"

"I know a place in *Ladaux*," Yan ventured, looking at her sidelong.

"Could certainly use a designer with expertise in small craft. And maybe occasional work as a test pilot, if she's crazy enough."

"Sounds lovely," she said with her first, true smile in hours.

"There is one catch," Yan said carefully. They had danced around the topic, but never confronted it.

"Oh?"

"If word gets out that I'm on the ground more or less permanently, people might come find me," he said. "Come looking, even. Depending on the technicalities, I do have two other wives out there. They might show up out of the blue someday."

"And they would hate me?" she asked slyly.

He could tell she was estimating her odds in close combat. He was from *Corynthe*.

"Worse," Yan countered. "Momoko probably would hate you, but I'm afraid that you and Aaliyah would turn into best friends and gang up on me."

She grinned and kissed him again. He could get lost, kissing this woman.

"Challenge accepted," she said.

"I appreciate your honesty, Commander van Gorzen," Vo said to the tall, thin officer standing across the pavilion space from him. "I would not have expected to say this, but I will be sorry not to have you with me. I think you would have made a good cohort commander for the 189th Legion."

"Thank you, General *zu* Arlo," the man replied crisply.

Van Gorzen did everything crisply, Vo had learned after watching the man for the last few months. Sharp, precise, concise. If the officer still had occasional issues with being a nobleman surrounded by jumped-up commoners, and being subordinate to a foreigner, as well, van Gorzen had proven himself a capable officer, routinely scoring in the top three in everything he tried from an academic standpoint. Not a man for a thirty kilometer march in full gear, but even then he had given credible performances.

"So what's next for you, Commander?" Vo asked.

The graduation ceremony had been relatively low-key, as these things went. Officers in dress uniform and a reception to congratulate them on surviving Field School. Less than one hundred people in attendance, all of them male, twenty-seven of whom were the students.

Vo had managed to get van Gorzen away from everyone for a private conversation. A pavilion that had been set up in case of rain, on what turned out to be a nice-enough day.

The commander beamed a rare smile, from what had turned out to be a focused, taciturn man, once Vo had spent time to really know him.

"My uncle, the Duke, raises horses, General," van Gorzen replied. "I have ridden since I was a child, but it was always for fun, rather than competition. The Grand Marshal wants to create something like your old unit, the Fourth Saxon Legion. He's tapped me to start recruiting ranchers to train war horses, and officers."

"Dragoons?" Vo asked, intrigued.

He had suggested something similar to Jenker when they first met. It was a pleasant surprise that the man was following up on it.

"Initially, yes," van Gorzen said. "Eventually, we'll transition to hussars, possibly lancers, although I expect that to take at least a decade. My mission is to start simple and work our way up. I cannot imagine the war will be over soon."

"I wish you the best of successes, Commander," Vo said. "And if I can be of assistance, please don't hesitate to ask."

"I will, sir," the man said. "It may be that we will want to recruit some retired Fourth Saxon troopers as training cadre, once we have a better understanding of the task. Thank you, again, for the generous offer."

And then he was gone.

Honestly, there had been times, especially during those first weeks of class and exercises, when Vo had expected the man to snap. Taking orders from a commoner?

Of course, the fact that their supreme commander, Grand Marshal Jenker, had started out as a simple man of middle class heritage, had worked wonders on those men. None would have made it this far in the Imperial Land Forces if they hadn't been able to overcome their snobbery.

A shadow at the edge of the pavilion.

Short. Broad. Present.

"Congratulations, General *zu* Arlo," the Grand Marshal said as he entered the space, apparently having observed van Gorzen depart while remaining unseen.

"Thank you, sir," Vo said. "What's next?"

It still amazed him to be able to stand next to the man, completely at ease. Growing up over the last few years had been a bitch, but the benefits were pretty good.

"*The 189th Legion, Expeditionary, Reinforced,*" the Marshal said conversationally.

Jenker was only smaller than Vo physically. He was still a giant, when you measured martial capabilities. Many people made the mistake of not understanding that. For some, it had been their last mistake.

"The Emperor approved, then?" Vo asked. It hadn't been a given, going in. Certainly, not in the hands of a foreigner.

But Vo and Karl VII had a bit of a…history.

"And the Grand Admiral," Jenker nodded. "I understand you were interested in having Olaf van Gorzen on your staff. That surprised me, considering how you two met, but I could still order it."

"That won't be necessary, Grand Marshal," Vo replied. "He's a damned good officer, and he will do a good job with what you have him on next. I don't think he'd be happy in the 189th long-term, given what I intend."

"A general officer, living in the field, eating the same food as his troops?" Jenker grinned knowingly. "No wine, no mistresses, nothing soft?"

"There will be many who resent me, sir," Vo said. "Resent my background, my class. My accent. Someone will figure out eventually that I was sentenced to the fleet instead of prison when I was seventeen."

"I'm aware of your past as a now-reformed cat burglar, Arlo," Jenker said. "We did a very deep investigation before any of this happened."

"And there are days I still think you and Wachturm are crazy for doing it," Vo replied. "But I understand my duty."

"Arlo, you understand dedication to duty better than anyone I have ever known," Grand Marshal Jenker stated firmly. "The only exceptions I am willing to grant are myself, the Grand Admiral, and most the Imperial Family. The locals, that is. Most of the more-remote cousins and uncles leave something to be desired, but they aren't in my chain of command, Good Lord Ever Willing."

"Thank you, Grand Marshal," Vo said simply.

"No," Jenker suddenly turned and saluted, fist over his heart in the ancient manner. "Thank you, *zu* Arlo. I cannot imagine where this galaxy would be right now, but for you."

EPILOGUE: JESSICA

She had survived.

Jessica had not been sure of that outcome, when *Steadfast at Dawn* came out of jump in a perfect kill position.

She had been aboard *IFV Amsel*, Wachturm's *Blackbird*, when a Mako had raked it with a single Mauler beam before escaping. *Auberon* had taken four hits, based on data from the after action report.

Casualties had been bad among the crew who had been closest to the outer hull when the storm broke. But even the Flag Bridge had not been immune.

As she sat on the side couch in her personal office, Jessica looked down at her left arm, currently encased in a soft cast from where she had somehow slammed it into the console hard enough to put a hairline fracture along her ulna and to bruise her radius. Plus her entire forearm was one massive purple-and-yellow blotch, but she could generally ignore the pain, if she focused on it.

While she had always tended toward ambidexterity, she was still left-handed enough that she reached for things that way, which hurt enough to stop her.

It was the frustration, more than anything. That and all the other bruises and bangs she had suffered when *Auberon's* entire hull seemed to flex.

Enej had been fine. Casey had a slight limp. Five or six others were moving tenderly, but she had suffered the worst. Denis and his bridge crew hadn't even noticed the immense whiplash that had snapped the Flag Bridge like a groundquake.

The random joys of starship combat. She had managed to cripple the battleship, the *Energiya Module*, and two of the cruisers, but *Auberon* was probably due for the wrecker, depending on what Oz and Moirrey reported about buckled frames.

And this ship had no business on the front lines with *Buran*. She could see that now. The others had all been designed for exactly this sort of combat, but she had been too headstrong to suggest traveling in anything less than her chariot. And this would be the third time she'd had a ship shot out from under her.

Brightoak had been rebuilt and then given to Robbie when she got *Auberon*. The Strike Carrier was still in orbit around *Ballard*, a monument to the defense of learning. The Star Controller was limping slowly back to Forward Base Delta, but that was to patch the big issues enough to get her into an Imperial Drydock somewhere.

Or a breaker's yard.

A chime at the outer hatch. Which was odd, since Marcelle and Willow should have been on duty, and either turning people away, or coming in to ask if she was taking visitors.

She found the cabin remote and unlocked the hatch, too tired to get up and walk over to see what was going on. And too depressed, if she was willing to be honest with herself.

This was a good night to brood.

The hatch opened and Captain Wald stepped into her cabin, holding a bottle of wine in one hand and two empty flutes in the other.

She fixed him with a curious look, but remained silent.

"Marcelle thought you could use some company," he said simply, one step inside the hatch but no further.

Marcelle thought?

"It is highly irregular for an Imperial officer to be visiting the quarters of a female in the dead of night," she observed, as if probing a worthy foe across the dojo floor.

"My reputation will be in tatters among the Grand Dames of *St. Legier*," he replied. "But it would be worse to leave you alone. And there is nobody you can talk to."

"Good point," she agreed.

Stoicism was one of the underlying pillars of the *Republic of Aquitaine*. A lesson she had learned early and well.

"So I thought perhaps some Malbec and light conversation might help you relax," Torsten said.

"Wine so you can seduce me?" she teased. At least as much as she could work herself up to it. It seemed important, but more work than reward.

"If I thought that would work, I would have tried it much earlier," he smiled. "Now, serious business, Jessica. I will leave if you desire."

"I would have thrown you out already if I wanted you gone," Jessica replied, as much to herself as to him.

It had been enough years, hadn't it? Wasn't she entitled to some level of personal happiness that didn't involve killing people as a profession?

"Emmerich Wachturm said something similar, once," Torsten said with a hint of a grin.

She watched him move closer with great deliberation. He no longer limped at all, even on tiring days, although his prosthetic was nothing but a titanium rod, so his pant legs always looked mismatched. And there were lines etched into his forehead that had not been there a week ago.

Worry for her, she supposed. It was an odd thought, someone worrying about her person.

He turned the flutes over and put them carefully on her desk. The bottle was sealed with a flip-top held in place by wires under tension, and it took two hands to open.

He poured a deep burgundy and handed it to her before filling his own glass and pulling one of the chairs close enough to sit with her. He seemed hesitant to encroach, violate her personal space, by joining her on the couch.

Perhaps she wanted her space violated?

Jessica couldn't make up her mind. She hid behind her glass and sipped.

It was a good vintage, and seemed possessed of magical powers capable of unraveling the knots across her shoulders and back. She had needed something, because the fighting robot was going to be off-limits for a month or more, to give all the muscles and tendons time to come back into alignment.

The best cure was still time, modern medicine's grumbling notwithstanding.

Torsten held up his glass in a toast. She stared blankly.

"You have done something no man in Imperial Service has ever done, you know," he said.

"What?" she replied, lost.

"Driven *Buran* out of a system," he noted. "We've only ever fought them off defensively, or broken our teeth trying to wear down *Ural* and *Samara*. This was the first offensive victory for us in a generation."

"And a woman did it," she retorted, returning the toast.

Imperial society still hadn't fully accepted her, even if much of the rest of the Empire had.

"Worse," he smiled, sipping. "Two women. Jessica Keller, the new Red Admiral, and the Lady Casey. The Queen of the Pirates and Emperor Karl VIII. Imagine the consternation back home when that that news arrives."

That did bring a smile to her face. Casey would never hold the throne, but she had captured the imagination of the people.

As Jessica had hoped.

The *Fribourg Empire* would survive, but it would never be what it had planned for itself a generation ago. Now she just had to protect them from an implacable *Sentience*, intent on recapturing the entire galaxy and yoking all humanity under its rule.

Jessica had known another *Immortal*, but Summer had explained over greasy burgers and thin beer on that last night, why that past should never be allowed to return.

"And what about you, Torsten Wald?" Jessica asked. "What part do you see for yourself in all this?"

"Whatever part you will let me play, Jessica Keller," he said with such seriousness that her breath caught.

"You understand what that means?" she probed.

"I probably will never return to the Imperial Staff," he said. "The rest of my career, the rest of my life, will be spent in other duties, other devotions, mostly involving following you around the galaxy and hoping for whatever scraps and leftovers I can get. The Beast will not be done with you for a very long time."

"Scraps?" she challenged, unsure how to take his words.

"It would be better than nothing at all, Jessica," he replied simply. "You cannot give up all this. I know that. The galaxy would not survive. But I can and will give up everything else, in order to be near you. Is that clear enough?"

She started to reach out her hand to him, the one not holding the glass. The left one.

That brought a stab of pain, so she put the wine glass down instead. He leaned forward and took her good hand carefully.

"You're crazy," she whispered.

"Yes," he agreed. "But that's beside the point. I will be whatever you need me to be."

She was breathless. Wordless.

Numb.

But not lost.

Found, perhaps.

It had been more than six years since she lost *Warlock*. In that time, she had conquered a world and defeated an Empire.

Now she would find time for herself, as well.

THE RED ADMIRAL CAST LIST

Name / Rank / Position

Corinth

- Jessica Marie Keller (F) / Fleet Centurion / Queen of Corynthe
- Marcelle Augustine Travere / Chief / Jessica's Personal Aide
- Willow Dolen / First Rate Spacer / Jessica's Bodyguard
- David Rodriguez / Vice Admiral / Regent to Queen Jessica
- Desianna Indah-Rodriguez / Counsel to the Crown / First Minister of Corynthe
- Uly Larionov (M) / Counsel to the Crown / Comptroller
- Galen Estevan (M) / Captain / Commander, *Marco Polo*

Kali-ma

- *Wiley* Shiori Ness (F) / Command Centurion / Captain, *Kali-ma*
- Anders Himura (M) / Executive Officer / EO, *Kali-ma*
- Bryn Maki (M) / Science Officer / *Kali-ma*
- Erik Doležal (M) / / Head Engineer
- *Rocket Frog* / Saša Binici / Pilot / Light Strike Wing

- *Neon Pink* / Asra Binici / Pilot / Light Strike Wing
- *Eel* / Gustav Marquez / Flight Lead / Heavy Wing

Auberon

- Denis Jež (M) / Command Centurion / Commander, *Auberon*
- Enej Zivkovic (M) / Centurion / Flag Centurion
- Nina Vanek (F) / Senior Centurion / First Officer
- Tobias Brewster (M) / Senior Centurion / Tactical Centurion
- Aleksander Afolayan(M) / Centurion / Gunner
- Nada Zupan (F) / Senior Centurion / Pilot
- Daniel Giroux (M) / Senior Centurion / Science Officer
- Vilis Ozolinsh (M) / Command Engineering Centurion / Chief Engineer
- Phillip Navin Crncevic (M) / Command Security Centurion / Dragoon
- Nadine Orly / Yeoman / Flag Marine
- Jackson Tawfeek / Chief / Marine
- Mahmud Astrauskas / Senior Centurion / Surgeon
- Moirrey *zu* Kermode / Centurion / Ritter / Engineer, detached duty, *Auberon*
- Nicolai Aoiki (M) / Master Chef / Master of the Wardroom
- Saana Robles / Centurion / Engineer

Pilots, Auberon

- Iskra Vlahovic / Command Flight Centurion / Flight Deck Commander
- *Jouster* : Milos Pavlovich / Command Flight Centurion / Flight Commander
- *Uller* : Friedhelm Hannes Förstner / Flight Centurion / *Jouster's* Wing
- *Vienna* : Avril Bouchard / Flight Centurion / *Jouster's* Wingmate
- *Bitter Kitten* : Darya Lagunov / Senior Flight Centurion / Wing Commander
- *Hànchén* : Murali Ma / Flight Centurion / *Bitter Kitten's* Wingmate

- *Furious* : Cho Ayaka Nakamura / Flight Centurion / *Bitter Kitten's* Wingmate
- *da Vinci* : Ainsley Barret / Senior Flight Centurion / Scout Pilot
- *Gaucho* : Hollis Dyson / Senior Flight Centurion / Commander, *Cayenne*
- Takouhi Taline Nazarian (F) / Chief / Loadmaster, *Cayenne*
- Murphy Alexandru (M) / First-Rate Spacer / Tower Gunner, *Cayenne*
- Branca Antía Rocha (F) / Flight Centurion / Commander, *Petron*
- Anastazja Slusarczyk (F) / Senior Flight Centurion / Commander, *Necromancer*
- Leila Ketevan (F) / Flight Centurion / Commander, *Damocles*

RAN Squadron

- Arott Whughy (M) / Fleet Centurion / Commander, Forward Base Delta
- Tomas Kigali (M) / Command Centurion / Commander, *CA-264*
- Arsen Lam (M) / Senior Centurion / Tactical Officer, *CA-264*
- Aki Ridwana Ali (F) / Centurion / Pilot, *CA-264*
- Alber d'Maine (M) / Command Centurion / Commander, *VI Victrix*
- Amala Bhattacharya / Senior Security Centurion / Ambassador to Trusski
- Pinchon Swarovski (M) / Yeoman / Security, *VI Victrix*
- Vibol Harmaajärvi (M) / First-Rate Spacer / Tailor, *VI Victrix*
- Robertson Aelieas (M) / Command Centurion / Commander, *VI Ferrata*
- Harden Glenraven (F) / Senior Centurion / First Officer, *VI Ferrata*
- Dalibor Radić (M) / Senior Centurion / Comm Officer, *VI Ferrata*
- Tamara Strnad / Command Centurion / Commander, *II Augusta*
- Merman (M) / Senior Flight Centurion / Wing Lead, *II Augusta*

- Doriane Matveev (F) / Command Centurion / Commander, *Ishfahan*
- Kanda Cosmina Lungu (F) / Command Centurion / Commander, *Ballard*
- Elzbet Aukley (F) / Senior Centurion / First Officer/Science Officer, *Ballard*
- Orn Nwokolo (M) / Centurion / Asst Science Officer, *Ballard*
- Mererid Stella Dimitriou (F) / Centurion, PhD / Security Marine. Geologist, *Ballard*
- Larsen Romanov (M) / Command Centurion / Commander, *Bulldog*
- Nero Yamakagi (M) / Command Centurion / Commander, *CT-9492*
- Waldemar Ihejirika (M) / Command Centurion / Commander, *Mendocino*
- Teuta Uzodimma (F) / Command Centurion / Commander, *Brightoak*
- Yezekael Jarogniew (M) / Command Centurion / Commander, *Rubicon*
- Siranush "Siran" Akpabio (F) / Command Centurion / Commander, *Vigilant*
- Tonći Östberg (M) / Command Centurion / Commander, *Andover*
- Calista Katsaros (F) / Command Centurion / Commander, *Albena*
- Ionuţ Yannic (M) / Command Centurion / Commander, *Advocate*
- Illiam Kovack (M) / Command Centurion / Commander, *Duncan*
- Anne Holgersen (F) / Command Centurion / Commander, *Andorra*
- Enfys El-Amin (F) / Command Centurion / Commander, *Wombat*
- Vendula Van Bueren / Command Centurion, retired / Former commander, *Audacity*
- Valerie Maikop (M) / Command Centurion / Commander, *CE-403*
- Phil Kosnett (M) / Command Centurion / Commander, *CS-405*

- Heather Lau (F) / Senior Centurion / First Officer, *CS-405*
- Siobhan Skokomish (F) / Centurion / Navigator/Second Officer, *CS-405*
- Jennifer Glenn (F) / Command Centurion / *CP-406*
- Takouhi Elouan (F) / Senior Centurion / Tactical Officer, *CP-406*
- Janel Rouge (M) / Centurion / Flight Deck Officer, *CP-406*
- Reese Steiner (F) / Centurion / Science Officer, *CP-406*
- Adnan Kristensen (M) / Yeoman / Gunner, *CP-406*
- Murdag Rasim (F) / Centurion / Pilot, *CP-406*
- Anmol Schwartzenwald (M) / Flight Centurion / *Black Prince*
- Erik Mosiondz (M) / Senior Flight Centurion / *Boomerang*
- Michelle Nystul (F) / Flight Centurion / *Grendel*

The Republic

- Indira (Chastain) Keller / Jessica's mother
- Miguel Keller / Jessica's father
- Petia Naoumov / First Centurion. / Commander, Home Fleet
- Nils Kasum / First Lord of the Fleet
- Kamil Miloslav / Senior Centurion / Personal Aide to First Lord Kasum
- Judit Margrét Chavarría / Premier, Republic Senate
- Tadej Marko Horvat / Senator, Republic Senate, Chairman
- Calina Szabolcsi / President of the Republic of Aquitaine
- Seth / Bartender, the Marquette Room
- Sigrún / Steward, the Marquette Room
- Yan Bedrov / Principle Engineer, Bedrov & Keller
- Svetlana Ognianov / Sergeant at Arms, Republic Senate
- Vresh Nalani / Senator, Republic Senate
- His Honor, Holman Metharom / Senior Judge, Retired, Anameleck Prime
- Alda Greet / Bailiff

The Fribourg Empire

- Johannes Arend Wiegand / Emperor / Karl VII
- Kasimira Ekaterina / Empress / Imperial Household

- Karl Ekkehard Szczęsny / Crown Prince Ekke / Imperial Household
- Kasimira Helena / HRH Lady Casey / Imperial Household
- Emmerich Wachturm / Grand Admiral, Duke / Commander of the Fleet
- Freya Wachturm / Duchess / Wife of Emmerich Wachturm
- Tiede Wachturm / Cmdr / Son of Emmerich Wachturm
- Jeltje Voight / *Burggraf* / Daughter of Emmerich Wachturm
- Carsten Voigt / Cmdr / Husband of Jeltje Voight
- Henrietta Anne Wachturm / "Lady Heike" / Daughter of Emmerich Wachturm
- Bernard Hourani / Lt. Cmdr / Fiancé of Heike Wachturm
- Hendrik Baumgärtner / Flag Captain / Aide to Admiral Wachturm
- Gunter Tifft / Lt. Cmdr / Aide to Admiral Wachturm
- Tomas Provst / Admiral of the White / IFV *Firehawk*
- Albert Benedikt Kistler / Captain / IFV *Firehawk*
- Vo *zu* Arlo / Centurion-*Ritter* / Commanding General, *189th Legion*

Imperial Land Forces

- Anthohn Jenker / Grand Marshal / Supreme Commander, ILF
- Anders Tsibin / Flag General / Commander, Field School
- Olaf van Gorzen / Commander / Imp Land Forces

Buran

- *The Eldest* : The Lord of Winter / God/Emperor / Ruler of Buran
- Xi Derag Ahma Kier (F) / Director / Commander, *Steadfast at Dawn*
- Ro Mashi Enok Torl (F) / War Advocate / *Steadfast at Dawn*
- Au Xixi Plana Gerd (M) / Entity Advocate / *Steadfast at Dawn*
- Ko Ashkhan Loren Miil (M) / Crew Advocate / *Steadfast at Dawn*
- Ve Klossak Marah Zaun (F) / Maneuver Advocate / *Steadfast at Dawn*

- Daniel St. Collins (M) / Master of Spies / *Steadfast at Dawn*
- Xi Ulan Atah Ahn (M) / Director / *Ural Starbase, Samara*
- Ko Gagan Vayak Ruus / Captain / Freighter *TO:557231455891*
- Ul Banop Cheani Yuur (M) / *Khan, Minister of the Eighth Rank / Trusski*
- Ve Gayav Chuluun Gan (M) / Scholar / Aide to the Khan, *Trusski*

ABOUT THE AUTHOR

Blaze Ward writes science fiction in the Alexandria Station universe: The Jessica Keller Chronicles, The Science Officer series, The Doyle Iwakuma Stories, and others. He also writes about The Collective as well as The Fairchild Stories and Modern Gods superhero myths. You can find out more at his website www.blazeward.com, as well as Facebook, Goodreads, and other places.

Blaze's works are available as ebooks, paper, and audio, and can be found at a variety of online vendors (Kobo, Amazon, iBooks, and others). His newsletter comes out quarterly, and you can also follow his blog on his website. He really enjoys interacting with fans, and looks forward to any and all questions-even ones about his books!

Never miss a release!

If you'd like to be notified of new releases, sign up for my newsletter.

I only send out newsletters once a quarter, will never spam you, or use your email for nefarious purposes. You can also unsubscribe at any time. http://www.blazeward.com/newsletter/

ABOUT KNOTTED ROAD PRESS

Knotted Road Press fiction specializes in dynamic writing set in mysterious, exotic locations.

Knotted Road Press non–fiction publishes autobiographies, business books, cookbooks, and how–to books with unique voices.

Knotted Road Press creates DRM–free ebooks as well as high–quality print books for readers around the world.

With authors in a variety of genres including literary, poetry, mystery, fantasy, and science fiction, Knotted Road Press has something for everyone.

Knotted Road Press
www.KnottedRoadPress.com